STRANGE

AND

EVER

AFTER

SUSAN DENNARD

HARPER TEEN
An Imprint of HarperCollins*Publishers*

HarperTeen is an imprint of HarperCollins Publishers.

STRANGE AND EVER AFTER

Copyright © 2014 by Susan Dennard

All rights reserved. Printed in the United States of America. No part of this book may be used or reproduced in any manner whatsoever without written permission except in the case of brief quotations embodied in critical articles and reviews. For information address HarperCollins Children's Books, a division of HarperCollins Publishers, 10 East 53rd Street, New York, NY 10022.

www.epicreads.com

Library of Congress Cataloging-in-Publication Data

Dennard, Susan.

Strange and ever after / Susan Dennard. — First edition.

pages cm

Sequel to: A darkness strange and lovely.

Summary: "Traveling to Egypt with the Spirit-Hunters, Eleanor Fitt must control her growing power, face her feelings for Daniel, and confront the evil necromancer Marcus—all before it's too late"— Provided by publisher.

ISBN 978-0-06-208332-6 (hardback)

[1.   Dead—Fiction.   2.   Magic—Fiction.   3.   Love—Fiction. 4. Egypt—History—19th century—Fiction.   5. Horror stories.]   I. Title.

PZ7.D42492St   2014   2013047946

[Fic]—dc23   CIP

                                                                              AC

Typography by Lissi Erwin

14 15 16 17 18 LP/RRDH 10 9 8 7 6 5 4 3 2 1

First Edition

For Sarah J. Maas, who taught me to seek out my darkest fears and to write them with courage

CHAPTER ONE

*I was not supposed to be here. Oliver would be furi-*ous. Joseph even more so. This dock was the no-man's-land between realms. It was a place for ghosts.

But my mother was dead.

And I, Eleanor, intended to find her.

Wood groaned beneath my feet as I shifted my weight. A soft, golden glow pulsed behind me. It was the curtain, a door back into the world of the living. I could almost catch a few sounds from that earthly realm—low voices and the hum of an airship engine—but the dark, lapping water beneath the dock was louder.

I took a single step forward. The curtain throbbed brighter, flickering in the corners of my vision. Then it pulled back— taking the sounds from earth with it.

Another step—the wood creaked again. At least this time I wore boots, unlike my last trip here. I'd been barefoot then, sleeping on a ship bound for France. At that time I had thought I merely dreamed this empty expanse of black water, with its driftwood dock and still air. Now I knew this place was a barrier and that I ought to turn back—I ought to leave this world before the Hell Hounds came.

Those giant, monstrous Hounds, guardians of the spirit realm. They kept the Dead on their side of the curtain . . . and the living on theirs.

But let the Hell Hounds come. Let them blast me far beyond this dock and the spirit world. Let them send my soul straight to the final afterlife.

For at this moment I *truly* did not care.

I glanced down and found I wore exactly what I had fallen asleep in: Daniel's loose shirt, tucked into a pair of his trousers and rolled up to expose my hands. I flexed my fingers before me. Everything about me looked hazy, as if my body were layered in fog.

All except for my right hand. My spirit hand. *That* was clear and crisp.

I examined it more closely. This hand had been amputated— cut off after a Hungry Dead had shredded it beyond repair. Though I had been without it for only three months before my demon, Oliver, had returned the hand to me. He had bound the *ghost* of my amputated hand in the earthly realm, leaving me with this phantom limb.

So perhaps my right hand appeared more real than any

other part of me because it was the only part of me that actually belonged in the spirit world.

With a deep breath, I lowered my arm and set off at a steady walk down the dock. I was here to find Mama, so that was what I would do.

Mama. Is dead. Mama. Is dead. The thought had not stopped pounding in my brain, beating in time to my heart.

Allison Wilcox had been the one to tell me, only a few hours ago. It felt like years. Or maybe only minutes . . .

It had been a beautiful, sunny morning in the Tuileries Gardens of Paris. The sort of sunny day that had made it impossible to believe I'd barely escaped the previous night with my life.

The Spirit-Hunters had come to Paris to stop a surge in walking corpses, only to learn too late that the source of *les Morts* was actually a demon—*Marcus*'s demon.

Yet the Spirit-Hunters, Oliver, and I had done our jobs well. We'd killed the demon named Madame Marineaux and saved the City of Light from hundreds of rabid Hungry Dead.

The following morning, Daniel's huge, egg-shaped balloon had creaked and swayed in the wind off the river Seine. Its shadow had drifted over me . . . then away . . . then over me once more. The long gondola hanging below gave it the look of a white-sailed ship with a wooden ladder dropping to earth.

"Hurry, Eleanor," a voice had called. I glanced up and found Joseph's head poking from the gondola thirty feet above. A bandage wrapped around his head; his black skin was sickly and puffy with exhaustion.

3

Madame Marineaux had cut off Joseph's ear in a blood sacrifice.

"There is no time to waste," Joseph added, with a final scratch at his bandages.

I nodded and tiredly grabbed at the first rung. The Spirit-Hunters and I were traveling south today—racing a train bound for Marseille that had departed the evening before with Marcus on board.

And with Jie on board too. He had taken her from us, so now *we* would take her back.

Then we would make the bastard pay for everything he'd done.

Yet the instant my boot hit the first rung to Daniel's airship, a new voice called, "Eleanor! *Eleanor!*" and my stomach plummeted.

I recognized that shrill pitch—and God, I'd so desperately prayed I would not have to hear it.

Allison Wilcox.

I had known she was coming from Philadelphia . . . but now? *Already?* It wasn't even eight o'clock in the morning, and nothing good could have brought her all the way to Paris.

Last I had seen her, only a few weeks before, I had confessed to her that my brother had killed *her* brother. Yet despite that awful truth, Allison had still helped me reach the Philadelphia wharf when I needed to get to Paris—though she had also promised to call in the debt one day.

This day, it would seem, when speed was needed above all else to rescue Jie.

I slowly twisted away from the airship ladder. Allison stalked toward me, dressed in black. In mourning. Though she certainly looked healthier than she had a few weeks before, she was still a bony, angled version of herself.

"Why weren't you in the hotel?" she demanded, stomping across the gravel and swinging her parasol. "I *told* you," she continued, "that I would arrive this morning, yet when I read the letter at the front desk, I learned you are leaving the city!" Her gaze raked over me, her nose wrinkling up. "What the dickens are you wearing, Eleanor? And . . . is that a hand? How did you get your hand back?"

"Allison," I said, forcing a smile onto my lips. It felt more like a wince. "I apologize for leaving town, but I must do so immediately." I motioned up, to the airship.

She followed my finger and started—as if she hadn't yet noticed the enormous balloon.

"So," I continued, in the proper tone that etiquette demanded though my brain *shrieked* at me to make haste, "if you will please excuse me, I must go. Good day." I turned back to the first rung.

"Is this some sort of joke?" She stomped quickly to my side. The feather on her hat bobbed in the breeze. "You cannot possibly leave! Do you realize how far I have come?"

"I am truly sorry." I was not sorry at all. "But I cannot stay—"

"Then bring me with you," she blurted.

At those words I froze. It was such an absurd, unexpected request. And so impossible—even *she* had to realize that.

"Please," she begged, her harshness shifting to desperation.

"Do not leave me here, Eleanor. I have traveled all the way from Philadelphia to see you because I bear news that I *must* give."

"Then tell me your news." My words sounded distant beneath the growing boom of blood in my ears. "And then return to the hotel."

Allison's lips suddenly pressed tight. She shook her head.

"Allison, tell me what happened so that I may go." Another headshake, and this time, tears shone in her eyes.

I leaned closer, and the world seemed to slow. Her feathers left black trails in my vision. "Who is it, Allison? Who *died*?"

She still would not reply. "Who is it, Allison?" Horrified by my violence yet unable to stop it, I grabbed her arms and shook. "*Who?* Tell me!"

"Eleanor!" Joseph's voice crashed down from above. "Control yourself!"

But I could not. All control had slipped through my fingers as quickly as the splintered hole in my gut had opened.

I knew *exactly* who had died—and with her death, there was no one left for me in Philadelphia.

"Your mother," Allison rasped. "Just like Clarence. Just like the other boys." Her chest shuddered. "Eleanor, your mother was murdered. Decapitated."

"Ah." I released Allison. *De-cap-i-tated.* Such a strange word. It knocked around meaninglessly in my skull. . . . And in a cold, slow clench, everything went numb.

No thoughts. No sounds. No pain.

I twisted back to the ladder, and I climbed. Allison shouted

6

after me, but it was gibberish. All I saw was the next rung. All I heard was my heartbeat. When I reached the open gondola hatch, Joseph tried to speak to me—Daniel too. But it was all still gibberish.

A quick scan of the airship showed a metal room the size of my bedroom back in Philadelphia. It was crammed with sandbags and pulleys, with familiar crates that held Daniel's latest inventions—and presumably supplies.

A cargo hold, I thought vaguely, aiming straight ahead, toward a narrow hallway of wood-plank walls.

"Empress." Daniel's hand reached for me. "Talk to me."

But I couldn't even look at him as I walked past.

My feet reached the hall. Doors hung open on either side, spaced close together, while at the end of the hall was a glass-walled room with an enormous steering wheel. The pilothouse.

"Please," Daniel called after me. I remained silent. All I needed was a moment alone, to remember who I was—and to remember what I was doing. . . .

I drifted past open doors. On the left, a tiny galley. An even tinier washroom. A cabin with two bunks. On the right, three more cabins . . . and then finally, a fourth with only one bunk inside.

I stumbled in, my fingers brushing against the doorframe, against the left wall. I gaped at the tiny porthole opposite me. The buildings of Paris were just visible outside, their beige fronts and gray roofs melting together. I looked down at the wooden floor instead. But it looked equally as fuzzy. It did not help that

7

the gondola listed and swayed with the wind.

I felt sick.

Footsteps pounded in the hall outside. "Empress. Eleanor. *Please*—"

I toed the door shut. Then I locked it. But Daniel would not go away.

"Please talk to me." His voice was muffled through the door. Through the roar of blood in my ears. "Please, Eleanor."

"I just need a minute," I mumbled. "A minute alone." I stared at the closed door and barely managed to choke out a final word. "Please."

I turned around, and a fresh numbness engulfed me. My posture deflated; my knees buckled; I slumped to the floor. I planted my hands on the wood, and stared vaguely at the swirls and grooves in the planks.

No. No. I refused to believe Mama was dead. Not her—not my dragon mother.

I needed proof. I would not accept this until I had evidence.

Or . . . until I had said good-bye.

I leaned right, curling into a ball against the low bunk.

Daniel pounded on the door. Then Joseph. Then Oliver. I ignored them. Even when Allison's voice began to mingle with theirs, even when the engines started to rumble and the airship's gondola swayed more wildly, even when my ears popped painfully from the rapid change in altitude, I stayed firmly curled on the floor.

Until eventually, I had fallen asleep. And when I had opened my eyes again, the floorboards had been replaced by a golden, glowing dock.

Though I knew entering the spirit realm meant certain death, I did not care. Now that I was here—now that I was in this no-man's-land—I could find my mother. And I could say good-bye.

My boots struck the dock, muffled in the heavy air. Unnatural. I risked a backward glance. The golden door was distant now—much farther away than it should have been, given I had moved only twenty paces or so. . . .

Fear rippled down my spine, and for the first time since I had crossed into this world, my numbness pulled back.

Then it *reared* back, and panic crashed over me. Was this truly what I wanted: to find Mama? Was it worth the risk of the Hell Hounds? Of final, explosive death as they protected the spirit realm from the unwelcome living?

Yes, my heart told me. I wanted to see her so fiercely, I thought my lungs would burst and my ribs snap. For my mother's final words to me had been filled with hate and rage. . . . How could I go on living if that was all I had for a good-bye? How could I accept that Marcus had *sacrificed* Mama? Decapitated her just as Elijah had decapitated all those young men. . . .

Suddenly, a whine sounded, and I jolted forward. A dog stood on the dock.

I scooted back two steps. This was not a Hell Hound—this dog was much too small. Yet it was *something*, and it was here. In a no-man's-land that should be empty.

"Go away," I croaked, stumbling farther back. "Go."

It did not move.

I gaped at it, my heartbeat throbbing in my skull. This dog was much too *real*—just like my phantom hand. Its black-and-yellow fur was scruffy, its body lean and wild, its ears tall and erect. For whatever purpose, it belonged here.

Jackal. He is a jackal.

The words formed in my mind almost as if . . . as if they had been *planted* there. From somewhere else.

My throat pinched tight. "You're . . . a jackal?"

The jackal gave another keening whine. Then it . . . no, *he* sank onto his haunches and very distinctly nodded his head.

My jaw went slack, surprise replacing panic. And when the jackal's yellow eyes latched on to mine expectantly, I eased out a breath—relaxing slightly.

Why are you here?

I flinched at the second blast of thought that was *not* my own. "You . . . want to know why I'm here?"

The jackal nodded.

"I'm looking for my mother. She . . ." My fingers curled into fists. "She died several weeks ago. She would have crossed this dock to enter the spirit realm."

And?

"And I heard that those who are not ready to die will stay here. On the dock. My brother did it—he stayed here and did not pass to the final afterlife. Since . . ." I swallowed. "Since I do not *think* my mother was ready to die, then perhaps I can find her on the dock too."

The jackal shook his head. *She is gone.*

My heart sank like a stone. Heavy. Choking. "So you have not seen her?" I could not keep the tremor from my words. "She is taller than I—broad shouldered and . . ."

The jackal saw her pass on, and you are too late.

"But maybe she is here anyway." I insisted. "How do you *know* she's gone? Who are you? *What* are you?"

The jackal is a messenger, and the jackal knows. *Your mother is gone, and you are too late.*

The thought burned in my skull, bright and penetrating. I stared stupidly at him. . . . But then the words shifted and sank. Down they slid, like clotted oil into my throat. Into my chest.

My mother was dead, and I was too late. She had left the dock, and I would never, ever see her again.

It was over; she was over; my family was over.

Everything inside me went limp. My legs stopped working, and I fell forward. My knees hit the dock, my hands too. My wrists snapped back.

I did not care.

Because I could not have my good-bye. My final "I love you." There would be *nothing*.

My lungs spasmed. No air in, no air out. I would suffocate, and I would not care.

I clutched at the dock, digging my fingers into the weathered wood. Splinters sliced beneath my fingernails. Into my knuckles. Blood welled.

You are angry, the voice said in my head. And he was right. I *was* angry. I was angrier than I'd ever thought possible.

When Marcus had taken my brother's dead body and *donned* it like some ill-fitting suit, I had wanted to kill him. When he had murdered all those people in Paris and then *kidnapped* my best friend, Jie, I had wanted to destroy him.

But now he had sacrificed my mother's blood for his own power. Now . . . the fury blistered inside me.

I would crush Marcus. I would slice him open, and I would laugh as he bled out. I would rip his soul apart bit by bit.

He had stolen my good-bye, and I would obliterate him.

A growl sounded.

Dazed, I looked up. The jackal's lips were drawn back, and the hair on his spine was high. He lurched at me.

I blundered back onto my knees. He lunged again—biting the air before my face. I scuttled upright.

Then for half a heartbeat, the jackal paused. His ears twisted behind, and the motionless air seemed to pause too. . . .

Go. You must go. In a rush of movement, he thrust at me again.

My feet shambled backward, my eyes locked on the jackal's bared teeth. *Go, go.* And that was when I heard them. A new, layered snarling echoed over the water. . . .

The Hell Hounds were coming.

The jackal dived at me once more. *You must run. NOW.*

In a blind scramble, I turned and charged for the distant curtain. Terror and grief coiled together at the nape of my neck, as heavy and inescapable as the Hounds.

I pounded my feet harder. Each step was like a drum, and

my knees kicked up higher, higher. I was out of breath before I was halfway down the dock, yet I barely noticed the scorch of air in my throat.

For as the curtain drew closer, the Hounds grew louder.

Then a wet, frozen wind slammed into me, and the baying of the Hounds shattered through my skull. I staggered, listing dangerously to one side—toward dark waves speckled with starlight. But my arms windmilled, and I maintained my course.

The Hounds were so close now. Inescapable . . . except that the curtain was close too. Its golden light shimmered brighter with each slam of my heels.

I would reach it. I *had* to reach it. . . .

Then the glow bathed over me. The snarling Hounds faded . . . faded. . . .

I glanced back once, to lock eyes with the jackal's. He loped behind me and paused just before the curtain, unperturbed and almost . . . *smug*. Yes, that was what that lolling tongue meant.

"Tell her good-bye," I said to him. "Please, if you are truly a messenger, then tell her good-bye."

If he can, the jackal will.

Then I stepped completely through the curtain and into the earthly realm once more.

CHAPTER TWO

My eyelids snapped open. I stood in the middle of my cabin on the airship. My chest quaked. My pulse shrieked in my ears, and with each gasp for air, the echoing howl of the Hounds vanished. . . .

A dull throb pricked at my senses. I glanced down . . . and blinked. My hands bled. Splinters poked out from my knuckles, yet I barely felt them. Elation and surprise hummed through me, dominating every other sensation.

I had just crossed into the spirit realm by my *own* power— something Oliver had sworn to me was impossible—and I had come out alive.

Though . . . I might not have escaped if not for the jackal.

Jackal.

I frowned. I hadn't seen him when I'd crossed to the dock

15

before, yanked there by Marcus's magic. Was the jackal *truly* a messenger? And if so, to whom could he relay messages? Of course, in order to give a message, I would have to return to the dock again. . . .

As my mind ran through possibilities—of how I could ask Elijah about necromancy, how I could beg for Clarence's forgiveness, how I could tell Mama I loved her—a scratch began to sound at my cabin door.

I ignored it, focusing instead on all the things I could ask the jackal to share with my family.

Splat. I looked down. A fat droplet of blood had hit the wood and now sank into the grain. My forehead knit. The engines on this airship were so quiet I could actually hear my own blood fall. I glanced to the porthole—the view outside was one of wispy clouds and green, patchwork farmland. We could have been anywhere in France right now. Presumably, though, we were south and east of Paris.

And, good God, we were *flying*. I shuffled two steps closer to the porthole, but the lush, pale green only served to confuse me. To distance me further from the moment. For seeing the land so far below and streaming by so fast . . . it did not feel real.

The scratching sound came again at my door, and this time there was a loud *click*. I whirled around just as the door banged open.

Daniel stood in the doorway, face flushed and lock pick in hand. Beside him, with his yellow eyes wide, was Oliver.

At the sight of them, anger sparked in my shoulders. "What the *blazes*," I began, "are you two doing——"

"You're hurt," Daniel interrupted. He strode forward, and I didn't miss the leather wallet of lock picks he slid into his pocket. He reached for me. "What the hell happened?"

I skittered back. "You broke into my room."

"We were worried," Oliver snarled. He stalked through the doorway. "You didn't answer our shouts, and then I heard . . . *something*." He did not elaborate, but the sudden flash of gold around his eyes told me he knew exactly where I had been.

Inwardly, I swore.

Our souls were bound—it was the magic of a demon and a master. So Oliver must have sensed my absence. Or perhaps he had even *heard* the Hell Hounds since he always knew when the guardians of the spirit realm were near. His existence depended on making sure they never found him.

"We need to tend these wounds." Daniel's voice cut into my thoughts. He gripped my wrists and flipped my palms upward. "This is bad. Your hands are destroyed." He pushed me toward the porthole, toward daylight. Then his grassy-green eyes bored into my face. "What did you do?"

"Nothing," I murmured.

His jaw clenched. "This ain't nothing, Empress. Talk to me."

"It doesn't matter," Oliver declared. Yet there was a forced nonchalance to his tone. "I will heal her."

Daniel's eyes clouded with resentment. He did not like my magic. He did not like that I was bound to a demon. Yet I could see in the twitching of his lips that he was trying to keep his hatred separate from this moment.

"How about," he said slowly, "I just get you some bandages instead. I'll heal you the old-fashioned way."

"It's fine." I wriggled from his grasp. "It doesn't hurt."

"Of course it does," he argued. "And it won't take me but a second—"

"It's *fine*," I repeated more forcefully. I did not want bandages. I wanted Oliver's magic—warm and safe. Then I wanted solitude.

"Please, Daniel," I added. "You should get back to flying."

"Joseph's at the helm. He'll be fine for a few more minutes." He lowered his voice and dipped in close. "Please, just heal yourself the normal way—"

"Magic *is* the normal way for her." Oliver's drawl held the same false apathy.

Daniel's teeth gritted, but he held my gaze. "Please, Empress?"

For half a breath I considered bandages and salves. It would please Daniel, and I wanted that. . . . But then another *splat!* filled the cabin. More blood on the floor. Traditional healing would take weeks; I did not have weeks.

So I said, "No, Daniel."

Hurt flashed over his face. His body tensed . . . but he made no move to leave. He simply stared at me, pain and frustration and . . . *disgust* warring in his gaze.

I understood his feelings—he believed, as Joseph did, that

my magic corrupted me. That necromancy festered inside my soul.

But he and Joseph were wrong, and if Daniel truly wanted to help me, he would accept my magic as it was. Just as I accepted *him* for who he was: a man with a criminal past and dark memories.

"You heard her," Oliver said, sauntering closer. He wore a smile as fake as his voice. "She asked you to go, Danny Boy."

Red exploded on Daniel's cheeks. In a violent twist, he rounded on Oliver and slammed him to the wall. "You have poisoned her mind, Demon."

Oliver's eyes flared bright gold. "And you," he growled, all his indifference gone, "have poisoned her heart."

Daniel's fist reared back . . .

And I finally moved. "Stop!" I staggered toward them. "Just *stop!*"

Daniel froze, his gaze fixed on Oliver's face. . . . Then his breath whooshed out. His fist fell. "I-I'm sorry, Empress—"

"Empress," Oliver said with a snort. "That's so bloody obnoxious."

Daniel flung him a sneer. "Go to hell, Demon."

"If only I could," Oliver retorted.

"Enough," I snapped at Oliver. Then to Daniel. "Please. Let me heal the way I wish to be healed."

Daniel eyed me slantwise, and his chest rose and fell as he visibly tried to gain control of his temper.

But he lost; his temper won.

"Fine," he muttered. "Use your magic. I have an airship to fly." Then, shoulders tensed, he strode through the door.

Oliver waited until Daniel was out of sight, then he eased the door shut and turned to me. Any semblance of nonchalance was gone entirely now. "What," he hissed, "just happened?"

"He doesn't like you," I said softly.

"*He* is not what I meant, and you know it."

I did know it.

"Though," Oliver went on, glaring at the door, "I will say that man is too volatile for you."

"Hmmm." I watched as another drop of blood spattered on the floor.

"Hmmm?" Oliver repeated, closing the space between us. "It does not bother you that he cannot control his temper?"

I lifted my gaze. "Daniel knows me better than anyone else."

Oliver's face hardened—his posture too. Even his single word, "Oh," was made of stone. Then suddenly he pushed his face into mine. "And does *Daniel* know you just crossed into the spirit realm? Because *I* know."

"I forgot to cast my dream ward."

"Really? After almost losing your life to the Hell Hounds several times, you simply *forgot* the one thing that keeps you safe. Sorry, El, but I do not believe you." He twisted away and stomped to the porthole. "Your grief makes you a fool."

I stretched my hands toward him. "Please heal me, Ollie." My voice cracked. I wanted his magic—and not just for the wounds. I *needed* it to soften the blade gouging out my insides.

20

"No." Oliver planted his hands on the wall and stared out the window. "What were you thinking, El? I can't protect you if you're in the spirit realm, and you can't set me free if you're dead. Recall: death already claimed your brother, and that is what got us in this demon-and-master tangle in the first place. So please—for my sake—stop being such a bloody *idiot*."

I flinched. "You are as volatile as Daniel is."

"Temperamental, perhaps," Oliver admitted, swinging his gaze to me. "But only when you have earned it. Daniel is cruel whenever his feelings are hurt."

"Do *not*," I spat, "try to turn me against Daniel. I love him, and your words will not change that."

Oliver snorted and turned back to the porthole. "He puts you through quite a lot of heartbreak for love—"

"Enough." I crossed the room and thrust my hands at him. "I want these cuts healed, so do it."

"You want me to heal your grief, you mean." He withdrew his flask and gulped back liquor. "Just admit it, El. You want me to erase all your sadness. Well, I fear I cannot. Nothing can heal that sort of wound. Though you might try this." He offered me the flask.

"*No.*" A frustrated hunger burned in my stomach, briefly erasing the stab of loss. The knife of regret. "You will heal me now, Ollie."

"Or what?" He straightened. "Will you *command* me?"

"Yes."

His eyes flashed. "Do it then. Command your tool. Just as

you did last night when you scorched away part of my very *being* with electricity. Just as you always do when you want something."

My breath hiccupped. I deserved Oliver's temper for what had happened in Paris. Yet when I had commanded him to grab a crystal clamp—a device that produced electricity from quartz—I hadn't known the electricity would kill a piece of his soul.

But *he* had been the one to manipulate me into binding to him. *He* had become my tool willingly, and *he* had given me a two-month deadline in which I had to set him free.

"Use me, Eleanor." Oliver leaned toward me. "*Betray* me so that for that brief moment while my magic keeps you warm, you can pretend your life is not broken. Why, I bet if you tried hard enough, you could even pretend your mother is still alive."

His words crashed into me. I rocked back on my heels, and all my guilt for mistreating him vanished.

"Heal me," I said. "Heal my wounds now, Oliver. *Sum veritas.*" The words of command slid off my tongue like snakes, and instantly Oliver's eyes ignited with bright blue magic.

His flask fell to the floor. He grabbed me and viciously squeezed my hands in his—so tightly that my cuts ripped wider and the splinters dug deeper.

Then through clenched teeth, he began to murmur. A heartbeat passed. Two more . . . until finally the warmth came—a sparkling, pure heat a thousand times more comforting than alcohol or an embrace. It washed over me, through me. It circled around my heart and then settled into every piece of my soul.

And one by one, the splinters wriggled out of my skin. The lacerations on my hands and knees closed up, and the pain around my heart eased. When the last cut was finally healed, Oliver flung away my hands and stalked to the door. "You will push everyone away," he growled beneath his breath. "Just like he did, you will lose us all."

He. Elijah. My brother.

Oliver grabbed for the doorknob.

"Wait," I called. I finally felt strong again. I finally felt *alive.*

Stooping down, I retrieved Oliver's flask. He drank too much, my demon. It might dull his grief, but he was wrong: magic *did* heal mine.

I stepped toward him. "I am not Elijah."

"Yet you are becoming him." His golden eyes met mine, glowing in time to his pulse. "All you care about is how the magic makes you feel. How is that so different from your brother?"

"You were the one who introduced me to power."

"Perhaps I did," he agreed, "and perhaps I inflated your ego too much in the process. You are strong, but you are not omnipotent." He pinched the bridge of his nose, and his eyes fluttered shut. "Nor does it atone for what you did to me last night—*forcing* me to touch electricity. . . . I can never forgive you."

Before I could open my mouth to argue—to explain how his power saved all of Paris—he said, "And what of Laure?" His eyes opened and latched on to mine. "She is your friend, yet you killed her—you actually *killed* her when you brought that corpse back to life. If I hadn't been there to save her, then Laure would be dead now. *And*"—his eyebrows rose—"as if that was not bad enough, you promised to explain everything to her. Yet instead, you left her in Paris with nothing but a note."

"That," I ground out, "was my only choice. We have to reach Marseille before Marcus does—you *know* that. And as for the butler's corpse, raising it was an accident."

"Accident or no, you have pushed Laure away." He ticked off one finger. "And you have pushed me away." He ticked off a second finger. "Who will be next, El? I understand how much you want to make Marcus pay, but at what cost—"

"How can you possibly comprehend?" I cut in, my pitch rising. "Do you have a family? Or loved ones? Or someone you would give your very *life* to protect? No," I went on, unconcerned when his nostrils flared or his breath hitched. "You have *none* of those things, so do not speak to me as if you understand."

For a long moment he stayed silent. His lips pressed tighter and tighter, turning into a white line.

Then I felt it. Felt the deep, agonizing pain that lived inside him.

He didn't mean for me to feel it—it simply shuddered over our bond and then instantly vanished again.

Yet I almost staggered back from the force of it. I had to bite the inside of my mouth to keep my face blank. I would not give him the satisfaction of thinking he had *gained* something with that display.

"You're dismissed," I said, swiveling away and crossing to the bunk.

"Am I?" Oliver barked a laugh. "You *will* push everyone away, El. Even your precious Danny Boy."

I flung myself onto the bunk and squeezed my eyes shut. "Do not act as if you care for my life, Oliver. You only want me around so I may set you free."

Fabric shifted and feet padded. I popped my eyes wide—to find Oliver only inches away, his body angled down. "You're right," he whispered. "I have no family. Yet I *do* have a home—a spirit realm that I will do anything to return to. You see me as your tool, Eleanor, and I see you as mine. After we destroy Marcus and my responsibilities are complete, do not forget: you owe me."

Then without another word and with his unnatural, demonic grace, he strode to the door and left.

I lay on my bunk for a time, staring at the curved, metal walls. Joseph's and Daniel's voices drifted through my open door from the pilothouse. Allison was, I assumed, on board as well, but where, I did not know—and I was too focused on Oliver's words to worry over it.

Was he right? *Would* I push everyone away as Elijah had? The way this bright, hot guilt burned along my shoulders and through my chest, the words felt all too true.

But maybe this was another of my demon's tricks—another cruel twist of words to keep me wallowing in pain and grief. Maybe *he* pushed my friends away.

I had accused him of that once before, in Paris. First Jie had discovered Oliver's existence and raced off in a rage. Then

Oliver had interrupted Daniel and me right before Daniel was going to kiss me. And of course, seeing Oliver had sent Daniel into a wild, red-faced fury.

One by one, Oliver had turned my friends against me, whittling away my allies until I had only him. Perhaps he did the same now.

You cannot give in to him, I ordered myself, and with a forceful huff of breath, I shoved aside all those black thoughts. I would focus on my magic instead. So warm, so perfect. The further I sank into it, the less I had to feel. The less I had to think.

Yet I could not seem to make the heady contentment come. It wasn't muffling my troubles as it usually did. The magic was fading too fast—so quickly, in fact, that I feared there was a hole in my chest through which it leaked. And if I looked down, I would see straight through to the other side.

I drew in a big breath, begging the thrum of power to stay . . . to *grow*, when my right hand slid into my pocket.

And my knuckles grazed against something grooved and smooth and palm sized.

I stiffened, then wrenched the ivory fist from my pocket and sat upright in bed. I had completely forgotten I had it, and as I traced the lifelike wrinkles and fingernails carved into it, I finally *felt* something.

I felt the air slide into my lungs. I felt my heart beat steadily in my chest. And I felt better. Stronger.

I didn't know what this artifact was—only that it was magical. And ancient. I had originally thought it was an amulet and that it contained a vast compulsion spell. But Madame Marineaux had told me I was wrong.

It is a far more powerful artifact than any amulet, she had said. And yet she'd offered no more explanation to what the carved ivory might be or what it might do. Then, just as the Hell Hounds were blasting her soul into oblivion, she had shown me where to find it. She had planted the image of the fist into my brain, and I had claimed the artifact for myself. There was something so appealing about it. As if whatever power that lived within was somehow pulsing out when I held it. When I watched it.

Footsteps sounded in the hall. I balked, and thrust the ivory fist back into my pocket. I would tell Oliver and the Spirit-Hunters about the fist eventually. But there was no need to tell them now—not when we would soon be in Marseille and dealing with Marcus. Whatever this strange artifact was, it could wait.

Someone cleared his throat, and I found Joseph standing in the doorway, fingers on his bandages.

I swung my legs off the bunk. "Yes?"

Joseph's hand dropped. "I came to offer you my condolences." His voice was gravelly with exhaustion. "The loss of a mother is something no one should have to endure."

"Yet we all must at some point," I said flatly.

"True." He sank into a bow. "Nonetheless, I am sorry, Eleanor. I feel . . ." He lifted, his forehead drawn tight. "I feel as if this is my fault. I could not see what Marcus was becoming all those years ago. I did not stop him until it was too late."

Marcus had been Joseph's childhood friend. They'd both

trained their magic with the Voodoo Queen of New Orleans. Yet Marcus had turned to a darker power—to necromancy and sacrifice—and all the while, the Voodoo Queen and Joseph had remained oblivious.

"That was years ago," I murmured.

"Yet guilt is the one wound time cannot heal." Joseph's fingers moved to a series of scars on his left cheek—gifts from Marcus. "Some days I catch myself missing his friendship. Such a mind—and a sense of humor too. We used to be inseparable. . . . But no one wants to believe their dearest friend is a murderer. Even when the facts are right before you."

Then Joseph surprised me—shocked me, really—for he heaved a sigh, and his posture slouched. For the first time since I had met him three months past, the Creole looked lost. And young.

"I cannot believe he has Jie," he said, shaking his head. "If you are right—if that hair clasp from Madame Marineaux was the amulet that compelled Jie to join Marcus—then it is one more thing I was too blind to see. One more person I foolishly trusted."

My chest tightened with a twinge of anger. Of hurt. And even a twinge of shame.

"I trusted Madame Marineaux too," I admitted. "None of us could have known what she really was, Joseph."

"No." His eyes thinned thoughtfully. Then he glanced into the hall and toward the airship's aft. Toward where Oliver had walked only minutes ago.

He was thinking that *I* trusted Oliver. That *I* did not know what my demon really was . . . and he was right. I trusted Oliver with my life, yet I understood nothing of his desires or motivations. I knew none of my demon's secrets.

But I would not speak of that with Joseph. Instead, I shuffled across the room and rested my hand on the doorknob. "Do you know how to stop the compulsion spell on Jie?"

He shrugged, another movement so out of character. "We must kill the necromancer who cast it. That is the only cure I have ever read."

"So we kill Marcus, then?"

"*Wi.*"

"Good." My lips slid up. "I am glad we agree."

For a moment Joseph only watched me. Then a grin spread over his own lips. "I do not think we ever *disagreed*. Marcus died years ago, and it is time he returned to the realm in which he belongs." Joseph rapped his knuckles against the door as if deciding this was a good note on which to end our talk . . . but then his eyebrows curved down. "Your friend Miss Wilcox," he added, leveling me with a stare, "has been sitting in the galley since we departed Paris. I do not know what to do with her, but she must be dealt with before we reach Marseille in an hour."

"Miss . . . Wilcox," I repeated. Even though speaking to her was the last thing I wanted to do, Joseph was right. Allison needed to be out of our way.

Joseph shifted his weight. "I realize you are upset, Eleanor, but Miss Wilcox has traveled a great distance to see you. Bad tidings or no, do not dismiss such a gesture, *non?* We have few enough friends in this life, and even fewer *true* friends."

I stayed silent as he drifted into the cabin next door. He was right—yet again—and I *knew* he was. Nonetheless, the thought of speaking to Allison . . . of discussing Philadelphia or why Allison had come . . .

It made my insides knot up.

But with a steeling breath, I forced myself to enter the hall. Each of the doors save one was closed. The galley, I assumed, so I crept to it . . . then poked my head inside.

On the right was a wall of cabinets, while against the left wall stood a squat, round table with stools tucked below it. The fourth stool was beside the porthole, and Allison Wilcox sat stiffly upon it.

I gave a low cough, slinking inside. "Allison . . ." I hesitated, for what should I say? At last, though, I managed a pathetic "Would you like something to eat?"

She did not look away from the porthole. "You," she said coolly, "are the first person to acknowledge my presence since we left Paris four hours ago. Everyone else pretends I do not exist."

"I am . . . sorry?" The apology came out as a question, and to cover the clear lack of pity in my tone, I hurried to the nearest cabinet and swung the door wide. Inside was jug upon jug of water. I moved to the next cabinet, which was filled with lumpy sacks of apples. I withdrew a bruised, red fruit, but when I turned to offer it to Allison, I found her still staring out the window.

"Two weeks, I traveled," she said. "Over the ocean and through France, but for what?" She swiveled toward me. "So that you could abandon me immediately."

I wet my lips as guilt—*always* the guilt—wriggled into my lungs. "I did not ask you to board this airship, Allison. Nor did I ask you to cross an ocean."

"Oh?" Her eyebrows shot up. "So should I have written a letter about your mother's death? Your maid—Mary or Marie or whatever her name is—intended to do just that. But I know from personal experience that death is not the sort of news one should drop upon another person."

My fingers tightened around the apple. "Is that a comment on my own behavior, Allison? When I told you Elijah killed Clarence, are you implying that I dropped that news on you?"

"Of course you did!" She shoved to her feet. "You left Philadelphia only moments later—"

"Because I was being *hunted*."

"I realize! But all the same, I wanted to do what you wouldn't do for me. Besides, I have nothing left for me in Philadelphia, Eleanor! I thought if I came to France, I could join you. In your travels. We could . . ." She wet her lips, and her shoulders sank. As quickly as her temper had grown, it now deflated. "I thought we could . . . mourn together, Eleanor."

"But what of your mother? You should stay with her." *For you never know when she might be gone.*

Allison shook her head. "Mother's only interest now is in marrying me off." She leaned expectantly toward me, knowing

I related to her predicament.

"I understand you don't want to get married," I admitted, "but the fact is that it makes no difference in the end. You cannot stay with us, Allison. You must return to Philadelphia. There's no place for you here."

"No place for me here," she said sharply. "Of course there isn't. You are Eleanor Fitt. You do not want me now, just as you never wanted my company before."

"That has *nothing* to do with it." I opened my hands, inwardly ordering my temper to stay cool. "The Spirit-Hunters and I almost lost our lives fighting a demon in Paris, Allison. Now we go to Marseille to fight her master. It is not safe."

Allison wilted back slightly. "A . . . demon? But I thought you were fleeing that necromancer. What happened to him?"

"Marcus," I said softly. I spun around and shuffled to the table to set down the apple. But then my hands felt too empty. I plucked it back up again and stared at the speckled peel. "The necromancer who died . . . and then returned to life. His name is Marcus."

"And he is the one who now possesses Elijah's body," Allison whispered.

I nodded. "And he was the reason the Spirit-Hunters were in Paris. It was his demon we fought. She was sacrificing people to help Marcus build a spell—a compulsion spell that we believe he used to kidnap Jie."

Allison's breath caught. "The Chinese boy?"

"Chinese *girl*," I corrected, looking back to Allison's face.

"Marcus and Jie boarded a train bound for Marseille, so now we intend to ambush him there. And we intend to kill him."

"But what if that is precisely what he wants?" Allison gestured south, toward Marseille. "Perhaps he kidnapped Jie just to lure you in."

I blinked, surprised Allison would jump to that conclusion so quickly. Of course Joseph, Daniel, and I had thought of that—but we were also intimately familiar with Marcus's tricks by now. Allison was not. . . .

Yet her cleverness had always managed to catch me off guard in the past—even after she had proven it time and time again.

"Marcus might be luring us," I finally acknowledged. "We did consider that, but since we have this balloon, we can travel much faster than any train. We intend to reach Marseille first and ambush *him*."

"Yet why is he even going to Marseille?" she pressed. "Why kidnap your friend only to carry her south?"

"He seeks a basilica in the city. One that might have information leading to the . . ." I hesitated. Allison did not need to know of the Black Pullet—a mythical creature of immortality and wealth my brother had once sought. Nor did she need to know of the Old Man in the Pyramids, who was said to be the only person who knew how to summon the Black Pullet.

And she *certainly* didn't need to know we had traveled all this way on mere guesses that the crypt in Marseille's Notre-Dame de la Garde would have answers leading us to the Old Man.

So at last I simply said, "He seeks a basilica with information leading to more power. *Black magic*," I added with a lift of my eyebrows. "So you must see how dangerous it will be, Allison, and why you cannot join us."

"But then where the blazes will I go? I am on this airship—Mr. Boyer allowed me to board—so I am bound for Marseille no matter what."

"Perhaps you can find a hotel when we arrive. Or a restaurant."

"Oh, so I shall go have lunch? While I wait for you to fight Marcus to the death?"

"Yes." I laughed drily. "That is exactly what you must do."

For several moments she was silent. Her lips pursed, her gaze darted around the room, and I thought the argument was blessedly over. But then she tipped her head to one side. "So Jie Chen is a girl . . . who dresses like a boy. For safety?"

I nodded, and Allison settled a disapproving stare on my trousers. "Is that why you do it? Or is your purse so empty you cannot afford a gown? You may borrow one of mine, you know. I have several in my luggage." She motioned to the rear of the balloon.

I scowled as shamed heat rushed through me. It infuriated me that Allison could *still* humiliate me over my family's poverty.

"My clothes," I said through gritted teeth, "have nothing to do with money. I cannot outrun the Dead in skirts and flounce."

"Oh?" She clicked her tongue. "And whose clothes are these? Clearly they are not your own since the sleeves and pants are far too long."

34

More heat scorched up my face. I had *nothing* to be ashamed of, yet my body reacted as if I did. As if Allison's opinion still mattered. But I forced myself to say in my smoothest tone, "These are Daniel's clothes."

"Ah." Her eyes widened melodramatically. "Your *beau*. The ex-convict you have chosen as your suitor. Or"—she jabbed a finger in the air—"is that other fellow your beau? They were both so very desperate to get into your cabin just now. And we all know how men fall at your feet for no apparent reason."

My jaw went slack. I knew she blamed me, at least partially, for her older brother's death. If Clarence had not been courting me, he might never have walked into Elijah's trap . . . and he might never have died.

But I had never loved Clarence, and Clarence had never loved me. He had courted me to make our mothers happy and to *bribe* me. His family had criminal connections; I knew about them; he had not wanted me to blab.

Yet Allison knew none of this. All she saw was someone who had chosen a ruffian over her older brother.

Yes, she blamed me for Clarence's death . . . and I supposed, deep down, I did too.

Still, no matter how much I understood her feelings—and perhaps even *appreciated* all she'd recently done for me—I could no longer keep the edge off my words. "His name is Oliver, and he is *not* my beau."

"Oliver what?" she demanded.

I flung my gaze around the room for inspiration. I could hardly say that Oliver was a demon—and *especially* not that he

35

was my demon. My eyes landed on the apple still clutched in my fingers. "McIntosh," I said gruffly. Then more firmly. "His name is Oliver McIntosh, and he is nothing more than a good friend."

"Oh?" Allison pushed out her chin. "Then why have I never seen him before? I know no McIntosh families in Philadelphia."

I squeezed the apple until my fingernails cut through the flesh. Until juice trickled out. "I met Oliver on my way to France. He helped me out of several dire situations." I left it at that.

"And now he is a part of your team?" Allison pretended to examine her gloves. "Mr. McIntosh helped you, and now he gets to stay with you?"

"Something like that."

A smug pucker settled on her lips.

"No, Allison." I shook my head frantically. "That does not mean *you* can join me too."

"Why not? After Marseille, then I can become a part of this little team as well."

"No." I set the apple on the table and wiped my hands on my pants. "You do not even like us. You do not know what we do. If you want a change, then visit Rome. Or London. But do not pester the Spirit-Hunters."

She planted a hand on her hip. "I was under the impression that Mr. Boyer was the leader."

"Allison, you cannot join us. When we reach Marseille, you will separate from us, and that is the end of this discussion." Her mouth opened to argue, so I powered on. "You have no reason to be here! I did not *ask* you to come to Paris! I did not *ask* you to tell me of my mother's death. And I most certainly did not *ask* you to board this airship. I. Do. Not. want you here. What is so hard for you to understand about that?"

My final words rang out, echoing above the airship's creak. Allison's face paled. For several long breaths she simply stared at me. Then her eyelids lowered icily, and she said, "Of course you do not want my company—just as I suspected all along. Forgive me, Eleanor, for hoping otherwise." Her chin tipped up, and she whirled around to return to her stool.

And my mouth bounced open. I had not intended to say that—at least not so cruelly. Yes, I wanted her to go away, but I had been better raised than this. My manners had failed me, and even if she was a girl I had grown up loathing, I appreciated what she had done.

But it was too late to withdraw my words. Allison was seated once more, her gaze latched on to the grassy patchworks outside and her posture unyielding.

I turned and dragged my feet to the door . . . then into the hall. And as I returned to my cabin, Oliver's words shrieked in my mind, over and over again.

You will push everyone away. Just like he did, you will lose us all.

CHAPTER THREE

I was shaking by the time I reached my cabin. I had lost my hard-earned balance, and though I squeezed the ivory fist in a death grip, it did not soothe me.

I didn't *want* to push everyone away. I wanted to be alone, yes, but not forever. *It isn't your fault,* I told myself. *It is Oliver who pushes your friends away.* Yet Joseph was still my friend—and Daniel had regained his regard for me once more.

Shoving the fist into my pocket, I marched from my room to the pilothouse. I would *prove* this was Oliver's doing and not my own.

But I paused in the pilothouse doorway, blinded by the onslaught of light and squinting as I waited for my eyes to adjust. Daniel stood at the steering wheel, its multiple spokes reaching up to his chest. At his right were two brass handles, waist high and fastened to some unseen mechanism below the floor. At his left were two more levers, and as my vision finally cleared, I watched him shift both levers forward and then spin the steering wheel sharply right.

The balloon swayed slightly and then shifted its course, heading south . . . and revealing the dark-blue waters of the Mediterranean.

For half a breath I simply stared—finally feeling a sense of wonder twine through me. I was seeing the Mediterranean. From above. I was *flying*.

"For every beauty," I murmured beneath my breath, "there *is* an eye somewhere to see it."

Daniel stiffened . . . and then turned very slowly toward me. *Clack, clack, clack.* He extended a worn, dented spyglass. Then *thwump!* He snapped it shut. "How are you?" His voice was rough, as if he hadn't spoken in hours.

"All right," I lied. He nodded, but I could tell from the flick of his eyebrows that he didn't believe me.

I moved fully into the room and craned my neck to examine the view outside. It was unlike anything I had ever seen. Such blue waters and craggy cliffs. A few scrubby plants eked out an existence in the dry landscape, and though there were still farms, the patches of green were localized and small. Most of this Provençal world was one of dusty hills, dustier roads, and bleached-out houses—and no wonder, with such a hot, bright sun.

And it was doubly hot and bright in the pilothouse thanks to all the windows. A sheen of sweat covered Daniel's forehead.

I shifted my gaze to the back of the room, to where charts and maps covered two low tables. Above, hanging on hooks, were white satchels with leather straps.

"What are those?" I asked, pointing at the packs.

Daniel made an apologetic smile. "It's a bit late now—I should've told you about 'em before we left Paris, but then . . . you know. . . ." He trailed off, clearly wishing to avoid mention of Mama's death.

That was fine by me. "What are they then?"

"Parachutes." At my blank look, he explained, "They're for safety. If for some reason we have to hightail it from the ship but we're still in the air, then you put one of those on your back. When you yank that piece of fabric beside the strap"—he motioned to a dangling flap of canvas—"a parachute will come flyin' out. It'll fill with air and stop your fall."

"Oh." My forehead creased as I tried to imagine how a piece of fabric could possibly fight gravity.

"Like I said," Daniel added, "it's a bit late to tell you since we'll reach Marseille in a few minutes." He turned back to the wheel, fidgeting with the spyglass. Then messing with a chain around his neck—a monocle.

Anger tickled down my spine at the sight of it. "Why do you keep that, Daniel?" It was one of many opulent gifts from Madame Marineaux and the Marquis. They had heaped us with new gowns and suits and jewelry, and they'd distracted us from

41

les Morts with parties and meetings and meals.

And it had all been a part of Marcus's carefully laid plans to get information on the Black Pullet. Once we had realized that the Marquis was none other than Marcus's uncle—when Joseph had seen a portrait of the Marquis's sister and recognized her as Marcus's mother—it had been too late to stop what was already in motion. Jie was gone; the Marquis was dead.

Daniel glanced at the monocle as if surprised. "I keep it because it's useful. It lets me see all the small details on my work."

"But it was from Madame Marineaux."

"So is that shirt you're wearing." He frowned and flicked a finger at his thigh. "These pants are too. Besides, have *you* ever tried to turn a screw the size of a pinhead?"

I gave a soft "hmmm." He had a point. . . .

Clack, clack, clack. He was back to messing with the spyglass.

"Daniel." I scooted closer to him.

His shoulders rose; his fidgeting quickened.

I moved even closer until Daniel's fingers—and the spyglass—froze.

"Are you angry with me?" I asked quietly. "For earlier? With . . . Oliver?"

"No." He closed the spyglass. "I'm just confused, I reckon. One minute you're hard as nails and don't need help from anyone. Then the next you're . . ." He blushed. "Well, the next minute you're *soft*." His voice almost cracked on that word. "And it's only then that you seem to want me around."

42

"Soft?" I repeated in a squeaky tone. His blush brightened, and I could only assume he referred to our kiss from the night before. I had initiated it; he had responded—perhaps too much. We had fallen so deeply into the taste and feel of each other that we'd lost sight of the real world.

"Daniel," I started, just as he said, "Empress."

Our mouths clamped shut, and we stared at each other. "Y-you first," I finally said.

"Are you . . ." He coughed lightly and pushed the spyglass into his pocket. "Don't get mad, all right? But I gotta ask this." His breath huffed out, and then he blurted, "Are you in love with him?"

I cocked my head, not understanding the question. "In love with whom?"

"Oliver."

I reared back. "Why would you ask that? Or even think that?"

"It's just . . . That is . . ." He moaned and rubbed the back of his neck. "You're so close to him."

"Are you jealous?"

"No," he insisted. But then he shook his head. "Well, maybe I am. I lost someone that way—to another man. So I want to know *now* if anyone's out there with designs on your heart. I can't handle all this back-and-forth between us, so I'd like a solid idea of where I stand." He nodded as if satisfied with this declaration.

But I was not satisfied. In fact, my breath seemed to trap

43

itself in my lungs as the meaning of his words slithered through my brain.

And as three months of hurt came rising to the surface.

"A solid idea?" My voice trembled. "You have no *right* to ask that of me, Daniel! Not after you left me in Philadelphia. I asked you for the same thing—do you recall? I wanted to know where I stood, and you crushed me. So pray tell, why should *I* make any promises to you now?"

His lips screwed shut, and he surprised me by lowering his gaze to his feet. "I thought I was doing what was best for you in Philadelphia. I thought you ought to find someone who your ma would like—who could make you happy. And keep you comfortable."

"And of course I had no say in the matter." I folded my arms over my chest and stared out the window. We were almost to the coastline now, and a series of jagged hills rose up and up to the east.

"I really did mean well." Daniel's voice was low and urgent. But I did not look his way, so he returned his hands to the wheel and shifted his own focus to the horizon.

"Mean well," I repeated to myself. Then louder, "And in Paris, when you screamed at me about my new hand—did you mean well then? Or in the lab, when you suggested that I *hurt* myself on the crystal clamp. Did you *mean well* then?"

His knuckles went white as he squeezed the wheel. "I know I don't always handle things right. I ain't . . . I mean, I *am not* polished. My temper always causes more trouble than I mean to. I'm just . . ." His eyes flicked to me then back ahead. "I'm protective

44

of the people I care about. *Too* protective. When I saw your new hand and your demon, my vision went red . . . and I didn't think before I spoke." Twisting the wheel left, he eased back one of the levers . . . and the balloon twisted sharply east.

We had reached the water now, and the steep hillsides alongside the sea were lined with green vineyards and olive groves. It was peaceful and beautiful—and *nothing* like what warred in my heart.

I wanted to forgive Daniel for leaving me in Philadelphia. Love was about forgiveness, right? Yet I could not seem to forget how much he had *hurt* me.

After shoving the second lever in place, Daniel turned to me. "I'm sorry, Eleanor Fitt. Really. Truly. I'm sorry if I hurt you when I left Philadelphia. Or when I yelled at you in Paris. It ain't . . ." He ground his teeth. "I mean, *it is not* easy to change. But I'm trying, Eleanor. I *swear* I am."

I could not breathe. I could not move. I could not speak. He was offering an apology. A genuine apology that I so desperately wanted to accept. I would *not* push Daniel away as Oliver wanted.

Daniel seemed to understand my thoughts, for he took a long, hesitant step toward me. Then another, to fully close the space between us. "I am so sorry," he said softly. His fingers came up to twine a lock of my hair. "Once we stop Marcus and get Jie back . . . well, then you can break this thing you have with Oliver, and it can be just us."

It's not so simple, I thought. Oliver was bound to me until I learned the magic to set him free, and I prayed that Daniel would

45

push the subject no further.

But he was Daniel, and he had no idea when enough was enough.

"And then Joseph says, with the proper trainin', we can fix your magic too."

Ice shivered through my body. My hair pricked up. "Fix my magic."

"Mm-hmmm. Joseph says—"

"But what if I don't want to?" I pulled free from Daniel. "I realize you follow Joseph blindly, but—"

"It ain't blind, Empress. He knows best, so I take his lead."

"But *does* he know best?" I gestured between Daniel and me. "Joseph knows nothing about what we feel, and he knows *nothing* of my magic. I do not need fixing, Daniel. This is who I am now. Magic is a part of me—a part of my very soul—and I wish you and Joseph could accept that."

Daniel reached for me, his eyes wide and lips parted . . . but the hole in my chest was back. It was bigger and meaner than before—and it was so, *so* cold. As I staggered around and marched for the door, tears burned my eyes. Stinging, ridiculous tears that I did not want to cry any more than I wanted to hear Daniel's inevitable apology.

Perhaps Oliver was right: perhaps I *did* push my friends away—but it was not only me. They pushed back. From all directions, everyone wanted something from me. Oliver wanted his freedom, Allison wanted companionship, and Daniel wanted my heart. Joseph was the only person on this ship who seemed to

46

understand that all that mattered right now was Jie and Marcus.

But even Joseph wanted me to stay away from necromancy—even Joseph made stupid demands regarding friendship and power that I could not meet.

I dug the heels of my hands into my eyes as I stumbled into my cabin. The only thing I had that I could still rely on was my magic. It had gotten me to the spirit realm and back, hadn't it? It had helped me destroy Madame Marineaux and save Daniel and Joseph. My magic had stopped the Dead in Philadelphia as well as in Paris, and it would stop the Dead again.

Lose you all in the end? I thought miserably, stopping before my porthole. Yes, perhaps I would, and perhaps it was precisely what Oliver wanted. But at least with no one telling me what to do, I would be left with the lone person who could kill Marcus and get this job done.

Me.

When the airship crested the final hill to Marseille, my thoughts were in another world—one in which Marcus was before me and my revenge finally had its outlet.

It was then, just as I reached for the ivory fist, that all of Marseille appeared. My hand jerked from my pocket, and I pressed my face against the porthole. Crowded with white buildings and red roofs, Marseille rose up and outward like a bowl. It sat right on the Mediterranean's edge, hugging a long harbor on all sides—and then the Gulf of Lion beyond.

Steamers and sailing boats dotted the waters, and the closer we puttered, the more clearly I could make out the huge merchant vessels and the more picturesque fishing boats. After the empty expanse of the Provençal desert, Marseille was a flourishing, vibrant place.

Soon I could even see individual people and carts, all scurrying about like ants on the cobblestone streets of the city. Faces turned up toward us, hands over brows like visors. . . . But strangely enough, they almost immediately snapped back down.

The airship slowed and then stopped completely above an oblong wharf running into the heart of the city. If my history lessons served me right, that was the Old Port: the very first harbor upon which Marseille had been founded thousands of years before.

I ran my gaze over the dirty waters of the Old Port, then east to the elegant buildings along the harbor—and then farther east and up the hill . . .

Until I gasped and had to clutch at the porthole to stay upright.

For there was the Notre-Dame de La Garde. It was impossible to miss, the enormous white basilica rising above the rooftops of Marseille. Upon its limestone outcropping and with an ornate bell tower that gleamed in the sunlight, the Notre-Dame stood higher than anything. And at its top, shining like fire, was a huge copper statue of the Virgin Mary. She stood guard over the entire city: *Notre-Dame de la Garde*, Our Lady of the Guard.

I tried to swallow, but I suddenly found my throat tight as two thoughts warred for space in my brain.

It looks just like the watercolor Mama had in the parlor. That thought flickered, an uninvited, vicious reminder that my mother would never get to see Marseille. Or anywhere.

The second thought was a better one—and I made myself latch on to it. *Marcus will be here soon. And I will slash open his throat.*

I scanned the city streets for any sign of the train depot. For any sign of where Marcus and Jie would arrive. . . . But then we began to drop, and the port surged in closer as my ears shrieked painfully. I winced, clapping my hands over them. Even my stomach felt as if it had been left a hundred feet above.

Then, in an abrupt jolt, we stopped moving. I peered through the porthole once more and found us floating over the harbor, over the ships tied to the pier. A confused fisherman gaped up beneath our shadow. When our ladder suddenly clacked down, he scurried below his boat's deck.

As Daniel shinnied down to the dock and set to roping us into place, I examined the shop fronts around the Old Port and the narrow, cobblestoned roads branching behind. Carts and carriages hurried away—as if their drivers all had somewhere to be. *Jobs, perhaps?* Yet even as this thought flittered through my brain, I knew it was not right.

But before I could consider the strange exodus of afternoon traffic, the airship's engines were cut . . .

And the wind *hurtled* into us, grabbing hold of the balloon. My face hit the porthole with a crunch—then I wobbled backward. Side to side, up and down, the wind did not let us go. If it had not been for the seething hunger in my gut, I did not think I would have the nerve to climb down that listing ladder.

But Marcus was so close.

Once Daniel, Joseph, and Oliver were off the airship, I left Allison chewing her lip in the cargo hold, and I battled the wind and the swinging ladder. When at last I dropped onto the street, I felt absolutely ill—so much so that I had to bend over, rest my hands on my knees, and stare into the murky depths of the harbor.

But looking at the water only seemed to make my stomach revolt more. It was *filthy*, and the oppressive afternoon heat sent a stench rising up that, if I stared hard enough, I imagined I could see.

Ultimately, I pressed a hand over my mouth and shuffled to Oliver nearby. He stood in the middle of the wide cobblestone boulevard—the Quai de Rive Neuve, according to a placard on the nearest building—with his hands in his pockets and looking for all the world like a tourist.

Daniel, meanwhile, was several feet away, inspecting a map of the city. His forehead was scrunched up, and he seemed to be mumbling to himself about "no direct route in this blasted city." He wore his leather bandolier, and the four holsters held loaded pulse pistols.

Beside him was Joseph, who could not seem to keep his gaze still. North, into the city, then south . . . then east up the hill, then west into the sun. He fidgeted with his bandages, tugged at his jacket, and looked as anxious as I felt. On one arm hung his physician's bag, and I could only guess that there were pulse bombs, pulse pistols, and crystal clamps within.

The pulse bombs and pistols created an electromagnetic pulse that acted very much as Joseph's electricity did: it blasted the Dead back to the spirit realm. They could be unwieldy and inefficient, but there was no denying they were effective.

As for the crystal clamps, they operated on piezoelectricity. It was brilliant really—as all of Daniel's inventions tended to be. A copper clamp held a large chunk of quartz that, when squeezed, produced an electric current. The electricity then moved through the copper and into Joseph's arm.

Or into *my* arm, except . . .

Joseph met my eyes, and as if reading my mind, he walked to me and unbuckled his bag. "I know the crystal clamp is hard for you to use, Eleanor." His gaze flitted to Oliver. "But you should take one anyway. As a precaution, *non*?"

He withdrew the crooked, copper clamp with its spring-loaded handle. The uncut crystal the size of my fist glittered in the sun. For Joseph, this was an invaluable tool—a constant and immediate source of electricity. But for me . . .

"I am not comfortable with electricity," I said, meeting his dark, serious eyes. "You keep it."

His head shook once. "I may only use one clamp at a time." He wiggled his right hand. "I need these fingers to expel the power I draw in. So please, take it." He pressed it into my palm, and, with a frown, I closed my hand around it.

I could sense Oliver's displeasure—his *hatred* for the

device—so I quickly shoved it into my pocket. I wanted my demon to know that I would not use it unless I absolutely had to—assuming, of course, I could even use it properly.

My first attempt to use the clamp had ended in too much power. I had accidentally raised a corpse. . . . And of course, my second attempt had stripped away part of Oliver's soul.

But when Oliver stepped close to Joseph and me, it was not the clamp that seemed to be bothering him. "Something isn't right," he said in a hushed tone—as if he feared being over-heard. "Either we have scared everyone off, or something *else* has." He dipped his head to the *quai*.

I started—and Joseph flinched too. Whatever traffic had claimed the streets when we had landed was absent now. The stores and cobblestones held only a few weathered souls, and they were hurrying toward shaded alleys or ship decks as fast as their feet could carry them.

"Perhaps," Joseph said as we watched a fisherman slink belowdecks, "it is merely time for an afternoon nap. The sun *is* quite intense. . . ." Yet even as he spoke, he frowned as if he knew a break could not possibly draw away the entire city.

Daniel approached. His map swooshed in the wind. He briefly met my eyes . . . then turned to Joseph. "Maybe we should just be glad everyone is gone. It makes things easier."

I gulped and swept my gaze up to the Notre-Dame. Figures still scurried in the streets . . . *away* from the Old Port. Away from us.

But before I could speak my concerns, Allison's voice lashed out. "Eleanor."

I twisted around—and winced. She was wobbling off the ladder, and her face looked as green as mine must have been. Yet, unlike me, she forced her chin high and extended her parasol toward me like a rapier. A master beckoning her servant. I hurried over.

"Someone will have to collect my bags," she declared. "I refuse to leave my things unprotected on that airship while I wait for you." She threw me a sideways glare. "And I *suppose* I shall hire a carriage to take me to the nearest hotel. Though I see no one about. What sort of city . . ."

A wind kicked up, even rougher than before, and carried her final words away.

"What?" I shouted, moving closer.

"Where are all the carriages?" she yelled back, but the wind thundered even harder. It swept at her petticoats. She shrieked and grabbed at her skirts—only to drop her parasol. It clattered and rolled toward the edge of the dock.

I dived for it—as did she. But with her hands pressed awkwardly to her knees, she stumbled forward. . . .

The wind shoved her over completely. She hit the ground with a scream, and I snatched up the parasol.

"My gloves," she screeched as I helped her stand. "They're ruined!"

Another gust of wind slammed into us. She almost toppled over again—as did I.

I glanced at the sky. No clouds marred the perfect blue. Nonetheless, there was an electric charge in the air now. That feeling of a storm about to hit.

My grip tightened on the parasol's handle. "I don't like this weather."

"Who cares about the weather?" Allison snapped. "These gloves cost me a fortune."

"I've got it!" Daniel shouted. "The fastest route to the Notre-Dame is definitely up the hill." I peered over my shoulder at him. He shook the map in the air. "We head due east."

"Obviously," Oliver groaned, pointing at the basilica. "We can all see where it is."

"Hush." I glowered at Oliver. "Don't pick on——"

Suddenly, a scream ripped from Allison.

I wrenched toward her—and found her arms outstretched. She shrieked again, and her fingers clawed for me. I seized her hands . . . but she was being dragged away from me.

I held tight, and with all my might I pulled and *pulled* . . . until at last, in a sudden burst of released speed, Allison fell forward and tumbled against me.

That was when I saw what had grabbed her.

Two putrid hands rose from the water and scratched at the cobblestones. Scratched at *us*. And as I watched, my stomach climbing into my chest, hundreds of other fingers splashed through the harbor's surface—and far in the distance, a single scream tore through the city.

"Les Morts! Les Morts!"

The Dead had risen in Marseille.

CHAPTER FOUR

The corpse that had grabbed Allison clawed at the street. I towed Allison behind me as her screams pierced the wind.

Its arms grappled closer. Then its rotten face appeared above the water. Broken teeth chomped, and fingers grated on the cobblestones.

Without thinking, I stabbed Allison's parasol into the corpse's empty eye socket. The metal tip squished in, clunking against bone.

I shoved, and the body toppled back into the water, its hands catching empty air as I skittered out of reach. But my heels hit something. I jerked around—it was Oliver, yanking me to safety.

"Stupid," he snarled, his eyes locked on the water. "There are hundreds of them!" He grabbed at Allison's arm next, and then pitched us both toward Joseph and Daniel.

"What do we do?" Allison wailed. "The Dead are everywhere!" She clutched her face and scrabbled closer to Joseph. "What do we *do*?"

"This changes our plans," Joseph said, shouting to be heard over the splashing and crunching bones of the Dead—and the distant echoes of a shrieking city. "Our duty now lies in retrieving Jie and protecting Marseille. Marcus is second priority to that."

"No." The word rushed from my mouth. We had come here to *kill* Marcus. "If we have to stop all these Dead, then he wins!"

Joseph shook his head grimly. "And if we do not stop the Dead, then we leave an entire city at risk. Daniel." He glanced at the inventor and pointed to the harbor. "Deal with those, please."

"Gladly." With a grim slant to his lips, Daniel unholstered two pistols and marched away from us. Corpses grabbed at the pier, but their bone fingers had not yet gained purchase. So with a steady arm, Daniel took aim at the nearest set of yellow skulls and matted hair. . . .

Pop! One pistol fired, and the heads sank beneath the waves.

I wheeled back on Joseph. "Marcus wants us to give up on him—you know he does. This is just a distraction."

"She's right," Oliver inserted. "He has ambushed us instead of the other way around."

"Be that as it may," Joseph said, "but this is my duty. My

job. I find Jie and protect the city first. That is what the Spirit-Hunters do."

"What about me?" Allison cried. "What do *I* do?"

I pointed up. "You get back on the airship." At that exact moment, the balloon shifted in the wind, and its shadow moved over us, blocking out the sun. "Climb the ladder, Allison, and then pull it inside once you're on board."

"But—"

"You will be safe there," Joseph added. "No one can get to you that high."

Her lips clapped shut, and I could see her trying to find a reason to protest—but before she could summon any words, Oliver's hand shot up.

"Look." He pointed to the end of the Old Port, to where a large avenue hit the open *quai*.

And to where two figures strolled into the sunlight . . . followed by row upon row of shambling corpses.

My stomach curdled. I knew who it was—even from this distance. That broad-shouldered shape could only be the necromancer wearing my brother's skin.

I launched myself toward Daniel. "Spyglass," I shouted.

He whipped around, a pulse bullet clenched between his teeth as he reloaded his pistols. Without waiting for a response, I thrust my hand into his pocket and snatched the spyglass from within. I ignored his shocked stare and stalked down the pier, pushing the glass to my eye.

First I found Marcus. God, he looked so much like Elijah still . . . and yet *so* different. So large. And while the auburn hair that waved in the wind was like my brother's, the way Marcus tugged at the black sleeves on his perfectly tailored suit was nothing like my unfashionable older brother had once been.

Then, several paces back, I found Jie.

Bile rose into my throat. She looked nothing like herself. She wore a dress—her waist pulled in unnaturally tight. Painfully tight, while the dress was a monstrosity of a gown. Gold, enormous, and with a wide, trailing skirt. And her hair—her *hair*. It had been piled on top of her head, a column of black with enormous orchids pinned in at all angles.

She looked like a puppet. A doll dressed up to walk alongside a monster.

I jerked down the spyglass. "I will *kill* him—"

Arms lashed around my waist, holding me back. "What are you doing?" Daniel bellowed. "We need a plan!"

I pushed him off, rage boiling in my lungs and up my throat. Marcus would die—and he would die *now*.

But then Oliver jumped in front of me and grabbed my shoulders. His yellow eyes blazed in the sunlight. "This is what Marcus wants, El. To be seen. To make you furious and careless. We can't give in—we must stick to our original plan and go to the Notre-Dame."

"Go without me—"

"You will both go," Joseph said, appearing beside me.

"I. Want. Marcus." I shoved the glass at Joseph. "You and Daniel can go to the Notre-Dame—"

"Are you insane?" Daniel demanded as Joseph lifted the

spyglass to his eye. "Joseph and I don't know what to look for there!"

"*Marcus*"—I snarled the name—"has made a plaything of Jie. I will not allow him to get away with that."

Joseph's breath caught, and he swore as he wrenched down the spyglass. "He will pay for this. He will *die* for this."

Yes. I grinned, drawing in a breath to start running again— but then Joseph turned to me. "Daniel and I will make sure Marcus pays; yet if he gets through us, then you and your demon *must* be waiting at the Notre-Dame, Eleanor. Whatever it is Marcus seeks, you must destroy it."

"What about the compulsion spell?" I demanded. "You cannot break it without killing Marcus—"

"I said," Joseph roared, his eyes bulging, "that Daniel and I will make Marcus pay. There is no time to lose, Eleanor. You go to the Notre-Dame, and you go *now*."

Oliver's fingers clamped on my bicep. "Joseph is right. If these corpses are meant to distract us, then we cannot lose sight of our original course: the crypt."

I swallowed, groping for any excuse I could conjure to face Marcus.

But I found none, because Joseph and Oliver *were* right.

"Fine. I will go to the Notre-Dame." I jerked from Oliver's grasp, and then I lurched around to stomp toward Allison. She stood, arms over her chest and skirts flipping. Her gaze never left the thrashing waters of the harbor.

"Get on the airship," I shouted at her, "and do not lower the ladder unless you see one of us return. Do you understand?"

She trembled, and for half a breath I feared she might argue. But then she gave a strangled cry and bolted for the dangling ladder.

I waited until she had ascended all the way into the airship, pulled up the ladder, and slammed the hatch shut. Then I angled my head up and east, toward the Notre-Dame. No matter what lay ahead, I would *not* leave this city without destroying what Marcus sought.

And not without rescuing Jie.

"Empress!" Daniel's voice whipped out, and I glanced over my shoulder as he jogged to me. "Take these." He fumbled with something in his pocket . . . and then withdrew his goggles— the lenses that allowed us to see when spirits and the Dead were near.

But I didn't need them anymore; I had my magic, and it was far more effective. So I shook my head. "Keep them, Daniel."

His lips pressed thin—a grave mask, not an angry one— and he lowered his hand. "Stay safe."

"You too." Then, with nothing more than a beckoning finger in Oliver's direction and a final, hard nod at Joseph, I set off up the hill.

It took longer than I had expected to ascend to the Notre-Dame—the hill was steep and the wind was rough. We passed beige, gray, and cream-colored buildings, but they all had their shutters closed tight and doors locked.

Which terrified me. How did the city *know* to flee indoors? It was as if they had expected the Dead to come.

As we pounded up a curvy road called Montée des Oblats, Oliver and I both had to lean into the wind to keep from tipping backward and tumbling down the hill. Just as we reached the first cliff of limestone jutting up from the hillside, the road twisted left . . . and a newspaper came flapping toward us.

It slapped into Oliver's face—but not before I caught sight of the headline: "*Les Spirit-Hunters amènent les Morts où ils vont.*"

My feet slowed to a stop, and I yanked the newspaper off Oliver. Below the headline was a hazy photograph of Daniel's airship on the day he had landed in Paris. "What does this say?" I shouted, thrusting the article at Oliver.

He took the shaking pages and quickly scanned them. Then his face paled with fury, and he flung the paper into the wind. "It says the Spirit-Hunters bring the Dead. It says they were feared in Paris and that the city should hide at first sight of the balloon. It claims Joseph and his team raised *les Morts.*"

My stomach flipped. How could such a story have reached Marseille? We had only left Paris a few hours ago. Oliver must have thought the same thing, for he said, "Telegraph travels faster than train—or airship. Marcus must have sent the story ahead."

"But . . . why?" I clutched at my stomach . . . and then my fingers moved instinctively to my pocket. To the ivory fist.

But the fist's trill of magic held no comfort for me right then. Not when my brain couldn't slow. Questions scattered

61

and twisted every which way. Because truly, why would Marcus want to get the citizens of Marseille locked inside? Unless it was to make things easier. To make this a final battle between him . . . and *us*.

Yet even if this was the reason, how far in advance must Marcus have planned to coordinate such a feat?

I spun around to face the Old Port—as if I might be able to catch a glimpse of the necromancer and his corpse army. But at this angle all I could see were buildings and shadowy streets.

"Come on," I said, turning back to Oliver. He nodded once, jaw set, and we launched back up the hill.

But we moved faster this time, our heads down and bodies angled. I felt Oliver's fear as clearly as my own, pulsing over our bond—a sudden certainty that we were, yet again, walking into a trap. That we were helpless flies clambering up the web and directly into the spider's maw.

The road led us around the exposed, craggy limestone before finally spitting us out before an old fortress wall. The heavy stone base rose up, bisected by two stairwells leading to the church itself. We darted for the nearest set. Higher, higher we went—Oliver skipping two steps at a time and me gasping to keep up—until we finally reached the summit of our climb.

And we almost toppled over, for now we were fully exposed to the erratic wind. It careened into me, and if not for Oliver twirling around at the last moment, I would have plummeted right back down the stairs.

But he caught me, and his fingers slid around my wrist to

grab tight and hard. . . . Then we heaved ourselves against the wind and toward the nearest door.

When at last we stumbled into an opening below the bell tower, I almost crumpled to my knees from the sudden *lack* of wind. The gusts continued overhead and resounded deep within my eardrums.

Oliver pointed warily ahead, to a dark doorway beneath an arch of gray stone. Gold letters above said CRYPTE.

"Well," I said between pants, "at least that was . . . easy . . . to find."

He snorted, a harsh sound, and looked back toward the city. I followed his gaze. Marseille sloped below us. But all I could see at this angle were red rooftops and distant mountains.

Oliver's fingers laced through mine, and he tugged me beneath the crypt's arched entrance into a shadowy entry room. Two white statues flanked another doorway, but it was too dark to see farther than the glow of the statues. I moved to a sconce beside the entrance and carefully eased off a candle. Then, in a low voice, I asked, "Should I cast an awareness spell?"

Like Daniel's goggles, the spell would alert me to the presence of the Dead—or the living too. But since spirits and bodies were more likely to be found in a crypt, the Dead were what I sought awareness of.

"Cast the spell," Oliver said, his gaze whipping forward and then behind. He actually seemed tenser than I was. I squeezed his hand once, reassuring, but other than a flash of gold in his eyes, he did not relax.

So I let him keep guard while I focused on drawing in my magic. It trickled in from my fingers and toes, warming my veins as it slithered into my heart. Then I whispered, "*Sentio omnia quae me circumentur.*" The words of the spell slid off my tongue like a snake. *I feel all around me. I feel all around me.*

And my magic expelled, like a throbbing, living fisherman's net, before finally settling many feet away.

"We're alone," I murmured. "Let's light this candle and proceed."

Oliver nodded, and after searching the other sconces, he found a matchbox. Once the orange flame of the candle flickered before my face, strangely warm against the cool air rolling in from the darkness ahead, we set off.

Then we were through the second archway. "At least it's not big," Oliver declared.

I squinted, straining to see what his demon eyes could, but all I found were flagstones like those in the foyer and a low, vaulted ceiling. The candlelight flickered and made shapes in the shadows around us.

Ice ran down my neck—and it was not from the crypt's cool air, but from fear. After chasing through the quarries beneath Paris, I had had quite enough with dark, damp places.

Yet fear had never stopped me before.

"If it's not big," I said, "then it will not take long to explore. Do you see anywhere worth starting?"

"More important," he countered, handing the candle to me, "do you have any specific ideas for what we seek?"

"All Elijah's letter said was that you told him a joke in this crypt. About Jack and the beanstalk."

"Which I didn't do," he muttered. "So we have assumed that a single throwaway comment is a clue. *Wonderful*."

"But you said yourself that the Black Pullet is a chicken-type monster—"

"A cockatrice more like," he inserted.

"—and just as the chicken in Jack and the beanstalk offered its master endless wealth, so does the Pullet. Elijah's letter *must* have pointed us here for a reason, Oliver."

"We shall see soon, I suppose." Oliver eased into a careful walk into the darkness. "You go right, El. I'll go left—I can see well enough in the shadows."

I gulped, watching his figure fade away. He might have declared it a small space, but it was also pitch-black and with only one doorway in or out.

If Marcus wanted to trap us, this was an excellent place in which to do it.

My pulse kicked up at that thought, and I flung my senses along my awareness web. . . . *No one. Nothing.* The crypt was as empty as it had been two minutes ago.

"Coward," I muttered to myself, rolling my shoulders and bouncing on my toes. "There's no one here." My words ricocheted off the low ceiling, sounding all too much like whispers and moans. But I forced my brain to task and set off to the right. I didn't have far to go, though, before I reached a wall of plaques. Or I thought they were plaques; yet as I approached, I realized the marble slabs were held in place by fat screws—and that each was labeled with a name.

These were the tombs of the crypt.

My breath fogged, spiraling out in time to my slow steps. There were corpses everywhere, but they were fully dead. There was no spark of magic flickering on my awareness spell.

Still, being near *potential* Dead was never ideal.

I hugged the wall, waving the candle up and down—until a figure appeared in the corner of my vision.

I shrieked, jerking back. But it was only a statue.

"El?" Oliver's footsteps rang out. "El, are you all right?"

"Fine," I squeaked. The statue was nothing more than a praying saint—and I was nothing more than a coward.

Oliver scrambled to my side, his eyes wide and glowing gold. "What happened?"

"Nothing. I am an enormous fool. . . ." My words died on my tongue, for just beyond the saint's halo was a tomb with a giant chunk of rock missing from its corner. I darted around the statue and held the candle aloft.

Oliver joined me, his brow furrowed. "It looks like someone has opened it."

I nodded, suddenly unable to speak. All my earlier panic had vanished, replaced with a surge of excitement.

For the tomb read JACQUES GIRARD.

"I know this name," I murmured, thinking back to Paris. "Take this." I shoved the candle into Oliver's hand and then brought my nose to the broken marble. "Do you remember when you found Daniel and me near the library in Paris?"

"Yes," Oliver muttered, an edge to the word. It was the same day I'd accused him of *wanting* me to be alone.

"Daniel and I had been researching the Black Pullet," I continued, "trying to retrace Elijah's steps. What we discovered was that the man who found *Le Dragon Noir* in Egypt was a necromancer in Napoleon's army. His name"—I tapped the plaque—"was Jacques Girard. Or *Jack*."

"Jack and the beanstalk." Oliver's breath hissed out, shaking the candle's flame. "And *Le Dragon Noir* was the grimoire Elijah sought."

"Exactly. And it's the grimoire Marcus wanted because it supposedly told one how to raise the Black Pullet. Endless wealth and immortality—what isn't to like about the creature?"

"The fact that it's supposedly a serpent-like bird, for one. Endless wealth and immortality do not seem worth raising a monster."

"That is easy for you to say," I retorted. "*You* already have an immortal soul."

Oliver gave a halfhearted snort as I beckoned for him to hold the flame closer to the broken edge of the tomb. The chipped edges were raw, but when I ran my thumb along them, old dust came away.

Oliver leaned in close to the hole as well, yet his gaze was on my face when he said, "If this Jacques Girard truly discovered *Le Dragon Noir*, then he must have read the grimoire—and he must have known how to find the Old Man."

I drew back slightly, meeting Oliver's eyes. The Old Man was the only person in the world who knew how to raise the Black Pullet.

"That was Elijah's final command for me," Oliver went on. "To find the Old Man in the Pyramids. I cannot rest until I fulfill that order from your brother, so if Girard's corpse is really in there"—he jabbed a finger at the plaque—"I must speak to his ghost."

"But how?" I asked.

"We have his body."

For a moment I simply stared at Oliver. Then understanding crashed over me. I gasped. "You told me that once, didn't you? The only way to contact a spirit is with the corpse. And, oh God"—I clutched at Oliver's sleeve—"Elijah *was* here. That's why the tomb is broken! He tried to *speak* to Jacques Girard. He hinted at it in one of his letters to me. *Monsieur Girard was not home today.*"

I closed my eyes and tried to summon the exact words of the letter. "*I fear I wrote the wrong address. If I cannot find him, then I will have no choice but to find the pages.*" My eyes snapped wide-open. "He *was* here, but he couldn't speak to Girard's ghost—the spirit 'wasn't home.' I bet he thought he had the wrong body, the—the wrong *address*."

"Blessed eternity," Oliver swore. "You might be right." He waved the candle back toward the crumbling corner of the tomb. "And Marcus must have figured it all out. That's why he's coming here."

My mouth went dry. "He wants to raise Girard and learn how to find the Old Man . . . which means we have to destroy the body."

Oliver recoiled. "Why?"

"If the body is gone, then Marcus cannot speak to Jacques's spirit. No one can." I reached up and dug my fingers into the gouged-out hole. "Help me remove the casket."

"Wait." Oliver's hand fell on my forearm. "*I* want to speak to the spirit. Before we destroy the body."

"Yes," I said without glancing away. "I know you do."

His fingers slid up my arm and then wrapped around my bicep. He twisted my body toward him. "Look at me."

I complied, leveling him with a stare.

"We use *my* magic to raise him," he said.

"No." The word lashed out.

Oliver's grip tightened. "Yes."

I drew in a deep breath, my eyes never leaving his. "I want to use *mine* because——"

"I know bloody well what you want and why. Magic feels so good, doesn't it?" His nose wrinkled up. "Magic helps you keep all that pain and guilt away. Yet you're incapable of controlling your power, El. You're too impulsive." Before I could argue, he brought his face near mine. "Elijah could not raise this body, which means it must have required a huge amount of magic *and* skill. Yes, you have the power, but you do not have the discipline."

"Why would you think——"

"Yesterday," he spoke over me, "you betrayed me. Twice. You were careless with Elijah's letters, and you forced me to touch electricity. You killed a piece of my immortal soul, and *then*"—he dipped closer—"only hours ago, you crossed into the spirit realm with no concern for your life or mine. I must learn how to find the Old Man in the Pyramids, Eleanor, and I will not let your recklessness and bloodlust stand in the way of fulfilling my final command from Elijah. This is my *only* remaining way to learn where the Old Man is, so *I* will raise Jacques Girard, and *you* will stand by and observe."

"What if," I snarled, "I refuse to command you? You cannot use your magic otherwise."

Oliver's eyes blazed even brighter than the candle. "If you refuse me in this, Eleanor, then you have *truly* become Elijah—and even you can no longer deny it."

For several heartbeats I held his stare. I wanted to be the one to summon Jacques because I wanted to use my magic. And . . . a throbbing, tender part of me wanted to do it to spite Oliver. To prove to him that I could control my magic—that I *was* powerful.

And that I was *not* Elijah.

But at last I simply lifted one shoulder and schooled my face into apathy. "Fine, Oliver. You raise Jacques." I flipped my hand in the air. *"Sum veritas."*

Oliver's eyes flashed blue, and the magic from my command spun through my chest. Then my demon bared his teeth in a triumphant grin and shoved the candle back into my hand.

Bracing one leg on the wall for leverage, Oliver dug his fingers into the broken tomb cover.

Minutes passed, and the only sounds were Oliver's breaths and bits of rubble breaking. I watched, silent and fuming. My fingers held the ivory fist, but as before, its usual magical hum did not comfort me.

Just when my lips parted to bark "Faster!" at Oliver, something deep within the wall snapped. Rock grated on rock, and with each fresh heave, the casket—or rather the stone slab on which it lay—began to move. In minutes Oliver had the wooden casket exposed.

The top half of its lid was missing. Oliver peeked inside . . . and instantly flinched back. "Nothing left but a skeleton." He rubbed his forehead on his sleeve. "But it will be enough." He did not look at me or wait for any sort of go-ahead or nod. He simply eased one hand into the open casket, his face scrunched up, and began to chant.

His eyes slowly shifted to blue—a gradual glow of his magic instead of the usual, explosive flare—and as his mouth moved, his skin took on a soft, ethereal sheen as well.

But then thunder boomed.

His words broke off. I jolted toward the crypt's entrance. It had been a distant sound, but there was no mistaking it—I knew that explosive sound too well.

"Dynamite," I whispered. Then I turned back to Oliver. "It's a pulse bomb. Keep going."

Oliver's nostrils flared, but he did as he was told.

71

As his words picked up once more, a rhythmic song that filled the crypt, I lifted my candle and crept back toward the entrance. My senses slid along the length of my awareness spell, but I felt nothing. We were still alone . . . yet for how long?

The hairs on my neck pricked up, and each of my footsteps seemed oddly muffled. There was electricity in this crypt. *It's just Oliver's magic,* I told myself. But I wasn't convinced. This had a different feel—a layered, coated feel that was nothing like the pure, bright surge of Oliver's magic.

The rattle of bones suddenly filled the crypt. I stopped mid-stride just as Oliver roared out, "He's awake!"

In a frantic scramble, I hurtled back to his side—and told myself the fuzzy wrongness was all in my head. *Just the humidity and coldness of a crypt.*

The casket formed before me . . . and Jacques's skeleton too. He sat upright—a brittle, fleshless creature held together by ancient, fraying sinews. Even the hair on his head had long since rotted away.

Jacques Girard, Napoleon's necromancer, was nothing more than a dusty, old museum skeleton.

Until his jaw creaked open, and a voice began to rumble out. "*Pharaon, pharaon, pharaon.*"

"Pharaoh?" I looked at Oliver. "Is that what he says?"

"The French word for it, yes." Oliver's brow creased—and still the skeleton said, "*Pharaon, pharaon, pharaon.*"

Oliver's frown deepened. "*Arrêtez,*" he growled. Jacques's teeth clacked shut.

72

And another explosion shook through the crypt. Oliver locked eyes with me. "That was closer."

I bobbed my head. "Hurry, Oliver. Ask your questions *fast*."

He launched into a quick stream of French. I caught the words *le vieil homme* and *pyramides* before another sound—a new sound—tickled my ears. It had come from the other side of the crypt.

I tensed and swiveled my head toward the noise . . . but all I could hear were Oliver and the mechanical, gravelly responses of Girard. I lifted the candle, and with wary steps, I began to cross to the other side.

The clattering, rhythmic sound came again, and a chill shivered through me.

I scooted closer. The pattering was louder now—and with an added *scratch*. All I could think of were rats clawing at marble.

It was then, as I stood in the middle of the crypt, my candle aloft and flickering over the flagstones, that I realized the electricity that coated things only moments before was now gone.

My blood ran cold, and I sent my magic scrambling down the lines of my awareness spell . . . before my senses exploded with static. It rolled over me in a cloying wave. I swayed back.

Then the spell seemed to regain its focus and settle into individual spots of magic.

Hundreds of them.

"Dead!" I roared, lurching around. *"Dead!"*

"Where?" Oliver shouted.

I sprinted toward him, the candle almost winking out. "In

the tombs! Marcus must have awakened them—every corpse has come to life!"

"Then they're trapped," Oliver said as I skidded to his side. He slapped a hand on the nearest tomb. "They can't get through the caskets—"

A loud crack suddenly shook through the marble. Then another—and this time bits of stone chipped outward.

"Oh hell," Oliver hissed. Then he rounded on Girard, and French poured off his tongue.

Crack. Crack. More rubble scattered, and every tomb started to shiver and shake at a constant speed. It wouldn't last long at this rate.

"Ollie," I yelled, scanning the nearest tombs, "you need to hurry!"

He waved at me to stay quiet, and Girard's jaw snapped open with a long, gravelly response. Then he stopped speaking, and Oliver snatched for a skeletal shoulder. He was going to lay the body to rest.

But an idea flamed through my brain. If Girard was truly a skilled necromancer, then he must know other things. . . .

"Wait!" I lunged to Oliver's side. "Ask him how to cancel a compulsion spell."

Oliver blinked at me, briefly shuttering the glow of his eyes. Then he nodded slowly, and the question rushed out.

Crack. Crack. CRUNCH.

Metal hit the floor with a *ping* that bounced off the walls. One of the plaques had been punched out . . . and now the crunching of stone was louder than the banging of bone fists.

"I have an answer," Oliver blurted, slamming his hand on Girard's shoulder. "I'm laying him back to rest now, El. Is there anything else?"

"No," I shrieked, twirling toward another *ping!* One of the magical spots in my awareness spell—no two . . . *three* spots— had started to move. If the bodies weren't already out of their tombs, they would be at any moment. "Destroy him and come on!"

The words of Oliver's spell shimmered through the air, a soft, countering magic to the grating stuff that filled my lungs and scraped at my skin. His eyes glowed that piercing blue of spiritual energy—of clean, natural magic. He shifted his gaze to me as he spoke, and then he eased his hand into his pocket.

He withdrew his flask, never pausing in his incantation, and extended it to me. I yanked it from his grasp, pushed the candle into Oliver's now-free fingers, and then set to screwing off the top. The burn of alcohol flew up my nose. Coughing, I splashed the bones haphazardly. There were too many crunches coming from around the crypt, and I didn't think I was imagining the sliding shamble of skeletal feet heading this way.

Oliver finished his chant just as I reached the bottom of the flask. Jacques Girard's bones crumpled backward, and Oliver dropped our lone flame into the tomb. In a whoosh of air and heat, the bones ignited.

We skittered back two steps, squinting in the light. I grabbed Oliver's wrist, lifting my voice to be heard over the flames and beating fists. "The Dead are everywhere."

"Then command me to fight them." He shoved into a jog—and pulled me with him. All around us, chunks of marble hit the ground.

"No," I shouted. "We need to save our strength for the true enemy."

He did not argue, and as we raced back to the entrance, I felt a single thought pulse from Oliver's mind into mine.

Finally I know how to find the Old Man.

CHAPTER FIVE

I had never seen so many Dead in my life.

We stood at the edge of the fortress-like base of the Notre-Dame, the stairs down the cliff before us and all of Marseille beyond—and hundreds upon hundreds of walking Dead. For as far as I could see, there were rows of them advancing up the hill—silently, for the wind carried away all sounds.

And they were coming toward the Notre-Dame. To us.

Marcus had raised every corpse in the city. Even at this distance I could see fresh dirt and silt from the buried and the drowned. Gleaming bones and green flesh from the long dead and the newly deceased.

I flung a backward glance to the crypt's entrance. The skeletons within had not reached the door. *Yet.*

"He raised them too," Oliver said, following my gaze. "I do not know how he did it from such a distance—I didn't know a human could even possess so much power."

"He is not human." I shook my head, my eyes never leaving the crypt door. "He was dead for years, a spirit waiting for a chance to come back. And we have been fools—all of us—dancing to Marcus's tune like puppets." I wet my lips. "What do we do, Ollie?"

"Try to leave here alive." He pointed slightly north. "See that speck of gold? In that big intersection by the *quai*? I think that's your Chinese friend."

The wind was rough as I turned my gaze into it. I had to blink constantly . . . but yes, I could just make out the flamboyant gold of Jie's gown. Which meant that black-clad speck beside her was Marcus.

A growl bubbled up my throat. He was so close. And Joseph could not stop me now.

I dragged my eyes away from Jie and over the streets. Daniel and Joseph were somewhere among all those writhing bodies, but until another pulse bomb detonated, I had no way of knowing where.

"We go to Marcus," I said. "Back the way we came. Down the hill, left onto that main avenue, then—"

"Are you insane?" Oliver cried. The wind carried his words away. "We need to flee Marcus—not walk right up to him."

I shook my head, a sharp movement. "This ends now, Oliver."

"*No.*" He cupped my face in his hands. His eyes blazed golden. "Listen to me, Eleanor. Marcus *knew* we were coming. He has us outnumbered and far, *far* outmatched. We will die if we try to stop him today."

"But we came all this way. I . . . I can't just leave. And what about Jie?"

Oliver winced, his hand dropping from my face, and I knew he'd been hoping I would forget her. Yet he did not argue. He simply said, "Fine. We get her and go." He glanced back at the crypt and pressed his lips tight. "The bodies are here, so whatever you're planning, we need to do it soon."

Holding my breath, I turned . . . and everything inside me hardened at the sight of the skeletons scraping into daylight. Unaffected by the wind, they moved in a single-file line—like an army—toward us.

I tugged the crystal clamp from my pocket. I would use it only if I had to, but it was better to have it ready.

An explosion thundered, trembling through the air. Oliver and I spun our heads toward the sound. Smoke billowed up from only a few streets away—but the wind instantly scattered it.

Daniel. Joseph. And only a few hundred corpses between us.

I had been planning to kill Marcus, certain that I could do it. Yet the fact of the matter was, I could not. But I would still use this power and this resolve to rescue Jie.

I had the rage and the skills inside me. So did the Spirit-Hunters. We could do this.

"Together," I said, "we can make a path to Daniel and Joseph."

"All right." Oliver's head swiveled once more to the skeletons leaving the crypt. Then he grabbed my sleeve and pinned me beneath a stare. "We must put aside our differences, El. Right now. Otherwise we'll never survive this."

"Yes—"

"I mean it." He yanked me closer, looking nothing like his boyish self. This was the *demon* in him speaking. "Your friend's life is of no consequence to me. But *your* life is. I will follow you to the end of this, whatever that may be. So I beg you, Eleanor— *beg you*—to do the same for me."

"I . . . will."

"Then for now we are partners and allies once more." Abruptly, he pulled back, and a cold, lethal expression settled over his features. "Command me, Eleanor, so I may use my magic, and let us see how long we can survive."

"Yes." The word growled out, hungry. Ready. And as I turned to face the oncoming tide of putrid faces, I said, "Let's lay these Dead to rest, Oliver. *Sum veritas*."

Once we'd descended the stairs, it was a blur of bodies. Gray skin, mottled with maggots and buzzing with flies. Frayed fingertips and tattered lips. Everywhere my gaze landed, I met the Dead.

But I faced them, and I was unafraid.

Magic coursed through my veins, pure spiritual energy.

Pure *power*. Then it exploded from me, a whip of necromancy to slay each corpse that crossed my path. I did not use the crystal clamp, but my left hand kept a firm hold while magic thrashed from my right.

"Sleep, sleep, sleep." The words rushed from my mouth, nothing more than a whisper. And though I could barely hear Oliver over the scraping of bones, I knew he chanted the same thing. "*Dormi, dormi, dormi.*" Building walls glowed with the blue light of our magic.

As soon as one corpse fell, blasted by my magic into the final afterlife, Oliver would attack the next. Yet for every body that collapsed, another would take its place. Marcus had truly woken every cemetery in Marseille.

When we reached the first intersection at the bottom of the winding cliff path, I realized with a rush of dismay—a dark explosion in my chest—that I had lost all sense of where the Spirit-Hunters were. We had aimed toward that one explosion, but I had neither seen nor heard a pulse bomb since. The wind covered almost all sounds. It rattled through trees and bushes, it roared in my ears, and there was no ignoring the gray clouds that it now carried in. A storm to block out the sun. Though rain wouldn't stop us, it wouldn't help us either.

And the Dead—milky eyes and ripped skin were everywhere.

"Sleep," I said, panting. "Sleep." Blue light flew from my fingers and slashed at the power animating each corpse in my way. An old woman. Then a soldier. Then two half-eaten sailors.

When the first fat drops of rain hit my shoulder, a shiver slid through my body. We had reached a grid of smaller roads and intersections, and it was only a matter of time before the skeletons from the crypt reached us or the Dead came at us from the side streets.

Lightning from the storm cracked nearby. No—not lightning. Electricity. *Joseph*.

Oliver's face snapped to me, his eyes triumphant. That sound had been close. It was the push we needed to keep going. To charge at more corpses until at last—

Crack! Blazing lines of electricity burst before us, lighting up shop fronts and closed doors. The Dead crumpled to the ground—felled by Joseph's electricity.

My chest heaving, I gaped at the Creole. The rain was picking up speed; his shirt was soaked through. Mine too, I realized with a jolt.

And through the misty rain I could just make out a hazy figure with pistols firing at the nearest lines of bodies. Daniel.

"Marcus is northwest," I shouted. "Only a few blocks from here." I pointed in what I hoped was the general direction. "We can't stop his army, Joseph. I know you want to protect the city, but . . ."

"I realize." Joseph scrubbed at his bandages and scanned the building fronts. Curtains shifted in windows, and pale faces appeared. "Thus far they are only targeting us. And it is so many—more than we have ever faced before. We will have to hope that fleeing Marseille will be enough for Marcus to call off his corpses. But first we rescue Jie. Somehow."

"Not somehow." I beckoned Oliver to my side. "What did you learn about compulsion spells?"

Without shifting his focus from the streets behind us, Oliver said, "There's no way to cancel one, but you can temporarily *block* it. You have to pierce a part of Jie's body, and as the blood falls, you cast a spell—*Dormi!*" His magic laced out, felling four bodies at once. Then he wet his lips and continued, "It will be like resting an hourglass on its side—the compulsion spell will pause, but *only* as long as she continues to bleed—just a little. If the bleeding staunches, then your friend will fall right back under Marcus's power."

Joseph and I exchanged grim glances through the rain. "That means," I said, "that we will need to get close enough to Jie to cut her."

Joseph nodded. "The question is, how do we do that?"

"I'll do it," said a new voice. Daniel. He stalked to Joseph's side, his clothes soaked through. The rain was a storm now.

"And how will you reach her?" Oliver demanded, looking at Daniel. "You have no powers, and your pistols are too sl—" His voice snapped off, his hands shooting up.

Daniel jumped around—but Oliver had already cried *"Dormi!"* and blue light was already streaking through the rain. A corpse fell only feet away.

"Your pistols," Oliver finished, his voice a snarl, "are too slow."

Daniel glared. "I can still make a blood wound. I just need

Marcus distracted. You go through the Dead together. I come up from behind."

"Then you," Joseph looked at me, "will cast the spell from afar." Before I could agree, Joseph's eyes shifted beyond me, and his fingers squeezed the crystal clamp. Electricity snaked through the rain. *Crack!*

I whirled around just as the bodies fell. Some were skeletons from the crypt, but most were not.

The Dead had us completely surrounded.

I twisted back to Daniel. "Cut any exposed skin on Jie that you can get to. Then shoot your pistol. I'll hear it and cast the spell—"

"But again," Oliver inserted, "how will you get to her?" He thrust a pointed finger at the never-ending lines of Dead tramping toward us.

"Take all the pulse bombs," Joseph said, shoving his physician's bag into Daniel's hands. "And prepare all your pistols now."

Nodding, Daniel hefted the bag onto his shoulder and began to load his weapons.

"Eleanor," Joseph continued, "you and I will clear a wide, *distracting* path to Marcus. Oliver will protect our rear. Daniel can break away from us at the nearest intersection. Then, after he gets Jie, we will make our way for the harbor and the airship."

Everyone nodded.

"Now, let us go." He marched off, Daniel beside him. I moved to follow, but Oliver's fingers landed on my shoulder.

"This isn't right," he said, his voice a mere murmur over the rain and blasts of Joseph's electricity. "We walk straight into Marcus's hands, Eleanor."

"Allies," I reminded him. "To the end."

His teeth gritted, but he nodded. "To the end."

"What are the words to cancel the compulsion spell?"

"It's just one word: *resiste*. But you have to focus on *what* you're trying to stop. In this case it's Marcus's spell. Can you do it?"

"Yes."

His eyes raked over my face. "Be careful." Then he pivoted backward to blast away the approaching corpses.

I stalked to Joseph's side. My attacks were pitiful compared to his—a handful of corpses toppled for the dozens he could destroy at once. But we moved onward.

At the first branching alleyway, Daniel veered away from us to make his own path. But he only went two steps before he paused . . . then bent around and ran back to us. To me.

I watched him, momentarily confused. Then, in a fast, hard movement, he yanked me to him and pressed his lips to mine.

Rain ran over our cheeks. Our chests were slick and cold. Wind howled. But Daniel kissed me fiercely. All teeth and desperation, and hard enough to steal my breath and show me all the things we never had time to share.

Half a moment later, he pulled away and, without a word, shot off for the alley. Joseph's bag swung on Daniel's back, and before he vanished into the shadows, he withdrew two pulse pistols and took aim.

I sent a silent prayer after him—because, by God, I wanted him to come back to me—before turning to the battle once more. The rain was collecting in the streets, soaking into the fallen Dead. My feet slipped and ankles wrenched on jellied flesh.

Yet I did not slow or stop.

Several blocks, we worked and fought. Every few minutes I would peek at the building fronts. People watched us, safe in their homes.

I was glad we would have none of their blood on our hands, and though I did not think protecting Marseille had been Marcus's purpose when he set up the newspaper article, it did make this fight easier.

"Sleep." The magic hurled from my fingers to snap the Dead leashes all around. My veins pumped with spiritual energy and something . . . darker. Something hungry.

Marcus was so close.

We rounded the final corner, and the buildings opened up in a wide intersection surrounded by more thin, red-roofed buildings. We had reached Marcus.

Kill him.

The blinding crush of hatred burst before my eyes . . . and then we were through the Dead. Like blades of grass in the wind, the last row of corpses between us and Marcus crumpled beneath Joseph's blazing attack.

The blue light left trails in my eyes, but I didn't care—as soon as I saw the shape of Jie's enormous gown, the twisting rise of her hair, and the blank stare in her eyes, I moved.

Joseph and Oliver did not stop me. In fact, they fell back and vanished from my awareness. All I saw was Jie . . . and Marcus.

He stood, a lazy slant to his posture and his attention on his fingernails. It was a pose—a slouch of such disinterest that I knew it had to be fake. He was aware of every step I made.

But I was not trying for stealth—or for anything, really, other than getting close enough to utter the words of the spell.

So I stomped directly toward Marcus, my gut on fire and my eyes never leaving his face. *Elijah*'s face. But there was nothing of my brother left in that jawline. Marcus had grown even larger—feasting off sacrificial power. Off my *mother*'s blood. He had burgeoned like some fat leech, and his shoulders were twice as broad as the old Elijah's.

I lifted the crystal clamp, wielding it before me like a gun.

But suddenly a flash of pain lurched through my stomach. Pierced my chest.

My footsteps faltered, then stopped completely. Agony coiled through me and threatened to cut off my air.

But it was not my own pain.

Oliver! I shrieked with my mind. *Stop!* For this hurt was his. This was *his* soul-deep rage at Marcus. . . . No, at Elijah. It coursed through me like worms. *Stop, Oliver. Stop!*

I fell forward, my hands flying out. . . .

The blackness rushed back, but it was too late. I hit the wet cobblestones. My palms ripped open. The crystal clamp clattered away from me—straight to Marcus.

Casually he kicked it to the opposite end of the intersection.

Then he laughed, a rumbling sound of genuine amusement. I remembered that sound from Laurel Hill. I remembered it from my nightmares. I pushed unsteadily to my feet.

"You think to stop me, *Mamzel*?" Marcus's heavy Creole accent oozed through the rain and over the crack of Joseph's electricity. "You think that you and *Joseph*"—Marcus hissed the name with venom—"can fight me? Do you not see the extent of my army?"

"We see your army," I growled. "We are not afraid." With a rough swipe at my pants, blood streaked and the skin ripped wider. It felt good. "You kidnapped Jie. Why?"

"Because I have a weakness for the beautiful." He threw an almost fond smile at Jie. She stood as immobile and disinterested as a statue. "Does she not look lovely? I have enjoyed her company so much—"

"What have you done to her?" The words screeched from my throat. I lunged two desperate steps toward him.

Without thinking, I drew my magic into a well, let it pulse into my chest. If Marcus had laid a hand on Jie—if he had touched her in any way, I would destroy him right now. I didn't care about Marseille or the Spirit-Hunters. If Marcus had violated Jie, he would die *now*.

As if reading my thoughts, Marcus's lips curved into a smile, and his eyes crinkled to glowing, yellow slits. He crooked one finger, an invitation to attack.

White blinked at the corner of my vision—Daniel. He stood just behind Jie, a knife in hand. I forced myself to ignore him.

Forced my eyes to stay locked on Marcus's. Forced my magic to stay contained.

"You," I said to Marcus, "will pay. In Philadelphia, I promised to send you to the hottest pits of hell, and I meant every word." My voice trickled out, a bare whisper beneath the rain. As I hoped, Marcus took a step closer. Then another. He looked as smug as ever—always in control—yet he *did* want to know what I said. He liked hearing his prey's final words.

It was as he took his third step toward me that Daniel struck. A blur of white, then a pistol shot.

Marcus flinched, but either he did not realize Daniel's proximity or he did not consider Daniel a threat. He continued to stalk toward me.

"Resiste," I murmured beneath my breath, never breaking my stare with Marcus. I fixed my thoughts on whatever sick power kept Jie trapped in place . . . and my magic slid through my body to trickle off my fingertips.

But I never looked away from Marcus.

He thought this would end today, and as much as I wanted it to—wanted to shred that smile off his face and feel his flesh beneath my fingernails—I felt a deep satisfaction at his inevitable disappointment. It was time he chased *me*. It was time for *me* to be in charge.

So, smiling, I finally let my eyes drift from Marcus's unnatural face—just as Jie, her gown rustling and her face streaming with bright-red blood and rain, swept up behind him. In a single, vicious movement, she slammed her cupped palms over his ears.

Then her foot kicked up between his legs. Into his groin.

A cry burst from Marcus's lips, but when he whirled around to attack, his face met Daniel's knife. With unnatural speed, Marcus slipped backward—out of Daniel's or Jie's reach. But I did not miss the sway in his step. Jie's blow had landed where it needed to.

"Go!" I bellowed at Jie and Daniel. I pointed to the harbor. *"Go!"*

Then, before Marcus could try to recover, I attacked.

I don't know how the magic came to me—like it always seemed to be, it was an instinctive pull. A natural understanding. A gentle slash at the nearest corpses to snip their leashes . . . and then bind them to me.

"Attack," I whispered. "Attack." Four corpses turned away from their steady march at me and aimed for Marcus instead.

Then another pistol popped. Blood burst in Marcus's chest, and I had enough time to see Daniel's arm lower—and then grab hold of Jie. Together, they raced away.

Meanwhile, my corpses shuffled toward Marcus—distracting him from healing his chest wound. Then Joseph's power cracked into the intersection.

The world spun before me, and my heart was a husk of exhaustion. Yet my legs carried me away from Marcus and after the rapidly fading figures of Jie and Daniel.

Until I rounded a building and came face-to-face with a wall of corpses. Their gray arms were outstretched, and bone fingers clawed for me.

I scrambled back, swiveling for another street—but it was closed off too. I must have chosen the wrong path. Somehow, I would have to backtrack.

But when I tried to retreat, I saw more bodies and that shock of auburn hair I knew so well. I was trapped.

"*Oliver!*" The name scratched up my throat, and with it came a mental shout for my demon, a tug over our bond. Then I drew in every inch of my soul, but instead of bolstering my courage, it seemed to weaken me. I had nothing left—not even enough to stop the nearest body.

I staggered in a circle. My head rolled back—the roof seeming so safe and distant.

"*Empress!*"

The cry roared out over everything and pierced my heart. I wrenched my gaze to a rooftop behind me—to Daniel. How he'd gotten up there I didn't know—didn't care. He skidded to the edge of the sloping shale and heaved something in my direction.

I watched it fly in an arc—a glittery rock surrounded by copper. A crystal clamp. Without a thought, my hands swung up and snatched it from the air.

I rounded on Marcus; my fingers squeezed. Electricity exploded in my veins—a burning buzz that set my brain on fire. But it gave me no time to dwell, no time to think how this device might fail me once more. I would have to let my instincts guide me. My hand shot up, and instantly, lines of blue sizzled out.

For a moment I felt every Dead in my way—ten, fifteen,

twenty corpses all animated by slivers of soul. Then, in a crashing burn that scorched through my vision, the souls shattered into a million pieces. The fragments slammed into the spirit curtain . . . then melted through. Gone forever.

Bodies toppled. Marcus ducked. By the time I could attack again, he had slithered into his army.

"Coward!" I screamed, launching after him. *"Coward!"*

Hands grabbed my waist. "No!" Oliver's voice bellowed in my ear, his grip unrelenting. He wrenched me around and toward the leftmost street. "This way, El. *Come on!*"

I threw a final glance after Marcus. I didn't understand why he fled when he obviously had enough power to fight us and to keep his army going. . . . But he *was* leaving.

And I would have to let him go.

So with a nod at Oliver, I shoved onward. Together, we pounded over the cobblestones . . . and directly toward the Dead.

"Duck!" Daniel's voice thundered from above. Then a glowing red pulse bomb arced through the rain.

Oliver and I dropped to our knees in the street.

Boom!

Flesh, bone, and congealed blood slapped the cobblestones, our backs, our heads. Then we were on our feet once more. The explosion echoed in my ears—but it faded fast as we sprinted ahead.

Daniel's pulse bomb had emptied the street. Each slam of my heels brought the smell of sewage and fish into sharper focus. We were almost to the harbor.

A jolt of acknowledgment burst in my gut—Oliver's emotions. He knew we were near too.

Then we hit a new street, and the airship—huge and white—appeared before us. It swayed and twirled, fighting the wind. The ladder dangled down; Allison must have lowered it.

We passed intersections and alleyways. Rotting flesh streamed along the corners of my eyes. My breath burned in my chest, and even as I pumped my legs harder, I knew the Dead would pour into our path at any moment.

But if I had thought there were too many Dead before, it was worse once we hit the *quai*. They came at us from all angles, and those that did not fit simply toppled into the water.

I pulled up short, and before Oliver could notice, I squeezed the clamp. For half a moment the world seemed to hold its breath—or perhaps *I* held my breath.

Then electricity burst from my fingertips to blaze over the nearest Dead. They toppled . . . but were instantly replaced by hundreds more. Ahead, behind, and beside, the corpses shambled into the street. They separated me from Oliver.

"Eleanor!" Oliver shouted. Waves of panic coursed through our bond. "Where are you? *Eleanor!* Don't stop!"

My heels punched through waxy flesh; my toes tripped over skulls. Yet my legs could go no faster. I had no magic left inside me at this point, and not even the explosive power of electricity could carry me the rest of the way to the pier.

Fingers clawed at me. Teeth chomped. My hair ripped from my skull in chunks.

But on I went, forcing one leg in front of the other and simply trying to *shove* the bodies aside.

Oliver's magic snaked out. The nearest Dead crashed back, and for a brief moment I had a clear path to him . . . and to the balloon. Down the pier, a mere twenty paces away, was the airship ladder.

"Come on!" Oliver roared. Then he charged to the ladder and began to climb.

I tried to run faster, but to my horror, the rope holding the airship snapped free. I blinked, my footsteps stumbling. Were they leaving?

Oliver paused midclimb and spun toward me, his eyes bulging.

Then fingers—human and alive—grabbed my arm.

"Go!" Daniel's voice ripped into my ears. He dashed in front of me—*dragging* me. And when he yelled "You're gonna have to jump, Empress," I nodded.

Rain fell into my open lips. My body had lost all feeling. The world was a haze of gray corpses and churning harbor. An orchestra of gasping breaths and scraping feet.

And shouts—Oliver, now at the top of the ladder, was screaming at me to go faster. But why the devil was the airship moving *away* from us? How would I ever reach it at this rate?

Daniel's fingers released me. His feet kicked up, and as his heels lifted toward the ladder, I shoved all my strength into my own legs and jumped.

Air whipped past my ears. I rose as if underwater: slow,

heavy. Daniel grabbed hold of the rising ladder rungs.

But I did not.

I wasn't even close—I had not jumped hard enough. Hadn't gauged the distance properly. The final rung of the ladder slid through my grasp and flew away.

Yet Daniel would never let me fall. His knees sank, his arm swung down. He reached; I reached.

Our hands clasped, and he tugged me with more power than I ever thought he might have.

Then I flew up the final inches and slammed against the ladder beside him.

As we stood there, clinging for our lives and shaking with exhaustion, the Old Port of Marseille and Marcus's army shrank away beneath us.

CHAPTER SIX

The gondola hatch slammed shut, and all sound abruptly vanished. It was as if my senses were blanked out—no roaring wind in my ears, no sting in my eyes, and no gulping for the next breath. I just lay there, shivering and wet and blessedly, *blessedly* safe.

My last sight after Oliver had pulled me into the cargo hold had been one of blue Mediterranean waves with whitecaps hundreds of feet below. No land. No ships.

It had felt like hours of climbing to ascend the airship ladder. Daniel had refused to move ahead—or even release me—so every rung had been a trial. Yet now we were here, my eyes locked on Daniel's.

"Thank you," I tried to say, but the words wouldn't come.

I wanted to ask him about the kiss in the street. About how he knew to come back for me. But I could summon no voice before Joseph shouted, "Daniel! I have lost sight of land!"

Daniel hauled himself to his feet, threw me a final, anxious glance, and then hurried into the hall.

I twisted my gaze to Oliver, kneeling beside me. His eyes roved over me. Checking for injuries, but it was not the outside of me that ached. I felt . . . torn apart. Something inside me had shifted. Something had been pushed too far—like a muscle too often unused.

"Where's Jie?" I asked, trying to rise onto my elbows.

"She's with your friend."

"Allison?" My eyes widened, and I jerked farther upright . . . but instantly swayed.

"Should I heal you?" Oliver asked.

"No." I shook my head. "But are you all right?"

He eased a breath through his teeth. Then he dropped his gaze. "I'm sorry. I thought you were right behind me. Back there." He jerked his shoulder in what I could only assume was the direction of Marseille. "I would never have left you like that." His gaze climbed back to mine. "*Never*, El."

"I know."

"Good." He stood and offered me his hands. "For once I'm grateful to your inventor." With a grunt, he hefted me to my unsteady feet. "You need dry clothes."

"Jie" was my only response, so Oliver guided me into the hall. At the galley, gold flashed in my eyes and skirts rustled.

Jie stood in the middle of the room, rainwater pooling beneath her. Blood trickled down both sides of her neck—though one cut was already clotting.

"Jie." I pulled free from Oliver and lurched inside. "Are you all right?"

She blinked and met my eyes, but it was as if she didn't even know me. She stayed perfectly still. Perfectly flat.

Until Oliver leaned into the room. Then a shudder exploded through her. "Demon," she breathed. *"Demon."* Her gaze fell and locked on her dress. "Oh God. Get it off me." With frantic movements, she yanked at her bodice. "Get it *off* me!"

I darted to her, grasping her arms. "Settle down—"

"Get it off!" Her fingers grabbed fistfuls of skirt, and she yanked. I flung a glance at the door—but Oliver was already gone. So I simply moved behind Jie and set to ripping off the hundreds of buttons that closed the gold silk. She stayed silent, but her fingers were flexed taut and quivering—as if she feared to touch anything. Minutes later I had the gown mostly off her.

Heels clacked and Allison strode in, a metal case in her hands. At my harsh stare she halted and held up the tin. "A first aid kit. To bind Miss Chen's wounds."

"No. The cuts must be left to bleed."

"Why?"

"If they heal, the compulsion spell will take control again—and do *not* ask why," I hastened to add as Allison's mouth opened. "I do not know. All I know is that it's necromancy, and as long as Marcus is still alive, the compulsion spell still exists."

"Seventy-three days," Jie mumbled. "It'll last seventy-three days—one for each of Marcus's victims in Paris."

A knot swelled in my throat. "Was it the hair clasp?" I asked quietly. "The one Madame Marineaux gave you. Was it an amulet?"

"I . . . I guess." Jie lifted her shoulder almost imperceptibly. "I don't remember everything. I just know he was proud of the length of the spell. He bragged about all the people he'd killed to make it." She inhaled a shaking breath, and it sent her shoulders almost to her ears. Her whalebone corset had cinched her waist so tight that her chest overflowed from the top. I grabbed for the first lace.

"Wait," Allison said. She fumbled in the case and withdrew scissors. Then, after a frightened glance at Jie's face, she offered them to me.

With each snip the laces snapped free—and Jie's ribs slowly shuddered back into their natural form. But even when the final pieces of the corset tumbled to the floor, her breaths remained too shallow and her skin too pale from lack of blood.

And all I could think of was Marcus. Of *destroying* him for this. I wanted to know how he had beaten us to Marseille. How he had gotten that newspaper article printed.

But above all, I needed to know what he had planned next.

"What else do you remember?" I asked as gently as I could.

"Too much," Jie whispered. "Boarding a train. Leaving a train. Being . . . being *stuck* while he raised all the Dead. While he . . . *put* me in this dress."

100

Suddenly, her fingers bent into claws, and she heaved at her undershirt. She was halfway out of it before I managed to skitter toward Allison. "Clothes," I ordered. "Find her clothes."

Allison nodded and hurried into the hall.

Jie cried out. I spun around . . . only to find her falling forward. She wore nothing but her pantaloons, and her body was covered in gooseflesh. Her legs buckled beneath her, and she cried out again.

I dived for her but was too slow. Her knees hit the ground, and the two orchids in her hair toppled to the floor. Her eyes landed on the wilted flowers. In a burst of sudden speed, she snatched the scissors from my hands and scuttled back. Gripping a fistful of her long, black hair, she lifted the scissors high.

"Oh God." I crawled to her. "Stop, Jie. Stop—you don't have to cut your hair."

"He touched it. He *touched* my hair, and I don't want it on me anymore." She squeezed the scissors, and a grating sound filled the galley.

She sawed. She hacked. And her hair fell in clumps and strands.

I grabbed her wrist. "Let me do it." She flinched away, her eyes bulging.

I held up my hands, palms out. "I won't hurt you, Jie, but let me cut your hair. *Let me do it.*"

Her eyes grew wider . . . but then sank shut. Her posture dropped, and she offered me the scissors. I took them and kneeled behind her.

"All of it," she whispered, staring ahead at the wall. "Cut all of it."

"I will." I gathered up her hair, staring at the fluffy wisps growing on her forehead. It had always been shaved bald.

For some reason, that made the moment all the more real. Something as fundamental to Jie as her shaved head was gone. My best friend was here, but she was still *gone*.

And then, to my horror, a sob shuddered through Jie's shoulders. "You can't stop him," she said breathily. "It doesn't matter what you do—he's always one step ahead. He'll raise the Black Pullet, and then he'll take anything and . . . and . . . *every*thing he wants."

The scissor blades gritted through the last bit of hair, and Jie's head toppled forward. Movement flickered at the door. I glanced up just as Allison reappeared, clothes in her arms. Her lips were drawn up to one side, her eyebrows tight with horror. But she moved to Jie, and in a quick, efficient move, she draped a loose shirt over Jie's shoulders. Together, we got her arms into the sleeves.

But as I worked to do up the buttons, I stared hard into Jie's eyes. "Marcus cannot get the Black Pullet now, Jie. I promise you. We destroyed the only clue left in Marseille."

"No." She pulled back, the buttons only half clasped. "You can't stop him. He knows where the Old Man is already. He went to the crypt before you—before he went to Paris."

Cold wrapped around my heart.

"He even has his own ship," Jie went on. "To cross the

Mediterranean. He can raise the Black Pullet, and he will."
With a slight lift of her head, she met my eyes. "One step
ahead, Eleanor. He's *always* one step ahead. And you *can't stop
him.*"

"We can stop him." Joseph's voice cracked into the room,
firm and loud. He strode in, and Allison scurried aside. "We *will*
stop him, Jie—even if it means going to Egypt."

With a cry, Jie shoved off the floor and pushed past me.
Joseph opened his arms, and she burrowed her face in his chest.
He pulled her close, his chin resting on the top of her jaggedly
shorn hair.

Joseph did not look young or lost now. There was a darkness
in his gaze that I had never seen before . . . but that I knew.

The true hunger for retribution.

"We will stop him," he said. "We will stop Marcus, and he
will *pay* for this, Jie."

Fingers clasped my elbow. I started, but it was only Allison.
"Miss Chen's wounds will fester."

I shook my head vaguely. "All the same, we must keep her
bleeding. To keep the spell from regaining control."

"You want her to bleed . . . all the time?" At my nod, she
dropped her hand. "Then Miss Chen needs a scarificator. And a
cup." At my vacant look she added, "They're devices for bloodletting." She waved to the inside of her forearm. "My father used
to bleed daily—small cuts on his arm to balance his humors. The
blood would free his negative emotions. I know how to make the
cuts, and I even know how to keep them from scabbing over.

I . . . I could cut Miss Chen. Every few hours, so that she never stops bleeding."

Joseph eyed Allison, his knuckles pale around Jie's shoulders—and my stomach turned to lead. He was going to invite Allison to stay.

Yet before I could open my mouth to protest, Allison plowed on. "And if we could get ginger, or turmeric, or garlic, we can help her bleed longer. Certain foods keep blood from clotting."

"Then I will see to it that we get these foods," Joseph said, peering down at Jie. Then he squeezed her even closer. "Can you tell me if her wounds will heal soon, Miss Wilcox?"

Allison's eyes flicked to me, excited and . . . *triumphant*. Then she bustled to Jie's side and inspected the cuts.

I gaped at Joseph. He could not truly consider allowing Allison to stay. Yet as I watched, Joseph removed Jie's arms from his waist and held her face. "Miss Wilcox will tend to your wounds, Jie." Then he leveled a firm stare at Allison. "You will make fresh incisions, Miss Wilcox, and then you will tend these wounds. I will ensure we get a . . . scarificator?"

"And a wet cup to produce suction," Allison added. She took Jie's hands in her own and gently guided her to a stool.

Joseph gave a final once-over to the scene before moving to the door. I followed, gripping at his sleeve, yet he pulled away to stride into his cabin across the hall.

I hurried after him. "You cannot let Allison stay," I hissed. "She will slow us—"

Joseph paused in the middle of his room. Then, in a careful, controlled movement, he pivoted toward me. "Eleanor, I will say this to you only once, so listen closely. I protect people—it is what I do. I fight the Dead so that others may live, and there is nothing I value more than a human life. *Except*"—his voice dropped to a whisper, and he bowed his head toward me—"for Jie and Daniel. I will always, *always* put their lives above others. And above mine. I would *kill* for them." He leaned in closer. "So if Miss Wilcox can keep Jie safe, then she will remain a part of this team. And that is the end of this discussion. Do you understand?"

For a moment I was speechless—unsure I actually *did* understand. Would I put Jie's and Daniel's lives above finding Marcus?

Of course you would, my heart nudged. And it was right. So I nodded at Joseph. "I understand."

"Good." He straightened. Then he ran a hand along his bandages—along the space where his ear had been.

I flinched. "You're bleeding."

"*Wi.*" His hand fell. "I will have Miss Wilcox change the bandages once she has dealt with Jie." He turned, as if to dismiss me—but I had one more question.

"Do we go to Egypt?"

Without looking back at me, he nodded. "If Marcus seeks the Old Man in the Pyramids, then so do we. Somehow, we will find the Old Man first."

With cautious steps, I moved to Joseph's side. "I . . . or rather, Oliver knows how to find him."

Joseph watched me slantwise. "How?"

I hesitated. He would be angry; he would not like that Oliver had interrogated Jacques Girard.

My right hand moved to my pocket, seeking the ivory fist's calming power. For two heartbeats I simply savored the way it eased my nerves. Then, in a rush of soft words, I told Joseph what Oliver and I had done in Marseille. "Girard gave Oliver instructions," I finished. "Oliver knows what to do to find the Old Man."

For several breaths, Joseph was silent—and I feared furious. But then his lips pursed. "Learn what your demon knows so we may set a course."

My breath kicked out, relief overwhelming me. "Yes. I will."

Joseph angled his body toward me, and in a voice devoid of emotion, he said, "Mark my words, Eleanor. Every fresh cut we must make on Jie's skin, I will give to Marcus. He will feel the deepest pain imaginable—over and over until he has paid for what he has done. Until his soul and his body are nothing but dust."

My mouth went dry. "We go to Egypt to *end* this," I rasped out.

And Joseph stared at me with unfocused eyes. "Yes, Eleanor. We go to end this. And *this* time we end it once and for all."

After leaving Joseph, I staggered to the washroom. Even the simple acts of relieving myself and scrubbing blood off my hands almost destroyed me. I barely had enough energy to reach Oliver's cabin and peer in.

He sat on his bunk, his elbows on his knees and his flask in his hands. He glanced up and briefly met my eyes. . . . Then he blinked once and returned his attention to the flask.

He wanted to be alone, and I was more than happy to comply. By the time I finally shambled into my own cabin and fell onto the bunk, I was too exhausted to dwell on him or Allison or Egypt. I could not even bother to change from my damp clothes. It took every last ounce of my energy to crawl beneath a blanket and summon the magical words of a dream ward. . . .

Then I slept.

Hours later I awoke, cold and hungry. All was dark outside. I hauled myself to my feet and stumbled for the door. A light shone dimly around the edges, and when I opened it, I found jars of glowworms roped along the ceiling outside.

A snort broke through my lips. How typically clever of Daniel—no open flames in an airship. At the end of the hall, a brighter light gleamed. The galley. I crept toward it, and the sound of a slicing knife hit my ears.

Someone was cooking. Perfect.

Of course, when I peeked my head through the doorway, I found an electric lamp glowing over a sandy-haired boy hunched at the table. With a surprising *lack* of coordination, Daniel chopped at a piece of garlic.

"What are you making?"

He jerked around, the knife flying up. His eyes met mine; his breath whooshed out. "It's just you, Empress. Sorry." He lowered the knife.

107

"Who else would it be? I do not think even Marcus could reach us this high."

He huffed a humorless laugh. "I'm antsy is all. I don't like having a Wilcox on board. I don't trust her."

As his words sank in, horror solidified in my gut. I had not *once* thought about the Wilcox family's connection to Daniel. That Allison's father and brother had tried to kill him.

I dug my hands into my eyes. I had been so preoccupied with myself, I had forgotten the one piece of Daniel's past that he wished to escape more than anything: the accidental death at his hands, the dynamite factory explosion, and the prison time he'd served when the Wilcoxes had framed him for murder.

And now a Wilcox was on the ship.

"I'm so sorry, Daniel. I didn't even think about Allison——"

"It's fine," he cut in. "If Joseph says she can stay, so be it. But it *doesn't* mean I trust her."

"A-all right." I frowned, for once grateful that Daniel did—and felt—anything Joseph commanded. At least he wouldn't make trouble with Allison.

I leaned back into the hall and strained to see through the dim light. "Who is at the wheel?"

"Jie." Daniel's voice was low, and when I twisted back toward him, he shrugged one shoulder. "We're just coasting over the Mediterranean for now. Ain't difficult to fly, and . . . well, she doesn't want to sleep."

"Ah." I slipped into the room, rubbing at my arms for warmth. "How long was I asleep?"

"Six hours? Seven?" His eyes landed on my shivering arms. He frowned and dropped the knife on the table. "Let me get you fresh clothes."

I opened my mouth, a natural protest forming . . . but then fading. I *did* want warm, dry clothes. So I nodded and held out my hand for the knife.

"I'll cut the garlic. And perhaps . . . some potatoes? Or bread?"

Another huffed laugh—but this one genuine. "Absolutely, Empress." With a playful, almost tender smile, he popped my chin with his knuckle. "Potatoes, bread, and clothes. I can do that." Then he handed me the knife and strode from the galley.

And as I watched him go, my heart was shaking almost as much as the rest of me. Despite how he felt about my magic, I could not forget the absolute honesty in his apology yesterday. Nor could I forget our kiss in the rain . . . or that, yet again, he had come to my rescue. I owed him so very, *very* much.

He was trying—he really was.

Yet it was so hard to be light after what we'd faced in Marseille. After seeing Jie's blank face and shorn hair. After learning of Mama . . .

My mind could not seem to move forward. Jie. Mama. Jie. Then Marcus, with his gloating grin . . . then back to Jie.

With a tight breath, I returned to the garlic. At least there was comfort in the mundane. In how easily the knife sliced through. At how the sharp tang of garlic filled the room. I could almost pretend I was back home. That it was May. . . . Elijah would be home any day, and Mary would be bringing in the evening paper as I made supper.

Clack, clack. I sank into that familiar sound. The familiar feel of cooking. Of course, just as I finished chopping, Daniel returned, and my daydream vanished like a popped soap bubble. I wiped my hands on my pants, dragging my mind back to the present and burying reality beneath layers of careful control.

Yet as I looked at Daniel, I froze. For atop a fresh shirt and trousers was an ornate, cream-colored hatbox.

I knew what was in that box—I had accidentally seen its contents in Paris. But why Daniel would show it to me now, I couldn't guess. I wanted it—oh God, how I *wanted* it—but now did not feel like the right time. I was so tired, so heartbroken.

Daniel set down the box and offered me the clothes. "While you dress, I'll cut some potatoes. I don't *like* cooking, since open flames ain't exactly safe on a balloon, but I'll do it. For you." He flashed me a lopsided grin.

"Daniel," I said, my voice tight. "Is that for me?" I motioned to the box. "Are you going to give it to me?"

His smile faltered. "Yeah. It's for you." His eyes skipped from my face to the box and back. "It's somethin' I wanted to give you in Paris, but . . . I couldn't."

"And perhaps you shouldn't now. Perhaps you ought to wait until the time is right." My blood pounded in my ears.

"I need to do it, Empress." His chest rose as he inhaled. Then he yanked off the lid, and, cringing, he held it out to me. "This is for you."

Ever so slowly, I dragged my eyes from his tightened face . . . down his strong shoulder and long arm . . . to the box.

Nestled within and burning bright in the electric light was a mechanical hand.

A sob trembled up from my stomach, but I bit it back. Even though I'd seen the hand before—when Laure had accidentally knocked over the box in Paris—it gutted me to see it again. The wire tendons, the bronze knuckles, and the seamlessly carved wooden fingertips . . .

There was so much meaning held within this creation—all the tenderness and thought that could characterize Daniel. And also all the anger and bleakness, for when he'd first seen me in Paris and realized I didn't need the mechanical hand, he had let his temper break loose.

This hand symbolized everything about our relationship. The good, the bad, and that inevitable, frightening truth that I would one day need the hand, when Oliver was gone.

"It's perfect," I finally croaked.

Daniel's face relaxed, and he plucked the hand from the box to hold it to the light. Then he groaned. "There's a spot on it. Goddamned grease gets on everything. . . ." He trailed off, his eyes widening to meet mine. "Er, I mean, gol' . . . dern?"

I forced a laugh and reached for the hand. "I don't care if there's a stain, Daniel. I still want it."

The edge of his lips curving up, he laid it on my palms. The metal was cool, and as I examined it more closely, I found the carvings even more meticulously intricate than I'd first thought.

"This is a masterpiece, Daniel." I shook my head, awe taking over all emotion, and caressed the small, curved fingernails. "You should patent it."

"Maybe. Plenty of time for that later."

Something about his voice made me lift my eyes . . . and I found his face had gone very still. As if he had stopped breathing.

I swallowed.

He took a step toward me. "Empress. I need you to know something." Then a long inhale, and he closed the space between us. I did not move. Not even when I had to hold the mechanical hand to my chest because he stood so near. Not even when I had to roll my head back to see his face. And not even when his fingers reached up to brush my hair lightly from my eyes . . . and then linger down my jaw.

"A few years ago," he said, lowering his hand, "when I first met Joseph, I made a promise to myself. I swore I would live my life unflinching. Unafraid. Just like Joseph does. No matter how hard I try, though, I never seem to do that with you. Whenever you're near, I flinch. Whenever I want you most, I always pull away. But . . . no more." He shook his head once. "I'm going to tell you exactly how I feel—right now—and you can take it or you can leave it. I just want you to know. . . . I *need* you to know."

My fingers tightened around the mechanical hand, squeezing it until the gears cut into my palm. I knew what was about to come. I had wanted it for so long, and now would be the perfect moment if not for *everything* else.

Yet before I could open my mouth, Daniel forged ahead.

"I don't know what's coming," he went on, "but I do know what's behind us. We go back and forth all the time—me and you. Saving each other, fighting, flirtin' . . . and then saving each other again. But this time, in Marseille, it was too close."

"I . . . don't follow," I said. This wasn't what I had expected him to say.

"I barely got to you in time, Empress. You almost didn't get out of that city alive, and . . ." He inhaled sharply—as if he was imagining what would have happened if I *hadn't* made it out of Marseille. "I never could've forgiven myself if I'd lost you—don't you see that?" His eyes captured mine once more. "Especially if you never knew how I feel about you. So, unflinching and . . ." He swallowed. "And unafraid, I . . . am . . . in love with you."

Now the sob did come—I could not stifle it. For months these were the words I had dreamed Daniel would say to me. Even after he broke my heart in Philadelphia, I had wanted these three words: "I love you."

Yet now that he was saying them, my chest felt like it might crush beneath the weight of it. *I'm in love with you too*, I wanted to say. *I have been since Philadelphia.*

But the words would not come—they seemed trapped inside, and all I could manage was a shuddering exhale. A pitiful nod. This one desire—a taut strand among many—had finally been released, and it felt all . . . wrong.

Wrong to speak of love with Mama's death fresh on my heart.

Wrong to feel happy when Jie's vacant eyes burned in my brain.

I finally had Daniel's love, yet I could not summon the voice to say it back.

And sweet Daniel did not move. He did not press me; he did not breathe. He simply watched me and waited.

My lips parted; his eyes lit up.

Nothing came. Though my brain shrieked *You must say you love him too! You will lose him if you don't!* my mouth closed and nothing came.

Daniel's face slowly hardened with each passing second—not angrily but . . . acceptingly. He was fighting whatever roiled inside, and with a slight bob of his head, he murmured, "I should check on Jie." Then he walked stiffly from the room.

My breath writhed up my throat as if to call after him—yet still I could summon *nothing*. I gaped down at the mechanical hand, wondering what the hell was wrong with me. I had wanted his love for months, and now I suddenly couldn't speak it aloud?

Tears blurred my vision, cutting and deserved, and through them I could just make out the small grease spot. On the back of the hand, right above the wrist and the various tendons trickling out, there was a black smudge.

Halfheartedly, I rubbed at it with my thumb. It did not move. I rubbed harder . . . then scratched with a fingernail. But the grease would be stuck there forever.

And I supposed that was all right.

* * *

I opened my eyelids groggily . . . and started. Wood creaked beneath my feet; waves lapped gently around me; the air was motionless and thick.

No-man's-land.

I had gone to bed after Daniel gave me the mechanical hand—and I had cast a dream ward as Oliver had ordered. So this shouldn't be possible. I should not be standing on this gray dock that vanished off into darkness. And yet here I was with the jackal beside me, his ears erect and head low.

Hurry, he said to my mind.

I sat up. "Hurry where? And how did I get here?" A glance behind me showed the shimmering curtain only paces away, and I could hear no snarling of Hell Hounds. I turned back to the jackal—but he was jogging away from me in a steady lope. I scrabbled to my feet.

"Did you see my mother?" I called, pushing into a run. He did not answer, nor did he slow. I squinted ahead, my vision bouncing with each step, but I saw only the dock disappearing into a distant fog.

The wood scraped at my bare feet. But I ignored the splinters that dug into my heels and continued on. The heavy, static air made each breath feel too shallow, while the wooden slats blurred and the dock shivered with each of my steps.

The jackal looked back. *Faster.*

"Where . . . are we going?" I shouted between gasps for air.

Hurry. He darted back into a run—and I now had to sprint to keep up.

But I had gone only a few bounding steps when I heard the

first howl—far off yet unmistakable.

My footsteps faltered. I almost tripped over my feet. "I can't follow you anymore," I shouted after him. "The Hounds are coming!"

The lone howl had transformed into two. Then three. They grew in volume with each step—and my heart lurched into my throat.

"I need to go back!" I shrieked, stumbling to a halt. I flung a glance behind me . . . and balked.

The curtain was so distant, I could not see it. All I could see was gray dock and endless waves. Blind panic rushed through my brain.

Hands shaking, I grabbed a chunk of flesh on my bicep. Maybe I could wake myself up. It had worked when I had first crossed into the realm, and Oliver had shouted me back to the earthly realm.

No. The jackal will show you.

My gaze lurched ahead—and a frozen wind gusted into me. *Hard.* I tipped to one side, squinting to see through stinging eyes.

The jackal had stopped only twenty paces ahead. His ears lay flat against his head, and with a dipping motion of his snout, he shifted his gaze down.

He was pointing at something.

But the Hounds were so close now. The icy wind ripped through my hair and yanked at my loose shirt.

And, God, they were so loud. Echoing in my skull.

Look! The jackal's voice burned behind my eyes. *Look NOW.*

My fingers fell from my bicep, and in a burst of speed, I launched myself toward the jackal—toward whatever it was he wanted me to see.

I reached him. I looked down . . .

And I saw into a hole. A gaping, jagged expanse in the middle of the dock. Beneath it I could just make out the dark, swirling waters of . . . of I didn't know—whatever it was that surrounded this no-man's-land between realms.

I looked at the jackal. "This is what you wanted me to see?"

He shook his head once, and then—with a high-pitched whine that somehow pierced deep into my mind—he jerked his snout down, into the shadowy waters below.

And that's when I saw it: a boat. As old and splintered as the dock, it was hidden just out of sight at the edge of the hole.

"Wake up!" Clarence Wilcox's voice slid into my ears. I spun around, my heart rising—with hope. With fear.

He raced toward me wearing the dress suit he had died in, and his coattails whipped like icicles behind him.

And on his heels, barreling toward me with the strength of a thousand cyclones, were the Hell Hounds.

Clarence flung his hands up, his knees kicking high with each step. And he screamed, "It's not time, Eleanor! Not yet! Wake up! WAKE UP!"

The jackal jumped at me. Fangs snapped in front of my face. I stumbled backward, and somehow golden streaks reared up along the sides of my vision.

"No!" I planted my feet. Wind and frozen mist thundered

over me and through me. But I would not move until I could speak to Clarence. "The boat—I can get in the boat!"

The jackal jumped again. I held my ground even as the world turned black before my eyes and howls shattered my ears.

But then Clarence's figure vanished in a swirl of black and gray—and the jackal's heavy feet slammed against my chest. The jackal's glowing eyes surged into my face. . . .

I fell backward, and in a rush of light and silence, I plummeted through the curtain.

CHAPTER SEVEN

Hands gripped my shoulders—shaking. Jarring me awake. My eyelids burst open, and I stared dazedly into burning yellow eyes.

Oliver gaped at me, his breathing rough. Then fury scored into his face. He flung me back as if scalded. "You returned," he hissed.

I didn't answer. The Hell Hounds' growls echoed in my ears, and my pulse still skittered. I squinted at the porthole. An orange glow filtered through. Dawn.

"You went *back*," Oliver repeated, "after I told you not to."

"Not on purpose," I croaked. "I cast a dream ward."

"Liar." His face sank into a sneer.

"I *swear*, Ollie."

Doubt flickered on his face, and I pushed on. "All I know is that I cast a dream ward, fell asleep, and awoke on the dock." I rose roughly onto my elbows. "And . . . Clarence Wilcox was there. I saw him."

Oliver's sneer finally vanished, replaced with weary resignation. He strode to the porthole, and the sunrise disappeared. He became a silhouette of blazing orange. "Let them go, El. Let Clarence go. Let your mother go. And for God's sake, let Elijah go."

"Because you have let Elijah go?"

"Master your grief," he continued dully, "and then *let them go.*"

Though the room spun, I stumbled to him. "Are you such a master of *your* grief?" I jabbed my hand into his waistcoat and yanked out the flask. He jolted toward me but made no move to reclaim it.

He simply barked a stony laugh. "My loss is a part of me, El. I cope with it as best I can. But you?" His gaze roamed over my face. "You fight to keep what you cannot have back." His hands rose, and almost languidly, he pried each of my fingers from the flask. "Crossing realms will not return your family."

"And I did not cross on purpose." I relaxed my grasp, and the flask fell into his palms. "Marcus's spell must be drawing me over the curtain still." Even as the words fell from my tongue, I sensed they were not true. Marcus was not the one pulling me over the curtain. Somehow, these trips were linked to the jackal.

But I kept that to myself, for at that moment Oliver said,

"Revenge will not bring back your family either, Eleanor."

"Revenge?" I repeated, incredulous. "Marcus must be purged from this earth, and it has nothing to do with revenge. Even you said he no longer belongs here—that his time has already come."

"Huh." Oliver unscrewed the flask top, twisting back to the porthole. "I did say that, didn't I? And it was only two days ago. How funny." He gulped back liquor, and his cheeks briefly brightened with drink. His yellow eyes too.

"What is funny?"

"How much has changed in two days." He returned the flask to his pocket.

And I gritted my teeth. He had come here to wake me . . . and to scold me. Yet now he was a wall of defiance. "And *what* precisely has changed?"

No response at first. Then with his focus still on the shining sea outside, he said, "I saw what Elijah truly was. I saw the black soul inside him and what sort of necromancer he had become."

I reared back. "That was not Elijah in Marseille."

"Close enough," Oliver muttered to himself. "It is what he would have become." Then louder, "I am not on this team, Eleanor. I will *never* be on this team any more than I will ever be human. Remember that."

Demon. Jie's voice whispered through my brain—the way she had looked at Oliver. The way he had vanished afterward.

"Once I find the Old Man," he went on, "then I am done with this. Jacques Girard told me what must be done, and once

121

this command"—he clutched at his stomach, his teeth clench-ing—"is complete, then I can go home. You may set me free, and I can return to my peaceful existence in the spirit realm. Finally."

"But what of Marcus? He must be stopped."

"I do not *care* about Marcus."

"He stole Elijah's body." I grabbed Oliver's shoulder, tried to turn him toward me. "I thought that mattered to you."

"No." The word shot out. Then, faster than I could react, Oliver closed me in against the wall. "Elijah," he whispered, "got exactly what he deserved, El. Can you not see that? There is *nothing* to avenge."

"You loved him. You *told* me you loved him."

"And he betrayed me." Oliver moved back, and he glared at me through half-closed lids. "First loves are blind. And second loves . . ." He snorted, shifting back to the porthole once more. "Second loves are even more so."

"So you will leave me?" I grabbed at his arm.

"Yes," he said simply.

"H-how? I have to set you free—within two months. That was the deal." My fingers fisted around the fabric of his sleeve. "If I do not set you free, then you cannot leave me."

"Is that what you think?" The edge of his lip twitched up. "Oh, naive Eleanor. You only ever see what you want to see, don't you? Take me, for example." His face angled toward me. "You only see a demon bound to his master—and you're right. I may *not* be a man . . . but it does not mean I lack for feelings.

"I have wants too," he went on, "and the more I'm trapped in this human body, the more I find myself *wanting* like a man wants. Feeling like a man feels. As if the demon pieces of my soul are rubbing off and washing away." He dipped in closer, his voice dropping to a mere whisper. "So be careful, El. Be careful how you treat me, for one day you may find you've pushed me too far."

You might wake up and find me gone.

His threat pulsed through my skull. Actual words—just like the jackal's.

I gasped, releasing his sleeve. "How did you do that? Put your thought inside my mind?"

"There is much I can do that you do not know about." Oliver flourished his hands and sauntered back two steps—though a stiffness marked the movement, as if he too might have been surprised.

"But . . . you *cannot* leave me," I insisted. "You *need* me—to command your magic."

"Then I suppose you will have to push me too far, El, and see what happens. *Or*"—his eyes narrowed—"if you bear me any affection at all, then simply be kind. And *please*, do not go into the spirit realm. You risk us both each time you do." Then, with a graceful twirl, he moved toward the door. "What is the line, El? From *A Midsummer Night's Dream*? Something about a spaniel . . ."

"'I am your spaniel,'" I said hollowly, watching him cross the cabin. "'And the more you beat me, I will fawn on you.'"

He snapped his fingers. "That's the one. Except . . ." He pulled the door lightly open and glanced back at me with a pained smile. "I am not a spaniel, and the more you beat me, I will *run*."

I stared at the sunrise for what felt like hours. Oliver's words had cut deep, and though I did not see how he could leave me—*I was the master; he was bound to* me—I was scared to test his threat. If he could speak straight into my mind, what else could he do?

As selfish as I knew it was, Oliver was the only thing I had left from my former life. The only thing that still tied me to Elijah. I *needed* that bond, for in just two short weeks, my magical link to this demon had become as familiar to me as my pulse.

I did not want to push him so far away that he was gone forever. At least not until this was over. Not until Marcus was gone and the world was right again.

Eventually I withdrew the ivory fist from my pocket and held it to the porthole. It almost looked as if its shape had shifted—as if the fingers were beginning to unfurl. My brow wrinkled, and I examined it more closely . . . until I forgot what I was doing.

Whatever strange artifact this was, at least while I looked at it I did not have to think about Oliver. Or Mama. Or Daniel's mechanical hand, now lying beneath my pillow. Or Jie's broken gaze. Or anything at all. Somehow, simply staring at the fist made my heart settle and my brain ease. I lost track of time and thoughts, and I smiled.

But eventually I heard voices in the hall. Jie's soft voice. It called me back to the present—I wanted to speak to her. I *missed* her.

So I returned the fist to my pocket and hurried into the hall. Jie was just walking into the pilothouse, and by the time I reached the glass room, she was at the wheel. She leaned on the spokes, her head in her hands. Though she stiffened slightly at my approach, she did not look my way.

"Have you slept?" I asked gently, moving to her side.

"No." Her fingers curled around one of the spokes. "I . . . don't want to."

"You're safe here."

She turned her face toward me. In the bright morning sun, her eyes looked like endless pools of amber. "Am I?" She lifted her left arm, and a lump bulged beneath her sleeve. "I'm completely dependent on this." She rolled back her sleeve to reveal a metal canister not much larger than a thimble. At one end was a round bit of rubber.

"What is that?"

"It's called a cup." Jie tapped the rubber. "This makes a suction—or I think that's what Daniel said. It pulls out a few droplets of blood every second."

"So Daniel made it?"

Jie nodded. "Based on what Miss Wilcox described."

"Does it work?"

"Yeah." She wet her lips, staring at it with blank eyes. "For now. But when I sleep? When I dream?"

I frowned. "What do you mean?"

"Is it worse to go to sleep and drown in the terror?" She swung her head forward, her gaze so distant, I thought she saw another world entirely. "Or is it worse to wake up and find it's real?"

I swallowed, unsure what to say. At last I simply asked. "Were you . . . *aware* when you were with him?"

"Sometimes I would return to my mind, frozen in place and seeing him. Sometimes we would be walking. Sometimes he would be speaking to me . . . or dressing m—" She broke off and shuddered. "I-I never knew if those moments were intentional. If he let me be in my brain and see from my eyes so I would know how helpless I was. Or maybe he just lost control of his magic from time to time. At least I was only with him for one day." She inhaled deeply. "At least you came for me."

"Of *course* we came for you."

"Right," she said absently. Then she sighed through her nose and gave an empty smile. "Daniel speaking to a Wilcox. It's hard to believe, yeah?"

I blinked at the sudden change in subject.

"And Miss Wilcox isn't the only strange thing I found on here," Jie went on. "Your, uh . . . *demon* is here too." There was a tightness—a bitterness even—in her voice.

And guilt grated against my insides. So much had happened in such a short time—Jie had returned to a world upheaved.

"Joseph explained Oliver to me," she added. "He says the demon helped us."

"He has." I lowered my hands.

"Then I guess it's all right if he's here." Yet nothing in her voice said she felt all right. Especially when she murmured again, "Yeah, it'll be all right."

We descended into silence. The only sound was the engine, the occasional whip of wind against the gondola, and the opening and closing of doors. Soon enough, Allison bustled into the pilothouse, her chin up. "It is time for more bloodletting," she declared with all the authority of a doctor. "Roll up your sleeve, Miss Chen."

My eyebrows lifted. And with a deftness I never would have expected, Allison released the suction on Jie's vacuum, slipped a clean bandage over the wound, and quickly bound it up. "Other arm," she said, and Jie extended her right arm. Allison patted the soft skin below her elbow and then extended a sharp lancet.

Jie inhaled. Allison slashed. Blood blossomed. Then Allison set a second suctioning cup against the wound, squeezed the rubber tip to draw out the air . . . and released.

The cup stayed sucked firmly against Jie's arm.

"If only we had leeches," Allison murmured, shooting Jie an apologetic look. "Then we could just pop one of those on you, and I would not have to cut you every hour before the old incisions scab over. But if we cannot find leeches in Egypt, then a scarificator will do. It won't hurt as much, at least." Her gaze slid to me, lips puffing out. "Thank *goodness* I was here to help Miss Chen, no?"

Before I could offer a response, Jie made a guttural sound.

Her face was unusually pale. "I don't feel good," she said.

Allison whipped an apple from her pocket. "Because you must eat."

Jie accepted the fruit, and I cleared my throat. "So you learned about this"—I motioned to the thimble filled with blood that now rested in Allison's palm—"because of your father?"

"Yes. Our doctor insisted it would get rid of his . . ." Allison hesitated, as if searching for a delicate word. But she gave up and shrugged. "Violence." She scoffed, and after capping the used thimble with rubber and placing it in her medical kit, she muttered to herself, "It didn't work."

And with those three words the world shifted. My view of Allison came into such a clear, sharp focus, I stopped breathing. I had spent my entire childhood envying her. Everything always seemed to come so easily—from friendship to comfort. When I had scrimped and saved, she had flaunted her wealth in my face.

But I had never—not once—considered what happened inside her home.

I gulped, suddenly hot and uncomfortable. Maybe Allison and I were not so different. Maybe we both had nightmares in our pasts.

And maybe all that time I had hated Clarence for bullying Elijah, I should have considered who might be bullying Clarence.

"Land." Jie's voice broke through my thoughts. She pointed. "Look—*land*!"

Allison darted to the glass, and I rubbed my palms on my pants—physically pushing away my distress. Then I moved to the windows as well and squinted into the bright morning light. I could just make out a shift in the horizon to our left—due south.

"Daniel!" Jie shouted, scrabbling toward the hall. "We're approaching land!"

"Shhhh." Joseph's voice hissed into the pilothouse as he entered. "Daniel sleeps, and I believe I can manage to get us aimed for Cairo." His eyes landed briefly on me. "Am I correct in assuming this is where we must go?"

"I . . ." My mouth bobbed shut. I did not know—Oliver had not yet told me.

Fortunately, Joseph did not wait for an answer. He strode to the left table of charts and thumbed through pages.

Giza. Oliver's thought flashed in my mind. Startling and clear. *We must go to the pyramids.* For half a breath I saw through Oliver's eyes—through his porthole. He watched the approaching craggy, yellow land. . . .

And then a sharp *stab* hit my lungs. Aching, wrenching pain impaled me. *Impaled him.* For this was the place where Elijah had chosen power and revenge instead of Oliver.

I held my lips tight and tamped down on our bond. Shoved it deep inside until I could not feel how much Oliver hurt.

"Giza," I ground out. "We must go to the pyramids."

"Which are beside Cairo," Joseph said, tapping at a map. Then he spun around and moved to the steering wheel. "We must head farther south then, and less east." With great care and a pensive expression, he shifted the wheel right, shoved in two of the levers, and then waited. . . .

We *all* waited, feeling the airship adjust its course . . . and then aim us directly for long strips of beach.

Minutes trickled past until at last the turquoise water vanished beneath us, and we puttered into a flat country, as smooth as glass.

We were in *Egypt*.

The airship left a perfect, egg-shaped shadow on the barren sands below, and for a time it seemed this desert land must be empty . . .

Until Allison spotted the first mud village. We all crowded against the right side of the pilothouse and stared while robed figures came out, hands over their heads, to gape up at us. When Joseph pointed out the first mosque, we rushed to the other side to stare at its elaborate minaret. And at the first string of camels, led by the nomadic Bedouin, I ogled with as much wonderment as Allison. Even Jie managed a twitch of a smile.

Over the dry earth we traveled. We passed fields of colorful corn and groves of green dates, tended by women and donkeys and irrigated with long channels that eventually wound and snaked like silver threads to the mighty Nile.

"I have always wanted to go to Egypt," Allison said in a reverent tone as we floated over a waving field of wheat. "Ever since Father invested in an expedition when I was a little girl, I have *dreamed* of seeing it."

"What was the expedition?" I asked, watching the cloaked women and donkeys move through the field.

"It was led by a professor at the University of Philadelphia. Rodney . . . Milton—yes, that was it." Her lips slid into a frown. "Do you recall him? They made a big fuss over him in the local paper, and I think they had one of his mummies on display at the Centennial Exhibition. He found some special burial ground a few years back. Since Father funded the trip, we were supposed to receive half of whatever treasure he uncovered."

She paused for a dramatic eye roll. "Of *course*, we never received anything, and Mother still complains of it. Clarence even hired a detective to find Milton, but when a man is all the way in Cairo, it is hard to actually demand a debt be paid."

"You could try to find him now," I offered, fighting to ignore the way Clarence's name made my chest squeeze with guilt. "You *are* near to Cairo."

"Perhaps," Allison mumbled, her attention already focused back outside. Then she gasped. "Look! It's the Nile!"

I snapped my gaze ahead—and my own breath caught in my throat. For *never* had I seen a river so powerful. Its brown, muddy waters moved so gently, with the age and patience of a river that had seen more civilizations rise and fall than any other. The rich, green landscape only grew denser the closer we came to it, and there was no missing how black the soil became.

The sun reached its zenith soon after Joseph shifted the airship directly south, to follow the Nile's path to Cairo. The room had grown hot—a veritable greenhouse—and I was sweating. We were *all* sweating.

Wiping a sleeve over my forehead, I wandered into the

hall to get water from the galley. Yet Daniel strode out just as I turned in.

I pulled up short, and he lurched to a stop. Once I'd freed my heart from my esophagus, I scanned his face for some sign of how he felt. . . .

But I did not need to search, for he made it abundantly clear right away that he harbored no harsh feelings.

"I made potatoes for everyone. I ain't the best cook, but . . ." He motioned vaguely into the galley. "Hopefully they'll fill you up. Oh!" He spun toward the table. "I also cut some bread. I think it might be a bit stale, but I slathered enough butter on there that you shouldn't notice."

"Th-thank you," I stammered.

He gave a half smile and rubbed his hands together. "Well, I reckon I should get flyin'. Eat up before it goes cold." He side-stepped me into the hall. "Jie! Your garlic mash is ready!"

I watched him go, a mixture of gratitude and affection and . . . and love rolling in my heart.

Not for the first time, regret twined through me for last night. Did a grieving heart stop what I felt for him? No. So why had summoning the words been so impossible?

In a daze of hunger and muddled emotions, I moved to a metal pot on the table. Inside were boiled potatoes—unpeeled, but appetizing. As long as there was silverware (there was) and butter (heaps of it), I was happy.

As I munched beside the porthole, I pondered how best to confess my feelings to Daniel. What to say. When to say it.

Soon Jie joined me to eat her raw garlic mashed with potatoes. She grimaced as she ate but didn't complain, and we watched the view drift by.

Steamers and boats sailed below us, and the farther south we went—and the closer to Cairo we came—the more traffic there was on the Nile. And the more people on the riverbanks. Fishing, bathing, washing clothes—it seemed to be a part of each and every person's life. It was so unlike the Delaware River back in Philadelphia—a fickle, wild force—or the river Seine in Paris, with its elegant, structured waterways. The Nile seemed to be the very lifeblood of Egypt.

"It's kinda cloudy, yeah?" Jie smacked her lips and tipped back a glass of water. "I thought Egypt was always sunny."

"Well, it must rain sometime," I replied, leaning into the glass. "But you're right. It *is* cloudy. And windy." I motioned to gusting palm trees below. "There must be quite a storm coming."

"And coming in fast." She frowned. "It's getting darker by the second. I've never seen clouds move so fast."

I tugged at my earlobe, alarm prickling along my neck. Then, without a word, I scrambled into the hall. Daniel and Joseph stood side by side at the wheel, their shoulders tense.

"The storm," I said, hurrying into the pilothouse—and catching full sight of the rolling gray clouds ahead. "It isn't right."

"We know," Daniel replied, his gaze intent on the horizon. "But we're only a few minutes outside of Cairo."

Joseph offered me the spyglass. "That rise in the distance is where the city is."

I pressed the glass to my eye . . . and a thousand tiny turrets appeared. At the foot of a white mountain, Cairo was a sprawling city of towers, domes, and layered, flat-roofed buildings.

I swung the glass farther left, to the east and toward the desert. Arid, lonely, and empty. Swinging right, to the west, I saw beyond the Nile, to fields of brilliant green and a rocky plateau with three sharp pyramids rising to the sky.

Suddenly, a cloud spun across my field of view. A cloud of darkness and death in the shape of a wild hound.

The Hell Hounds were here.

Everything inside me froze. Blood, pulse, thought. Just as when the Hounds had found me on the boat to France, they had somehow entered the earthly realm once more—and I had no doubt they were after us. . . .

My brain—and my body—roared back to full speed. Faster, even. "We need to land!" I snapped down the spyglass. "*Now*, Daniel!"

He winced. "We're almost there, and I think I can navigate—"

"No." I thrust the spyglass to him. "*Now!*"

Daniel glanced to Joseph—and Joseph nodded. "Do it."

With a spin of the steering wheel and a wrenching of levers, the airship lurched left—to the east bank of the Nile—and began a descent.

We would not be fast enough—not to outrun the Hell Hounds. But what I could not figure out was *why* they were here. On the boat to France, Marcus's spell had called them through. Had he done that again?

"El!" Oliver's voice bellowed through the airship. Then he charged into the pilothouse, his eyes huge. "Is this your doing? Are they here because of you?"

"Is who here?" Joseph demanded. "And why is it Eleanor's fa—"

His words were cut off by a single, long howl.

A hound's howl.

My stomach punched into my lungs. I doubled over. And beside me, Oliver whispered, "God save us all. It's the Hell Hounds."

No one moved. A frantic glance to the front showed Daniel looking puzzled while Joseph had paled to near-deathly white.

"Hell Hounds?" Daniel asked. "You mean those creatures that killed Madame Marineaux?"

"Those are the ones!" Oliver answered, while I shrieked at Daniel: "Land the airship!"

"I'm trying." Daniel twisted back to the wheel. "Everyone hold on!"

But no one had time to hold on. The storm rammed into us. The airship snapped sideways like a kite, and I reeled into the wall.

"Right lever!" Daniel yelled, spinning the wheel left as Joseph hurtled for the levers. "Now left lever, halfway!"

I staggered around to Oliver. "What do we do?"

"Figure out what they want," he yelled back.

I lifted my right hand. That was how Marcus had set the Hounds on me before—by casting a spell on my amputated ghost hand. But the fingers were not glowing, and no pain coursed through me. "It isn't me. Could it be you, Oliver?"

My demon wrenched out his locket—the necklace that kept him magically trapped in the earthly realm. But the locket was not glowing either.

Lightning cracked, flashing over miles of farmland. Thunder rumbled through the metal. It was close—far too close.

"What's happening?" Allison cried, running in from the hall and pushing past Oliver.

Behind me, Daniel kept bellowing commands at Joseph— "Middle lever, down!"—and spinning the wheel as hard as he could against the wind. But then he jolted back as if struck . . . and he began to shout.

"Oh shit, oh shit—get it off me! Get it off!" He yanked at something around his neck. Something that glowed bright blue.

I lunged for him. "What is that?"

His eyes met mine, wide with panic. "Monocle."

"Oh God." I snatched at the chain and tried to snap it off his neck. It held fast. "Oliver!" I screamed. "Help us!"

"Why is it stuck?" Daniel cried. "Why can't I get it off?"

Oliver paled. "It must be *bound* to you. A spell."

"But Madame Marineaux is dead!" I argued. "How can the spell still work?" Even as the words fell from my mouth, I knew the answer. The monocle might have come from Madame Marineaux and the Marquis, but just like Jie's hair clasp, it must have been bewitched by Marcus. And now whatever spell it contained was calling the Hell Hounds to us.

Daniel gaped, first at Oliver, then at me. "How do I get it off?"

Oliver shook his head. "You don't. Only the spell caster can break a spell like this."

"Will we die?" Allison screeched.

Jie clambered into the room. "Should we put on parachutes?"

"Yes." Daniel stumbled toward the hall. "Everyone put on a parachute. Joseph, you take the wheel while I go back and pull the sandbags to the—"

Another gale hit the airship, and everyone went flying across the pilothouse. I hit the glass with a thud, and before I could scrabble back to my feet, my nose was filled with the stench of grave dirt.

Against my will I gagged. We were out of time. After all this, the Hounds were going to pluck us from the sky, and there was nothing we could do.

Daniel rounded back on Oliver. The chain clenched in his fingers, he yelled over the roaring Hounds, "This is what they want?"

Oliver nodded.

"And they'll rip through the airship trying to reach it?"

"Yes!"

"So if I'm not here——"

"Distraction!" I screamed. "We can distract you, and that would break the spell!"

"And then we might be able to get the monocle off," Oliver finished, nodding faster.

I grabbed Daniel's chin and made him look at me. "Sometimes you can stop a necromantic spell with distraction. Think of something else!"

"Like what?" His eyes were so wide, his pupils dilated fully.

"Anything! Just *think* of something that isn't the Hell Hounds!"

"Hurry!" Allison shrieked. "They're coming." She pointed out the window. I dropped Daniel's face as everything inside me went blank with fear. For there they were. Four curs galloped amid a gray squall, growing larger and closer each second.

Then a new sound filled the gondola—a blast of wind. The howls and the thunder were suddenly doubled in volume, and I knew before I even looked down the hall what I would find.

The hatch in the cargo hold was open, and Daniel stood on the edge. He glanced back only once, and his eyes met mine.

"*No!*" I launched myself after him. But I was too slow, too far away.

Daniel jumped.

And that was when I realized—in a half-formed thought that flitted through my mind before I'd gone two steps: he had no parachute.

And I could not let him die.

I skittered back, yanked a parachute off the hook, and then sprinted. Each kick of my legs brought me closer to the open hatch—and just before I reached it, I swung the parachute on.

Then I jumped too.

CHAPTER EIGHT

I was weightless. I wasn't falling! I wasn't moving!
I was lost in an endless, gray world of clouds.

And Daniel—I couldn't see him anywhere.

But then I broke through. The lush vegetation of farms opened up before me like a jungle. Wind slashed into my face and forced its way into my nose, my mouth, my eyes—I couldn't see, couldn't breathe—and I knew, with horrifying certainty, that I *was* falling.

Fast.

I forced my eyes to stay open though tears poured from the sides, and I searched for Daniel. How could I have lost him so easily?

Then there he was, off to my left, arms flailing out to his

sides. His hands clawed as if he grasped for something—anything—to slow his fall.

I closed my arms into my body and aimed, willing myself to fall faster. *Faster.*

I risked turning my head. But I instantly wished I hadn't—the Hell Hounds were there. Gray storm clouds with jaws of death. They careened straight for Daniel.

I had to reach him first.

I *would* reach him first. *Faster, faster, faster!* He was so close now. Through my watering eyes, I could see his hair lashing.

And I could see the monocle glowing.

I slammed into his back and threw my arms around his chest, clinging as tightly as I could.

A scream ripped from his lips—and was instantly lost behind us.

"It's me!" I shrieked in his ear. "Eleanor!" And in that moment he was distracted. The blue glow died; the spell lost its hold. I gripped the monocle and yanked, snapping it free.

Then, with all my strength, I slung it into the sky.

But the Hell Hounds' open jaws were still cycloning for us.

"Parachute!" Daniel roared.

My fingers wrapped around the canvas cord, and in a single move I squeezed Daniel tighter and ripped the parachute open.

Fabric whipped out, billowing wide. In a neck-wrenching movement, we tore backward, our bodies yanked straight up, shooting us above the Hell Hounds.

They screeched beneath us, a gust of wind bursting up as their thunderous jaws snapped onto a dim, glowing chain.

The wind blasted us, swelling into the parachute with a roar. We rocketed even higher, pushed off far from the Hounds' fury.

But not before I saw the glowing chain—and the Hounds—explode in a flash of blinding blue.

The instant the Hounds were gone, Daniel cried out, "I can't believe you, you stupid, stupid girl!" He was shouting in my ear, and I realized from the shudders in his chest that he was sobbing. "Stupid, stupid Eleanor—why?"

His arms came backward, and I felt his hands clasp behind my back; but he couldn't get much of a grip at this angle. So I squeezed tighter and wrapped my legs around his waist. "Can these parachutes hold two?"

"No!" he screamed. "You just killed yourself too!"

"Isn't there *something* we can do?" The only thing keeping Daniel alive was my arms—and my strength was draining fast.

It wouldn't matter that I had just saved Daniel's life, and he had saved the airship—

The airship!

I wrenched my head up, hoping to see it, but my entire, watery vision was filled with white fabric. And my ears were filled with the creaking parachute lines. It was the only sound over our heavy gasps for air.

"Can Joseph land?"

"We have other things to worry about right now!" Daniel tried to look up.

"Stay still!" I clutched him more tightly. "If you squirm, I'll drop you!"

"You need to drop me anyway!"

"Absolutely not." We were alive, and that was not something I was going to give up.

"Let go," Daniel shouted, but I noticed he made no move to break free.

"I didn't catch you so I could drop you again."

"Well," he growled, "this parachute isn't gonna hold us much longer. We'll start falling faster real soon. Got any more genius ideas?"

"Not if you keep insulting me," I hissed in his ear. "I just saved your wretched skin, Daniel Sheridan. The least you could do is thank me."

"I'll only thank you if we get to the ground alive." There was a new note of terror in his voice, and I realized by the quickening whistle of wind in my ears, by the growing funnel of air in the parachute, that gravity had taken its hold once more. I looked out over the land—yellow rock, jagged hills in the distance, and far to the east, the muddy Nile. I had no idea where we were now or how we would find the others, but I'd be damned if I'd let my heroic jump go to waste.

Screwing my eyes shut, I focused on my spiritual energy. If I could strengthen *myself*, why not the parachute? Necromancers transferred spells to inanimate objects—that was the purpose of an amulet—so surely I could find some way to make this work. . . .

My arm muscles scorched with strain. My fingers were weakening. I made myself inhale deeply—stretch my lungs to the limit—and draw in a full breath. My power spiraled up from the tips of my body.

And from something warm that pulsed in my pocket. The ivory fist. It was *feeding* me magic. But I did not have time to dwell on this. I simply gathered and grabbed at all the power I could.

A trickle of blue warmth turned to a rush and then to a torrent. I gathered it in my chest, letting it whorl around my heart as I called up more . . . until my well of power was pressing against my lungs, pushing out my oxygen. Until soon enough I would have nothing left to breathe.

"Daniel," I said, surprised by how calm and smooth my voice was—not that it much mattered. We had picked up substantial speed now, and the air cut into my face and eyes. "Daniel, I need you to hold on as tight as you can. I'm releasing one hand."

He nodded, and I quickly checked that my left arm wouldn't give out—but it was fine. I felt shockingly strong. My legs too— they squeezed his waist with unrelenting power. The magic had not only refreshed my strength but *increased* it.

I released my right hand, instantly grabbing hold of a parachute line. Then I willed every ounce of power I had into it. *Stronger, stronger, stronger. Hold us a little longer until we reach the ground.*

Instantly, the magic responded. It slipped from my fingers, and though I didn't look up to watch, blue flared in the top of my vision.

"What did you just do?" Daniel demanded—though he

had the good sense not to squirm. "Why . . . why are we fallin' slower?"

For two heartbeats I remained silent. I waited for the rest of my magic to twine itself around the parachute, to hold the cloth open and keep the strings from snapping. The ground below—leafy farms and distant desert—was still so far away.

At last I yanked my arm down and clutched Daniel's chest once more, and the heady perfection of the spell bubbled over me as it always did.

"Empress?"

Daniel's voice pierced my happy warmth. "Hmmm?"

"What did you just do?"

"Magic. To keep the parachute intact."

He didn't answer, but I felt the muscles in his back tighten. Yet if he was worried about the necromancy, I didn't care. I had saved his life—what did it matter *how*?

In the back of my mind, though, something nagged—something bleak that wanted my attention, but I gave it none.

Because, for heaven's sake, we were flying! The slightest wind gusted over us, and hawks glided at eye level. My heart swelled with joy, and I couldn't keep from grinning. I was *flying*! And I had saved Daniel's life, and he had saved the airship.

It didn't take long before the ground stopped looking like indistinguishable plants, and the sugarcane leaves and patches of scrubby forest came into focus. Even a clay farmhouse in the distance. Then, faster and faster, the ground approached—and I realized that despite my stroke of genius that would get us *to* the ground, we weren't going to arrive softly.

Daniel seemed to have the same thought, for he suddenly started shouting, "Steer left—left, Empress!"

"How?" A wicked-looking sycamore was directly beneath us, and the clicks of insects were doubling in volume each second.

"Left, *left*! You need to pull—" His words broke off as the leaves raced toward us . . . and then we were on them. I had no choice: I dropped Daniel into the sycamore, and he immediately grabbed a branch. But without his weight, my speed decreased and spiraled even more sharply right.

Then I plummeted between two acacia trees. The thorns sliced into my skin, but I barely noticed—I was too busy trying to grab hold of a branch to stop my fall.

Then my parachute strings snagged, and with a final, gut-wrenching jerk, I stopped moving altogether.

The ground was a solid ten feet beneath me.

"Daniel," I yelled. "Are you all right?" He didn't answer, and panic stole my breath. With my fingers flying, I unfastened the sack's harness. "Daniel? Dan—" My yell became a yelp as I plummeted to the earth.

I hit with a thump. Shock jolted through my legs. I toppled forward onto my hands—and they sank into the soft, rich soil. Bugs hummed everywhere, and the humidity was so intense, it seemed to muffle all sounds.

"Empress!" Daniel's voice cut through the air and the insects. He was alive—we were both *alive*.

But what about everyone else? Now that *we* had landed, what of the airship? I dragged myself into a kneeling position, lowered my eyelids, and felt for Oliver. Felt for the bond of power that connected us. . . .

There it was, tugging in my gut. I reached out along it, trying to gauge where the demon might be.

South. Southeast, actually. At least two miles . . . but not moving. He wasn't in the sky anymore, and I could only hope that meant he was safe.

For half a breath our bond shimmered more brightly, and a fresh surge of magic pulsed through me. I smiled. Oliver was looking for me too—I could follow our connection until I found him.

Just as I opened my eyes and leaned back to dust off my hands, footsteps beat on the dark earth. I twisted my head left, knowing who came.

And then there he was, his face jubilant. Cheeks flushed and eyes bright, Daniel sprinted to me. Before I could tell him to slow, to give me a moment to breathe, he had me in his arms. He spun me, laughing and crying.

One twirl, two twirls, and the leaves blurred into a world of green and yellow.

But just as suddenly as he'd picked me up, he lowered me onto my toes and clasped the sides of my face. "Empress," he said, his voice stern—though tears pooled in his eyes, "that was the stupidest, *stupidest* thing you have ever done."

I gave a hoarse laugh. "I saved your life."

"I know—oh God, I know." He tugged me into an embrace, so tight I could barely breathe. "But please, don't ever do something that foolish again. *Ever.* Do you hear me?"

"You're only mad because I've rescued you more times than you've rescued me." I laughed again, this time more deeply. I still burned with the power I'd cast on the parachute. It was a happy drunk that made me bold—made me draw back and flick his chin, like he always did to me.

But he grabbed my wrist and pulled me to him. Our bodies met. "That's not true." His voice was suddenly rougher. Lower. All sign of his tears were gone. "How many times have you saved me?"

My heart was thrashing erratically, but not because we'd almost died. Or even because Daniel held me. I was *finally* going to get what I wanted, and this time I would not balk.

"I've saved your life three times now." I splayed three fingers on his chest. Beneath the thin cotton of his shirt, his pulse bounced as fast as mine. "First at the dynamite factory, then in the Paris underground, and now this."

His lips quirked up. "That makes us even, then." His smile faltered . . . and then fell again. "Promise me something." He reached up and ran his knuckles down my jaw. I held my breath and strained to listen. "Promise me you'll never do something like that again."

"I can't promise that, Daniel."

His fingers paused. "Why?"

"Why do you think?"

He swallowed, glancing down at my hand on his chest. Then he flinched. "You're hurt—oh hell, you're *bleeding*." He yanked up my right sleeve, and, sure enough, blood was sliding down my arm from my elbow.

A giggle broke through my lips. "I must have cut myself on the acacia thorns."

Daniel's brow furrowed. "I don't see why it's funny."

"It doesn't hurt," I declared, but Daniel ignored me. He set to rolling up my sleeve, and moments later, once my forearm was exposed, his breath came hissing out. It was a huge gash—the sort that would need cleaning and salves. The sort that *should* be causing pain.

"We need to bind that immediately." Daniel met my eyes, worried. "And your demon ain't here, so it's got to be the normal way."

"Pshaw." I pulled my arm free from his. It was tender, but nothing I couldn't handle. "I told you: it doesn't hurt."

"And I don't care." Avoiding my eyes and with his jaw muscles twitching, he ripped off the bottom half of my sleeve. It was stained with blood but not yet soaked through. So he wrapped it tightly around the wound.

When he was finished, he pointed east. "Walk."

"To where?" I glowered. "And since when are you in charge?"

"Since you got drunk off your black magic and lost the ability to think clearly." He sighed . . . then groaned. "I don't want to fight about this, all right? I am so, so, *so* grateful that you saved me, but that"—he pointed at my arm—"scares the hell out of me. So please, just do as I say. And walk."

I eyed him. A thousand retorts lay on the tip of my tongue, but I swallowed them back. I would not shout at him. And I would *not* cry. I would cling to this magical strength for as long as it would let me.

But then panic jolted through me. My hand shot into my pocket to search for . . .

My breath whooshed out, relieved. The ivory fist was still there . . . though a fist no longer. Tracing the feel of its carvings, I could tell the fingers had further unfurled.

I had no idea what it meant, and I wasn't in the mood to contemplate it. "Fine, Daniel," I declared. "I'll do as you say, and I will walk. But you follow me. I know where Oliver is—I can sense him through our bond."

Daniel's face tightened, but he did not argue. So with an unhappy inventor on my heels, I felt for Oliver—closer, ever closer—and set off at a steady march through the fields of sugarcane.

It took us almost an hour to find Oliver—and the balloon. Endless fields of sugarcane, dates, and cotton . . . endless mosquitoes and flies. Endless heat. Hawks glided overhead, while lapwings fluttered everywhere like butterflies.

I was desperate for water within minutes—especially seeing all the canals from the Nile that separated farms in place of hedges. But I doubted it was drinkable, and there was no one to ask. The fields were abandoned—likely to avoid the afternoon heat—and the few veiled women still out tending the crops did not seem open to conversation.

My arm began to hurt by the third farm—not badly, but it did throb as blood seeped out. The magic had already worn off. I was desperate for more, but too ashamed to use it with Daniel there. I tried, albeit halfheartedly, to speak—about the landscape or the bugs—but he only gave me one-word answers. He did not seem angry with me. Only sad. And silent.

But he did check on me several times, to rewrap the wound or to inspect me for other injuries. I think he could tell the magic had faded, but neither he nor I knew how to make amends. So silence it was until we finally crested a hill and reached a sprawling village of flat-roofed buildings and sycamore trees. In the distance, ruins crumbled—Greek, by the look of the ornate columns thrusting up amid fields of grass and dust.

But what caught my eye was an obelisk that jutted out of the ruins. Much like the one in the Place de la Concorde in Paris, it towered over everything—even the small city. Sycamores grew all around it, and draped over one gnarled tree was a sprawling heap of white fabric. It billowed in the breeze like a sail.

The airship.

Daniel and I pushed into a jog. People were clustered around the covered sycamore . . . and the gondola behind it. As we approached, I could see that it lay in the grass like a ship run aground.

A whoop sounded—Jie's voice. Then Joseph's. In moments they were racing through the knee-high grass toward us.

Never had I seen them look so happy. But it was not to me that they ran. It was to Daniel. They flung their arms around him in a frenzied embrace, and I saw tears pouring from Joseph's eyes. Jie's as well.

"Foolish man," Joseph cried over and over. "Foolish, foolish man! I could never forgive you—or myself—if you were to sacrifice yourself like that. *Foolish* man."

Daniel pulled back, his eyes shining and head shaking. "My life's nothin' compared to yours."

Jie punched him in the arm—*hard*. "Don't ever say that again, yeah?" Then she yanked him back into a hug.

For a moment, hurt wrangled through me. Were they not happy to see me? Or at least *grateful* I had saved Daniel's life?

But then Joseph's tear-filled eyes—and Jie's too—landed on me, and there was no denying the gratitude in their smiles.

So I grinned back before turning my gaze to the balloon to find Oliver. He lounged against the gondola, his eyes firmly on me. Even from here I could see his nonchalance was an act—and not only because of the flush in his cheeks, but also the absolute stillness in his face. Grass waved around his legs, and his curls kicked up in the breeze.

I lifted my fingers in a tentative wave . . . and a subtle, tender warmth bathed over me. Oliver's happiness. His relief.

My smile grew. It was *good* to be alive.

Then Allison appeared around the gondola and spotted me. She bounced on her toes and clapped—looking beyond ecstatic that I was returned.

I gave the Spirit-Hunters a final look. They were still

caught up in their tearful reunion, so I jogged the rest of the way through the shimmering grass. The locals noticed me soon enough, and after pointed fingers and chattered words, several children darted at me.

"*Baksheesh!*" they cried, pushing their open hands to me. "*Baksheesh! Baksheesh!*"

I smiled, my face bunching up in confusion, and scooted onward until I finally popped out before Oliver, Allison, and the gleaming gondola.

"What do they want?" I cried, shooing at a child who *refused* to let go of my pants.

"*Baksheesh,*" Oliver said with an amused smirk. "It means 'charitable gift.' The Egyptians expect it from everyone." He sauntered toward me, and his eyes flickered to the children's. And thank the merciful heavens my demon knew so many languages, for after a few barked words of Arabic, the children finally released me—and shot straight for Allison.

I looked up at Oliver with a smile. "You survived," I said.

He stepped to me and brushed a light, almost casual kiss over my forehead. "As did you."

My heart stumbled—just a tiny catch. He was *very* happy to see me.

But then his gaze settled on my arm, and a frown creased his forehead. "Should I heal you?"

"No." I glanced at Allison. She gestured wildly at the children, but they refused to stop yanking at her skirts.

I turned back to Oliver. "I'll go with normal healing this time."

"Ah," he said with a knowing arch of his eyebrow. Luckily, he dropped the subject and simply turned a snarl on the Egyptian kids—and in a flurry of shouts and laughter, they finally scampered back toward town.

Allison threw her arms around me. "I thought you were dead! You just *jumped* right off the balloon, and then I didn't see you again." She lurched back, gripping my shoulders. "What the blazes were you thinking? Mr. McIntosh kept insisting you were fine, but I do not see how he could possibly know. And yet here you are!" She hugged me again. "You are fine! And you are alive! And, oh goodness, Eleanor, I do not ever want to experience that again."

"What happened?" I asked.

"Well," she said, her expression animated as she pulled away, "Mr. Boyer managed to land us, but not before those awful creatures hurtled into us. What were they called again, Mr. McIntosh?"

"Hell Hounds," Oliver offered with an almost indulgent smile. I could only suppose that near-death had made him and Allison tentative allies—and that Oliver had realized he now wore a last name. He responded to Mr. McIntosh as if born to it.

Allison shivered. "*Hell Hounds*. They hit us, Eleanor, and we were spinning and spinning for at least a hundred feet—"

"More like fifty," Oliver amended.

"—until we hit the ground so hard, I thought my teeth would break. And then the balloon just . . . *poof*." She flicked her wrists up. "I do not know how we'll *ever* get off the ground now."

I glanced at Oliver. "Is it that bad?"

He shrugged one shoulder. "That will be for your inventor to decide, but . . . it certainly won't be easy to fix."

Oliver was right. Once Daniel had assessed the damage, we learned the engine had been so knocked about that it would take at *least* the rest of the day to repair. But more concerning was that we needed fuel—the only way to inflate the balloon was with heated air. A lot of it.

After a great deal of asking around, Oliver managed to find a vendor in the nearby village who had sufficient oil . . . but not at an affordable price. "The man wants two hundred British pounds," Oliver told Joseph, "and I cannot talk him down."

Joseph, Allison, and I stood beside the open gondola hatch while Daniel and Jie yanked out floorboards in the cargo hold— Daniel needed better access to his engine. Meanwhile, our robed fuel salesman leaned on his donkey beneath a sycamore tree nearby. He stroked his mustache and looked very pleased by the inevitable fortune coming his way.

Joseph massaged his forehead. "We cannot possibly afford that. I do not even have a quarter of it."

"Perhaps we could try a different village," I suggested, but the grim slant to Oliver's brow told me we weren't likely to find a better price anywhere. Swatting at flies that kept attacking my bleeding arm, I turned to Allison. "How much money do *you* have?"

She winced and shrank back. "Not much more than Mr. Boyer."

I blinked. "Your mother let you leave Philadelphia with less than fifty dollars?"

Her wince deepened, and she stoutly refused to meet my eyes. "My mother did not precisely *approve* of my trip. In fact, she swore she would not contribute a dime. What little money I have is what I managed to save myself."

My breath wuffed out, and I fought to keep the disappointment off my face—it was hardly Allison's fault we were poor. "Do we have any idea how long it would take to reach Giza from here?" I asked Oliver.

He hollered the question over to our new Egyptian friend—who quickly hollered back an answer.

"Half a day by horse," Oliver translated.

I lowered my hands. "That is not so bad then. If we had horses, I mean."

"But it would be better if we had the airship," Joseph muttered. He shook his head. "What if we must make another escape like Marseille? This balloon has been invaluable to us so far, and I do not want to abandon it if we can help it."

"Well," Allison inserted hesitantly, "we can assume this Marcus fellow is at *least* a day or two behind us, no? A boat cannot possibly cross the Mediterranean as quickly as an airship. So you could feasibly fix the balloon and still reach Giza before him."

"Except for the money," Oliver reminded. "And I do not think we can convince this man that *donating* his fuel is a worthwhile investment."

Investment. The word jostled around in my brain . . . and then solidified into an idea. "Investment!" I gripped at Allison's hands. "That professor you mentioned—we could find him! You could collect your debt, and we could use the money to repair the balloon."

"You mean Professor Milton?" Allison's eyes widened. "B-but he probably isn't around anymore. And even if he was, I haven't the faintest idea where to begin looking. Clarence's detective found him at . . . at some hotel. Shepheard's, I believe."

"Shepheard's?" Oliver asked, eyebrows rising with interest. "You are certain?"

"No!" she wailed. "It was a year ago, and I wasn't very interested. And who knows if he is still there after all this time?"

"Well, Shepheard's is *in* Cairo, Miss Wilcox. It's, uh . . ." Oliver waved a mosquito from his face. "It's a hotel where all the Westerners stay, and if your professor is still in the area, it's very likely he would stay there. Someone at the hotel will surely know."

Joseph folded his arms over his chest, his face screwed up with concentration. For several moments, the only sound was the wind in the grass, the huffing of the donkey, and the groaning of resistant gondola floorboards.

"I suppose," Allison mused aloud, "that if we went into Cairo, then we could also get Miss Chen a scarificator."

Joseph remained silent, but his eyes twitched.

"And," Allison went on, an undeniable layer of syrup in her tone, "we could find turmeric to thin her blood. Perhaps we

158

could also find fresh bandages for you, Mr. Boyer."

Another eyelid twitch. Then Joseph nodded once, his eyes coming back into focus. "All right. It is decided then. Allison and Oliver . . . and you as well, Eleanor. You must go to Cairo and try to acquire enough funding for fuel—*or* possibly find a cheaper fuel source." Joseph's gaze settled on Oliver. "Perhaps you could find transportation into the city."

My demon nodded, a hint of a smile on his lips, and strode off toward the Egyptian and his donkey.

"And *I*," I said, holding out my wounded arm for Allison, "will let you bind this cut. It stings like the dickens, and the flies simply will not leave me alone."

Once my arm was cleaned and bound up, there was only one thing more I wished to do before leaving the airship. One person I wished to see.

Because now that my magic had worn off, and we were all so happy to be alive—and now that I had almost lost *him*—I was ready to say what needed saying. *Now* was the right moment for me. Finally.

I found Daniel in the engine. Half the floorboards had been ripped out and tossed to one side, and his blond head was hunkered over a vast array of valves, tubes, and gears.

I knelt at the edge of the planks. "Daniel."

His head whipped up. Grease and sweat streaked across his cheeks. He looked absolutely *himself*.

"Look." I extended my right arm, now wrapped in bandages.

"Old-fashioned healing at its best."

Slowly, his lips spread into a grin. His forehead relaxed, and his eyes crinkled. "I'm glad." Wiping at his face, he rose to his full height—which brought his eyes level with mine.

And the awkwardness took over. Unflinching and unafraid might work well for him, but *I* suddenly felt very exposed.

So I dropped my gaze as I forced the proper words to come. "Back in the woods, you asked me why I could not promise to never save you again."

He swallowed. "And?"

"And . . ." I bit my lip. This had really seemed quite easy to say in my head. "And the reason I cannot promise is . . ."

His face tightened as if bracing for the worst. "Yes?"

"Because I am in love with you." The words blasted out, and I cringed. Then, to make it all the more mortifying, I stupidly added, "Too."

"You're in love with me," he repeated. "Too."

"Too."

His face relaxed, and his eyes flicked to my lips . . . then to my eyes . . . then *back* to my lips. "If it's all right with you then . . ." He moved slightly closer. "I'm going to ki—"

A tremor shook through him.

"Daniel?" I grabbed for him, alarmed. But the shudder subsided—and with it went all the discomfort of the moment.

"Are you ill?" I asked.

"I'm fine." He exhaled through his teeth. "Just . . . just a chill. Nothing to worry about." In a quick, easy move, he hopped up and twisted around to sit beside me. His legs hung into the open hole, and I swung my legs forward to mimic his.

Then he took my hand and wove his fingers through mine. "Sorry if I scared you."

"It's all right." Feeling bold—and relieved it was just a chill—I traced a finger up his arm, relishing how it raised gooseflesh on his skin. "Perhaps someone is walking over your grave."

"Or maybe," he said, bringing his forehead down to mine, "I just don't like it when we split up."

"I can take care of myself."

"Don't I know it, Empress." He pressed a soft kiss to my forehead, and his lips murmured against my brow, "You're the toughest girl in the world."

I drew back, grinning up at him. My heart banged, and my cheeks hurt. This was it. What I had wanted all along. Daniel and I acting as normal lovers do. No fights or problems in sight.

"Eleanor?" Allison's voice cut into the cargo hold—and right through the moment. "Are you in there? Mr. McIntosh and I are waiting."

Daniel's expression darkened. His jaw muscles tensed. "I don't trust her."

"She isn't like her father," I said softly, pushing to my feet. "Or like Clarence."

"That doesn't make her trustworthy." Daniel peered at me sideways. "Be careful, Empress, all right? I mean it. Fixing this engine is absolutely mindless, and I'll have nothing to do but

161

worry about you while you're away."

"I'll be careful. I promise." I bobbed him a curtsy, and as I turned to go, he flashed me a fond, happy smile.

I found Allison and Oliver waiting beside a rickety old cart filled with sticks of sugarcane and towed by two donkeys.

Jie stood beside them, examining the sugarcane. Her face showed more animation than it had since Paris.

Hope swelled in my chest, and I scurried toward her. "Are you coming with us into Cairo?"

She hesitated.

"Please?" I pressed. "When else will you get to see this city?"

Her eyes ran over the cart, then flicked west toward the distant towers. And then to my absolute joy, her lips actually quirked up.

"Yeah," she said with a slight nod. "I guess I'll go. Let me just tell Joseph." She strode off, her head a bit higher than it had been a few minutes before; and as I watched her walk, my heart soared into my throat. Into my brain.

She would be all right. Bit by bit, my best friend would feel like herself again, and she would be all right.

With a happy hum, I twirled around the cart to join Allison and Oliver. Of course, my hum instantly cut off when Allison caught sight of me. "You intend to wear your trousers *into* the city?" she demanded.

I scowled and hopped onto the back of the cart as Oliver slid up beside me. "I have nothing else, and Jie will also be in trousers."

"Miss Chen can at least pass as a boy. *You*"—she stared meaningfully at my chest—"cannot. You could have borrowed one of my dresses, you know."

I glared. "I could not possibly fit into one of your dresses, *you know*."

She didn't argue with that—nor would she stop her complaints as she clambered onto the cart beside Oliver. Nor would she stop as she popped up her parasol.

Not even as Jie climbed beside me and Oliver shouted for our driver to get going would Allison pause her torrent of nasty words. Indeed, her complaints regarding my person only stopped once children squealing for *baksheesh* chased after us—giving her a new target for her endless displeasure.

CHAPTER NINE

As our cart rattled from town—which, it turned out, was none other than Heliopolis, ancient city of the Greeks— Oliver happily donned the role of tour guide and began to point out various Egyptian sights. Allison fed his ego with enthusiastic questions, and soon we had seen a fountain of sweet water in which, according to Oliver, the Virgin Mary bathed her feet; a fig tree beneath which Mary rested; and then a garden supposedly planted by Cleopatra.

"How do you know all these places?" Jie asked softly. Her eyes slid to Oliver's face, challenging. "Is it some kind of demon knowledge?"

Oliver paused, and for a moment he looked genuinely offended. But then he swatted the question aside with that careful nonchalance only he could manage. "Other than an ability to speak all languages, Miss Chen, I fear demons have no more special knowledge than you have. I only know these places because I have *been* here before."

I blinked, shocked that he had answered her so frankly— and even more shocked that Jie seemed to accept this answer, for with nothing more than a scrutinizing look, her posture relaxed. She settled back onto the sugarcane and laced her hands behind her head.

Allison's posture, on the other hand, locked up completely. "Demon?" Her voice was as squeaky as the cart's wheels. "Pardon me, did I hear that properly? *Demon?*"

My mouth bounced open dumbly, and Jie's eyebrows lurched high. Oliver, however, simply flipped up his hand and drawled, "It is a euphemism, Miss Wilcox. For a . . ." He lowered his voice and whispered, "*bastard*. No father, you know."

Allison stiffened even more, statuesque if not for the breeze through her curls. "Oh? And since when do bastards speak all languages?"

"That was a joke, Miss Wilcox." Oliver gave her a look of such withering disbelief, even *I* thought it was all in jest. "Sarcasm," he added. "You have heard of it, I daresay?"

As Allison's cheeks scorched pink, Oliver's gold eyes met mine.

Well played, I thought at him, wondering if he could hear my thoughts.

His smile told me that he could.

166

We continued on until Heliopolis had passed behind us and cornfields slid by. Jie pointed out flocks of white birds with black, plumed heads and long, curved beaks hovering above the fields. "What are those?" she asked, and Oliver resumed his role as tour guide.

"Ah, that is the Sacred Ibis, Miss Chen. They once protected Egypt from a great winged serpent—or so the story goes."

"Wasn't there a god with an ibis head?" Allison's forehead scrunched up.

"Thoth, I think." I wasn't sure why I knew that, yet Oliver nodded as if I were a particularly apt pupil.

"Precisely, El." He leaned into me with a playful nudge. "Thoth is the god of wisdom and balance. He and Anubis judge your soul in the afterlife."

"You speak as if they are real," Allison said with giggle.

He flashed her an arch smile. "And how do you know they are not, Miss Wilcox? Perhaps they speak all languages too."

Yet again Allison's cheeks turned bright red. I glared at Oliver—and at Jie too when she actually *snorted* into her hand. Jie quickly covered her laugh with an overly interested point at a series of donkeys with buckets, and the conversation shifted to the primitive—though effective—irrigation system of Egyptian farms.

Eventually we left the farms only to pass a modern train depot packed with people . . . and then *finally* we trudged beneath an enormous gate of wide stones into Cairo.

"One of the Babs al-Cairo," Oliver declared, pointing at the fortress-like archway above us. "From the Middle Ages. And look—over there are remnants of the Turkish city." He motioned to a series of narrow lanes that shot off beyond the gate. Houses hung over the streets, meeting in the middle, and their elaborate lattice screens spoke of another time—a world like the one from Scheherazade's tales.

But I'd barely caught a glimpse of that exotic, old Cairo before our sugarcane cart carried us into a fantastically *modern* city. Wide boulevards were lined with hotels and theaters, while gardens and trees hid behind new buildings and gates. Cairo had an almost Parisian flair to it, and the pigeons fluttering everywhere were identical to those back home in Philadelphia. If it weren't for the *people*, I might have forgotten where we were entirely.

But there was no missing the people—there were faces of every color and type, from as white as mine to darker than Joseph's. And the clothes! Some women wore veils, some wore Western-style dresses; some men donned turbans and fezzes, and others went exposed. Children trotted around on donkeys, and carriages raced behind horses.

For a brief time all I could do was stare. During the quarter of an hour we clattered through Cairo, I was simply Eleanor again—and finally traveling the world.

And the best part was that I had friends with me. There was already more color in Jie's cheeks than I'd seen in two days. She was here, she was trying to move past what Marcus had done, and I would be at her side for each step of that journey.

Just when I thought things in Cairo were quite exotic enough, the road split off in either direction to ring an enormous park.

"Ezbekieh Gardens," Oliver declared as we veered left to circle it. "A popular spot—as you can see."

And I *could* see. The pathways winding into the park teemed with people. Antiquity merchants shouted their wares beside mimosa trees, while charmers prodded at their snakes next to chrysanthemums. I had never in my life seen such vividness of color or people: jugglers and puppeteers, cucumber vendors and flower girls. Everywhere my eyes fell, I saw something new.

At last our cart slowed before a palatial building. Four stories of elegant balconies and awnings made it look both modern—like a Western hotel—but also classically old, like a sheikh's palace. Patios out front were covered with cushioned wicker armchairs as well as the well-dressed and well-to-do.

"Here we are," Oliver declared.

"*That* is Shepheard's?" It was even more elegant than the Hotel Le Meurice. I scrambled off the cart and wiped at the dust on my pants.

"That is Shepheard's," Oliver confirmed.

"Finally," Jie muttered. She rubbed at her head. "My scalp is getting sunburned."

"That is why I have a parasol," Allison said primly.

Jie and I exchanged arched eyebrows.

But Allison was not yet finished. As she launched into a march for the entrance, she flashed me a mischievous grin over her shoulder. "Are you regretting your wardrobe selection yet, Eleanor?"

"No," I lied, scowling and brushing at my hair with my fingers. Jie only laughed, a loud, clear sound; and as she kicked off toward the entrance too, all my frustration with Allison slipped away.

Today was becoming a good day.

Oliver strolled up beside me, his elbow extended. "Shall I escort you, milady?"

With a grin, I hooked my arm in his. "You're in an unusually fine humor this afternoon, aren't you?"

"Hmmm." His lips pressed into a vague, private smile, and he guided me up the front steps. "You are as well, Eleanor."

"Because my best friend is here, and she seems to be feeling better. But what reason is there for your happiness?"

As he twirled us around a shoe shiner singing for *baksheesh*, he flashed his eyebrows. "Let us simply say, Eleanor, that on this particular day, I am very glad to be alive." He towed me through a lattice-screened door. "Your palace awaits, milady."

"That is all?" I demanded. "You are simply glad to be alive?"

"Mmm."

I dug my heels into the ground, trying to get him to stop. But Oliver simply slipped his arm free, wiggled his fingers mockingly, and strode ahead, cryptic and confusing.

I hurried after him, through the entrance doors . . . but my stride instantly failed me. The hotel was even more luxurious inside. Potted narcissi and elegant leather sofas were crowded amid golden Persian rugs. The orange-sunburst tiles clicked beneath hundreds of feet, and above it all was the soft murmur of voices—primarily, I was surprised to note, speaking English.

While sportsmen in khakis and artists toting their paint-brushes streamed by, Oliver informed Jie and Allison from several paces ahead of me that it was likely everyone in and around Shepheard's spoke English. The hotel was a haven for Americans and British abroad.

Allison tipped up her chin. "I daresay that will make our investigation easier then. We should start with the concierge."

"Yes," Oliver said slowly. "You inquire at the front, and, uh . . . I shall do a bit of snooping elsewhere." With his hands sliding into his pockets, he slunk off into the crowds.

I craned my neck for sight of the concierge beyond the throngs of people. At last I found the dark-wood desk. "It's at the far end of the room."

"Let me do the talking, please." Allison ran a disgusted eye over Jie's and my clothing. "In fact, you two ought to simply wait here." She trotted away.

Jie and I shared more arched eyebrows.

Then Jie shrugged. "Well, *I'm* not waiting."

"Good. Nor am I." With our jaws set, we moved out after Allison. Jie was especially adept at swatting people aside like they were obnoxious insects, and we soon reached the desk. Allison threw us scowls. Then, while the decidedly European concierge was subjected to the full power of Allison's arrogance and command, Jie strolled over to a rack of newspapers nearby.

Almost instantly, though, Jie hunched over and snatched up a paper. "Eleanor," she called. "You'd better come look at this." She lifted the paper as I scurried to her side. Today's *Egyptian Gazette*, an English paper, read "Dead Rise in Marseille."

My stomach flipped, and with trembling hands, I took the page. The article stated that the Spirit-Hunters were not being blamed for the mass rising of corpses in France—thank God. Enough people had seen us *battling* the Dead to know which side we were on.

"But it doesn't say what happened to all the Dead after we left." I glanced at Jie.

Her forehead furrowed. "The news was probably just telegraphed in this morning. Maybe the rest of the story hasn't reached here yet."

"I hope Marseille is all right." My eyes skimmed over the article once more . . .

Until a hand slapped the back of my neck.

"Ouch!" I cried, whirling around.

It was only Allison. "Sorry." She grinned, not seeming even remotely sorry, and offered me her gloved palm—on which was the smashed form of a mosquito. "They're everywhere."

I returned the *Gazette* to its rack, watching as Jie wriggled and scratched as if there were suddenly mosquitoes all over her.

"We ought to pick up a tansy salve at the apothecary," Allison declared matter-of-factly. "It will keep the tiny monsters away."

I nodded absently, rubbing at my neck. "Did you learn anything from the concierge?"

Allison's lips pruned. "Only that information on guests is completely confidential and no amount of sharp disapproval will change that blasted man's mind . . ." She trailed off, her mouth dropping open. Then she lunged at the rack of newspapers and yanked up a flimsy paper booklet. "This is Milton! This is that *rotten* man who owes my family!" She thrust the booklet at Jie— then at me.

I barely had time to see the title, *The Exploits and Adventures of Rodney Milton, Greatest Egyptologist of the Century*, before she had whipped open the booklet and was scanning the contents.

"Here it is!" she exclaimed. "Saqqara. *That* was the excavation father invested in." Clearing her throat, she began to read. "'Saqqara was a well-known site that had barely been touched before the esteemed Professor Rodney Milton'"—she made a gagging face—"'excavated the ruins in 1870. With funding from the University of Philadelphia and other donors, Milton bravely explored many pyramids at the site. During his excavations, Milton uncovered an entire necropolis, or city of the dead, where hundreds of catacombs were built to honor ancient Egyptian deities.'" Her eyes snapped to mine as she shoved the booklet into her pocket. "'Esteemed professor,' indeed! And how very kind of this book to lump my father under 'other donors'! Oh, I will find this double-crossing Milton if it's the last thing I do. And I *will* get that concierge to talk—"

"Wait!" I snagged her wrist before she could slay the poor

man with her words. "Perhaps Oliver has had better luck. Let's find him first."

Yet as I turned to go search for him, my gaze landed on two ridiculous-looking girls marching toward the front desk. They were close in age to Allison and me, but their matching red hair and freckles indicated they were sisters.

One was tall and lithe, the other small and plump, much like Mercy and Patience Virtue back in Philadelphia—and with quite the same airs. They stopped imperiously before the concierge.

"We are expecting a delivery from Swan & Edgar," said the taller, prettier of the two sisters. "When it arrives, please have it sent back."

"Tell them we will not be needing the dresses," inserted the plump sister, her expression dramatic and forlorn.

"Your names?" the concierge asked.

"Deborah and Denise Mock." The taller one's face flushed with annoyance. "*Surely* you know us by now. We have been staying here for *ages*." With a scathing glare, she spun on her heel and scurried back past us. "Come on, Denise," she trilled.

Denise hustled after. "Oh, I am still *so* overcome that Mother will not let us go to the party."

"Do not speak of it," Deborah snapped. "I was looking forward to seeing the professor's latest artifact, and now *everyone* will be talking of it without us."

"And here I was," Denise went on dismally, "so certain that my new rose silk would catch Mr. Chaplin's eye. . . ."

The girls rounded an urn and slipped from earshot.

And Allison and I exchanged wide-eyed glances—and I knew she thought as I did. It was not so long ago that we behaved like those sisters, and that dresses and bachelors had dominated *our* conversations too. For all that girls like the Virtue sisters enraged me, I had once been just like them.

"Ladies."

Jie, Allison, and I jumped. But it was only Oliver behind us. "The professor isn't here," he said, sliding to my side. "But he *does* dine here every week, and the staff knows all about him. Today he is at the Bulaq Museum."

"Then let us go there," Allison cried. "Can we afford the carriage fare?"

"Ah, but the cost does not matter." Oliver opened his hands apologetically. "There is a party tonight, hosted in your professor's honor. Apparently he has discovered some wondrous artifact, and he intends to unveil it."

My breath hissed out, for certainly this was the same party the Mock sisters would be missing. . . .

"A party?" Allison snarled, stamping her foot. *"Esteemed professor, indeed!"*

"Can we try to get in?" Jie asked.

"Doubtful." Oliver's eyebrows dipped down. "Security will be very strict. They aren't letting anyone in without an invitation."

Allison ground her toe in the tiles, as if they might be Milton's nose. "So we must wait until after this party to speak to Milton?"

"Or we return tomorrow."

"We cannot wait," I inserted. "We have to assume Marcus is on his way to Egypt right now. We have certainly gained some time from the airship, but how much? A full day is already lost because of the Hell Hounds—losing any more is too much risk." I rubbed at my earlobe, considering our options. Giza was not *so* far away, so we *could* hire a carriage . . . though that still would require more money than we currently possessed.

It was then, as I was frowning into space, that Jie nudged me.

"Look." She dipped her head at two well-dressed gentlemen with large boxes striding toward the concierge. The boxes read SWAN & EDGAR.

"Brilliant," I whispered, flashing Jie a bright grin. Then I snatched at Allison's arm. "Go tell them you're Deborah Mock." At her oblivious stare, I pointed at the dressmakers. "Tell them you're Debbie and those gowns are *yours*."

Understanding brightened her eyes, and without wasting a heartbeat, she puffed out her chest and swept toward the men.

"Hullo," she sang, "I am Deborah Mock, and if I am not mistaken, these gowns belong to me. Thank you so *very* much for delivering them."

Allison managed to get the dresses in mere moments, so we promptly aimed for the hotel's washroom. Professor Milton's party would begin at six—and it was already a quarter until.

"And we still gotta find a Western apothecary," Jie reminded us as we strutted around a row of potted violets. Allison and I

176

had the two dress boxes, while Jie and Oliver sauntered behind us. "If that scar . . . scarifi . . ."

"Scarificator," Allison inserted.

"That," Jie said. "If it will make these cuts hurt less—"

"It will," Allison chimed.

"—then I want to get one."

"Eleanor and I promise to hurry," Allison said.

My eyebrows lifted at her.

"What?" she demanded, stopping before an ornate door marked LADIES.

"I am merely surprised, is all. You are quite good as a nurse."

"Humbug," she scoffed—but there was no denying the pleased flush on her cheeks before she pushed into the water closet.

I threw a backward glance at Jie and Oliver. "Stand guard?"

Jie chuckled, as if it were stupid I even mentioned it, while Oliver gave an elegant shrug. "I always do, don't I?"

I blinked, briefly struck by how different he seemed. With his fitted charcoal suit (somehow always impeccably clean) and his top hat (stolen in Le Havre), he looked as he always did. . . . And yet when I'd first met him two weeks ago, he had reminded me of Elijah—young, silly Elijah.

He did not remind me of Elijah anymore. Now Oliver seemed like a man. His *own* man.

"Enjoying the view?" He smirked at me. "If you continue to stare, Eleanor, you might give me the wrong impression."

My cheeks warmed, and to my even greater shame, Jie

snickered. I scowled and turned toward the water closet. "I do not know what you mean."

"No," he murmured as I pushed through the doorway, "you never seem to."

Yes, there was definitely something different about my demon these days. And Jie. It was not just what Marcus had done to her—though perhaps that had triggered this shift—but she seemed . . .

Well, she actually seemed to *like* Oliver. Or at the very least, she did not seem to mind him. Had it only been two days ago that she had screamed at me in the burned-out Tuileries Palace? That she had raced off to tell Joseph? And had it only been yesterday that she had hissed *demon* and cowered?

The door softly clicked shut behind me, and I found myself in a washroom as ornate as the lobby. The space was open, long, and filled with comfortable wicker seating. At the back was a low counter with multiple china washbasins, and to the right were several doors leading to individual toilet closets.

Allison laid her box on a sofa, and with my help, we had her down to her small clothes in mere minutes. Then as she donned Deborah's gown, I stripped free of Daniel's trousers . . .

And thought of my inventor, back at the airship. He would be slaving over the broken engine, while Joseph fretted over each detail. . . .

And while Marcus drew ever closer, seeking the same Old Man my brother had sought and hoping to gain immortality and wealth from some ancient, mythical monster.

But soon—so soon—we would give Marcus what he deserved. We would crush him, and then everything could return to normal. Or a broken version of it, at least.

Pivoting toward Allison, my fingers moved to my trousers' pocket to check on the ivory fist. . . .

And I froze, my jaw sagging.

For Allison was dressed in Deborah Mock's gown, and though it was not yet laced up and was at least four inches too long, it was *stunning*. The jade muslin was decorated with sky-blue flowers sewn along the shoulder-baring collar—and larger flowers were fastened onto the bustle.

"Heavens," I breathed, dropping the trousers on a chair and approaching her. "Jade is most certainly your shade, Allison." I was so used to seeing her in mourning, I had quite forgotten how well she looked in such colors. . . . And I realized with an inward frown that this was likely the first time she had donned anything but black since Clarence's death.

A smile tugged at her lips, and she ran a hand over the skirts. "It is nice. These Mock sisters certainly have taste. . . . Now your turn."

"So that I may look the fool next to you?" I grinned, and Allison blinked.

"Whatever do you mean?"

"Do not pretend you aren't prettier than I." Still smiling, I moved to my dress box and towed off the top.

A rose silk gown with lace trim met my eyes.

"Prettier than you," Allison repeated softly, and I glanced at her in surprise. Her forehead was creased. "Do you really think that?"

"It's the truth, isn't it?" I shrugged helplessly. "In all honesty, Allison, I have always envied your beauty. And all your friends. *And*," I continued, since clearly I was in a confessing mood, "your wealth."

She shook her head, her frown only deepening. "People were not *really* my friends, Eleanor. It was all because of Father. Mercy, Patience—I spent all my time with them, but they were never like . . . like your friendship. With Miss Chen." She barked a harsh laugh. "And here I was, always envying *you*. All the clever things you would say. How you could always make people laugh. And how you never seemed to care what they thought of you."

"But . . . I did care." I tilted my head to the side, now eyeing *her* with surprise. "I cared very much and merely pretended not to."

For several long moments she watched me, her expression inscrutable. Something was happening here. A shift in a wind I had not even noticed was there. But then a huge grin suddenly split her face.

And she laughed. A full, rippling sound that sent her hands to her lips and her shoulders bouncing. "Can . . . you . . . believe it? We're in the middle of Egypt, wearing stolen dresses and discussing how much we envy each other! Can you conjure a more absurd situation? And," she went on, snorting, "we're about to sneak into a party so I may demand money! It is like something out of a novel."

I cracked a wry smile. "I suppose you *are* a Portia with no sense of mercy now."

Her laughter paused . . . then she doubled over even harder. "I . . . forgot . . . you called me that! I had to ask Clarence what it was, you know—and of *course* it was Shakespeare. Heavens, it feels like ages ago."

Because it was, I thought. *It was a lifetime ago.*

Bang, bang, bang! A fist hammered on the door. Allison and I flinched.

"Eleanor!" Oliver called. "What is taking so long? It is past six o'clock now, and we still must find an apothecary."

Allison and I exchanged winces. Then we dived into action—I laced up Allison's gown, and she helped me don mine. The gowns did not fit *well*, but they were at least manageable. Though it did take a great deal of sucking in and grinding my teeth before I eventually managed to squeeze into the rose silk. It was harder than it *should* have been thanks to my corset-less waist, but soon enough, Allison had all the buttons fastened.

Of course, the gown was at least three inches too short, and though it made walking easier, it revealed my worn boots. But even more obvious was the huge bandage wrapped around my forearm.

"Maybe . . . no one will notice?" Allison said, but from the way her face screwed up as we pushed back into the lobby, I knew she was lying.

"Finally," Jie groused as Oliver gave Allison and me a once-over. His eyes caught on my bandage . . . then drifted down to my boots.

"Nice ankles, El." He bared a rakish grin that left Allison blushing and Jie smirking. Then, after gathering up the dress boxes that now held our old clothes, he loped off toward the street. Allison, Jie, and I hurried after.

"I managed to secure a carriage," he said as we scampered down the steps and back into the seething array of beggars, donkeys, and street vendors. "I promised the fellow payment after our party—as well as loads of *baksheesh*." He turned a high eyebrow on Allison. "Let us hope your professor pays up."

Allison's teeth clenched—as did mine. When we had left Paris, the last thing on my mind had been money. After facing armies of Dead, I never would have guessed our largest obstacle to be funding.

"Here we are." Oliver motioned to a dingy, dangerous-looking carriage pulled by a pathetic horse covered in open wounds and festering sores.

My stomach rebelled. And when I saw that one of the horse's legs was lame, I flung a furious glance at the driver. I *knew* this was simply a cultural disparity—this horse was a work animal and nothing more—yet I could not accept it.

Jie winced as well when she noticed the horse's sores, and even Allison wrinkled her nose.

So I turned desperately to Oliver as Jie and Allison ascended into the carriage.

"Can you help the horse?" I whispered. "Heal it or something?"

"How?" he asked without looking at me. "Recall: Mr. McIntosh is nothing more than a regular person with regular powers. Now, up we go." His hands clasped my waist, and with surprising strength, he hefted me into the carriage. Then he hopped up beside me, hunkered down, and ordered our driver onward.

But not before his yellow eyes met mine and a thought flickered through my brain—*his* thought.

Command me once the party begins and Miss Wilcox is out of sight. Then I will heal the horse.

I was amazed. Delighted, even. My demon really was in quite an unusual mood. A generous one, and though I could not understand why, I was grateful for it.

And I could not deny that I liked seeing Oliver happy. It made my heart warm—even more so because my best friend was at my side and an Egyptian sun beamed down upon us.

So as the carriage rattled to a start, I shifted my body toward him, and I smiled.

And Oliver smiled his beautiful smile back.

CHAPTER TEN

We found a British apothecary easily enough and spent *all* our remaining money on bandages, a scarificator, and bloodletting cups. Allison was like a child in a toy shop, and had I not forcibly *yanked* her out, she easily could have spent ten hours examining the various scarificators and newest salves.

The sun was just setting when we headed back out through Cairo, aiming west. I was able to forget the poor horse's plight—and how blasted uncomfortable my dress was—for the closer we came to the Nile, the thicker traffic grew.

"Why are there so many people out?" I leaned over the carriage's side—and was almost clipped by a camel. "The streets were busy earlier, but this is madness!"

"The *adhan* will begin soon," Oliver answered. At our

vacant-eyed stares, he explained, "The muezzin call." We continued to stare dumbly. "Egads, ladies, the call to *prayer* in Islam. It happens five times a day, and sunset is one of those times. A man will stand atop a minaret and shout 'God is greatest' so that our faithful Muslim friends may hurry to the mosques to pray."

"Oh," I mumbled, watching the passersby with new interest. I could rattle off Shakespeare as if the words were engraved in my skull, but when it came to the world's religions, I was woefully ignorant. Just as we clattered onto a bridge flanked by two huge lions that ran over the Nile, the *adhan* did begin . . . and my heart lifted.

"*Allahu Akbar, Allahu Akbar,*" shouted muezzins all over the city—*hundreds* of them, and everyone around us picked up their paces.

I caught Allison's eyes. She grinned. Then Jie smiled that smug, catlike smile of hers, and I let my own lips curve up. I could briefly release some of the darkness that always clotted my lungs. I could let it float away on the Nile breeze and pretend I was simply *me* again.

It took our driver a solid half hour to navigate what was actually a short distance to the Bulaq district—and if we thought the crowds were bad, it was nothing compared to the *droves* of bugs coming out for twilight feasting.

"Can't you make them go away?" Allison cried, smacking a mosquito off her wrist. "With your magic or something." She threw me a pleading glance.

I gulped. At the word *magic*, the old hunger had awakened in my stomach. Instinctively, I reached for my pocket . . . but of course I wore a dress now. I had slipped the ivory fist into my bodice, so I could hardly grope for it.

Allison slapped a fly on her neck. "We will be eaten alive before we even reach the party!"

She was right, of course. Small, itchy bumps speckled our flesh by the time we pulled to a stop before the Bulaq Museum, and Jie's fingers seemed permanently fastened to her scalp with all the scratching.

"Well," Oliver grumbled, eyeing Allison and me with disapproval as we disembarked from the carriage toward a building of yellow and umber sandstone, "you certainly will not be the *cleanest* girls at the party, but hopefully the quality of the gowns and the prettiness of your faces"—he pinched my cheeks with an almost vicious force—"will more than compensate."

"Ouch." I slapped his hand away, my cheeks stinging . . . but the pain almost instantly vanished from thought. For I now had a full view of the museum.

It was guarded by two enormous statues, both wearing the typical ancient Egyptian headdress and garb. Spotlights shone brightly on them, illuminating their weathered edges and severe expressions. A breeze whispered through palm trees and then over us, drying sweat and soothing bug bites.

Several guests milled about outside—suited men speaking in low voices or Egyptians tending carriages and horses—but the bulk of sounds came from within the museum.

I turned to Jie. "Will you be all right waiting here with him?" I glanced at Oliver.

"Yeah," she said simply, following my gaze. Then an almost wicked smile spread over her lips. "In fact, I have a few questions to ask *Mr. McIntosh*. Now seems a good time, when it's just the two of us."

I frowned, not liking the sound of that, but then Allison shot me a panicked look. "We are late. Everyone will see us arriving, and we look hideous, Eleanor." As if to prove the point, she gave an indelicate scratch at a mosquito bite on her collarbone.

"You look lovely," I said in what I hoped was a soothing tone. And for good measure, I lifted one heel—showing my dusty boots and a thoroughly indecent amount of calf. "At least your gown covers your ankles."

"Hush," Oliver groaned, stepping behind me. "Did you not hear me say that you look perfect? You do"—he glowered at me—"and you need to act like it. Otherwise that fellow checking invitations is never going to believe you're the Mock sisters." He pointed to a suited man directly beside the wide entrance doors.

"Right." I hooked my arm in Allison's. "We must pretend this is nothing more than the Continental Hotel back in Philadelphia, and those men are simply porters."

She drew in a fortifying breath and set her jaw. "Yes. I do believe we can manage that. Come on." She set off, her arm slipping from mine.

Yet before I could follow, Jie punched me lightly. "When you get inside, find a good hiding place. And all the exits—just in case things go bad, yeah?"

I nodded. "Right. A hiding place."

"Come on," Allison screeched at me, so I flashed a final smile at Jie and scurried off. My skirts rattled like palm fronds, yet I had only gone ten paces when a strange *twist* began in my stomach. I paused and glanced back, thinking it must be Oliver.

He leaned against our carriage, Jie beside him, and at my stare he lifted an eyebrow. "Heal the horse," I whispered. "*Sum veritas.*"

He bowed his head, giving me a lazy smile, and I resumed my stride.

But the twisting began again, and with each step after, it grew more intense. Clearly it was not coming from Oliver . . . so from where? My forehead crinkled as I focused on the sensation. It was not unpleasant. In fact, it was quite the contrary. It was . . . exciting. As if I anticipated something.

I towed all thoughts of it aside, for I had caught up to Allison before the museum doors.

"Invitations?" said the mustached doorman. His suit was too large and his accent too thick.

Allison twittered. "We seem to have forgotten them."

"Then I cannot let you in." He bowed. "I am sorry."

"What do you mean cannot let us in?" Allison gave a derisive snort. "I am Deborah Mock of *the* Mocks, and Professor Milton is expecting me."

The doorman cringed.

"And I am Denise Mock," I crowed, cocking my chin high

with a bit too much drama. "Surely you recognize us *now*."

But the doorman only looked more wretched, and it was clear he did not *want* to say what came next. "I really cannot let you enter without an invitation—"

"Of course you can!" Allison interrupted. Then she snapped toward me. "This is all *your* fault. You left our invitations at home."

"Me?" I squealed, poking her a bit too sharply in the ribs—though it did make her mask of annoyance all the more genuine. "*You* were the one who was supposed to bring them."

The doorman coughed. "Please, *Mesdemoiselles*, you are making a scene—"

"This is not a scene!" I screeched, wheeling on him. "You shall see a scene very soon, indeed."

"Do not make me call the guards." The doorman looked truly ill at the thought.

"Let them pass," said a new voice. Allison and I spun around to find Oliver marching toward us. Arabic poured from his mouth, and his face was so red, even *I* flinched. His arms went up, down, and out. Then as if deciding the man was too stupid to comprehend Arabic, he shifted into French.

And as he stormed, presumably letting this doorman know exactly what he thought of him, his eyes slid to mine. A brief flash of gold, the tiniest of winks—maybe even a hint of a smile—and I realized exactly what he was doing.

My hand latched on to Allison's wrist, and while Oliver directed the man's gaze away from us, I yanked her along toward the doors, *through* the doors ... and then inside—into a room of tiled floors and artifacts.

Allison's breath burst out. "We *did* it," she whispered, her eyes gleaming.

Do not get too excited, I thought. *That was only the beginning.* And with a scrutinizing eye, I examined our surroundings.

Enormous walls rose up, mosaicked and lined with glass cases and open shelves. Directly before us was an octagonal case filled with old relics. Beyond, surrounded by a low iron fence, was a small statue of a hunched old man with a cane. And behind him was a curtained doorway that led into an even larger room—and, judging by the sound of voices and a string quartet (to say *nothing* of the delicious scent of fresh bread), it was where the party was.

I moved farther into the room, and it was like a gulp of champagne. A pleasant buzz surged into my lungs and up my throat. Empowering and warm.

I met Allison's eyes—her cheeks were flushed, her expression triumphant. Perhaps this feeling inside me was merely a shared victory at getting inside ... but I did not think so. It felt too much like magic.

Pushing aside the intoxicating hum in my chest, I forced myself to scan the museum further. To find the exits and a hiding place.

Amid all the glass cases were statues with hard faces and stiff poses. They were useless for hiding—too small and crammed together. But on either end of the entrance rooms there were more curtained doorways. I crept to the nearest one and peeked through. It was a long room lit by skylights.

Allison moved to my side, and I jerked my thumb into the room. "If we get separated for any reason, we'll meet in there, all right?"

Allison nodded. "Next to that large stone thing."

"You mean the sarcophagus? The one beside all those maces and clubs?" I squinted into the gloom. The sheer size and rect-angular shape certainly *suggested* an Egyptian coffin.

Allison's hand slipped into mine, distracting me. "Come on, before I lose my nerve." She squeezed with bone-breaking strength. "And I daresay, I hope you are ready for a scene, for I fear I am about to make one."

"And *I* daresay," I said, squeezing back just as fiercely, "that if you can handle an airship crash and Hell Hounds, then a mere scene will be child's play."

She eked out a tiny smile, and we set off into the gala.

It turned out to be an *incredibly* elegant affair. Cases and shelves were everywhere in the huge, high-ceilinged room, but they had been pushed aside to make room for a dance floor and small orchestra. Bright red and blue tiles blended into orange sandstone on the walls, the columns, the floor. Hieroglyphs and gold seemed to pop from the cases and shelves, but as far as I could see, there was no rhyme or reason to the placement of items *within* their displays.

Men and women in black suits and pastel gowns swept past us as we hugged the edge of the room and moved toward the center.

My memories of the party at the Palais Garnier were hazy, but even that opulence seemed tame compared to this. Perhaps it was simply the Arabian atmosphere—that surreal feeling that I was in a completely different time.

But of course, the music was as Western as possible—a standard polka redowa—and the faces streaming past were no different from those of Paris or Philadelphia. Or rather, the *wealthiest* of Paris or Philadelphia.

Professor Milton was clearly a very important person.

And for some reason this amused me. As did Allison's hand in my own. And the yellow glow of the lamps and dull murmur of voices. For some reason a giggle tickled my throat, and I had to clasp a hand over my mouth to trap it inside. There was nothing funny about this situation—was there? Yet I felt drunk off the moment.

I examined Allison, now awash in warm lamplight. She looked as determined as always. Yet unlike me, she did *not* look as if she might burst into laughter. I schooled my face into the same severe expression she wore: lips puffed out, chin up, gaze challenging.

Act normal, I ordered. Now was not the time to let this odd burst of giddiness take control.

"There he is," Allison hissed, drawing to a sudden stop. She motioned to the very center of the room, to a stone sarcophagus—like the one we had seen earlier. This one, though, had its top *off*, and I could only guess that Milton's surprise artifact lay within.

Behind the sarcophagus was a long table overflowing with exotic and traditional foods alike, and chatting happily beside it, a glass of champagne in hand, was Professor Milton.

Or I assumed the monocled man with the neat, peppery beard was he, for he was surrounded by a gaggle of fascinated men and women. And his tan, seamed skin was precisely as I imagined an Egyptologist must look.

He seemed to be telling a story, so I tugged Allison along, and we navigated our way around people and dancers until we were also in his crowd of listeners.

Yet before I could hone in on his story, I had to appease my curiosity. I slunk close to the sarcophagus. A placard before it read THUTMOSE II, and excitement flickered through me. Milton's unveiled artifact was a mummy!

Rolling onto my toes, I peered inside . . . and instantly recoiled.

I do not know what I expected since I had obviously seen many corpses before. Nonetheless, I suppose I'd hoped a mummy might be more impressive.

But it was not. Its skin was blackened and shriveled, with ancient bindings that were mostly disintegrated. One of its legs was actually missing from the knee down, and it looked more like a sad skeleton (with skin and patches of curly hair) than it did a former pharaoh.

I glanced back at the placard. It would seem Mr. Thutmose II had died around 1480 BC.

At least *that* was impressive.

Allison's fingers clamped onto my shoulder and wrenched me back to the circle of Milton's admirers.

"And there I was," Milton said, his voice quite bass and pleasant to the ear, "standing face-to-face with an imperial guard's mummy! I daresay, it's not often they come to life, but this one was most certainly awake—and ready to kill me for stealing his pharaoh here."

"Oh my," a woman squealed. "Was it one of Thutmose's own guards?"

"In all likelihood, no." Milton patted the edge of the sarcophagus with a proprietary fondness and sipped his champagne. "The mummies that guard many of the tombs are meant to protect *any* of the pharaohs, and judging by the mummy's headdress, he was a nineteenth-dynasty guard."

"And wha dynath-ty wath Thutmoth the Thecond?" asked a tiny man through a mouth full of pastry.

Milton smiled indulgently. "Eighteenth."

"But," the first woman said, "whatever did you do about the awakened mummy?"

"Why, I ran, of course!" Milton gave a deep, throaty laugh, and the party guests all giggled along with him.

Allison and I exchanged glances of mutual disdain—which only turned darker when Milton proceeded to say, "Once I was out of the cave, I hurried to our camp—which was all the way at the *southern edge* of the Valley of the Kings. Then I sent my dragoman, which is what we call a native Egyptian guide, of course." A second indulgent smile. "I sent the dragoman back

195

to deal with the wretched thing. I daresay, I have never run so fast or so far in my life. Though it could have been much worse had I awakened one of the *queens'* guards. I never would have survived."

"Zey are more dangerous?" asked an elderly woman with a French accent.

"Absolutely," answered a British gentleman with muttonchops. "The queens' guards were all women, and for whatever reason, their mummies are much better preserved than the kings'."

"Just so," Milton agreed. "They also carry much more frightening weapons. I try to avoid any excavations that might bring me near queens' guards. I *always* send my dragoman instead." He gave a smug chortle, and his listeners joined in.

Allison's nostrils flared, and with no warning, her mouth popped wide in a shrill shout. "How very cowardly of you, Professor Milton."

Instantly his laughter and the crowd's broke off. Despite the low, almost magical hum that still remained at the base of my spine, I suddenly felt quite sober. I had not considered how very outnumbered we were or how exposed one feels with so many eyes turned upon you.

Milton's lips pruned, but he did not bother to move—or even shift his body our way. He merely met Allison's gaze and asked, "I beg your pardon?"

"I said," Allison declared, lifting her voice even higher, "that it was very *cowardly* of you to run from the mummies. And to force your poor dragoman to deal with them—why, that's not so different from how you treated the Wilcoxes, is it?"

Milton's eyes narrowed even more. "I am afraid I haven't the faintest idea to what you refer."

"Clay Wilcox of Philadelphia. He invested ten thousand dollars in your excavation of . . . of . . ."

"Saqqara," I whispered, thinking back to the booklet at Shepheard's.

"Saqqara!" Allison thrust a finger in the air. "Ten thousand dollars, and yet you never paid him back. What do you say to that, sir?" She cast him her nastiest stare . . . yet Milton showed no sign of embarrassment.

In fact, after a moment, his lips burst wide in a laugh. "Of course! That's why you look so familiar—you must be Clay's *daughter*." He took a step toward Allison, his gaze raking over her. "You do look like him, don't you? Same coloring. Same *ridiculous* demands."

"*Ridiculous?* You promised my father you would double his money."

"Yes, well." Milton tugged at his waistcoat. "Some investments do not pay off as well as others. I would imagine a man such as Clay could find other sources of income—if you take my meaning."

"I most certainly do not take your meaning." She advanced on him, her face scarlet and eyes bulging. But before she could part her lips, Milton called out, "Guards! Get this nuisance of a *child* out of my party."

And with that simple command, everyone reared away from

us. A moment of panic seized my lungs. . . .

Then came cool action. Getting thrown from the museum would leave us with no airship and no carriage ride, so we must *not* be thrown out. Snatching Allison's wrist, I yanked her—*hard*—after me.

"We're leaving!" I shouted, in case anyone cared enough to listen. Then I dragged her back through the dancers. Fortunately, people cleared out of our way.

"You're a criminal!" Allison shrieked over her shoulder. "I hope a mummy eats you, you *coward*!" I wrenched her into the entrance hall just as two guards reached Milton's side.

"Hush," I snarled, "and *run*."

She must have spotted the guards as well, for she instantly shut pan and bolted behind me. Our heels hammered much too loudly for stealth, but we raced into the dim side room . . . and back, back, *back* until we finally ducked behind our chosen sarcophagus.

Then, my heart pounding against my lungs, I held my breath and listened. The orchestra had stopped playing, the party guests had grown quiet, and there was no missing Milton's bellows to find us.

"Eleanor," Allison whispered.

"Shhhh." I poked my head around the sarcophagus and squinted to see into the entrance hall. Yet it was hard to tell which distant figures were statues and which were people.

"There's something glowing in your dress."

"What?" I jerked my gaze to her . . . then down. Sure

enough, a faint blue glow pulsed inside my bodice.

I fidgeted with the fabric over my chest and finally withdrew the ivory fist. My jaw went slack, for it flared with a throbbing, blue light.

I gasped, and my fingers jumped to my throat. To the heartbeat that pulsed at the exact same speed.

Allison gawked at me. "What is that?"

"It's only a . . . an artifact." I lifted one shoulder. "I found it in Paris—but it has never glowed like this!"

"Put it away." Allison shrank back, covering her eyes. "It's too bright, and someone will see."

But someone seeing us was the least of our worries, for at that moment, a shriek—rattling and desperate—ripped through the museum.

I met Allison's wide eyes through the glowing blue light.

Another scream broke out, followed by another.

With no concern for caution, I scrambled around the sarcophagus—for something was happening, and it was *bad*. Through the distant curtains, I could see figures racing for the door.

"Eleanor." Allison's fingers latched on to my bicep and squeezed.

"What?" I snapped. But then I saw what had caught her eye. The ivory fist was pulsing twice as fast now.

I shoved the fist deep into my bodice. The light dulled, but even the layers of silk could not hide it completely. "I think it's time to go—we can get out while everyone is fleeing."

"But what about my money?" Allison cried. "And we don't even know *why* they're fleeing."

"We'll find out soon enough." I had to shout now to be heard over shrieking party guests. Yet as I crept back toward the entrance, I saw that the main hall was blocked—too many people were trying to get out. I watched in horror as one man tripped and fell, hitting the tiles hard . . . and no one stopped to help. They simply *climbed* over him.

I tried to swallow. Tried to breathe. My feet stumbled two steps forward, and my hand waved dumbly for Allison to follow. Two more steps . . . then one more. . . .

Then I stopped trying to move at all, for now I could see what had sparked the panic. His rotted, cloth-draped body had reached the octagonal case in the entrance, hopping along on one leg.

Thutmose II had woken up.

People kicked and heaved to get away as he clawed with skeletal fingers for anyone in his path. Then a guttural groan poured from a lipless mouth . . . and his head snapped toward Allison and me. In a twist of ancient sinew and bone, he lurched toward us.

A scream tore from Allison's throat—then her hands shoved against my back. "Go! *Go!*"

But I stayed glued to my spot, unable to look away from the approaching mummy. There was something in his hand—something in each hand . . .

And the items were glowing blue—identical to the ivory fist.

"Do something," Allison screeched. "Stop it—lay it to rest."

"Not yet." My hand moved toward my bodice.

"Yes yet!" Allison yelled at me. "Do *something*!"

But I did not do something. At least not what Allison likely wanted. And it was certainly not what Oliver or Jie would recommend. But they were not here to stop me.

I tried to swallow. Tried to nod, but the old hunger for magic was beating to life—and it was as loud and insistent as the mummy's moans. Somehow Thutmose II was walking again—and somehow he was linked to the ivory fist.

And I needed to know why.

Then my eyes landed on the display of maces, and an idea ignited. I dived for the nearest one, its head of spiked bronze looking particularly effective.

For half a breath Allison gaped at me, her mouth hanging open—and in a flicker of a half-formed thought, I realized how *much* I would rather have had Jie beside me at that moment. She would know instantly what to do.

But then Allison caught onto my plan, and she snatched up another mace. "Now what?"

My only response was to slink back into the middle of the hall, for the mummy was close now. His groans—a sound like ancient wind—grated against my skin. The glowing items in his hands burned my eyes with their light. There was a heaviness in the air. An electrical shimmer. It set my teeth to grinding, and my hairs pricked up.

This wasn't simply one of the Dead—the mummy reeked of power.

With a deep inhale, I sank low into my stance. But then Allison's hand thrust up, pointing ahead to a lone figure limping through the entrance hall. "Milton," she growled. "And he's getting away."

She was right. Why the professor was the last to leave—and why it looked like he could barely shamble out, I had no idea. But this was our chance to get what we'd come for.

"All right." I tightened my grip on the mace. "I'll distract the mummy, and you go after Milton."

She nodded once, and a stiffening in her body told me she was ready—and absolutely unafraid.

"We'll run straight at it," I said, taking a single slow step. "And when I say 'move,' you'll slip around it. Can you do that?"

She gave another sharp nod, and without another word we set off. Our heels clicked in unison, picking up speed until we ran almost as fast as the pounding light.

And the mummy hopped onward. Its moans grew louder and louder until they vibrated up my body, through my chest. The glowing items in his hands—whatever they might be—glowed more brightly. Blinding.

Then we were to Thutmose, and my arm was swinging back to aim for its one and only leg. . . .

"Move!" I swung out just as Allison skittered left. As if on instinct, she threw in a twirl and ducked low to glide around the mummy. Then she was behind it and barreling onward.

My mace connected with its knee.

Shock waves thundered up through me. Thutmose II did

not move—*I* moved, thrown backward as if caught in an explosion. A shout burst from my lips. My back hit the tiles, my head cracked down, and as a thousand stars fell over my vision, I knew with deep certainty that I had made a mistake.

Oliver! Help! Sum veritas! My mind screamed the command, unbidden yet absolutely needed.

Instantly, a sensual, explosive heat rushed over me. Perfect and pure. Oliver was coming, and I felt a tug in my gut that said he was approaching fast.

So I tried to sit up, tried to draw in my elbows. But when I lifted my torso, I instantly froze.

For the mummy had reached me. His twisted form was bent halfway, his closed eyes shifting as if the eyeballs behind could see me. I had the definite impression that Thutmose II was inspecting me.

"Dormi!" Oliver's voice trickled into my ears, a million miles away and strangely drawn out.

"Eleanor!" That was Jie, also far off and dulled. When I squinted to see beyond the mummy and the pulsing glow, I found them running toward me—but each of their steps seemed to take an eternity.

It was as if Thutmose and I were trapped outside time—outside the earthly realm entirely.

The mummy straightened and extended his hands. I shrank back. The sandstone walls were bathed in blue flashes from whatever it was Thutmose held. Without thinking, my fingers eased into my bodice and withdrew the ivory fist.

"Is this what you want?" I held it out. The ivory blazed as brightly as whatever Thutmose held—and at the exact same tempo. "Is this why you came to life? Take it."

He did not take it. Instead the light blinked faster and flared so brightly, my eyes screwed shut.

And like a breath held too long, magic burst from my chest—unsummoned and scalding, it poured out of me. I had to gasp to breathe, and my eyes could not squeeze tight enough against the light.

Two long heartbeats passed until suddenly I found I *could* breathe again. My eyelids peeled back—the light was gone. My vision was clouded with shadows, yet I could see.

And what I saw made my bowels turn to water.

For the mummy knelt. Its head was bowed, and in its skeletal fingers were two curved tusks. No longer glowing with light yet undeniably offered to *me*.

I stared at the ivory, each the length of my forearm. One was topped with an open hand—a flat palm that looked exactly as my own ivory fist had when I'd first seen it in Paris. The other curved piece was topped with a jagged, knobby end . . .

As if it had lost its hand.

I wet my lips, and, with great care, I reached out . . . and plucked the broken ivory piece. When Thutmose II did not move, I peered beyond once more—but Oliver and Jie looked no closer than they had moments before.

Time had truly stopped.

So with a steeling breath, I slowly brought the broken tusk

to the half-clenched ivory fist. My fingers trembled, and my eyes shuttered over and over . . . until at last the pieces touched.

A strange, slithery sensation oozed up from the ivory. It felt like I was holding a snake—scaly and frantic—that wanted freedom. But then the feeling stopped, and with it time lurched back to its normal pace.

"Dormi!" Oliver's voice slammed into me, and his footsteps pounded into life. Drumming loud and coming in fast. *"Dormi!"* Oliver was close now, Jie just behind him, and blue light blazed from my demon's fingertips. His magic was finally working—this time he *would* be able to lay the mummy to rest.

But before he could do that and before he could reach my side, I yanked the second ivory piece from Thutmose II's hand. Then, though they hardly fit, I shoved both ivory artifacts into my boots.

I could not say why, but for some reason I wanted no one to see these. Madame Marineaux had given *me* the ivory fist back in Paris, and the mummy of Thutmose II had woken up and given *me* the tusks. They were mine.

I had just gotten the folds of my skirt wrapped around the ivory when Oliver and Jie reached me—and the mummy collapsed in a heap of bones and shredded cloth.

"Eleanor." Oliver dropped to the floor beside me. His arms flung around me, crushing my ribs in an embrace while Jie kicked at the heap of mummy bones—presumably for good measure.

Oliver quickly jerked back and examined me. His face shone

with an unearthly beauty—the result of his magic—yet his cheeks were flushed with worry.

"What the hell happened?" Jie demanded, crouching beside us.

"I-I don't know," I finally stammered out, yet before I had to offer up any pathetic explanation, Allison's shouts echoed through the room.

"And that," she roared, "is why you should never mistreat a Wilcox. Or *anyone*, for that matter, you sniveling excuse for a man!"

"Allison!" I shouted. Jie hauled me to my feet. "Don't hurt him—we need his money!" Jie's hand slid into one of my own, Oliver's into the other, and we sprinted down the hall, toward Allison, towering over a sprawled figure.

"Get his wallet!" Jie cried.

"I did," Allison yelled. "Don't worry, I have this completely under control." Yet her tone was anything but reassuring. There was a brutal edge to her words that sounded . . . *deadly*.

Oliver and I scrambled into the entrance hall. Milton's nose gushed blood, and his lip was cracked in two. The mace lay several feet away.

"What did you do?" Oliver demanded, lurching toward the man. Milton was barely breathing.

"I didn't do it," Allison snapped. "He was like that when I found him—the mummy must have done it."

My gaze darted to the mace—one side of it was covered in blood. But I didn't say anything, for at that moment the professor's eyes fluttered open.

"Bitch," he snarled. "Daughter of a whore. I won't give your pathetic family a thing. May you all rot in—"

Allison's foot came up faster than I could even see. With a thud, her toes hit the professor's temple.

His eyes rolled back in his head.

"Dammit, Allison." I grabbed for her, but she skidded back. "You knocked him out!"

"He deserved it."

"He may have," Oliver said through grinding teeth, "but an unconscious man is no help to us. So unless his wallet is over-flowing with money, we're no better off than we were before."

"It *is* overflowing." She tossed a black leather purse at Jie. Coins clanked as she caught it. "And," Allison said, lifting her voice haughtily, "you should all be *thanking* me. You got exactly what you came for." She bared her teeth in a smile. "And so did I."

CHAPTER ELEVEN

"Did you heal the horse?" *I asked Oliver. We were* nestled back in our carriage. Allison's head was slumped over with sleep—as was Jie's—and the darkened gate into Cairo lumbered overhead.

"Yes," Oliver said softly. In the shadows I could see nothing but his glowing eyes. "Did you not feel it? Or *see* it?"

"I didn't feel it," I murmured, twisting around to glance at the horse. He trotted into the moonlight, towing us out through the gate . . . and yes, he looked fit and clean.

I glanced back to Oliver. "Thank you."

His eyelids twitched, and he yanked out his flask. Then he gulped back several enormous swigs of liquor, exhaled sharply, and offered it to me. "Zabib?"

My nose curled up. "What's zabib?"

"Alcohol, of course. I got it at the apothecary."

Something about the way he said "got" gave me pause. My mouth fell open. "You stole it, didn't you, Oliver?"

His only response was to return his flask to his waistcoat and lace his hands behind his head.

"*Oliver—*"

"Do. Not. Judge me," he growled. "Not when you are just as morally decrepit as I. Neither of us would survive the final judgment. Remember that." His eyes fluttered shut. But I knew he did not sleep. Whatever generous kindness had possessed my demon earlier, it was gone now.

"What bothers you?" I asked once Cairo had faded away behind us. "Oliver, is something the matter? You were so happy earlier," I pressed. "What has changed?"

He refused to answer me . . . yet I knew he listened. "All was so good in the city. We were friends and getting along so well. For once you worked *with* everyone instead of turning me against—"

"Enough." His eyes snapped wide, glowing and furious. "Stop speaking before you say something you will regret and force *me* to say something I will regret." Then he sank even farther into his seat and did not move the rest of the journey. All I had for companionship were windy silence and moonlight— though at least we made better time on our return. The newly healed horse was quick and lively.

We reached Heliopolis in an hour and a half, and as we approached, I felt a change in the air. A heightening of my senses, as if I were entering another world. Or another *time*.

The wheat fields around the ruins seemed spun from silver as they listed and swayed in the night wind. Even the crumbling walls seemed to glow from within.

Our fuel salesman had fallen asleep beside his donkey—which had, in turn, fallen asleep beside a sycamore. I left Oliver to deal with him while Allison, Jie, and I hurried into the gondola. We found Joseph laying planks back over the engine.

His face lit up at the sight of us—especially at the sight of Jie. "You are well?" At her nod, he smiled wide. But then his eyes settled on our evening gowns. His forehead puckered. "I *do* hope you did not spend our funds on dresses."

"Not at all," Allison declared with a laugh. "We now have one hundred eleven American dollars, two hundred thirty-four Turkish sovereigns, ninety-seven British pounds, and four hundred twenty-one Egyptian *gineih*. And it is all with Mr. McIntosh now, so he may secure our fuel."

Joseph huffed a relieved laugh. "That is good. We were beginning to worry when it grew so late." He picked at his bandages.

"Oh, do stop," Allison scolded, flurrying toward him. "You will bring infection if you continue." She leaned in and scrutinized. "Actually, we ought to change those wrappings now. Our trip was very fruitful, and we managed to buy both fresh bandages as well as a scarificator." She twirled around, motioning to Jie. "Come along, both of you. We shall clean you up, Mr. Boyer, and try out the new scarificator, Miss Chen."

She strode into the hall, and Jie tiredly followed. Before

Joseph could join, though, I snagged his sleeve. "Where is Daniel?"

"I believe he went for a walk in the ruins." Joseph glanced at the open hatch. "He only *just* finished fixing the engine."

Good. I could find Daniel later then.

I let Joseph, Jie, and Allison vanish into the washroom before I hurried to my cabin. Then, in a rush, I closed the door and yanked the ivory tusks from my boots. My curiosity had been eating me up since the Bulaq Museum, and now I could finally examine these artifacts. I wanted to see how the fist had fused onto the carved, flat piece. I wanted to *know* what an ancient pharaoh had awoken to give me.

Moving to the porthole, I held both tusks in the moonlight.

The tusk with the half-clenched fist—*my* fist on it—looked as if it had never been broken. I squinted, my eyes still adjusting to the dimness of the cabin, but a careful scrutiny showed no sign of fracture. If I had not seen the two pieces fuse together, I would never have believed they were ever separated.

The next thing I noticed was that my ivory fist was the right hand, and the other was the left. Clearly, the two pieces were a set. The question was: a set for *what*?

A yawn cracked through my jaws. I was too tired and confused to examine the artifacts properly, so I stowed them beneath my pillow for later inspection. Yet as I moved to undress, I glimpsed a figure outside, ambling along a distant wall; and as I watched, he hunkered down, craned his neck back, and stared up at the stars.

Daniel.

I could change into practical clothes later; right now I did not want to miss seeing him. So I hurried from the gondola and into the night. The cool air clung to my bare shoulders, my exposed collarbone, refreshing and alive.

My skirts rustled with each step—and the sounds grew louder as I glided through the grass, dug my heels into crumbled gravel. The nearer I drew to the ruins, the more the world seemed to melt away—fade into a dream.

For this moment—dressed in a beautiful gown, gliding through silver wheat toward the ancient remains of a temple— seemed too fantastic to be real.

And yet it *was* real.

As was Daniel when I rounded a row of broken columns and reached him. At the sound of my approach, he twisted . . . and then his eyes widened.

"Empress," he breathed, kicking off the wall. His feet crunched onto the rubble, yet he did not move toward me. He simply watched, looking stunned. Lost.

So I moved to him, bold and unafraid, and stopped two paces away. The breeze ruffled through his hair, billowed through his shirt.

"Is this real?" he asked softly. "Or am I sleeping?"

I laughed, a soft but genuine *laugh*. "It's real."

Ever so slowly, as if he feared the moment might break, Daniel eased closer.

The breeze kept sweeping; the grass kept singing.

He shook his head, almost in wonderment. "I have no idea where that dress came from, but I would say it was made for you."

I gave a shy smile, and happy heat warmed my face.

He grinned back and swooped into a graceful bow. "May I have this dance?"

"There's no music."

"We don't need music." Narrowing the space between us, he slid one arm tentatively around my waist. When I didn't pull away, he grew braver and tugged me close. Then his left hand gently clasped my right. "The last time we danced," he said, "at that ball in Paris, you were bewitched. I want you to have a new memory of dancin' with me." He eased into a slow one-two-three, one-two-three. "And"—he briefly touched his forehead to mine—"*I* want to have a new memory too."

I could summon no worthy response. I could only shake my head and stare up at him. This *had* to be a dream. He still had grease streaks on his cheeks, and he smelled so very much like himself—of outdoors and machines.

Daniel. My Daniel.

One-two-three. He whisked me through the grass, past fallen columns, beneath wide sycamore limbs. One-two-three.

We left the ruins behind. Spinning. Stepping. Smiling. Until at last Daniel twirled me once, my skirt swirling out, and then . . . he stopped. And the only sound was our rhythmic breaths and the wind shimmying through the grass.

His eyes ran over my face. Then he barked a low laugh.

214

"What?" I asked, unable to look away from him.

"I can't believe this is happening," he said quietly. "You, lookin' like this . . . and being with *me*."

"And standing in the middle of an Egyptian wheat field."

"Yeah." He nodded slowly and wet his lips. "I never thought I would be this lucky. Not a fellow like me."

"A fellow like you," I said, lifting my hands to grab his collar. "Which is what?"

His lips curved into a half smile. "I believe you once called me a scalawag."

"Then I suppose it's good I like scalawags." I rose onto my toes and brought my lips *almost* to his.

He stayed quiet. Frozen. If he spoke . . . if he breathed, our mouths would touch—and it would be over the cliff for us.

He knew it. I knew it. Magical moments like this did not happen every day. They meant something. They *changed* something, and once we crossed this line, there would be no going back.

And then his mouth moved. He spoke one word: "Yes." Our lips grazed, our breaths mingled, and we fell utterly and completely into each other.

Slow. Determined. Unflinching.

Our bodies moved together, our lips feasted, and the grass around us vanished. My fingers explored the shape of him—the muscles in his back, the bones of his hips . . . the power of his thighs. And his hands roamed fiercely—hungrily—over every inch of me.

For the minutes or hours or years we spent tumbling into each other, I shared everything I had with Daniel—*my* Daniel.

And he shared back.

But as always happened, our dream came to an end. When Joseph shouted for Daniel to get the balloon inflated, Daniel had to disentangle himself from my limbs, my skirts, my fingers. And the instant he pulled away, I wanted him back. I wanted his mouth, his hands, his strength *back* . . . but I understood he was needed elsewhere.

And I understood we had our entire lives to drown in each other. We had started something—together—and there was no taking it back.

So I gave Daniel a lingering, full kiss, and I sent him on his way. Then I lay back in the grass and stared up at the moon. I was not ready for sleep—not yet. I wanted to savor this night. Replay every moment in my head.

For it had been perfection.

Wind caressed me. I turned my head to the side and caught sight of the obelisk. It gleamed like a knife, and behind it, the balloon was just starting to inflate.

I climbed to my feet, not even bothering to dust off my gown. There was no salvaging it at this point, and it had served its purpose.

Then, in a dreamlike haze, I wandered toward the obelisk. Something about it called to me. When I reached its base, I craned my head back and stared up to its tip.

This carved granite had stood here, inflicting awe, for

thousands of years. It was ancient. As immortal as my demon.

At the thought of Oliver, the obelisk seemed to flicker—to *drift* mistily before me like a beam of clouded sunlight—and I had an urge to explore the monument more closely. To trace the hieroglyphs and try to decode its secrets. . . .

"A perfect night, huh?"

I jolted around. Oliver stood only paces away, his yellow eyes bleary and flask in hand. He tipped back a swallow and listed to one side.

I frowned. "You're drunk."

"Yes," he admitted. "I believe I consumed enough zabib to kill a small donkey."

I sniffed and turned back to the obelisk.

Oliver stalked in closer. "I need to speak with you."

"Speak to me when you are sober." I planted my hands on the cool granite and stared back to the top.

"Or . . ." Oliver paused beside my outstretched arms. His eyes seemed silver in this light. "I will speak to you now." His lips curled back. "There is something we need to . . . discuss."

"And what is that?" I asked in an indifferent tone.

"Tomorrow, at the pyramids, I cannot find the Old Man."

I stiffened, then slowly dragged my hands down the smooth granite. "What," I growled, "do you mean?"

"*You* must find him." He slipped into the space between me and the obelisk. "Remember how Jacques Girard called you *pharaon*?"

"Yes."

"Well, I was puzzled by it. *Pharaon*. Pharaoh." He licked his lips as if tasting the word. The breeze twined through his hair, brushing strands onto his forehead. Into his eyes.

He did not seem drunk now. He seemed poised. Dominant. *Demon*. His legs slid into a slow, predatory gait around me.

"You are not even male," he murmured, his gaze roving up and down the length of me as he paced. "So why would Girard label you with such a title?"

"I don't know," I said, keeping my eyes firmly ahead. I would *not* let Oliver take control of this moment.

"Well, I asked Girard that question." Oliver stalked behind me and then leaned in toward my ear. "Imagine my surprise," he whispered, "when he said you carry an artifact. An *imperial* artifact that marks you as pharaoh."

Cold slid through me. Yet I stayed very still and kept my face blank.

Oliver resumed his careful walk until he was back in front of me. Until his glowing eyes bored into mine. "Girard told me this artifact is an ivory hand, and funnily enough, I recalled someone else with such a hand. Someone in Paris who is now *dead*."

"If you have known so long," I said coolly, "then why have you said nothing until now?"

"Because you said nothing to me." He cocked his head to one side. "I thought I would see how long before you *did* share—for surely you would tell me eventually. Me. Your demon. But then what should happen tonight?" His eyebrows lifted. "I watched as you received the final pieces of the artifact." He tipped his face

218

toward me. "Yet you still. Said. *Nothing.*"

"You . . . you saw?" My mind raced back to that frozen moment when Thutmose II had knelt and offered me the ivory tusks. "How did you see? O-or know?"

"Time might have slowed, El. My brain, my eyes—they did not."

"You should have said something."

His nostrils flared. "No, *you* should have said something."

I compressed my lips. I owed him no apology.

He pulled back, and with a forced nonchalance, he leaned against the obelisk. "But why ruin this perfect night, hmm? You and your inventor. So happy." He spread his hands. "It amazes me how easily you forget all the darkness surrounding you, El. How blind you are to your own corruption. Luckily, I am here to remind you. Let us see. . . ." He ticked off one finger. "First, your brother killed Miss Wilcox's brother—among many other victims, murdered at his hands."

My teeth gritted as Oliver ticked off a second finger. "Then *he* died, and a necromancer took possession of his body."

My teeth gritted harder. *Why* could he never let me have one moment's peace? "*Stop.*"

A third and fourth finger unfurled. "That same necromancer wearing Elijah's skin then *killed* your mother and compelled your best friend—"

My hand cracked out. I slapped him. Pain lanced up my arm, and he lolled against the obelisk. Yet he did not stop speaking. "You are as blackened as Elijah now, Eleanor, and no matter how fast you run, you cannot escape what you are becom—"

I attacked.

It was as if a switch went off inside me. I lost all sense of who I was. I simply saw Oliver's gloating, perfect face, and I wanted to shred it.

My fingers grabbed at his cheeks. He spun away—but I expected it. We were *connected*. I knew what he would do.

I lashed out with my leg and tripped him. He tumbled forward, tangling in my skirts, and I sprang onto his back—pummeling. Scratching. *Hissing*.

His chest hit the earth. I landed on him, clutching for his neck—for the soft flesh above his pulse.

He flipped me. In half a breath, wheat and grass streamed along the sides of my vision. I crashed onto my back. My breath punched out. Oliver pinned my arms over my head.

I fought. I kicked.

But my demon was strong. He held me firmly trapped.

"What do you want?" I screeched at him, writhing. "Why do you do this?"

"Let's call it a final attempt to reclaim my dignity."

"But *why* do you torment me?" I fought harder. I kicked harder. "You know what shadows chase me—why can I have no happiness?"

"Because *I* cannot, and I am a petty soul."

"What?" My fury burst out in a sigh of confusion—and the wind carried it all away.

"I am unhappy, and I am petty." Oliver spat into the grass,

and in a careful, deliberate move, he released my arms . . . and then wiped his mouth on his sleeve. "You do not know what it is like to live completely *driven* by a command."

"You're wrong," I rasped, my lungs heaving for air. "I *do* know what . . . it feels like. I am driven every day to . . . obliterate Marcus."

"Exactly." Oliver planted his hands on either side of my head and leaned down. His eyes throbbed with golden light. "You live by what moves *you*. I live by what moves my master. I have no drive of my own. No loyalties. And no love."

"Still . . . wrong." I swallowed and wet my lips. "You have me."

"Do I?" he said softly. Then he rolled off me and collapsed on the grass beside me. "I do not have you at all, Eleanor, and you were right. He *does* know you better."

"Who?"

"Your inventor." Oliver draped his hand over his eyes. "You *invite* him in . . . and he invites you. I understand now. It isn't about knowing facts or secrets. It's about knowing where you fit. Too bad for me, I fit nowhere." He gave a gruff laugh. "Oh, what a bitter thing it is to look into happiness through another man's eyes."

I sat up. The night sky spun, but I made myself tilt over Oliver—and I pushed his hands off his face. None of this night made sense to me, but I wanted at least to *try* to understand. "You are angry because I didn't tell you about the ivory fist."

"Yes," he muttered, pushing onto his elbows and bringing

221

his face nearer. "But it is not only that. I cannot fully blame you for hiding the fist. Items of power warp the mind. *Power* warps the mind. I am mostly angry because I am alone. Again, after briefly glimpsing what the other side held."

My brow furrowed. "I do not understand. How could you feel alone when we are bound? I always sense our connection, a pulsing line of magic here." I clutched at my stomach.

He stared at me unwavering. "For a moment today, El, none of you saw me as a demon. You saw me as *me*. Yet now that we are back here, among the frightened distrust of Joseph and your inventor, I am alone once more."

I let my gaze roam over his inhumanly perfect face. Such beautiful lips, such an elegant jaw.

There was truly nothing left of the Oliver from two weeks ago—and I recalled his words from a few days before. *The more I'm trapped in this human body, the more I find myself wanting like a man wants. Feeling like a man feels.*

And that was when I finally began to understand it. He *was* lonely, and the more he felt like a man, the more his otherness grated inside. He wanted to be one of us; he never could be.

"I don't mean to push you away," I said roughly. "I don't want you to be alone."

"Then help me go home, El. Set me free so I may return to a world that welcomes me."

"But . . . but then *I'll* be alone." *And then this familiar pulse of connection will be gone. Forever.*

He gave a sad shake of his head. "Remember this, El: not

222

everyone who you invite in will wish to be there. And no matter what you might want, I will one day have to leave."

I blinked, and my mouth went dry. "But you won't leave me now, right?" My voice was a whisper. "Allies . . . still?"

He did not answer. He merely sat up all the way, his cheek brushing past mine, and glided to his feet. When he offered me his hand, I almost laughed at how much dust was on his suit. He so hated being dirty. . . .

But I was too cold inside to laugh.

I took his hand. Air whizzed past my ears, and suddenly I was standing . . . and only inches from him.

"I am sorry for provoking you tonight." He spoke in a distant voice. "It was wrong of me, El. It would seem I am just as cruel as your inventor when my feelings are hurt."

My lips parted to speak, but Oliver wasn't finished. "Tomorrow we find the Old Man. It's so close. *So* close. Please live long enough for that, secrets or no." He cupped my face with a single hand, his face so motionless that he looked carved from stone. "And for the love of eternity, please cast a dream ward tonight, all right?"

He lowered his hand, nodded once, and then set off toward the airship's gondola. And as he walked, the grass whispered and the balloon continued to grow. It rose and rose until Oliver was long out of sight.

Until it had blocked out the moon and plunged my world into shadowy darkness.

CHAPTER TWELVE

I awoke with the gray light of dawn at my porthole and the dregs of heavy sleep trying to tow me under. The airship hummed, and I knew by the groan of wind over the gondola that we were flying once more.

I had cast a dream ward the night before, and it had left my mind fuzzy. Confused. Then a memory flickered through my brain—one of shallow breaths and sweat. Of skin against skin and fingernails . . .

Daniel. I sighed, rolling onto my side and squeezing my eyes shut. It hadn't been a dream, had it?

My eyes popped wide. Oh, it had certainly happened—as had my fight with Oliver.

For two heartbeats I wished I could erase the memory of the

fight and keep only Daniel. . . . But I couldn't, and Oliver was right: we were *so* close to the Old Man. We were *so* close to ending this. I simply had to get through today.

I hauled myself from bed and donned Daniel's clothes once more—dusty, ripped, and stinking of yesterday's trip in the city. I tucked an ivory artifact into each boot, and though it was stiff and conspicuous, should anyone look, I felt better having the pieces touch my skin. And somehow, knowing that Oliver knew of them only bolstered me more. It was one less secret to carry alone. . . .

I crept into the hall and toward the pilothouse. Joseph stood at the steering wheel, his perfect posture outlined by the foggy light of dawn. My eyes were drawn straight ahead—to the pyramids on the dark horizon, yet as I stepped into the pilothouse, I peered from the windows to the world below. In the gray light, the mosques looked like Gothic towers, and they cloaked the narrow roads in shadows. Yet even at this hour people moved about, clogging the streets with a thousand hues.

Joseph glanced back at me. "Good. You are awake. We will be at the pyramids in mere minutes, and I must know where to land."

"Oh." Tugging at my earlobe, I moved to stand beside him. "I, uh, don't precisely know—"

"Good morning, Empress." Daniel's voice cut into the room, and when I spun around, I found him carrying a mug of steaming coffee—*and* a plate of buttered bread. With an earnest grin, he offered them to me. "Breakfast."

A happy lump formed in my throat, and I slowly wrapped my fingers around the warm mug. The coffee smelled divine. "Thank you, Daniel." My eyes flicked to his. "Truly—this means a lot."

"It's just breakfast," he mumbled. He scratched at his stubbly jaw, and then, with aching slowness, he leaned his lips to my forehead . . .

Only to pause. His gaze dropped back to mine. "Er, is that all right?"

For some reason the coffee and bread trembled in my hands. "Always," I whispered.

His lips twisted up, and then he pressed a gentle kiss to my brow.

"Really, Eleanor," Allison declared shrilly, striding into the room in a rustle of skirts. "You realize you have spectators?"

I stiffened, and Daniel scowled. But Allison had already strutted past.

I drew away from Daniel, ignoring the disappointed droop in his shoulders. Allison was right—we had spectators, and now *really* was not the time for romance. So with an energetic interest in the landscape, I set to eating my bread and watching the muddy Nile slide beneath us. The plateau and the three pointed structures rose up from a vast ocean of sand. So silent and lonely after the farms and bustle of the city. There was no sound in that arid world. No movement. Only the hazy light of dawn.

Soon we floated over a tree-lined path with tiny figures on the road. At the end of the path, where the complex of ruins began, I glimpsed a man and his donkey. . . .

My mouth fell open. The man was no larger than a *single stone* in the pyramid. These monuments were bigger than I ever could have guessed—larger than seemed possible. And the Great Pyramid—the biggest pyramid of all—surprised me most. Not only did our airship float as high as its peak, but our egg-shaped shadow wasn't even a *twentieth* of its size.

"What is it?" Daniel asked, moving to my side and sipping his own coffee. "See any sign of where we should land?"

"Uh . . ." I pressed my fingers to my lips and examined the pyramids. We were closing in fast now, and what had seemed to be only three pyramids were in fact nine. And the tawny limestone looked like bricks of gold in the dawn glow—misty and rich against the receding gray skies beyond—while the eroded head of the Sphinx poked up from the sand. She seemed almost . . . *longing*, as if staring at the same view for thousands of years was beginning to wear away at her soul.

I looked back to Daniel. He gazed upon the Great Pyramid, his face a mask of reverence. "You know," he said slowly, "the first time I ever went down the Mississippi, I thought the highest point in the world was a bluff in Missouri. It still stands out in my mind, Empress." His gaze darted to me—then right back to the Great Pyramid. "I thought that cliff was the biggest thing I'd ever seen. All the trees at the top looked so tiny. . . . But this pyramid? It makes that Missouri bluff look like a sand castle."

I smiled at him, but pink burned onto his cheeks. "I reckon I'm just showin' my ignorance."

"Pshaw." I nudged him with my elbow, but when I opened

my mouth to declare him absurd, Joseph called out, "Eleanor? I really must know where to land."

He, Daniel, and Allison all turned expectant eyes to me.

Oliver? I called mentally, thinking he might be able to hear my thoughts as I could sometimes hear his. *Where do we go?*

Three long breaths passed, and Oliver did not respond. No thought in my head, no hint of emotion over our bond.

My demon had cut me off, and with that realization, a spark of anger ignited in my shoulders. For all his threats and fickleness, I knew Oliver could not leave me until *I* broke his bond. So let him have another temper tantrum.

Hoping for inspiration, I flung a final look at the colossal, jagged pyramids and rocky plateau.

"Well," I began, cringing, "the truth of the matter is, I do not know where . . ." My words died on my tongue. The first orange beam of light was now spraying over the limestone. It lit up the pyramids as if they were sun's rays. So bright. So golden.

And movement was flashing before the Sphinx's head.

Hurry.

The word burst in my brain, as glaring and sharp as the sunrise.

"Spyglass," I croaked, lurching close to the window. Daniel pushed it to me, and I locked my magnified gaze on the Sphinx's eroded head just as a scruffy jackal trotted before her patient face, plopped down, and looked directly at me.

Hurry, he repeated, his yellow eyes trapping mine. *You must hurry.*

"Go to the Sphinx," I said.

"How do you know?" Daniel asked.

"I just . . . do," I murmured. No one would believe me about the jackal anyway. "Trust me, Daniel; we need to land beside the Sphinx."

We split up. Joseph, Oliver, Daniel, and I would find the Old Man; Jie and Allison would remain with the airship.

Jie was opposed to it—of course—but Joseph insisted someone ought to guard our things. And since Allison was adamantly unwilling to searching for the Old Man (Thutmose II and the Hell Hounds had sated her appetite for the Dead), that meant Jie had to be the one to stay back as well. She needed her hourly bleeding, and as Allison pointed out, what if more excitement should happen (like last night!) and we all forgot?

As these discussions were rambling on heatedly beside the airship's swaying ladder—which sent crisscrossed shadows over the Sphinx's face—I waited anxiously nearby. The morning air was quickly warming, and sand gritted in my eyes, coated my skin and my lips. I barely noticed. I simply hopped from foot to foot and stared up at the Great Pyramid. It towered above me like enormous steps. Up, up, until it blocked out the entire morning sky—and all the other pyramids too. Overwhelming, dominant, *ancient*.

And slowly ascending, one springing leap at a time, was the jackal.

For half a breath, awe and fear cramped together inside me. We were here—in Egypt at the *pyramids*. We were about to find the Old Man and learn the secrets of the Black Pullet. It was what Elijah had wanted. What Marcus wanted . . . and now it was what we wanted too.

And I was trusting a spirit jackal to guide me.

"You see something, don't you?" Oliver's voice snaked into my ear, almost carried off by the gusting wind.

I tensed. There was nothing cruel in his tone . . . yet there was nothing gentle either. His voice was empty—as was his expression when I glanced at him sideways.

"Yes," I admitted. If anyone would believe me, it was Oliver. "I see a jackal. We are supposed to be following him."

"You seem unimpressed by this jackal, so I presume you have seen him before." Oliver spoke it as a statement, not a question.

I grimaced. It was one more secret I had withheld from my demon.

But he did not seem angry—no flash of his eyes. No sharp words. As he swatted his hair from his eyes, he said, "He is not *a* jackal, El. He is *the* jackal, and it is best we not keep him waiting."

"You know him?"

Oliver gave a grunt of acknowledgment. "There are many creatures in the spirit realm. The jackal is a messenger of sorts . . . I think. He stayed on the dock; I lived beyond. We never interacted."

"You are not upset I didn't tell you about him?"

Oliver settled a flat-eyed gaze on me. "A bit. It would have

231

at least explained how you crossed the curtain despite your dream ward. But . . ." He chewed his lip for a moment. "I am less upset over the jackal and more worried about him. Ivory artifacts and spiritual messengers open many questions. Let us hope we find the answers here." He dipped his head toward the Great Pyramid before launching into long strides, his feet kicking up sand as he aimed for the first jagged level of enormous stones.

The need to chase after him swelled in my chest—to grab his sleeve and *beg* him to yell or drink from his flask or show any sign of what he felt. He was not *only* worried. Or if he was, it was a more terrifying, crippling worry than I had ever seen my demon wear.

But I simply set off behind him, assuming Joseph and Daniel would catch up soon enough.

Of course, climbing the Great Pyramid was no easy feat. Though the structure looked smooth from afar, the walls were actually comprised of steplike bricks that rose up to the peak. Each level of the bricks was as high as my head. So tall were the stones that I could not climb them unassisted.

"Help?" I called weakly, mortified heat rising in my face.

Oliver paused, already three levels up and with his clothes billowing in the sandy breeze.

He glanced back. Then, with seemingly no effort, he hopped to the level above me. He spoke no words, yet he offered me his hand. My heels were just digging into the rough rock when Daniel's hands gripped my waist.

"I'll help her," Daniel said roughly, pushing me up.

Oliver towed me the rest of the way, yet the instant I was steady, he backed off. And he even offered Daniel a nod, as if to say "She is all yours."

I did not like that. Oliver *always* jabbed at Daniel given the chance. His temper always ignited around my inventor. But there was no time to dwell on it, for Joseph joined us on the first level.

"Take these," he said, withdrawing a pulse pistol from his belt and a crystal clamp from his pocket. "We should all be armed. We do not know into what we are walking."

I accepted the pistol, placing it, exactly as Joseph had, in my belt and ignoring how the copper coils rubbed against my stomach. Then I shoved the crystal clamp into my pocket.

Joseph offered a pistol to Oliver. My demon pretended not to notice, and in an easy leap, he ascended to the next level. Daniel followed, offering me his hand—but his posture was stiff. His gaze constantly moving and checking our surroundings.

So up we went until I lost all track of time and the sun seared over Cairo. By the time the jackal had stopped his ascent, I was parched and sunburned. I thought surely we must be near the top . . . but a glance back showed we had barely risen half the way. The airship listed in the wind, and a lone figure paced in its shadow.

Jie.

Wiping sweat and sand from my eyes, I turned ahead . . . and found the jackal was now racing horizontally along the stone steps.

Hurry, he insisted. Then he hit the pyramid's corner and disappeared from view.

"This way," I said tiredly, kicking into a jog. Joseph, Daniel, and Oliver hurried behind. I was panting even more desperately by the time we rounded the pyramid's edge—and I caught sight of the jackal once more.

He had stopped halfway along the next ledge. Darkness cloaked this side of the Great Pyramid—and a pointed shadow ran off for what seemed like miles of rocky desert. I squinted into the sudden shade and chose my steps carefully. The stones were more eroded than on the south side, and loose pebbles were everywhere.

When we had crossed almost half the length of the pyramid, I realized with a start that the jackal had abandoned me yet again. I picked up my pace, my gaze darting up and down, ahead and behind. . . .

"What is it?" Oliver called after me.

"I do not know where—" My heel slipped on a rock. I toppled sideways, my arms flinging out. . . .

Oliver's hands grabbed my waist.

Time slowed. Electricity shot through me from his fingertips. His emotions—his absolute *anxiety* over this day—sizzled into my skin. Into my lungs.

He *was* scared, but not because of the unknown. Because of how long he had waited for this one moment—because of how much depended on it.

Oliver towed me around. Each fragment of a second lasted

a heartbeat—a full, *painful* heartbeat. And as I tumbled into his chest, each gust of dry wind was a lingering kiss.

My eyes latched on to Oliver's . . . and I was scared. *Terrified.* I thought each of my ribs would snap beneath the weight of his fear. Beneath the desperation in his gaze.

He had searched and fought for months to find the Old Man . . . and now he was about to fulfill that mission.

At last he could claim some peace. He could release this need—this burning, writhing drive in his gut from Elijah's final, unfulfilled command. . . . And he could feel normal again. He could return home to the spirit realm, and he could shed this human body with all its human feelings.

Yet no matter how bravely *I*, Eleanor, acted or how fearlessly *I* forged ahead, a single misstep would mark the end of everything Oliver had fought for.

If I failed now, I failed everyone—not just myself.

The dusty, shadowy steps blurred around me. I saw nothing but Oliver's blazing, golden eyes; I felt only his scorching fingertips.

Then a single word *thundered* into the front of my brain.

Hurry. And with that thought I spotted where the jackal had gone.

Two levels above us there was an unnatural crack in the rocks that had not been there moments before.

I had no doubt this entry into the pyramid was magical. Supernatural, even. It shimmered with a hazy blue light.

Time reclaimed its hold on the world, lurching forward in a

flurry of seconds, breaths, and whipping wind.

Oliver released me, his gaze pleading. His desires clear: *Do not ruin this for me.*

I stumbled back, my fears and his fears already melting away beneath the jackal's command. "There," I shouted, and then I set to scrambling up once more.

Oliver, Joseph, and Daniel followed, and in mere moments we reached a narrow gap between two stones. A black tunnel descended within—but it was not so dark that I could not see the jackal. His ears were back, his hackles risen.

Hurry.

I scrambled after him, but just as I wedged myself between the stones, Daniel called out, "Hold up! Be careful!"

Then came Joseph, clipped and wary: "You are certain about this, Eleanor?"

I ignored him—the jackal was already scampering off—and after I squeezed completely within, I found a tunnel before me. It sloped steeply down but was quickly swallowed up by darkness.

At the sound of Oliver crawling behind me, I hurried into the shadows. The ceiling, walls, and floors were made of smooth bricks, and just as the stone steps outside had become worn away and dangerous, the floor was littered with gravel and slick dust.

We had been so prepared with weapons . . . but lighting had never occurred to us.

Yet if the jackal had gone this way, then I would have to follow.

Footsteps echoed behind me, and soon we had lost the safety

of the sun's light. When I glanced back, all I saw was a dim glow around the others' silhouettes.

Oliver stepped in front of me. "I can still see." His hand slipped into mine—and then I grabbed Daniel's. He gave me a reassuring squeeze before reaching back for Joseph.

But we only made it three paces before a loud groan filled the tunnel. The sound of rock grinding on rock above us—and behind. Light flashed overhead . . . then shifted to fill the tunnel beyond. I squinted at the sudden onslaught, only to find a square mirror hanging from the ceiling. It had rotated to catch the light from outside, and though it was no larger than my head, it sent a sharp beam farther down the tunnel.

"Magic," Joseph murmured. "Those mirrors were triggered by magic."

I gulped. He was right. A gentle layer of power was settling along my skin like the finest of dusts. "But what triggered it?" I whispered.

"Does it matter?" Oliver's voice was edged with impatience. He pulled free from my grasp and scooted ahead. "Let us simply be grateful we can see. Now where is the jacka—"

A second groan broke out, and a series of cloth fans shaped like palm fronds dropped from the ceiling—then began to wave. How they had not decayed I could only guess at. Magic seemed the likely explanation.

No matter the cause, they kicked up a draft and brought in fresh air.

I gulped, and with the pretense of scratching my leg, I let

my fingers run over an ivory tusk. I instantly felt stronger. *We have light, we have air, and there is only one direction in which to go.* "Keep walking," I said, easing into a stride. "We should hurry."

After another fifty steps we reached a second mirror . . . and a second cloth fan. As the fresh light stabbed farther down the tunnel, I glimpsed an abrupt end to the brick walls. From here on the tunnel was hewn from the bedrock.

We would soon be underground.

And I could not help but think of the tunnels beneath Paris—especially when the dust thickened and muffled our footsteps. Or when Daniel's pistol would bounce high at every sound, his grip on my arm releasing and his body moving to protect Joseph. I knew, in those moments, that he thought of what Madame Marineaux had done—how he hadn't kept his leader safe from her claws.

And I knew Joseph thought of Madame Marineaux too, for he scrubbed at his bandaged head.

Another fifty paces and a mirror creaked into position . . . to reveal a brick doorway ahead. Its frame was lined with hieroglyphics: eyes, falcons, cobras, and thrones. Beyond was a long, low-ceilinged room carved from the bedrock. On either side, running the length of the room, were eight pairs of blocks, each as ornately carved as the doorway. And standing atop the blocks were man-size statues. With their bronze headdresses, they looked like miniature versions of the statues guarding the Bulaq Museum—except these ones held spears. *Real* spears with metal tips.

Oliver marched through the doorway, and he did not bother to dampen our bond. His anticipation *rolled* off him.

I scurried after . . . but quickly stumbled to a halt—for Oliver had paused between two statues, his head cocked as if listening.

"What is it?" I whispered.

"This room is . . . waiting." He tipped his head in the other direction. "There is magic, and it will soon be triggered."

I moved closer to him, a confused question on my tongue, but as soon as I crossed the first pair of statues, a loud *snap!* grated through the chamber—and dust billowed.

Instantly, I had my pulse pistol out and trained on the statue to my right. Its spear was now extended.

I held my breath, my pistol trembling, and when I glanced back, I saw Joseph with his crystal clamp up.

None of us moved. None of us breathed. The only sound was the flapping of the fans.

"Keep moving," Oliver hissed. "They respond to you. *You* are what the room waited for."

"Why?" I asked, locked in my stance.

"They serve you," Oliver said with a flicker of meaningful emotion across our bond. "*Pharaon*, recall?"

With a tight swallow, I nodded and stepped carefully onward. *Snap!* The next set of statues and spears shot out; dust exploded off them, and they did not move again.

Sand clogged my nose and mouth, yet as I stood there waving the air, I could just make out the various air currents. Dust twirled and twisted, carried away by the cloth fans.

"Again," Oliver ordered. So again I crept ahead until all sixteen statues had their spears thrust out.

Until I stood before a final pedestal with a stone chest on it. I motioned for Oliver, Daniel, and Joseph to join me; and as they warily stepped near, I hunched over the chest.

Its lid was shoved off, just like the open sarcophagus at the museum. Yet when I peered inside, there was nothing more than a thick coating of grime.

"It's empty," I said as the three young men materialized beside me.

"Excludin' all the dust," Daniel muttered.

Joseph bent closer. "It looks to have been empty for many years."

"Because it has," said a new voice. "It has been empty for many centuries."

CHAPTER THIRTEEN

I spun around... and jolted.

In the center of the chamber, hobbling with the aid of a cane, was a gnarled man with a stringy, white beard. His tattered gray robe was streaked with stains, and if not for the power oozing off him, I would have thought him nothing more than a beggar.

The Old Man in the Pyramids had arrived.

And the jackal now sat, tongue hanging out, by the room's entrance.

My pulse pistol was ready as the Old Man shuffled toward us, and Daniel's also stayed aimed at him—while Joseph held out his crystal clamp.

But then the Old Man paused ten feet away, lifting his chin to sniff the air like a dog.

His eyes landed on me—eyes that glowed golden. "Forgive

me, Pharaoh, if I do not bow. I am old and have been for millennia."

None of us moved. None of us answered—until a sudden, incredulous laugh broke from Oliver's lips. "You are a demon, aren't you? Bound in this world?"

"Not quite." The Old Man's eyes shifted to Oliver. "I was once a man, and I looked just as you see me now. But then I was blessed—or some might say *cursed*—with a demon soul. If you stripped away my skin, you would find a spirit like yours."

"But how is that possible?" Oliver frowned and approached the Old Man. "How can you have a demon soul?"

"In the same way that you could have a man's soul, demon boy." He bared a toothless grin. "All that separates man from demon is the *size* of our souls. When I was granted a *second* spirit, I stopped aging. Disease could no longer touch me."

My breath caught—something about his words sent all the pieces twirling into place. "The Black Pullet," I breathed. "That's what it does, isn't it? It grants a longer life by giving you a larger soul."

The Old Man nodded, his beard wiggling. "A second soul, to be precise." He flourished his hands like a performer. "I have twice the magic and twice the soul that you have. I can still be killed, certainly, but only if the injury is so vast I cannot heal. Disease . . ." He smiled. "It never ails me."

"What of the endless wealth?" Joseph asked, his expression tensed and his body ready. "How does the Black Pullet provide that?"

"It is not a magical reason," the Old Man answered. "Or even very interesting. Its feathers are made of gold." He shuffled toward me, passing by Oliver. "But you are not here for immortality or wealth, are you, Pharaoh?"

I shook my head slowly. "We are here to find you—so that we may learn how to destroy the Pullet."

"Hmmm." The Old Man twirled a knobby finger in the air. "Well, you have found me. Your first step is complete."

"Then tell me how we may dest—" My voice cut off, teeth chomping on my tongue. In a single, slamming heartbeat, rage crashed over me.

Oliver.

"It didn't work," he snarled, advancing on the Old Man. "Why didn't it *work*? I have found you, so why am I still in pain?" He lunged at the Old Man, grabbing for his throat.

"Oliver!" I shrieked.

Two of the statues dived off their pedestals.

Oliver stopped, fingers frozen at the Old Man's wrinkled neck . . . and the statues' spears frozen at Oliver's.

"Oh God." I stumbled toward Oliver, screeching at the Old Man, "Get the statues off!"

"Do it!" Daniel shouted, two pulse pistols now aimed at the Old Man.

"I did not call the guard." The Old Man turned a bemused eye on Oliver's fingers. "The girl is their pharaoh, and the mummies protect her. And you . . ." The Old Man's eyes slid to Joseph, then Daniel. "You should not even bother with your electricity.

243

It cannot kill an imperial guard."

"Then how do I call them off?" I cried.

"Command them, Pharaoh."

I wet my lips, tasting dust, and looked at the mummies.
"Uh . . . leave Oliver alone?"

As one, the two guards jerked back in a clank of armor and
marched to their pedestals on stomping, cloth-wrapped feet.

And all I could manage was a gawk. *I* had controlled them.

Oliver staggered away from the Old Man. His fury pulsed
off him, and like a scorching sun, I could not dampen our bond
enough to block what he felt.

And what he felt was a high-pitched, digging rage. He had
fulfilled his command to Elijah—he had found the Old Man—
yet the boiling in his gut had not lessened.

I clutched my hands to my ears and staggered to the nearest mummy, trying to stay in the moment. The dirt and armor
had made it seem carved from stone, but up close, I could see its
desiccated skin.

*The mummies that guard many of the tombs are meant to protect
any of the pharaohs.* Those had been Professor Milton's words
only the night before—and here I was, facing them. Controlling
them.

"Empress." Daniel laid a hand on my shoulder. "Empress,
are you all right?"

"Yes. No. I don't reall—"

No time. The jackal's voice sliced through my thoughts. *You
must hurry.*

244

I gulped. I had to hurry, so with a nod at Daniel, I forced myself to face the Old Man once more. "Why am I the guards' leader?"

He blinked. "You do not know?" At my glare, he hastened to add, "You wield the clappers of Hathor. The ivory artifacts made to look like hands."

Daniel stiffened behind me as Joseph repeated, "Ivory artifacts? She has no such things."

The Old Man's eyes crinkled with pleasure. "Yes, she does. Stuffed into her boots, she has two ivory clappers that were once gifts from a Hittite king to an Egyptian pharaoh. Whoever possesses the clappers possesses the power to control the imperial guards, the power to control *me*. And," his voice dropped to a whisper, "the power to raise the Black Pullet."

"Eleanor," Joseph said, his voice low. "Please tell me he is wrong."

I clamped my lips tight. What could I possibly say right now? Even when Daniel whispered "Is this true?" I simply replaced my pistol in my belt and slid the ivory pieces from my boots—before holding them out for Daniel and Joseph to see.

Daniel choked, the blood draining from his face. "No. *No*, Empress."

"How?" Joseph began, just as pale. "That fist was atop the Marquis's cane. How did you get it?"

"Madame Marineaux." It was all I could say right now. They could scold me later, but the jackal had said to hurry— and I knew I needed to listen. So, twisting back to the Old Man,

I thrust the clappers toward him. "You said Hathor had these. Who is Hathor? And why do *I* have his artifacts?"

"*She*. Hathor is a she, and *she* is one of the Annunaki."

"The what?" I demanded.

"The Annunaki," Oliver murmured nearby. His eyes flicked to me, a dull yellow. No anger keened off him now. Only defeat. "That was the magic Elijah told me about, El. The one even darker than necromancy, remember? I told you of it in Paris. Elijah called it the magic of the Annunaki."

"The Annunaki are not darker than necromancy." The Old Man wagged his head. "You should know that better than anyone else here, demon boy. They come from the spirit realm. *Your* world, and they wield *your* magic. It is simply stronger than yours or mine or any magic ever seen. They possess the purest energy of all: the power of life and death.

"So now you must see that *this* is how an ivory artifact can steal a man's soul. The power over life is inside Hathor's clappers. Which is why a closed fist"—he flourished his cane at the clappers—"can contain a soul. Or part of it." He flashed his white eyebrows at me. "Someone has been using the energy."

"*What?*" My voice cracked out. "I don't understand." Except I *did* understand. The ivory fist had held a person's soul inside; and every time I had touched it, stroked it, or gazed upon it, I had taken some of that soul. The ivory fist had made me feel strong because it was *bolstering* me—giving me power.

And I knew whose power I had used—whose power the fist had stolen.

The Marquis's.

We had found his body, shriveled and drained of life, in Madame Marineaux's sitting room. *That* was when Oliver had referred to the Annunaki as a magic darker than necromancy.

"The fist holds the Marquis's soul," I rasped. "It sucked the life from him and *killed* him, didn't it?" My breathing turned shallow. I grabbed at my stomach. Of course the fist had killed him. It made too much sense to be anything else. And then . . .

I had *used* the Marquis's soul. I had touched it. I had even *savored* the feeling as I used up bits of that soul. As the fingers had begun to unfurl once more.

Oh God. Nausea rose in my chest. I never wanted to touch the fist again. I wanted to fling it away and pretend I had never seen it.

But the jackal's voice blasted in my skull.

If you drop the clappers, then you are no longer Pharaoh. You will lose control over the Old Man.

I paused . . . and I grasped the clappers more tightly.

But Joseph stalked toward me, a furious Daniel at his heels. "Why did you not tell me of these artifacts?" he demanded. "How long have you carried them? It is one thing to lie about your magic, but to hide something that belonged to Madame Marineaux—"

"Enough," Oliver interrupted, appearing at my side. "Eleanor did what needed doing. You wish to stop Marcus, and she has led you to that."

Joseph's lips parted, but I spoke first. "*Please.* We can argue over this later, but not here. And not now. First"—I pointed at the Old Man—"he must finish his tale."

Joseph's nostrils flared, but he remained silent. Daniel would not even look at me.

The Old Man's lips twisted into a smile. "It all began some three thousand years ago. There was a foolish Annunaki named Hathor. Because she doted on an even more foolish mortal, she created a gift for her human lover: an enormous serpent with wings of gold called the Black Pullet. This creature would not only guard Hathor's lover, but it would grant him an immortal life and endless wealth. Yet as I said"—the Old Man lifted a hunched shoulder—"her mortal was a foolish man. As king of the Hittites, he cared only for gathering more land. He hoped to use the Black Pullet to conquer Egypt.

"So he asked Hathor to craft two sets of clappers. One pair would go to the Egyptian pharaoh; one would go to the Egyptian queen. And these clappers were beautiful—they begged to be touched. They also sucked away the wielder's soul with each caress, and through this the Hittite king could use the clappers to kill the pharaoh and his queen. Then the Hittite king would lay waste to Egypt with the Black Pullet at his side.

"But the Egyptian queen was clever. She realized the power of the clappers and had her necromancer tweak the magic. The clappers could still take the soul of whoever held them, but they also gave the queen power over the Black Pullet. She let the pharaoh's clappers kill him, and then when the Pullet arrived to destroy Egypt, she used her own clappers to control it.

"And because her necromancer was so adept, she became the

new master of the Black Pullet and crushed the Hittite king."

"You." I frowned. "*You* were that necromancer, weren't you?"

"Of course." The Old Man grinned, a wicked mask of shadows. "But for all my powers—even after I claimed the Pullet's gift of a demon soul—I could not kill the creature. Only another Annunaki can claim the creature's life. So I mummified it, exactly as I would any other being that wished to return to life one day. I removed its organs and bound its soul in eternal sleep."

"Where are the organs now?" Joseph asked. "If they are destroyed, then the Pullet cannot be raised."

The Old Man motioned to the empty chest. "Its organs used to rest here, but they were removed long ago. They now reside in the Valley of the Kings. A different pharaoh tried to bring the Pullet to life, but if you wish to raise the creature, you must have two human souls. The clappers must be filled, and both fists must be closed." He shrugged dismissively. "Right now you only have a single fist *partially* closed."

"We do not," Joseph growled, "intend to summon it. Eleanor told you; we wish to destroy it."

"And I told *you*." The Old Man sneered. "Only an Annunaki has the power to judge and kill the Pullet. Yet I can feel it. Someone here *does* wish to raise it. This person will travel to the Valley of the Kings today."

I opened my mouth to protest—but then a wave of static shivered over me. It prickled deep within my ears and laid over my tongue.

Run.

I blinked.

RUN.

Terror shocked through me. I dropped to the floor, and the clappers skittered from my hands. . . .

A pistol shot cracked—explosive in the small chamber. Blood burst from the Old Man's throat. He fell, and I crawled behind the nearest pedestal.

Then a rich Creole voice sang out, "I am the one bound for the Valley of the Kings. *Mèrsi* for telling me where to go."

CHAPTER FOURTEEN

My blood ran cold. My lungs choked off.

Marcus was here, and he had shot the only person who knew how to destroy the Black Pullet.

And now the Old Man was dying. His expanded soul could not keep the blood from pooling on the floor—this was an injury too vast.

The jackal shrieked in my brain. *RUN!*

But I couldn't run. I had nowhere to go. Marcus was striding toward us, his eyes as bright as torches in the darkness.

And even if I could run, I wouldn't. Marcus was alone. No army, no escape. Now was my chance to *destroy* him.

Joseph and Daniel crouched behind the pedestal opposite me, Oliver behind another nearby. I locked eyes with my demon.

Stop Marcus, I thought. *Sum veritas.*

Blue light flashed around his pupils—then from his fingertips. Marcus's pistol fired, but not before Oliver's magic slammed into him.

But the power had no effect. If anything, it sank into Marcus like water into sand . . . and the monster laughed.

My hand mindlessly shot into my pocket for the ivory fist. . . .

Shit. It was part of the clappers now, and *they* were on the floor. Next to the dying Old Man.

Thunder ripped through the room as Joseph's electricity blasted from his fingertips and Daniel's pistols fired.

Marcus stumbled this time—even toppled back several steps. But it wasn't enough. He had spotted the clappers, and he was moving toward them faster than Joseph or Oliver could mount another attack. Faster than Daniel could reload.

And faster than I could dive for the ivory.

I lurched at the Old Man anyway, clawing for the clappers. But as more electricity and magic blazed overhead, I lost sight of them. Lost sight of anything. My hands slapped through the Old Man's blood, through his robes . . .

But no clappers. *No clappers.* Where were they?

I could use them to lead the imperial guards. I could finally take down Marcus. Crush him from the body that was not his and watch as his soul burned—

Joseph's electricity snapped off—Oliver's magic too—and all that was left was Marcus's purring laughter. It rolled into my ears, and I knew with a sickening hitch in my gut that somehow *he* had found the clappers first.

Run! the jackal roared.

I shoved off the floor. Another gunshot exploded—blasting into the stone chest. I dived behind a mummy and yanked out my pulse pistol just as Daniel fired his.

But then a muffled voice screeched, *"Joseph!"* It was Jie, distant yet approaching. *"Joseph!"*

Marcus's head jerked toward the archway—just as Oliver's magic flashed.

But as before, the demon magic had no effect. When the blue light faded, I saw Marcus striding easily from the chamber, the ivory clappers held high. "Kill them!" he bellowed over his shoulder. "Now."

"Stop!" Joseph hurtled from behind a mummy, his crystal clamp flying upward. . . .

A spear swung out, and the handle smacked his stomach like a baseball bat. It was one of the guards—and it was *moving*. Joseph flew backward, barely darting aside before a second mummy slashed out.

That was when I noticed that the mummy before me was rearing back for an attack.

"Stop the guards!" I shrieked at Oliver, scrabbling backward. *"Sum veritas!"*

Oliver's magic crashed over me, spiking the mummy and its spear backward. But almost immediately, the guard clambered upright and lunged at me once more.

I fired my pistol—Daniel fired his. All the mummies in

the room froze . . . only to reanimate half a breath later. Just as fast and just as deadly. Left and right, they slashed at us with spears. Their attacks were jagged and stiff, but too quick for us to hold off.

Yet the pistol's pulse had given me enough time to yank out my crystal clamp, and as I clenched it tight, a hot, angry power rippled through me.

I let it loose. The nearest mummy toppled backward, its spear snapping in half, and before it could rise again I rounded on the next guards.

Yet they were everywhere. Oliver, Joseph, Daniel, and I— we twisted and blasted, kicked and ducked, but our magic and our weapons were ineffective.

We really had only one choice—exactly as the jackal had said: *Run.*

A pistol popped through the room, and then Jie's voice ripped out, *"Come on! I'll clear a path!"*

Yet as we bolted toward the archway, the jackal spoke once more—and this time his message was different. *Wait.*

I didn't wait. Except the message came again, reverberating with command. *WAIT.*

So I staggered around. The jackal's scruffy body was bent over the Old Man . . . and the Old Man's eyes were open.

Come.

I wanted to scream at the jackal—*No!*—but I knew I had to obey.

So, with a running leap, I slammed onto my knees and slid

through puddles of blood across the floor.

I bent over the Old Man. His throat was healing—but not quickly enough. Each of his ragged breaths sent too much blood spurting out. His hands bloodied but his eyes sharp, he grabbed my wrist and *yanked* me close. "Stop the Pullet," he rasped. "Stop that man who wants to raise it. You can get help on the dock. By blood . . . and moonlit sun. Get help and stop him."

Then the Old Man released me. The jackal vanished.

I clambered back to my feet, my fingers already gripping the crystal clamp. Half the mummies charged straight for me.

Briefly, Oliver's panic twisted through me. He knew I wasn't with everyone else. He was coming back for me.

No, I ordered. *I am coming.*

Then I let the electricity collect inside me. The guards were moving in fast—ancient spears and skeletal, sinewy bodies. One breath, two. The electricity scorched through my veins, boiled in my skull. Too much of it—too much . . .

I flung up my hands and let the magic loose. Like a thousand bees stabbing me, like a thousand voices shredding my throat, it erupted from my body. So much electricity—it erupted from my fingertips and my eyeballs. From my tongue and my chest. It was everywhere, and for a long, endless moment, I thought I had gone too far. Drawn in more power than my body could handle . . .

Then it broke off, and my scorched vision saw the faintest line of escape. A path through the mummies. I shambled forward, and the haze cleared with each step. I tripped over two spears—spears that were already drawing in and mummies that were already returning to life.

I reached the doorway. Blue light blazed ahead, and the *pop-pop!* of the pulse pistols slipped between the thunder in my ears.

I bolted up the narrow tunnel. Faster, I ran. Faster. There were mummies ahead, and there were mummies behind. Their armor clanked, and their bony feet clattered. Soon enough, the guards in front would realize I was behind them. They would turn around and swarm over me. . . .

And I could not call on Oliver's power—not while I used electricity. So I simply pushed more strength into my legs. One foot in front of the other, and one ragged, heaving breath after the next . . .

Until the mirrors shifted. As one, they rotated, and all light winked out.

Black, clotted panic surged up my throat. I couldn't see. I lost all sense of the tunnel or where anything was: the mummies, the Spirit-Hunters, the exit. All I could do was hear the guards' footsteps and armor. Closing in . . .

My feet slipped on the loose gravel. My hands hit the floor. My chin hit next. The crystal clamp fell and clattered back down the tunnel.

"Sleep!" The scream burned up my throat, and magic I hadn't even gathered rushed from me. It poured out of me in a great wave of blue light.

Oliver's magic. I pushed myself back up with bloodied

hands. In pulsing gusts of magic—*Sleep, sleep, sleep*—I kept the guards above slowed and slogging.

And through the light, in front of Daniel and Jie, I saw Oliver. His eyes glowed so brightly that the contours of his skull blazed.

I reached the next mummy, ducking below its spear. Then the next mummy and the next—they were slowed by Oliver's unrelenting power. It rolled off him, gushed from me. All the while, Jie kicked at knees, and Daniel heaved bodies aside.

And Joseph ran onward, chasing someone who always managed to outrun us.

I pushed past the final mummy, shoving its spear aside, and then Daniel's hand was latching on to mine and pulling. We reached Jie—Daniel grabbed her too. Then we were to Oliver, and it was my job to snatch his wrist.

My demon jolted, his magic roaring back and the glow leeching from his face. *"Run,"* I shouted.

He did run, shoving at me from behind while Daniel towed ahead. The mummies' speed was fast returning—and ours was fast *flagging*. . . .

But Joseph had already reached the sunlit door. With a final burst of strength, I pumped every ounce of life into my legs—into my grip on Oliver and my grip on Daniel. We were so near, so near. . . .

Then we were through, back on this high stone level of the Great Pyramid. The morning sun stabbed my eyes. Joseph had bolted left along the worn-pyramid side. We followed.

The mummies followed too.

I don't know why I'd thought daylight would be our salvation. The guards were not slowed in the least. They hopped the pyramid steps as easily as acrobats. In fact, the narrowness of the tunnel had slowed them—now that we were open and exposed, they doubled their speed, scuttling on all fours like bronze spiders.

"Faster!" I shrieked at Oliver. But he needed no prodding. His eyes flashed blue; his face paled; he lashed out with another attack.

It did nothing. With the extra space, the mummies simply fanned out. The magic licked harmlessly over them.

So on we ran. My ankles rolled, and the corner of the pyramid came into view. We would round the edge . . . and then what? Even jumping to the next level would be too slow, and at this point, the only thing that kept me going was Daniel's hand on mine—and Jie's hand on his.

We reached the edge, barreled around . . . and then as one skittered to a stop, our arms spinning.

For Joseph had halted, his gaze on the distance, his shoulders back.

"Run!" Jie screamed, bolting to him. She made it in three steps, her hands outstretched to shove him into action . . . and then she froze.

Midstride, her entire body locked up.

"Jie!" I screeched. *"Move!"* But she didn't move, and had it not been for our own motion—for Joseph's twisting body and

258

Daniel's beating steps—I would have thought the world had frozen once more.

But then Jie pivoted sharply left, and when she began to bound up the pyramid in great, inhuman leaps, I realized what was happening.

Somehow the compulsion spell had taken control once more.

I lunged after her. "Shoot her!" I screamed at Daniel. "Stop her!" In a frantic climb, I hauled myself up the stone and then the next. Mummies scrambled ahead of Jie, moving at the exact same speed and in the same direction.

She was so much faster than I was. Ten steps above me quickly became fifteen. . . .

Daniel's pulse pistol cracked. Jie's right leg ripped wide, the cloth shredded and turned instantly red. *"Resiste!"* I screamed, focusing all my magic on canceling the compulsion spell. My vocal cords snapped, yet over and over I shrieked at her, *"Resiste! Resiste!"*

For a moment her arms clapped to her sides and she stiffened like a plank . . . then she toppled forward. Her face hit the stones in a sickening thud.

I spared a single glance at the mummies—they were rounding the top of the pyramid now . . . and then they were gone. They followed something I could not see. So I continued my frenzied climb after Jie. Joseph passed me, reaching her long before I was even close. He eased her onto her back and shouted her name over and over.

Then Daniel was clambering by. He fell to Jie's side,

crying, "I'm so sorry. I'm so sorry."

By the time I finally climbed the last step to reach them, Daniel had wrapped Jie's leg tightly in his shirt . . . and her eyes were open. But they were empty.

I threw a glance at Oliver. He swayed with exhaustion, his face too pale and his expression was . . .

Heartbreaking. Something about him looked broken, I wet my lips, caked in sand and sweat, to call to him. . . .

His hand lifted. He pointed east, and when I followed his finger toward the morning sun, my knees almost dissolved beneath me.

For drifting up from the other side of the pyramid was a balloon. A simple, round one—much smaller than our airship and with nothing more than a basket beneath.

And there were two figures standing within. Marcus and . . . Allison.

"No," I whispered. My head shook, slowly . . . then faster. "No." I staggered into a run, passing Daniel and Joseph and Jie. And still the word fell off my tongue, louder each time. "No. No. *No.*"

It couldn't be. She had to be compelled—it was a spell. Allison wasn't with Marcus willingly—she just . . .

Couldn't be.

But the truth settled through my chest, spreading outward and inward like the blackest of oils. I couldn't breathe. I couldn't see. I stumbled. . . . I fell. My hands hit the stone steps.

I had trusted Allison. I had thought we were allies.

God, I had been so, *so* wrong.

A laugh splintered up my throat. I was a blind fool. Of course Allison and I were enemies; we had been since the day she had learned that Elijah had killed Clarence—and I had *known* it. Deep within, I had known it all along, but I'd refused to see. I had not wanted her to be the enemy even when the facts were all there—obvious and undeniable now that I truly looked at them.

Back in Philadelphia, when Allison had demanded answers about Clarence's death, I had thought it odd how she took the truth so stoically.

But she had already *known*—that was why her reaction had been so stiff. In fact, she had probably come to my house that day simply to ensure that I got on the steamer for France. . . . Marcus had dug his talons into Allison ages before I had spoken to her. Somehow, Marcus had found her, swayed her to his side, and then used her.

For not only had Allison goaded me into traveling to France—even *driving* me to the wharf—but then she had come to Paris to guarantee that I went on to Marseille. She had inserted herself into the group to make sure we traveled to Egypt. . . . And then finally, she had helped us reach the Old Man in the Pyramids.

Everything she had done, had said, had shared—it had all been a lie. She didn't care about Jie's incisions or Joseph's bandages. She didn't care about *me*. She had helped Marcus get what he wanted by manipulating us.

And Marcus must have wanted the clappers and the Old

Man all along. When Madame Marineaux had not arrived in Marseille with the ivory fist as Marcus had planned, then he no longer had the power to find the Old Man—he was not marked as Pharaoh.

Instead, *I* had arrived in Marseille, and Marcus had let me get the information from Jacques Girard. Then he had let me do all the dirty work, step by step, to finally summon the Old Man. All Marcus had had to do was show up and collect the final prizes: knowledge of where the Black Pullet was buried and the complete, unbroken clappers with which to raise it.

Marcus had coordinated everything. *Always one step ahead.*

It was like salt on a wound, and a hot scream writhed up my throat. I dug my fingers into my thighs and threw my head back to stare into the sun until my eyes were raw.

I wanted to *hurt* Allison. I wanted to rake my fingernails down her face and into her traitorous smile. I had trusted her; she had betrayed me, and now I wanted her to *die*.

The desire was so strong, it pushed against my ribs and swelled in my neck. But with that rage came sobs. They shuddered through me, threatening to explode at any moment. But crying had never served me well, and crying would not catch Marcus.

So, gritting my teeth, I hauled myself to my feet. My blurry vision latched on to the balloon—and then drifted down. . . .

Sixteen figures galloped over the sand, their spears erect and helmets glinting in the rising sun. Their inhuman strides kept pace with the balloon.

Movement flashed to the north, and when I twisted my head, I found even more guards streaming over the sand. They must have come from the other pyramids, answering the call of the clappers. Marcus had himself an army—one that our magic could not stop.

My breath sawed between my teeth. *He cannot win. I will not let him win.*

I dragged my gaze right to Daniel's airship, still hovering over the Sphinx. It swayed in the breeze, seemingly unharmed.

But there was blood all over the sand beneath it. And deep, dragging footprints as if someone had limped away—seeping blood with each step.

For a bleak, vicious moment, I *hoped* it was Allison's blood. *She cannot win. And neither can Marcus.*

In a rush of desire, I finally gave in to all the hunger and want that had writhed inside me since Paris.

This magic was who I was, and when I called to it, it came. Like a door burst wide, the power inside me *came*. The more I inhaled and tugged at the magic, the more it pulsed through me. To me. I gathered it in my chest. More, more, *more*.

A wind picked up. It twined around my legs and through my hair, as if the world itself were offering me its soul. . . .

Then I realized that it was. I was taking magic from the stones and the air and the sand. I was feasting off the living world around me.

I straightened. Magic rolled up my spine, and the wind kicked harder.

A shout came from behind me; I ignored it. The balloon was fading too fast.

My hands reached out; my fingers flexed. I would throw everything I had at that balloon. I would rip it from the sky. I would beat down Allison.

And I would *destroy* Marcus.

"Eleanor!" Oliver's voice snaked into my ears. "Stop!"

I did not stop. I narrowed my eyes to slits, focusing everything I had—everything I *was*—on that distant balloon. I had no spell in mind, but I did not need one. Death and power were close cousins—and I had *plenty* of power. More than I'd ever had inside me before. It surged in from the world. It breathed and squirmed like a living thing, and I gulped it in as if I were drowning.

"El!" Oliver's voice again, nagging like an insect. "You're hurting us—stop!" Hands grabbed my shoulders. *"STOP!"*

The command shuddered through me, reverberated in my skull. The demon I controlled was telling *me* what to do. His desperation poured through our bond—but with it came magic. I latched on to it like a lamprey.

And then his power gushed into me. Where his hands squeezed my shoulders, the skin boiled. Where his breath laced over my neck, the hair stood on end. He was so powerful—even weakened as he was, Oliver was *made* of soul.

And I would take it. I would take and I would crush Marcus—

Stop. Oliver's voice pierced my brain. *You will kill yourself.*

"I don't care," I tried to say, but the voice that came out was not my own. This voice was layered and charged like the rumble of heat lightning. "I would rather die," I went on, "than let him get away."

But what about me? he pressed, and there was an undercurrent of panic. It chafed against my skull. *You will kill me too if you do not stop. You will kill Joseph and Jie. You will kill Daniel. You will push us away forever. Stop, Eleanor. Stop and come back to us.*

"Marcus will get away."

And we will go after him, but you cannot stop him like this. I will not let you.

I almost laughed at that, for there was nothing Oliver could do to me—not when I was this strong. Not when I had *his* power coursing into me. "How will you stop me?"

Like this. He slid his arms around my waist, rested his cheek against the back of my head, and opened himself up.

My legs turned to water. My body collapsed beneath the tide of his magic.

But it was not only magic that weighed me down. It was *him*, and in a roar of sound and light, I crumbled beneath his being.

I am in a world of darkness and stars. It is a resting place before the final afterlife. I exist when moments before I did not—and this puzzles me. But I soon forget, for as I watch the stars drift by, I realize they are actually other beings. Some are pinpricks of light that swirl with power too intense to look upon. Some are weaker, like me. And floating amid us are wispy, fragile things.

The souls of the Dead.

For a century I watch, until one day I feel a tug inside me. It is like a pronged arrow in my gut, and it yanks me along. I fight, but it is stronger than me. Quicker and quicker it pulls, until the stars fade into a cloudy sky. Until an ancient, slatted dock rushes beneath me and a distant, golden door appears ahead. I try to gain purchase on the dock, try to slow this hurtling speed . . . but to no avail. The door zooms closer and closer. . . .

I am through, and I am in a world I never knew existed. I have a body—it wraps my soul around bones and traps it within skin. I do not like it, and though years will pass, I will never learn to like it.

Yet I am able to forget for a time, for the boy who called me through is fascinating. His laugh, his jokes, his mind—they are alive, *and it captivates me.*

I revere him. Even when he starts to shut me out, I love him. He is all I have, and though he commands me away, I cannot stop what I feel.

But then I meet her. She confuses me. Her laugh is just like his. Her wit and her heart—like his, *except brighter. She tells me my love is dead, and I hate her for it . . .*

Until I do not hate her anymore. One day I awaken in a city of lights and magic to find that she is no longer my bane but my beacon. Where I had thought myself neutral and indifferent, I have fallen onto a side. Her side.

And perhaps this is the worst part about being alive and trapped in a human form.

I do not know what I want, *much less how to get it. There is something writhing inside me—something that aches for fulfillment.*

I had thought it was the Old Man—I had thought fulfilling that command would solve everything. Make this hunger go away.

It didn't.

Now she is all I have, and that knowledge crushes me . . . yet also keeps me from drowning.

But I do not belong in this earthly realm, Eleanor, and if you die now, then I can never go home. Please, I will not let you do this to me or to yourself.

Come back to me, El. Come back to me.

I snapped into myself. Me—only *me*. No Oliver, no magic. It was my brain and my body . . . and it was shrieking at me to breathe.

Because I couldn't. I had pulled in so much magic, there was no space for my lungs to expand. My ribs were bowing beneath the pressure in my chest. I had no feeling in my skin—no sense of sand, no touch of wind.

"Give it to me," Oliver murmured. His words brushed through my hair, and he hugged me tighter to his chest. "Cast it into me, El, like any other spell."

Take it, I thought, sinking into him. *Take it, Oliver.* Sum veritas.

A howl like a tornado burst from my mouth. A wave of magic pulsed out of me, so strong, it lifted me off the stone step and *boomed* outward. I watched it rush forward in a great wind of power. Down the pyramid, it swept up sand and wind and daylight. The airship swung dangerously, and its shadow gusted over the earth . . . until the wave had moved on. Until it had reached the rows of far-off trees and finally vanished.

My legs turned to pudding beneath me. I fell into Oliver . . . and then together we collapsed onto the rock.

CHAPTER FIFTEEN

The sky was brilliantly blue behind Oliver's head. My chest quaked, and each breath was like fire, each blink acid.

His lips trembled as he gulped in air. His eyes shook, trying to stay latched on to mine. The wind twined through my hair—and through his—and sand collected on the pyramid steps around us.

But I could not look away.

He was so much more than I had ever thought or understood. So much soul—so much pure emotion. Each of his hurts was an agony and each tenderness a blistering flame. No human was meant to feel what he felt, and no body was made for it.

But worse—what scared me—was that I had *changed* him. I had irrevocably made him into a person he did not wish to be.

Slowly, his eyelids shuttered, and a flicker of a thought whispered through my mind. *And now I have changed you.*

"Eleanor!" Joseph's voice seeped into my ears, distant and fuzzy. He was shouting for me from the other end of the pyramid. "Eleanor! *Help!*"

I wet my lips and tried to swallow . . . but I was still falling into Oliver's eyes.

"Eleanor!" Joseph bellowed again, and this time he added: *"Oliver!"*

My demon looked behind me. Our moment slipped away. Like a punch to the gut, my breath burst out. I rocked back and gaped up at the sky.

I *was* changed. His thoughts and his feelings were inside me. Even if I didn't want them, they flailed in my lungs and in my skull—

"Eleanor! Oliver! Help!"

Oliver staggered to his feet and set off in a listing jog toward Joseph, Daniel . . . and Jie.

Jie.

My throat closed off. The world reeled and blurred, my blood rushed in my ears, and I had to grab at the stones to get upright. But I dragged my feet, and soon enough I reached the others.

Jie lay on her back, her head in Joseph's lap as he stroked her hair—over and over, he petted her forehead and murmured soft words. Daniel knelt beside her, his voice hoarse. "I'm sorry, Jie. I'm so sorry."

And Jie simply lay there, as pale as a corpse and with blood gathering in the stones. Bits of flesh and bone flecked her clothes, her skin, the ground. . . .

So much blood. So much damage.

"Heal her," Joseph said, his eyes locking on Oliver. "Please—you must heal her."

"I . . ." Oliver's hands opened helplessly.

"Please," Joseph begged us. "She will die."

Daniel gaped at Joseph. "No . . . not magic—she wouldn't want it."

"And she will die otherwise." Joseph's gaze never left my demon. "Please. Oliver. Please heal her."

Again Oliver gave a helpless, almost lost shrug and looked at me. "I cannot heal her unless you command me."

I stared down at Jie. My magic was gone. It had pulsed out, a harmless wind, and now all I had was Oliver's power. I would command him if I had to, but I didn't want to force him. Not now that I understood him.

"What do you want?" I asked him.

He cringed. "No. No, El. Do not put this on me."

"B-but . . ." I tried to moisten my mouth—each word was a blade in my throat. "I do not want to make you do—"

"You *can*," his voice hissed. "You must command me or I will leave her—"

"You won't." I searched his face, his eyes. "I know you now, and you *won't*."

Pain tightened his features—and something else . . .

something angry. "If you believe that, then you do not know me at *all*." He leaned in and gripped my elbow, rough and tight. "But command me, El, and command me fast or your friend will die."

My breaths came in quicker. Harsher. I refused to back down from his gaze. I *did* know him, and I did not believe for a second he would abandon Jie. "Oliver," I whispered, bringing my nose to his and driving the command into his eyes, "do what needs doing. *Sum veritas*."

His irises blazed blue. I blinked, and he released me—lurching around toward Jie.

But Daniel refused to move. "No," he mumbled, angling toward Joseph. "Please. We can heal Jie the natural way—"

"Get your inventor out of here," Oliver growled at me, "or this girl will bleed to death, and we will be too late."

I marched to Daniel. Blood splashed on my boots, on Jie's clothes. I grabbed his collar. "Come with me."

His head rolled back, his gaze uncomprehending. "Jie needs—"

"She'll be *fine*." I tugged harder. "We need to get the airship running, and you have to be the one to do it."

Understanding flickered through his eyes, and with a final, broken glance at Jie, he staggered to his feet.

Together, we descended the pyramid. Our boots scraped on the stones. The sun seared into our scalps, into our faces, while the wind carried away Oliver's chanting.

But I felt my demon's magic, so pure and gentle in my chest. He was tired—drained from the hell I put him through—yet he did as I had commanded, and each word he uttered pulsed through my veins.

And it made me strong.

Far to the south, small mounds poked up against the horizon . . . and a white dot floated above. Marcus. East was the Nile, a mirror of molten crimson. Sails moved along it like gliding gulls, and seas of orange grass fanned out along the banks as far as I could see.

My fingers closed and opened with each step. Curling, unfurling, and back again.

Why had Marcus done all this? Why had he pulled our strings like *this*?

So he can raise the Black Pullet.

But again, *why?* Were immortality and wealth worth all this planning and puppeteering?

"Empress?"

I looked down, my vision spotted and broken from the sun. Daniel was waiting for me, but his gaze was leveled high. On Jie.

"She'll be fine," I said to him, resuming my steady shamble. "Trust Oliver."

"That's exactly it." Daniel's lips twisted down. "I *don't* trust Oliver—any more than I trust a Wilcox. And I don't understand how *you* can." He spoke with such venom that I knew he only wanted a target—a focus for his rage.

"Oliver is saving her life," I said wearily, hopping down the next level. And then the next. "Come on. We have a balloon to follow."

"You could show some goddamned concern," Daniel snapped. "My best friend is bleedin' to death from a bullet *I* put in her leg. Sorry if I'm a little distracted from your revenge."

I slowed to a stop, my teeth grinding as I wrenched my gaze back to him. "I *am* concerned, Daniel. She is my best friend too, but we need to get the airship ready now or we will never catch up to Marcus."

"I don't give a damn about Marcus!" He vaulted easily to my level, his face lined with pain. "That's *your* mission. Not mine."

"My mission?" I threw my hands wide. "I'm not the only one who wants Marcus's blood. Joseph, Jie—they want their revenge just as much as I."

"No. You're wrong." Daniel stalked closer. "It's just *you*. You and your demon have poisoned everyone—"

"And did we poison you?" I thrust a finger at him. "Or are you so enamored by Joseph you simply follow everything he does?"

"Do *not*," Daniel snarled, "say that to me." He advanced on me, and I shrank back. *Never* had I seen him look so angry. "Joseph is the most honorable person in this entire world, and the day I met him was the day my life turned around. Even if you and that demon and that . . . that ivory *thing* have poisoned Joseph's thoughts, I will still follow him. To the grave."

For a long breath, Daniel's green eyes bored into mine, unrelenting and absolutely terrifying. But then his breath burst out, and his shoulders sank. "I don't want to fight. Not with you." He turned away, and as he padded down the final level to hit the sand, he called out, "But please think about it, Empress. This is what Marcus wants. If he's really one step ahead—and he sure has been so far—then he's expecting us to give chase. He'll be waitin' for us. *Again*. Just consider that, Empress. Think about what it means." Daniel shoved his hands into his pockets and hurried toward the airship.

And I watched him go, his words skating through my mind—leaping, twirling . . . and finally settling like silt on the bottom of a pond.

Because Daniel was *right*. If we followed Marcus, we walked directly into what he wanted.

I screwed my eyes shut and thought back to my earlier question: why did Marcus go to such great lengths?

It wasn't simply for immortality and wealth. If all Marcus cared about was the Black Pullet, then he easily could have killed us in Marseille or just now, in the pyramid. For that matter, Allison could have sabotaged us at any point before now and claimed the ivory fist.

I popped my eyes wide, casting my gaze on the airship. It floated, unharmed and safe—ready to fly at a moment's notice.

So what was the one thing Marcus wanted more than *anything*?

Swiveling my head, I peered back up the pyramid. At Joseph. He sat bowed over Jie; his face was pale with worry while Oliver continued a tired chant.

And as he always did, Joseph scratched at his bandages. They were now filthy with grit and sweat.

Your blood is very strong. That was what Madame Marineaux had said when she cut off his ear. *And when my master learns whom I have killed. Oh, how pleased he will be.*

I wet my lips, remembering one of the first things Marcus had done after taking Elijah's body: he had asked me where Joseph was. *He and I have unfinished business,* Marcus had said, *and I intend to settle it.*

"Marcus wants Joseph," I murmured. My head tipped to one side. The breeze carried strands of hair across my vision. "He wants his blood—and he has since the beginning."

But it was not only Joseph's blood he craved—no. It had to be something Allison wanted too. . . .

Revenge.

I had known it all along, yet until this moment I had never considered how far a person would go for vengeance.

But now I understood, because *I* was willing to do the same.

It was all so obvious—so *stupidly* apparent when I thought about it. Marcus knew we would follow him because we always did. Because, in the end, Joseph and I wanted the same thing that Marcus wanted. As such, all that Marcus had to do was imagine what *he* would do in our shoes and then lay the trap accordingly.

I bent forward, planting my hands on my knees and watching our balloon. Daniel scrabbled up the ladder, ready to take us south . . . exactly as Marcus expected.

I dropped my chin, staring at the pebbles on the crumbling stone. At the blood and dust on my boots.

If I were *Marcus* and my prey failed to walk into my next—and presumably final—trap, what would I do?

I would go after them. I would hunt them down and finally claim the one thing I had wanted all along: retribution.

As the realization solidified, I shoved off my thighs and tipped my head back to bask in the sudden surge of ideas.

The Spirit-Hunters, Oliver, and I were weak; Marcus knew that. He had beaten us time and time again, and now he had an invincible army of mummies. If he were to raise the Black Pullet, there would be no stopping him—not in our current, devastated condition.

And that meant we needed to even the odds. . . .

I dug my knuckles into my eyes, reveling in the Egyptian sun warming me so completely—and Oliver's magic, strong and sure.

There was a way to win this war, and all I needed to do was think it through. It was like Elijah's eight-queens puzzle from chess, but this was *real*. We needed a location we could defend and a way to defend it. . . .

And who defends the queen? An army.

Hunger spasmed in my belly, fierce and insistent. It was our turn to pull the strings—our turn to move the pawns on the board. We would raise an army of our own, and we would pick the place to defend.

"It's a good plan," Oliver rasped, lolling his head back against the Sphinx's paw. The airship creaked overhead. Less than an hour had passed since Marcus and Allison had fled, yet it felt like days.

Oliver had finished healing Jie, and now she slept. Daniel, Joseph, and I had toted her down the Great Pyramid on a makeshift stretcher of sheets from the airship beds. Then we'd hauled her rung by rung into the cargo hold.

And ever since then, Oliver had been resting. Even now, almost an hour later, his cheeks were much too sallow. His chestnut curls dull—though that might've been from all the dust.

I hunkered in the sand beside him, enjoying the airship's drifting shade. "But we will not know when Marcus returns." I pursed my lips. "It might be hours. It might be *months*."

"Call up a scout. A corpse scout."

I turned a frown on my demon. "I have no idea how to do something like that."

"You woke up something before," Oliver went on. "In Paris."

As he said that, an image of a teal-carpeted hallway—the Hotel Le Meurice in Paris—filled my brain. And scurrying through it were dead rats and cats and . . .

"Birds," I whispered.

"Exactly," Oliver said. "A bird corpse under your control could follow that balloon."

I chewed my chapped lip, considering where I could possibly find a dead bird—or if I had enough power left inside me to raise one.

"I will give you what magic I have," Oliver murmured, his eyelids fluttering shut.

"Which isn't much since you can barely stay awake." Gently, I laid a hand on his forearm. "I . . . I think I understand you now, Oliver."

"Really?" He snorted and cracked open one eye. "I highly doubt that since *I* do not even understand me."

I sighed. "Perhaps, but what I meant is that I cannot in good conscience take any more magic from you."

"Not in good conscience?" A laugh tickled over our bond. "That's a first for you."

I groaned tiredly and shoved to my feet. At least, despite the horrors of the morning, my demon still had his sense of humor.

I offered him my hand, my shadow slinking over his face. "Thank you, Oliver. For everything."

His eyes flashed, briefly brighter than the sun's light. "Don't thank me. Not yet."

"Then when?" With a grunt, I towed him upright.

He rolled his shoulders and set to brushing the dust off his suit. "How about when you free me? Perhaps then one of us will have sorted out exactly who I am." His eyebrow rose. "In the meantime, shall we summon a scout?"

I nodded, my jaw setting. Even if he didn't accept my gratitude, at least he knew he had it. "Help me find a scout, Oliver. *Sum veritas.*"

* * *

Our spell to find a scout was a strange, unexpected success. Rather than raise many animal corpses—as I'd accidentally done in Paris—when I sent out the call *Awake!*, Oliver helped me focus my magic. Together, we narrowed the necromantic leash from an almost weblike wildness into a single, targeted arrow.

And that arrow found a dead falcon. The magic plunged into the corpse, then with a gentle nudge—*Awake*—my necromancy latched on tight and sparked the body back into life. Suddenly I felt the falcon—its ragged wings, its ancient rib cage—and I sensed its surroundings of crypt-like darkness and other dead birds. And then, just as suddenly, I had absolute control over the corpse, almost like some extended limb.

So when I commanded the falcon to fly south after Marcus, south it flew.

But oddest of all, when I finally caught sight of the falcon, it was nothing more than a speck, far to the south and flapping from the distant mounds I had noticed earlier.

"Amazing," I breathed, watching the black spot vanish— and feeling the necromantic leash connecting us grow taut and thin. "I cannot believe I could reach a corpse so far away."

"I must admit I'm impressed," Oliver murmured. "Saqqara is miles south."

For some reason that name—Saqqara—sounded familiar. But I did not dwell on why. My mind was too consumed by the falcon's flight. On the fragile line of magic that bound my soul to it.

By the time Oliver and I clambered inside the airship, my falcon had caught up with Marcus's balloon. And by the time we had the hatch firmly shut and Daniel began gliding south, Marcus was many miles away.

Tourists and Egyptians watched us go. If any of them had seen Marcus and his army, I didn't know. Some of them must have felt my gust of vicious power. . . . Yet as we flew away, I saw no signs of damage. No fear from our spectators.

I only hoped Marcus and his army remained as unaggressive. I told Joseph as much when I explained what I had done with the falcon corpse—and why. Yet the idea of Marcus acting out of revenge seemed impossible to Joseph. Only after I pointed out the great lengths to which *we* were willing to stretch for vengeance did the idea seem plausible.

"So we lay the trap," Joseph mused, scratching the scars on his cheek as he, Daniel, and I bent over the table of charts. Jie still slept, her face as beautifully serene as when Joseph had draped her in her bunk an hour ago.

Oliver slept too.

"I don't like this idea," Daniel muttered. His gaze burned into the side of my face. "There are too many ways this could go wrong."

"And when," I retorted, "have we *ever* had a foolproof plan? We broke into Laurel Hill cemetery with only a *boat* and *baseball bat*. And we descended the tunnels of Paris with only pulse pistols and a crystal clamp. At least this time we may choose where our battle happens, and we can prepare."

Joseph's lips pinched tight, and ever so slowly he nodded. "Eleanor is right. We will have at least some advantage if we choose where to fight."

Daniel gave a strangled groan, but other than that, he brooked no argument.

And I knew it was not the ambush that bothered my inventor. It was the thought of *me* raising corpses. At the first mention of my falcon scout, he had balked, and at the mere word "army," he had gone deathly pale.

No matter how hard Daniel tried, no matter what had happened between us last night in the field, he still was not easy with my magic.

Joseph cleared his throat. "The first step will be to find a location. Preferably somewhere with old bodies."

I stared at the maps, my eyes catching on Cairo. Then dragging down to Saqqara. Again, something about the name scratched at my brain. Why did I know it?

I gasped. *Professor Milton*. It had been the excavation in which Clay Wilcox had invested. . . . It was far from civilization or people, and best of all, it had been a *necropolis*. A city of the dead.

Without a word, I darted from the pilothouse to Allison's cabin. Her trunks were still here, the lids tossed back. Her first aid kit was strewn on her bunk. In fact, it looked as if she might come back at any moment.

For a split second panic wound through me. What if Allison *was* compelled? Maybe we were abandoning her to Marcus by not following.

But my gut knew better. Allison wanted revenge, and like a patient spider, she'd spun her web . . . and then struck.

Fresh fury slid up my spine, gathering at the base of my neck. Scalding. Insistent. But I forced it aside and focused on what I'd come for.

The booklet about Professor Rodney Milton.

I found it quickly enough, tossed atop Allison's gowns. The pages were bent and ripped as if she had crushed the booklet viciously in a fist. Yet it was not too damaged to read, and I flipped ahead to the page I remembered her reading at Shepheard's.

During his excavations, Milton uncovered an entire necropolis, or city of the dead, where hundreds of catacombs were built to honor ancient Egyptian deities. He estimates thousands of mummified animals are buried below the dunes. However, due to a lack of tourist interest in the catacombs, Milton focused his excavation on the pyramids only. One day when funding permits, he hopes to uncover the animal tombs and reveal their secrets.

A grin spread over my face. Thousands of mummies. Even if they were animals, they could still do precisely what we needed: attack.

Now I merely had to convince Joseph—and I doubted I would find any resistance there.

My grin widened, and I sent out a pulse of magic to my falcon.

He was still flying south. Even if Marcus were to turn around now, we would have a few hours to prepare.

This time *we* were the ones in charge. As long as we screwed our courage to the sticking place, we could not fail.

CHAPTER SIXTEEN

To reach Saqqara, we followed the Nile six miles south, then moved east past cornfields and date groves. We must have drifted over a thousand palm trees, our shadow covering their latticework of shade before we finally reached a barren realm of yellow rocks and sand.

And it was a world of pyramids. One after another they rose up, with edges so old as to be curved now. The dunes around them were littered with shards and bricks—as if the entire necropolis had been smashed with a hammer and the pieces left to scatter in the wind.

Joseph, Daniel, and I stayed silent as we floated beneath the late-morning sun, the shifting of levers and the creaking steering wheel the only sounds as we focused on the ruins below and the pyramids passing by.

Joseph broke the quiet first. "That mound at the very north-western corner—beside the column."

We all squinted into the distance. On the far edge of the ruins was a mound rising up from a dune that I never would have thought man-made if not for the eroded column thrusting up beside it.

Except it wasn't a column. As we approached, I realized it was an obelisk, like the one at Heliopolis, and it burned like a candle flame beneath the sun. And the mound behind it was a pyramid, weathered almost to dust.

Joseph took the wheel, while Daniel went to the cargo hold to prepare us for mooring. Several minutes later, the ladder clacked down, and Daniel began anchoring us on a series of stones on the north side of the pyramid. The stones *almost* seemed to extend in a straight line, as if they'd once been a street, but now all they led to was a great, sloping dune.

I checked my falcon. It had been flying for hours now, yet it still diligently followed Marcus. If we were lucky, the necromancer would go all the way to the Valley of the Kings, wait some time, and *then* head north. We needed all the time we could get. . . .

But it was best never to rely on luck.

While Joseph slept, I sat with Jie in her cabin and fought to keep my eyes open. She looked so peaceful, and the remains of Oliver's magic gave her face an unearthly glow.

Eventually Daniel relieved me, and I staggered to my bunk

to enjoy a dreamless sleep of my own. When I awoke it was sunset, and after feasting on apples and hard bread, I wandered into the cargo hold. The hatch was open, and a rope swung through it. Daniel had set up a simple pulley system to lower his crates of equipment onto the orange earth below. He was tying off knots around several small boxes when I came in.

He smiled at me. "Where's your falcon?"

"South. Always south."

"Then good. Always good." He moved to the hatch and shouted, "These are the last ones, Joseph!" Then he shoved the crates through the hatch, the pulley's wheel squeaked, and the box lowered from sight.

"What are you doing?" I moved to the open hatch and waved down to Joseph. His hands full, he only nodded back.

"All these dunes around here will work in our favor." Daniel wiped at sweat on his brow. "I'm thinkin' I'll lay out copper wires—rig up something like our Dead alarm in Philadelphia. But these lines will trigger pulse bombs instead of a telegraph."

My breath caught. "And then when a mummy crosses, the spiritual energy will detonate a bomb. How very clever, Daniel."

He grinned, flushing.

"So what can I do?" a soft voice asked.

My head whipped to the door—to where Jie stood, her hands in her pockets.

She looked . . . *different*. There was a bright challenge in her eyes that I hadn't seen in days.

"You're awake!" I cried, stumbling toward her. "How do

287

you feel? You look all healed, but—" I hesitated. "Sorry. You're probably tired and don't want—"

"Oh, shut pan." She punched me lightly in the shoulder. "I feel great, yeah? Never—" Her next words were lost in the bear hug Daniel flung around her shoulders.

"I thought I'd killed you, Jie. I'm *so* sorry."

She made an uncomfortable grunt and pulled free. "Where's Joseph?"

"Here," he answered, rising up through the hatch. He gave her a small smile and moved slowly toward her. "I am . . . glad you are well. Immensely glad. Have you had a fresh incision to resist the compulsion spell?" He winced as he asked, and when she shook her head no, his wince only deepened.

"I know how to use the scarificator," Daniel said gruffly, moving toward Allison's cabin.

Jie's face fell at the prospect of more bloodletting, but she didn't argue when Daniel returned. And as he had her sit on one of the equipment crates in the cargo hold, she explained what had happened while we were inside the Great Pyramid.

"You had been gone awhile," Jie began. "I was getting nervous, so once it was time for another cut, I started calling for Allison. I was by the Sphinx, yeah? And she was still in the airship.

"When she didn't come to my call, I climbed the ladder. That was when I realized she wasn't on the airship at all. I saw her from the pilothouse, trekking around the dark side of the pyramid toward *another* balloon. . . ." Jie's voice faded as

Daniel pressed the scarificator to the inside of her arm, and *click!*

The blades popped out, and when the device pulled back, three narrow slices welled with blood on Jie's arm.

Daniel pressed a suctioning cup over the cuts and offered Jie an apple. She resumed her story, pausing every few moments to munch. "I took Daniel's spyglass and saw . . . Marcus in the balloon. I *saw* Marcus and realized you were all in danger. So I ran—as fast as I could up the pyramid and to you. But . . . I wasn't fast enough, I guess."

"Or you were just in time," drawled a new voice.

I started—we all did, snapping our heads to the door, to where Oliver lounged against the frame, intently focused on his shirt cuffs.

"Perhaps we would all be dead if you had not cleared a path," he added, glancing at Jie—and then quickly back down.

"Oliver." Jie smiled—a strangely happy crinkle around her eyes.

He sauntered into the hold, an unmistakable pink flush on his cheeks as his eyes dragged to mine. "There are a *lot* of mummies to be found, Eleanor, so if you are finished dillydallying here, I think we ought to get started. An army of Dead won't raise itself." He stalked to the exit hatch, and Jie skipped off her crate after him. Then they both shinnied down the ladder.

I glanced at Joseph, who merely nodded his approval. Though there was a confused furrow on his brow.

And Daniel's face was drawn. There was no doubt we all

wondered the same thing: what had Oliver done to Jie? He had healed her body . . . but was there something more? While she and Oliver had reached a tentative alliance before, *this* was entirely different.

"Here. Take these," Daniel said to me, though his gaze stayed on the hatch as he offered me a jar of glowworms. "It'll be dark soon," he added. "So be careful . . . and keep an eye on Jie."

"Of course," I murmured. Then, with Milton's book and the glowworms, I set off after Oliver and Jie in the sand.

"Oliver said we're gonna raise old mummies to make an army." She squinted into the darker east. "Where will we look first?"

"You, uh . . . don't mind if I raise the Dead?" I asked.

"Not if it will stop Marcus." She cracked her knuckles on her jaw. "Besides, Oliver won't let anything go wrong, will you?" She punched him fondly in the bicep.

He gave an uncomfortable grunt and looked at his toes. "Let's start our search over there." He waved east, toward the rest of the ruins. Far in the distance, palm trees and cornfields were alight with a flaming sunset, and if I looked hard enough north, I could see the Giza pyramids reaching for the sky.

Oliver and Jie trekked ahead of me, hopping walls and dunes with the ease of desert cats. I, of course, was boiling and coated in sticky sweat before we'd even reached the nearest, lumpy pyramid—a spot where Oliver *thought* there might be a catacomb of mummified birds. Yet after poking through the sand

and crumbling stone for what felt like hours, we found nothing.

By the almost-vanished sunlight and rising moon, I consulted Milton's booklet.

"There ought to be a temple devoted to Anubis," I said. "If we continue east, we'll hit a series of columns that were once his temple. Below that, we should find some tunnels."

"I see columns," Jie said. She pointed ahead, to a sad set of spikes surrounded by slanted dunes. Without waiting to see if we followed, she kicked into a jog.

Oliver moved to follow, but I snagged his sleeve. "Wait a moment." I let Jie step out of earshot. Then I hissed, "Why is Jie acting like this?"

His yellow eyes shuttered. "I haven't the faintest idea to what you refer." He tugged free and stomped ahead.

But I simply scurried after. My boots kicked up sand and pottery, but with long enough strides, I managed to keep pace with him.

"Did you *do* something when you healed her?"

A single pulse of unease flashed through our bond—but instantly cut off. "I did what needed doing," he mumbled. "That was the command you gave me."

"It was," I admitted, "yet why is she acting so . . . affectionate? She was tolerant of your presence before. Friendly, even, but now . . . now she seems to *adore* you."

"I didn't do anything." Oliver glared daggers at me. "I merely . . . Well, I showed her who I was. Just as I showed you. I suppose she saw something in me that was acceptable."

"Will this last? Or is her interest in you simply some magic that will fade—"

"I don't know." Oliver sidestepped before I could grab him and make him stay. "She decided she liked me because she wanted to. Now it's her choice to continue liking me or not."

"Oh," I murmured. "I . . . I guess . . . Thank you. For making her . . . happier."

He groaned, his gaze very focused on the dunes ahead, and for several moments our trek was filled with crunching footsteps and wind.

"I didn't do it on purpose," he muttered at last. "Whatever happened to Jie's mind was entirely by accident. You seem to think I am a *good* person now that you have seen my soul, but you're wrong, El. I care for no one but myself, and I care for nothing but going home."

I did not believe him in the slightest. Especially now that Jie had also seen his soul and deemed him worthy. Yet before I could speak, Jie shouted, "I think I found it!"

She stood before the columns, a shovel in her hand. Oliver and I darted to her, and sure enough, only a few feet from where Jie stood (and from where she had found the rusty shovel), there was a hole in the dune.

With a determined slant to her mouth, Jie dug up the sand while Oliver and I tried to paw our way in. . . . And eventually we managed to clear away enough of the dune to reveal a gloomy doorway—and a set of stairs descending into blackness.

Withdrawing the glowworms, I slunk inside. Oliver crept

behind me, while Jie took up the rear. The narrow stairwell only dropped thirty steps before opening into an intersection of three tunnels. The air was too warm, too dry. The darkness too complete. Within a few moments, however, my eyes had adjusted to the lack of light and the green shadows of the glowworms.

"I am getting tired of tunnels," Oliver said under his breath. I was inclined to agree.

"Which way do we go?" I whispered.

"Right," Jie said. "There are a bunch of paintings that way, yeah?"

Sure enough, when I swung my glowworms toward the rightmost tunnel, the light sprayed over a mural on the wall.

My jaw went slack, and I scooted toward it.

It was a mural of a jackal.

"It's him," I breathed, turning to Oliver. "That's the jackal I saw at the pyramids."

"Anubis." Oliver spoke with weary boredom. "He is one of the gods."

Jie's eyebrows drew together. "Anu-what?"

"Anubis," I whispered, tasting the name. A god. An Annunaki. Exhilaration shivered through me. "When you called him a messenger, Oliver, you did not say he was also a *god*."

My demon shrugged disinterestedly. "I only saw him a few times, speaking to the souls of the dead . . . or . . ." He frowned. "I *think* that's what I saw him doing. I find it harder and harder to remember these days."

A burst of longing twined through our bond. He was

forgetting the spirit realm; it frightened him. My mouth trembled shut. . . . The feeling snapped off.

"Come on," he said gruffly, as if nothing had happened. "We may as well start in this tunnel since we're already here." His glowing eyes narrowed, looking ahead. "And if I am not mistaken, there are some cloth-wrapped bundles ahead. . . ."

My glowworms were soon illuminating *hundreds* of miniature mummies. They were bound in swaddling like babies, their bodies completely hidden.

"What are they?" Jie asked, crouching beside one. It wasn't much larger than her torso.

"Dogs," Oliver answered. "They were sacrificed to Anubis. Just as falcons were sacrificed to Horus or bulls to Apis. Whatever the god supposedly looked like, that was what he or she got." He kicked at the sand on the floor. "It looks like there are even more bones beneath. This is a treasure trove for you, El." His eyes climbed to mine. "Command me, and we can begin to raise your army and get them into position."

I swallowed, my gaze flicking to Jie. But just as before, she showed no opposition. In fact, she seemed genuinely curious. For half a breath relief crushed through me that I had one more ally for my magic.

But then fear unwound. When Jie had first seen Oliver, she had gone berserk with terror and rage. Yet now her attitude toward necromancy had completely flipped, and it scared me.

What exactly had Oliver shown her?

I looked back at my demon. "I'll . . . do this spell myself."

His jaw clenched. "Not on my account, I hope."

"Of course not," I mumbled. "Let's go outside to do this." Without waiting for a response, I spun around and began the hike back to the entrance.

Once we were outside, I moved away from the sandy steps and began to call in my magic. Jie leaned against her shovel, and Oliver slouched, arms over his chest. The breeze gusted through our clothes, our hair. The moonlight colored us silver.

I inhaled, and my magic came. Balmy and smooth. I inhaled more, drawing in more power as I did.

Until the wind picked up speed. Until I felt magic course in from around me.

Fear rose in my throat. This wasn't right—this was what I had done earlier at the Great Pyramid, and I couldn't lose control like that again. I would hurt everyone, and only Oliver would be able to save me—

Calm. Oliver sauntered toward me, his pose indifferent but his gaze fierce. *You can control it. Just focus on the soul inside you.*

I tried to gulp, but my mouth felt coated in cotton. And magic continued to spiral in from the sand. The air. The ruins.

He paused in front of me, and as my ragged breaths turned shallow, he laid his fingers on my shoulder. *Focus on the magic in your fingertips, El. The magic in your toes. It's all you need to raise these mummies. Leave the world's power to the world.* Oliver's eyelids slowly lowered, his fingers pushing into my skin. *It is just you and me. Nothing else, no other power.*

I closed my eyes and focused on the feel of his four fingers on my shoulder. His thumb on my collarbone. Steady and sure.

The wind settled down. The magic in my chest stopped grabbing for more. I had a glowing, throbbing well of power. . . .

"Awake," I whispered, thinking about the dog mummies. The buried bones. "Awake."

It was like fireflies on a summer night. One by one, souls winked into being. I felt them twinkling and collecting below the sand. Ten, then twenty. Then hundreds. *Awake, awake, awake.*

"Look," Jie hissed, and cautiously I opened one eye.

A skeleton loped up the stairs. Its snout was lined with chipped fangs, and its barrel-like rib cage had broken in many places. Yet it ran with the ease of a living dog. . . .

And then it stopped before me.

One after the other—some wrapped in fabric, but most nothing more than bones—the dogs ascended the stairs. And just like an army, they gathered around me in rows.

"They're so fragile looking, yeah?" Jie's voice held a hint of awe; and, scooping up a handful of sand, she poured it over a skeleton waiting beside her. "It looks like they'll break from just a little wind, but they don't." She glanced at me. "What will you do with them?"

I shrugged. Sweat beaded on my brow. My magic was running dry. Yet more dogs continued to pour from the catacomb's mouth; more dogs sucked my soul into them and awoke.

"You should bury 'em," Jie declared matter-of-factly. Then she pointed back toward our distant airship and pyramid. I forced myself to squint, to listen to what she said. But blood roared in my ears. So many leashes binding these Dead to me.

"Blessed Eternity," Oliver swore. "That's bloody brilliant."

"What is?" I croaked out.

"Have them lay down in the sand around the pyramid," Jie said. "Then we cover 'em with sand. A surprise army."

It *was* a good idea. "Go," I mumbled, latching my eyes on to the dunes around the pyramid. On the obelisk. "Go."

In a great grinding of bones, the dogs moved. As one, they jogged over the sand, bony tails hanging and torn cloths swaying.

They shone like white gold, reflecting moonlight and moving in perfect unison. Shadows flickered beneath them, and their bone paws crunched easily through sand.

Jie nodded, her face lined with purpose, and after setting her shovel on her shoulder, she jogged after them.

And beside me, Oliver said, "Amazing what you can accomplish on your own two feet, El. Just . . . amazing."

"I cannot tell if that is a compliment." I turned toward him. "Or an insu—" My words died in my throat.

The wind had shifted—and the light had somehow moved with it to cast Oliver in a full, lustrous moon.

Wide shoulders, a narrow waist, curls whipping in the wind, and a profile with a slightly *hooked* nose.

My lips fell open. My heart slowed.

Oliver had changed. Again.

It was not just his nose either. His jaw was stronger. His lips rougher. His eyelashes not so full.

And it was my fault—I knew it was. When his demon soul had passed through the spirit curtain at my brother's command, Oliver had shifted into a human form. Like water solidifying into ice was how he had described it. And it was as if the more he stayed in that ice form, the more solid it became. The more familiar and used to a body he grew. And the less his soul—his spirit form—became the natural, familiar existence.

And it was *my* fault, because our bond was turning Oliver into a man. It was changing him into the one thing he did not want to be.

Which left me with only one course of action left. If only I could summon the courage to do what was right.

"The falcon has stopped moving," I said quietly to Joseph. Several hours had passed since raising the dogs, and it was midnight now. As Joseph unwound copper lines, walking backward so the wire rolled out, I followed behind and kicked sand over it. So far, two lines were buried in concentric circles around the obelisk—each ring twenty feet apart.

"You are certain it has stopped?" Joseph asked.

I nodded and followed behind Joseph to sweep sand over the wire.

Daniel was at a makeshift table on the other side of the pyramid. He had set up his crates below the balloon, and now glowworms illuminated gears, screws, and tools while he hammered away at pulse pistols.

He was crafting a spring-loaded cap that would catch the

fired bullets and force them back down the barrel to be fired again. When spiritual energy crossed the copper line, it would detonate the pulse and hold the mummies in place—and their souls would cause the pistols to detonate over and over. They would, we hoped, be trapped by their own energy.

Meanwhile, Jie shoveled sand over my dog army. They lay crumpled and lifeless. Twenty-five rows of twenty-five skeletons moving out beyond the copper booby traps. And then another fifteen rows on the other side of the pyramid, near Daniel and the balloon.

"Just in case," Jie had said.

"Can you sense *where* the falcon or Marcus is?" Joseph asked. "Is it the Valley of the Kings?"

I shrugged my shoulders. "I can only sense that they have stopped. And that the falcon has not lost sight of Marcus."

"All right. Let me know when he moves again."

"Of course."

El. Oliver's voice filled my mind. *I have found another cata-comb. Come quickly—you will see me beside the sphinxes.*

I sighed tiredly and set off once more into the silver, moonlit ruins.

Oliver had traveled far, though, and it took me almost ten minutes to find him. He stood beside a head-sized stone—a whole row of stones, actually, each ten paces apart.

"*This* is a sphinx?" I jogged to Oliver's side; and sure enough, as I approached, I could see the faintest shape of a head-dress . . . and then a face.

Oliver waved Milton's booklet at me, the pages flapping in the breeze. "There used to be an entire avenue lined with sphinxes on either side. And at the end of it, there was a temple dedicated to Apis. I suppose that vague bump over there is it."

"Dedicated to whom?" I asked, squinting at a mound in the distance.

"Apis. He was a god in the shape of a bull. And bull mummies seem formidable indeed."

I bit my lip, unsure what to say. I was so deeply grateful that Oliver continued to fight on my side—that he sought to help. . . .

But I could not let go of this coiling guilt inside me. I knew what needed doing—and this only confirmed it further.

Yet . . . I didn't want to.

So as Oliver walked onward . . . and then onward some more, I simply followed in silence. Sphinxes' heads poked up with regularity, some more intact than others. Whoever this Apis god was, he was clearly important. Soon the mound ahead began to look less like a pile of moonlit sand and more like a small building. Each step brought bricks into focus.

But that was not all.

There were footprints. Lots of them. And they were fresh too, since the wind had not blown them away.

Oliver and I exchanged a glance, but our pace did not slow. The prints led to the temple and descended into a dark hole like the entrance to the catacombs of Anubis. Oliver knelt and inspected the opening.

"Did something go in?" I asked.

"I'd say the reverse—something *left*." He pulled back, shoving Milton's booklet into his pocket. "The sand here has been pushed outward. Come on." He wriggled through the hole . . . and then vanished into the darkness.

"El," he shouted back, "there are stai—" His voice broke off, replaced by a yelp.

"Oliver!" I thrust into the hole. It was as black as pitch within. "Are you all right?"

"I'm . . . fine." His words were muffled and distant.

I scrabbled in, trusting my hands to guide me in the darkness.

"Be careful," he went on, sounding slightly closer. I scuttled faster, feeling a stone step. Yet just as he began to yell something else, the floor vanished.

And I toppled into nothingness.

CHAPTER SEVENTEEN

I did not hit the ground.

Instead, I hit *Oliver*, and he crumpled beneath me with a miserable *"Oomph."*

"Why didn't you warn me?" I snapped.

"Your hand is on my nose," he mumbled nasally. "And I *did* warn you. I said 'Watch out for the drop.' I'm sorry if you were already falling as I said it." He shoved me, and I toppled to the side of him.

As in the other catacomb—and the Great Pyramid—the air was hot and dusty, the darkness oppressive. But most concerning of all, our entrance hole was at least fifteen feet overhead. A circle of white light.

Oliver fumbled the glowworms from his pocket. Their

feeble green shimmer only illuminated a few feet around us, and as he rose to his feet, it sprayed and flickered unevenly—revealing a high, vaulted ceiling and a wide tunnel cut directly from the bedrock. It was much larger than Anubis's temple.

"How do we get out?" I asked as Oliver towed me upright. My voice echoed off the stone.

"Not sure . . ." Oliver swung the jar around, his eyes glowing bright—and then widening. "Thank you, Professor Milton." He strode away from me and revealed a ladder set against the wall. He snatched it up and toted it toward the hole of moonlight.

"How do you know it was Milton's?" I asked.

"It's either his or some treasure hunter's. Does it really matter?" He returned to my side, and together we set off into the catacombs.

"We seem to wind up this way often," I whispered over our padding feet.

"And what way is that?"

"You guiding me through the dark."

Oliver grunted a humorless laugh. A laugh that said *Are you just now noticing?*

My teeth gritted together. I should do it now—I should do what needed doing right now . . . and lose Oliver forever.

But I didn't. I couldn't, and after twenty paces we came to a three-way split in the tunnel. Yet no paintings adorned the walls here.

"I see figures ahead," Oliver said softly. "I think they might be statues."

His grip tightened around my fingers, and he towed me onward. Soon enough I could see the statues too. . . .

But they were not statues at all.

Oliver pulled up short and shoved me behind him.

For several long moments we simply stared, our breaths trapped. But then I eased mine out.

"They aren't imperial guards," I whispered. "They're holding swords—not spears. And they have shields too."

"You're right." Oliver crept forward—two cautious steps. "And I think they're smaller. Your size. And look." He pointed to vacant pedestals—one between each of the current statues. "That's where the imperial guards were."

Releasing his hand, I tiptoed closer and crouched beside one of the vacant blocks. There was an undeniable outline in the dust. "They left. They must have gone when Marcus summoned. And they're what left those footprints outside."

"Then who are these remaining mummies?" Oliver asked.

I stared at the nearest form—and then it hit me. I barked a soft laugh and scrabbled toward it. "It's a queens' guard. *She's* a queens' guard." I glanced back and found Oliver's eyes glowing behind me. "Professor Milton mentioned them at the party—how the queens' guards are even more deadly than the pharaoh's."

"Then let's be glad Marcus cannot control *them*. I wonder though. . . ." He paused, chewing his lip thoughtfully. "Well, it doesn't matter at this point. What matters is finding these bull mummies—or any others, for that matter."

He turned to go, the jar spewing beams over the long row of armored mummies. There were at least fifty in this tunnel alone . . . and perhaps twenty-five empty pedestals.

I gulped, my throat pinching tight. Marcus's army was going to be vast indeed.

"And a vast army has never stopped you before," I muttered to myself, folding my fingers into fists. We were going to face Marcus here, and we were going to *defeat* him. That was all there was to it.

"Are you coming?" Oliver called, glancing back. "I think I see a sarcophagus ahead."

I scooted after him, giving each of the queens' guards a wide berth. If they were as dangerous as Milton had declared, then we absolutely did not want to awaken them.

My footsteps faltered . . . and my breath huffed out. "Oh no."

Oliver wheeled back. "What's wrong, El?"

"We can't raise any bulls." I dug my knuckles into my eyes. "If we do that, we risk awakening the guards. They protect the mummies—that's what Professor Milton said. So if we touch these bulls, the guards will awaken. We are not pharaohs; we cannot control them."

For a breath, Oliver remained silent. Then he swore. "Dammit." Then louder. "*Dammit.* As useful as your dogs are, I don't think they'll be enough to keep us alive." He stomped toward me, and, yanking up my hand, he marched me back the way we'd come. "Maybe we can find another tomb that isn't guarded. The bulls *were* the most sacred animals in Egypt, but

Milton's booklet said he found birds. So there must be some birds . . . somewhere."

"And if not?" I asked quietly. "You do not think we can win this?"

Oliver didn't answer me . . . and he didn't have to. It was apparent in his voice. In his stride. He thought we would lose. That we would all die tonight.

And it had become his problem when it never should have been. He was trapped in a body he did not want, helping a girl he didn't want to help.

"Oliver," I murmured.

He slowed, then twisted back to face me. His face shimmered in the glowworm's light, but his eyes pulsed their steady gold. "Hmmm?"

"Earlier. At the Great Pyramid. What you did was—"

"Is this another thank-you?" he cut in. "Because I told you to hold off on gratitude until you set me free—and now is not the time."

"But it *is* the time," I insisted, my voice rising. "Everything has changed between us. Can't you see that?"

He simply turned back into his stalk. "You're wrong. Nothing has changed."

The glowworms flickered onward, and with a frustrated sigh, I trudged after him. A blinding silver ring of light was visible, and we would reach the ladder soon.

"Wait," I called, lengthening my steps. I had to say this to Oliver now, in the safety of darkness. If I went outside—if I had to do this in the barren, vulnerable ruins . . .

I couldn't.

"Oliver, please wait." I reached his side and grabbed at his elbow. "What you did this morning *does* change things. What you did to Jie too. I see how much I depend on you. It was never you who pushed my friends away—it was me. And I pushed *you* away too. Over and over again, but you always stayed true even when I didn't deserve it. I know that now." I tried to moisten my mouth. I *had* to say this. "And I know . . . I know I have no right to keep you."

The words whispered up from my chest. Over my tongue. Across my lips. *I have no right to keep you.*

His golden eyes twitched. I inhaled to continue. "I have called on your magic, on your friendship, on your mere *presence* more times than I can count. Yet this is not your fight. It was *never* your fight. Elijah made you come to this world, and I . . . I have to send you back before it's too late. Before you are too much a man and forget everything about your home." Tentatively, my hand trembling, I traced up his arm, over his shoulder, and to his collar. To the locket I knew rested around his neck.

His face stayed very still as I twined my fingers around the gold heart.

"Tell me how to do it, Oliver, and I will set you free."

His hand lifted; his fingers gripped around my wrist. "No." His voice was so quiet, I could barely hear it. But then he took a step closer, and his voice trickled in my ear. "I cannot let you do this. I was wrong about you. You are *not* Elijah. And I see that now."

I did not move—though my heart did. Something about those simple words made my pulse stumble and my gut tighten.

And when Oliver's free hand slipped behind my head, I still did not move. Nor when his fingers tangled in my hair or his forehead lowered to touch mine.

"You asked me how I could speak to your mind, El, and I told you that there were many things demons could do." He gave a dry, whispering laugh. "The truth was, I didn't know how I'd done it. I'd never done that with Elijah—and my thoughts had never reached you before either. Not until that moment when . . ."

"When?" I breathed.

"When I realized I . . ." His words died on his tongue, and he shook his head ever so slightly against mine. "It's our bond. Don't you see? It's so strong. So much *deeper* than what I had with Elijah. So much . . . bigger."

And you think that's why we can do this? I asked. *Speak to each other mind to mind?*

Yes. The word shimmered through my brain, bright and poignant. *That is why we can do this, so are you sure you want to give it all up?*

"I . . ." My voice cracked. "I want you to be happy. That means letting you go."

"But if you set me free," he whispered, "you will lose your hand."

"I know."

"And you will no longer be able to use my magic. Or even *touch* it."

"I know. But you were right, Oliver. Like you said on the airship, I must let go of everyone I love. And that includes you."

He smiled sadly. "I appreciate that you have listened to me for once, but I don't think this is what you *actually* want. You feel guilty—am I right? You saw my pain and my memories, and now you pity me." He shifted as if to draw away.

"No," I croaked, yanking him closer. "That isn't it at all. This . . . *this* is it."

I tipped up my chin and stared into his yellow eyes. . . .

And then I bared my soul to Oliver.

I poured everything I had through our deep, wide bond. My life in Philadelphia, before Father died. Then after. Before Elijah's return—then after that too.

I showed Oliver how much I had loved my brother—idolized him. He had been older and so clever, and I had always trusted everything he did or said.

I let my pain for Clarence crash out of me. My heartbreak when Daniel rejected me, and the tears when Mama disowned me. My bone-deep terror over Jie. My grinding *hatred* for Allison.

I gave Oliver everything I had—and I showed how much I loved him too. How much I loved and relied on him, both as a demon and as a man.

Yet I also showed him how fear lived inside me. Fear that

310

I had changed him, fear that he had changed me. Fear that we could never exist apart . . . unless I let him go now.

Bit by bit, memory by memory and heartbeat by heartbeat, I showed my soul to Oliver until there was nothing left to give.

Then as the final pieces of who I was washed over our bond, I tried to let him go. To pry my soul from his—and to release my grip on his locket.

"Wait," he rasped, squeezing my wrist and tightening his fingers in my hair. "Don't do it. Don't break the bond. Not yet."

"This is what you wanted."

His head nodded, his nose touching mine. *I want to go home,* he whispered to my mind. *But if you do this, I will leave you.*

"Then," I whispered, my lips skimming over his chin, "that is what you should do. Leave. No more commands. No more pain. Find what *you* want, and I will find what *I* want."

And with those words, I let him go completely. My fingers released the locket. My heart released his soul.

Oliver staggered back, his eyes brilliant as the sun. Then he began to cough.

And I began to cough too.

I was drowning . . . no—I was *suffocating*. There was a hole in my body, and it was real this time.

I gaped down, watching my chest billow ineffectively. Oliver was gone from me. I had lost him.

"Oh God," I wheezed. My gaze leaped back to him. But his yellow eyes swayed in my vision.

He stumbled close and gripped the sides of my face.

"Desperate measures." His words were rough and broken. "Desperate measures to do what needs to be done. Thank you. *Thank you.*"

Then he dropped his hands, pressed the glowworms into my left palm, and lurched to the ladder.

And for several agonizing seconds, all I could do was watch him climb the rungs and disappear. My lungs heaved and heaved. I tried to claw at my throat . . .

But I had no hand.

My right wrist was a puckered, shadowy scar. Green in the glowworms' light. "Stay," I tried to call after him.

I shambled to the ladder and clumsily ascended—only to topple up through the hole and into the harsh moonlight.

By the time I had crawled upright, Oliver was long gone.

My demon was gone. He would not be coming back.

And I had made my choice.

A sob burned in my chest. How could I have finally realized how much I relied on him yet been so utterly blind to it too?

I *needed* Oliver simply to keep standing.

Far to the west, something gleamed. The obelisk. It wavered and shone like a beam of silver sunlight. Without thinking, I scrambled upright and set off toward it.

Time passed. When I finally reached the obelisk, almost tripping over the sand piled around it, the Spirit-Hunters were nowhere to be seen. No doubt they were sleeping—and I was grateful for it.

I laid my left palm against the carved granite face. "You can do this, Eleanor. You are strong. You are an *empress*."

Nothing. No spark of strength. No surge of self-belief.

I rolled my head back to stare at the pointed tip. It swam and drifted in my vision.

"Can I, though?" I whispered to the stone. Then to the starry sky, to the moon, to anything that would listen. "*Can I?*" I had learned how to use my magic with Oliver's help—before him, I had been simply me. . . .

A girl with no hand and no family.

My fingers fell, dragging down the obelisk's surface.

"Eleanor?"

My head snapped sideways. Joseph stood at the base of the pyramid. The worried lines on his brow told me he'd heard my outbreak, seen me cry.

"Come," he said softly. "Join me." Without waiting to see if I would follow, he began a graceful ascent up the worn steps of the pyramid.

And I hurried after. There were only thirty steps to climb, and they were waist high—easier to rise than the Great Pyramid had been.

By the time we reached the top, I was sweating and my breath burned in my throat. But I welcomed it—any feeling that distracted me from the gaping hole in my heart.

Joseph settled onto the top stone and eased Daniel's spyglass from his pocket. I dropped down beside him, rubbing my face on my sleeve.

"He is gone," I said into the damp fabric. "He is gone for good." I risked a peek at Joseph.

313

But all he did was nod. Other than that, he showed no reaction.

And I was grateful. So *very* grateful. I lowered my arm, and as if Joseph were a priest to absolve my sins, I confessed. "I don't know why I did it, Joseph. I suppose I hated feeling like I was no one without him." I lifted my left hand helplessly. "But I *am* no one. His magic was everything that kept me alive."

"You do yourself an injustice," Joseph said softly, pressing the spyglass to his eye and scanning the horizon. "You saved all of Philadelphia without him. You battled spirits, you battled corpses, and you battled Marcus—all before you'd ever met Oliver." He lowered the spyglass. "I realize the loss hurts, but it will fade with time, Eleanor."

"But not soon enough. And there is such a vast emptiness where our bond used to be." I clutched at my belly. "It is like someone scooped out my insides. Like *he* scooped them out and took them away."

I sank forward and cradled my head. It was as if part of me had *not* let him go. As if this swelling in my chest was a desperate hope that he would return.

Joseph rested a hand on my shoulder—a brotherly gesture that was so unlike him . . . but that comforted me all the same. "Jie told me something," he said softly. "She said that when Oliver healed her, their minds met. She thinks it was by accident—that he was so upset by how close you went to the edge, he lost control of his feelings. They poured into Jie—and do you know what she felt?"

I shook my head.

"She felt lost and alone. Confused and angry. She felt a love so powerful, it branded her heart and reminded her why it was worth being alive."

"But I felt that too," I murmured. "He showed me his soul too."

"Ah, but I do not think he did, Eleanor. You felt what your demon wanted you to feel. Jie felt what he could not hide."

Joseph's hand withdrew, and I nodded—though I did not truly understand.

Remember this, El: not everyone who you invite in will wish to be there. And no matter what you might want, I will one day have to leave.

My eyelids flicked shut. Perhaps I *could* understand. He had warned me, time and time again.

"Marcus," I croaked, "could be here tomorrow. We are made weaker without Oliver's magic." I wet my lips and peeled my eyelids back. "We might not win this."

"Ah, but you forget something." Joseph leaned onto his knees. "Marcus wants only me. He will come to us because—as you rightfully saw—he wants revenge for what I did to him all those years ago. And so, should it seem that we are losing, then there is an obvious solution to change the tide."

A chill snaked through me. "No." I angled my body toward him. "*No*, Joseph. I will not let you consider that. It is not an option."

His eyebrows lifted, and the resignation in his eyes was

inescapable. "I will do *anything* for Daniel and Jie, remember? I will kill for them . . . and I will die for them. And so, should our plans fail, it will be your job to make Daniel and Jie go."

"Go?"

"They will never leave me behind." His eyes narrowed. "Marcus comes here for me, Eleanor, and I will give him what he wants if it will save the rest of you."

"So you're going to *hand* yourself to him?"

"No. I go into this battle to win. But I cannot . . ." He grimaced and rubbed at his bandages. "The truth is, I cannot face Marcus if I worry about the rest of you. This is a fight between him and me that goes back many years—and it is a fight I pulled you into. Marcus should never have been *your* problem. Or Daniel's or Jie's. Yet look at what he has done to all of you. Look at what he did to your family."

"Stop talking like this," I said. "As much as I may *want* to blame you—as easy as it would be for my conscience, I cannot lay this at your feet, Joseph. Not for a single moment do I see Marcus as your fault. My brother caused just as much damage as he. We are all here today because of the choices we made, good and bad. Nothing we say or think or feel can change that. So when Marcus arrives, we must *finally* finish what we set out to do."

The muscles in Joseph's jaw worked, as if he was trying to swallow back what he was about to say. But then it rushed out. "Except, I am not sure I can finish it, Eleanor."

I grabbed at his arm. "Of course *you* can. You are the strongest one here."

"Yet Marcus is much stronger than I. My electricity cannot hold up against his immense power."

My fingers tightened on Joseph's sleeve. "But you have us behind you."

"And that is what frightens me most—can you not see?" He exhaled, a pitiful, shaking sound. "I know you think me rigid, Eleanor. I know my avoidance of black magic confounds and frustrates you. But every man has his limit—a line he will not cross. And every man must choose what that limit is."

"And your line is self-power," I whispered, releasing him. "I understand that, but it does not mean we will lose against Marcus."

"But it is *very* likely, especially with Oliver gone. And that is why I am begging you to make sure Daniel and Jie leave if the battle should fall to me. Promise me this, Eleanor." He leveled me with a sad gaze. Yet the look on his face was the Joseph I had come to know. The unwavering poise that made him a leader. "Promise me that you will see them to safety."

I gazed into his glittering eyes, and ever so slowly I nodded. "I promise, Joseph. But only because you have a line—and that is what makes you worth following. It's what has earned you the unflinching love of Daniel and Jie. And it is what makes us believe in you. To the end. If I had such a limit, then . . ." I shrugged one shoulder. "Perhaps I would not be so lost without my demon. Or so scared—" My voice cracked. "Or so *scared* of what the future brings."

Joseph's lips twisted into a smile. "But you *do* have a limit,

Eleanor. Every man has one. Let us simply hope you are never faced with crossing it."

Joseph and I sat in silence until dawn, with no company but the stars and coarse wind. By the time the sun began to rise, its misty pink light bathing our left cheeks, I felt better. Though I kept reaching for things with my right hand: an itch, an errant curl. At least the stab in my gut had lessened. The choking in my lungs had tapered off.

Oliver was gone; I had let him go; I would move onward as I always did. Joseph was right: the loss *would* fade with enough time.

"Has the falcon moved?" Joseph asked, his voice a mere breath.

I closed my eyes, tested the leash. . . . "Not yet."

And we descended back into silence until the sun was fully risen and burning with heat. Until Daniel appeared with breakfast—and saw my missing hand. Until Jie followed behind him and asked about Oliver.

Until I could not handle the chatter or accusatory gazes a moment longer.

Then I claimed the need for sleep and stumbled down the north side of the pyramid.

But Daniel hurried after. "Empress," he called once my feet had dug into the warming sand.

I slowed, biting back a sigh. Ahead, the balloon shifted against its tethers, a graveyard of dogs now resting beneath its shade.

Daniel stopped beside me. The sun lit his face, his skin as golden as the pyramid now. His hair the same color as the tawny sand. His fresh white shirt billowed around his frame, and sunburn sprayed lightly over his nose and brow.

My frustration instantly dried up. And in an unexpected tide, grief buckled through me. Oliver was gone, we would soon face Marcus, and it all felt much, *much* too real.

So I turned and fell into Daniel's arms, and I wept.

For my brother. My mother. My old life. For Jie. Allison. Oliver.

And finally for me.

I cried and cried until Daniel's clean shirt was soaked through. And my wonderful inventor never said a word. He simply waited.

When at last I wiped my eyes and pulled away, he flicked my chin with his knuckle. "Cheer up, Empress. We'll be home soon."

"Home?" I croaked. "But . . . but we don't *have* a home."

"And that's just it. It's time to make one." He pulled me back into an embrace, and my cheek rested against tear-soaked cotton. "We're all family now, you know. None of us has anyone but one another. So I reckon it's time for me, you, Joseph, and Jie to make a home. Though, of *course*"—he smiled into my hair—"you and I will have our own little place. Just the two of us."

"Ah." My eyelids fluttered shut. It was such a blissful image. A *home*. With Daniel.

For a long moment I sank into the warmth of his body so near to mine. And I reveled in how his heart thumped against my cheek. How his ribs vibrated as he breathed. "I would like a home," I admitted.

"So let's go then."

I snapped my eyelids up. "You mean *after* all this."

"Let's leave Marcus behind, and just . . . go."

"Marcus will never let us leave," I said quietly. "You know that. He will chase us until he has gotten to Joseph. Until he has gotten to me, to you, and to Jie."

"I know." Daniel shrugged one shoulder. "But you can't blame a man for tryin'."

"What happened to unflinching and unafraid?"

He drew back slightly and peered into my face. "I ain't flinching, Empress. And I ain't afraid. Not while this"—he took my hand and curled my fingers inward—"can make a fist. And not while breath still burns here." He laid his other hand over my chest. "I will fight until the end, no matter where it takes us. But sometimes a man needs a few good dreams to warm his wicked nights."

"Then let us dream right now." My lips quirked up, and without thinking, I moved my arms back around his waist. "Let's dream about what we'll do when this is all over."

A soft laugh ruffled my hair. His arms slid around my shoulders and tugged me even tighter. "We should start by getting your hand attached. The surgeon I designed it with is in Munich."

My hand. Daniel's perfect, mechanical prosthesis. I had forgotten it.

320

"And then what?" I asked.

"Then let's go back to Paris so I can *finally* see the Louvre, and then . . . how do you feel about London?"

"I feel good about London." I grinned. "But we mustn't forget Vienna. Oh, and there's always Rome." I tipped my head back and rested my chin on his chest.

He smiled down at me, the breeze sweeping his hair in all directions. "And how about *after* we see the world with all that money we don't have?"

"Oh, we'll have money," I declared. "After we patent all your inventions and become disgustingly wealthy, we'll have heaps of it."

He chuckled. "In that case, after we see the world we'll open a school."

My eyebrows shot up.

"For all the kids like me," he added. "All the kids who got kicked around by life but want somethin' more." He twined his fingers through my hair. "For all the kids who never even *dared* to dream about a life as perfect as mine is right now."

I swallowed as cold crept over me. Nothing about our life was perfect. This sunny morning would end very soon, and the darkness would seep back in as it always did.

But for *now* it was good. For now I had my inventor. My Daniel.

I pressed my ear back to his heartbeat.

"I'll call it the Joanna Sheridan Institute," he declared. "After my mother, of course, and we can all be teachers there.

Joseph'll teach about magic, I'll teach about machines, and Jie can teach self-defense."

"And what will I teach?" I asked.

"What do you *want* to teach?"

I chewed on that for a moment—but then the obvious answer came. "Literature, of course. Oh, and geography. I daresay I am more than qualified to discuss that nowadays."

"I daresay you are," Daniel murmured.

"I like this dream," I whispered, my words sailing off with the sand and the sun and the wind.

"Me too," he whispered back. "And when this is all over, it's exactly what we'll do."

"Promise?"

"Yeah, Empress." He squeezed me just a bit tighter. "I promise."

I stood before the spirit curtain again. It was the strangest sensation—seeing my body stand in the middle of my cabin though I *knew* I was asleep.

I blinked. The curtain hovered before me instead of behind, and when I looked down, I was standing in the real world.

Cautiously, I reached for the shimmering doorway to the dock.

My hands hit a cool, flat surface.

I pushed. Nothing happened. For some reason I was trapped on the *earthly* side of the curtain. I leaned into the light, struggling to see the spirit dock. Yet it was like staring through a window in a thunderstorm—a thousand lines of gold trickled and slid down a pane I could not cross. The view on the other side was blurred.

Except . . . the more I squinted, the more I *thought* I could see an old man. No, *the* Old Man. He shook his cane in the air, and his mouth moved as if he was shouting at me.

I pressed in, straining to hear something from the other side. The hairs on my neck and face pricked up, and when I laid my ear flat against the curtain, it sparked with static.

But the faintest sound also crept through. A voice—the Old Man's voice.

I screwed my eyes shut and focused all my energy on shoving into the wall, on catching any strands of his words. . . .

Stupid girl!

It crashed into me. I straightened, the curtain flickering and fading—but briefly granting me absolute clarity.

The Old Man, cane in hand and toothless mouth wide, roared at me, *By blood and moonlit sun, stupid girl! You cannot enter without the clappers. Only by blood and moonlit sun.*

I stumbled back from the curtain. It flamed once, so brightly my eyes screwed shut. . . .

And they stayed shut, for with the disappearance of the curtain, my body fell into a deep and thoroughly dreamless sleep.

CHAPTER EIGHTEEN

I awoke, the Old Man's words resounding in my skull. *By blood and moonlit sun.* It was meaningless to me.

As I sat there staring at the ceiling, a hiccup caught in my throat. It was as if a taut line were slackening—whirling back into me.

I shot up in my bunk.

The falcon was returning. A day after I had raised it, the leash that bound us was drawing tight.

Scrambling from bed, I bolted to the cargo hold. Daniel's crates were back inside, the hatch open. In moments my feet sank into the sand, and I ran toward the pyramid. The sun was in the western sky—midafternoon—and if Marcus took as long returning here as he had traveling south . . .

He would arrive in the middle of the night.

I found Joseph pacing beside the obelisk—back and forth along the sand, up the pyramid, down again, and eventually in circles. Daniel waved at me, crouched beside the outermost buried copper line. Jie stalked among our buried army.

"He's . . . coming," I said breathlessly when I reached Joseph's side.

His lips pinched tight. He nodded once, and I could see him mentally counting the hours as I had done.

"What should I do?" I asked.

"What we have been doing." He opened his hands. "Waiting. Restoring our strength. And praying."

The day passed accordingly, with obsessive checking and rechecking of our traps. Then a meal. Then more checking and rechecking. But our ambush was as well laid as we could make it.

Three giant circles of copper wire were rigged to the pulse pistols, plus a final fourth line that would detonate the pulse bombs. My twenty-five rows of dogs before the obelisk and fifteen rows behind the pyramid were hidden and ready. They shimmered with dormant power, awaiting my command to reawaken.

And always, the falcon closed in.

Before the sun set, Daniel moved the balloon to a less obvious location farther in the ruins. He came shuffling back to us just as the moon started to rise. Joseph took up residence atop the pyramid, spyglass at his eye. Daniel, Jie, and I sat at the bottom—hand in hand. Then we all began our mind-numbing wait once more.

The moon slid by overhead. The stars twinkled. The breeze never stopped.

A *clack!* sounded from atop the pyramid. "He comes," Joseph shouted. Then he skipped quickly down the stone steps.

For a split second my heart clenched so tight, I couldn't breathe.

But then Jie pushed to her feet, cracked her knuckles, and said, "Hey, we aren't dead yet." And Daniel rose, his face tight but eyes bright.

Joseph dropped to the sand beside us. Beckoning a crooked finger at me, he strode toward the obelisk.

"Remember what I told you," he said once we were out of the others' hearing. "You take them and you leave."

"Only if it's the last option."

He did not reply. He simply offered me the spyglass and said, "The Pullet is with them. And it is worse than I feared, Eleanor. It is a true monster of darkness, so you must prepare your army now." Then he marched off to help Daniel.

Closing one eye, I lifted the spyglass . . . but Marcus was still so distant. His balloon was a mere white ball on the horizon with a snaking shadow below.

No, *not* a shadow.

My stomach lurched into my throat. I swayed back.

The long, winding shadow was the Black Pullet. Its wings gleamed—pure gold, as the Old Man had said. And the waves rippling alongside the Pullet were the mummified imperial guards. *Hundreds* of them.

"God save us," I whispered. But no sound would come. My lungs ached with a feeling I barely recognized—as if they were trapped beneath a thousand stones. How many villages and farms had they trampled as Marcus came north? How much waste had he left in his path? *At least Saqqara is isolated*, I thought. But it held no comfort.

For I was afraid.

Truly afraid.

I lowered the spyglass, clacked it shut against my chest, and thrust it into my pocket. Then, without thinking, my left hand reached for my other pocket—and my mind reached for Oliver.

But the ivory artifact was gone, and so was my demon.

And I *could* do this on my own.

So I withdrew my fingers, curling them into a vicious fist. And then I inhaled until my ribs bowed outward.

It was time to end this.

My heels dug into the sand as I picked up speed. Daniel flashed me a grim nod as I bolted past. . . .

But I barely noticed him. My attention was on my army now. They would topple beneath those imperial mummies, but at least they would be a distraction. As soon as I had crossed the final ring of copper lines, I began to draw in my power.

With each hot breath, I sucked in the magic. With each sliding step, I wrapped it around my heart.

I sprinted to the dogs, and when I sensed the skeletons beneath me, I slowed to a walk . . . then a careful creep. Bones rolled beneath my feet, and my magic throbbed in my chest.

At last, when I had reached the center of the dog graveyard, I stopped and opened my arms wide.

Dust billowed over me. Moonlight shone down. Then, with my left fingers flexed taut, I poured my magic from me. "Awake."

As before, the magic sifted into individual sparks. Hundreds upon hundreds spiraled out to each and every skeleton. Then they stabbed in, nestling deep within the dog's bones . . . and the strands of magic pulled tight. Over and over, my power gushed from my heart until every ancient hound was awake—and was *mine*.

Then, with a tired breath, I pushed back through the rows and jogged toward the pyramid—toward Jie. She waited at the obelisk, Joseph beside her. His face was unusually pale, his forehead pinched, but otherwise he looked ready.

Jie, on the other hand, fidgeted and swung something in her hand.

A sword.

"Take this," she said, extending it to me.

My forehead bunched up. It was a dented, chipped thing as long as her arm and double-edged.

A laugh escaped my throat. "This was from Philadelphia. The ancient Roman sword you stole from the Centennial Exhibition."

"Yeah." She bared a tight grin. "It still works fine, even if it is a thousand years old. I've kept it in my luggage since Philadelphia."

My left hand wrapped around the hilt. "But what will you fight with?"

She wiggled her fingers at me. "These will do fine. Here . . ." She moved to me and slid the sword behind my belt. It was stiff, but it was also accessible. Then she laid her hands on my shoulders. There was no missing the terror in her eyes.

"Be careful, Eleanor."

"You too, Jie."

She grunted her agreement and turned to Joseph. "I'm not much for prayer, but now seems like a good time, yeah?"

He nodded absently, his gaze locked on the southern horizon. As I set off toward the north side of the pyramid—toward the second dog graveyard—I heard him begin to chant beneath his breath. The words were Creole, but the message was clear: *Please let us survive this night.*

I reached the base of the pyramid and wheeled around it— only to skitter to a stop. Daniel marched toward me, his bandolier in hand, though only two pistols remained. His jaw was set, his spine straight.

In two long strides, he closed the space between us, dropped the bandolier to the sand, and tugged me into a fierce embrace.

His lips were on mine. It was a desperate kiss—a kiss to end the world on—and I thought I might crumble beneath it . . . except that I fought against the tide of need, and I kissed him just as hard in return.

I clutched him to myself, digging my fingers into his back,

into his hair, biting and tasting until our lips were raw and I could not breathe.

Until Daniel broke away. His lip bled, his chest heaved. But his fingers stayed in my hair, and he touched his nose to mine. "I love you."

"I love you too."

"Please survive this night. For me."

I nodded. Then he brushed a final kiss over my lips, hefted his bandolier, and strode around the pyramid without looking back.

And I did not watch him go. I kicked back into a run, the sword banging against my leg as I raced toward our secondary army.

As I had done before, I navigated to the center, called in my power as I moved, then *released* it. "Awake, awake."

In four thunderous heartbeats, the dogs awoke—and our army was complete. Now *I* simply had to get into position.

By the time I had ascended the pyramid, hunkering behind the top step and easing out the spyglass, the obelisk's shadow had shifted—and Marcus's balloon was fully in sight.

Holding my breath, I raised the spyglass to my eye.

The Black Pullet was undoubtedly worse than I had ever feared. It was no chicken, nor a cockatrice—nor any monster I had ever imagined. Such black scales seemed to absorb the light. And yet its wings were brilliant, blinding gold. It slithered over the sand on four talons, its snakelike form twice as long as the balloon's shadow.

And on either side of it, droves of imperial mummies marched in perfectly uniform lines. Each of their steps was a bounding leap.

I wrenched my gaze up and honed in on the balloon. On Marcus's face. He had a spyglass of his own, but he was focused on the obelisk. On Joseph standing beside it. And next to Marcus, her gaze also straight ahead, was Allison.

My blood curdled. Yet . . . Allison did not look like herself. Perhaps it was merely the shadows, but her face seemed withered. Skeletal even. And her posture was hunched, her arms clasped tight.

And the fleeting panic returned. Had she been compelled?

No, my gut told me. *She chose this. Long ago, she chose this path.*

I ducked behind the step, crouching out of sight. Daniel and Jie would be taking up their positions beside Joseph now, and there was nothing left for me to do . . . but wait.

And as Joseph had done only minutes ago, I prayed. I prayed to anyone or anything that would listen. The Annunaki, the jackal, the spirits of the dead—I begged for them to see us through the night.

But no warm, answering presence came to me. No reply or acknowledgment that a god listened or cared. And I suppose I hadn't expected one.

Time trickled past, painfully slow. I heard every scrape of wind over the pyramid, every murmur of Jie's voice, every spin of a pulse pistol chamber . . .

Until a steady thumping took over. Until rattling armor dominated all.

"Eleanor," Joseph roared. "Get ready!"

I scuttled to the edge of the step and peeked around the corner, pressing the spyglass to my eye.

Marcus's balloon floated closer, his army marching in their constant rows . . . and the Black Pullet sliding along like a cobra.

Then, five hundred paces away, the balloon stopped moving—and the mummies all froze. A rope heaved over the side of the balloon's basket, and in a quick move, the Black Pullet snapped the rope in its fangs. Then it towed the balloon down, bit by bit, until Marcus was close enough to jump out and tie the rope to a boulder.

My gut heaved. The Pullet was not just a creature of wealth and immortality. It was also a servant able to do its master's bidding.

Allison scrabbled from the basket next, but her body almost caved in when she hit the sand. Then, in aching movements, she hobbled around to face us. No shadows blanketed her face. Only pure moonlight.

My body went limp. The spyglass almost tumbled from my grasp.

Allison Wilcox was an old woman. Lines seamed her face, and white streaked through her hair.

The ivory fist.

With that thought, the image of the desiccated Marquis formed in my mind. The ivory had sucked away his life.

And now it had sucked away another's. Allison's. And I did not think it had been her choice.

I tried to look away from her, but I couldn't. No vengeful satisfaction moved through me. Only gaping horror.

I slid the spyglass back to Marcus. He was watching the obelisk, his eyes thinned. Suspicious. He was not a stupid man—he knew the Spirit-Hunters would not offer themselves up openly. Yet our traps were well laid, and he did not spot anything.

So with a dismissive arch of his eyebrow, he flicked his wrist toward the pyramid . . .

And half the mummies launched at us.

I shoved to my feet, pushing the spyglass deep into my pocket. Marcus's eyes lit on me, and a slight mask of surprise settled over his features. But otherwise he let his mummies continue their charge. . . .

They reached the edge of my dogs. Their feet stamped over, and I let them come. Closer, closer . . .

"Attack," I said.

In an explosion of sand, bones thrust upward. Skulls and spines, ribs and claws, the dogs erupted from the earth and careened headfirst into the guards. Fangs slashed into the mummies. Legs shredded, throats ripped wide, and the guards had no choice but to fight back.

Yet their spears poked through open ribs or smashed on sturdy spines. For every dog they managed to topple, two more would attack.

Marcus's face clouded with fury. His yellow eyes met mine,

and the message was clear: *This will not be tolerated.*

I bared my teeth at him. *Do your worst.*

He snapped his fingers, and a second surge of mummies moved. But they streamed around the dogs—looping out and avoiding my skeletons entirely.

"Attack," I whispered to the hounds at the edge of the battle—but they were too slow. The mummies moved with such inhuman speed and agility, they rocketed past my dogs in mere breaths.

I gulped and glanced down at the Spirit-Hunters. It was time to see how well Daniel's traps worked.

As if sensing my eyes, he glanced up at me. His green eyes shone, and he nodded once.

I nodded back. The guards scurried over the sand. Closer, closer they came. . . .

Pop! Pop! Pop!

As one, the guards locked into place—some with knees up, others with heels down; some with spears out, and some with spears low.

Pop! Pop! Pop!

The pulse pistols fired, over and over—exactly as Daniel had planned—and the mummies stayed trapped in place.

Or I thought they did, but as I watched, I realized that they did still move, just with such slowness, it was barely visible. They would break through the line *eventually.*

My gaze shot to Marcus. He fumed, his hands in fists and his lips curled back. He had realized he would have to come to us.

He shouted something, but the words were lost in the clashing of spears, armor, and bones. Then he stalked forward, Allison shivering as she watched him go.

And the Black Pullet slithered after.

My heart skipped. I had forgotten it. It was as if the pitch of its scales not only soaked up light but thoughts as well.

Marcus reached the edge of my dogs, and with a simple slashing attack of magic, he toppled ten. Then ten more.

I scrambled to draw in my power, but no matter how quickly I sent out new sparks of soul, I could not reanimate their skeletal forms as quickly as Marcus could fell them.

And at this rate he would surge through my army in a matter of minutes. Marcus's eyes climbed to mine. He smiled, and with a dramatic twirl of his hand, he pointed at me.

In a flurry of sand and a flash of gold, the Pullet hurled forward. Like the second wave of mummies, it charged around my dogs and aimed for a sideways attack.

I couldn't breathe. I couldn't move. I could only watch as it streaked over the silver sand. Then it thrust between two mummies . . .

And it crossed the copper line without slowing at all.

Because, of course, it was not *dead*. It was a living creature with a soul bound to a body—it could not be affected by electromagnetic pulses.

And now Marcus had sent it after us.

My brain exploded with panic—and with a spine-locking need to survive, I hurled around and I *ran*.

I stumbled down the pyramid, leaping and reaching. Each step jarred through my body and rattled my teeth—but I could not slow. I had no real plan in my brain other than a vague idea that it was already time for my second army to arise.

I hit the sand, crashing onto my left hand. But I bounded back up in an instant.

And then I was sprinting again. Every bit of power I had, I pushed into my legs. I could hear the Pullet. I could hear its claws scratching over the pyramid, its scales scraping over stone. . . .

God, it was so fast. So big. So close.

My feet cracked through skeletons—I was crushing my own army. But I could not stop. I just had to get the Pullet far enough into this graveyard. . . .

I tripped. A stone slammed into my shin—one of the stones we'd tied the balloon to. They were almost invisible by moonlight.

I flew forward, and the clattering of gold feathers filled every piece of my brain.

"Attack!" I screeched just as my chest plowed through sand. *"ATTACK!"*

Bones burst from the sand around me—vicious and fast.

And a keening wail erupted from the Pullet's mouth.

I crawled around, yanking my sword from my belt while the skeletons of a hundred dogs swarmed the Pullet. Gleaming bones covered the beast.

Distantly, the pulse pistols kept up their *Pop! Pop!*, occasionally broken apart by an explosive crack of Joseph's electricity.

But most sounds were swallowed up by the Pullet. It writhed and snapped, fighting the skeletons.

When at last I had my sword free, the moonlight flickered over the stone I'd tripped on.

It wasn't a stone. It was a sphinx's head.

I wrenched my gaze north, toward the large sand dune I had noticed two days ago. In a numb frenzy, I heaved back into a sprint, my sword hoisted high.

I bounded over sphinxes' heads. They weren't as well preserved or as consistent as the ones leading to the bull catacombs, but they were undoubtedly *here*. And if this was an avenue leading to another temple, then I would take it. I could at least try to hide within.

And if that outcropping ahead was nothing more than a sand dune, I would take that too.

Just before I reached the mound, I flung a glance back at the Pullet.

And I instantly wished I hadn't. It was moving again. Most of my dogs were snapped in half, and though they still writhed to reach the creature, they were too broken to succeed.

Shit, my brain screamed at me, and I pumped my legs faster. . . .

Then I was at the pile of sand, and my hands were connecting with stone. I brushed and swept and kicked and shoved, but I could not clear away sand fast enough—certainly not before the creature reached me.

So I climbed up onto the sand-covered temple, and I whirled

around to face the Black Pullet.

It barreled toward me, a line of blurring black and blinding gold. My sword out and my heart in my throat, I slowly backed away from the temple's edge. The serpent would have to rise onto its hind legs to climb, and I would have one shot. One shot to slash its throat.

And then the monster was to me. Its enormous, train-sized body was rearing up, and I was darting forward. My sword slipped between black, velvety scales . . .

But I had severely misjudged. The Pullet's neck was wider than I was. My sword was a mere bee sting. The creature lurched back, taking my sword with it.

I bolted. Away, over the sand and to the back edge of the temple. Then its front legs *slammed* onto the temple roof. Sand bounced, burning up my nose, into my eyes—and I bounced too. My legs crumpled beneath me. I had just enough time to wriggle onto my knees before the Pullet hefted its entire body onto the temple. Blood pooled around my embedded sword, and I briefly considered trying to retrieve the weapon. . . .

But then a loud *crack* tremored through the sand. The Pullet paused. I paused.

The roof collapsed.

In a roar of crunching bricks and dust, the temple caved in beneath us. The Pullet fell with an ear-shattering screech—and I fell too.

I hit a ground of rubble and bricks. A fall of twenty feet in less than a second. Debris knocked into me, and dust choked my vision, my lungs. But I kicked free easily—unlike the Pullet, which was too heavy and too layered beneath the broken roof. As it writhed ineffectually, I scrambled to my feet. Then, in a flash, I took in my surroundings. I was in a catacomb, but it was narrow and shallow like the dogs' tunnels.

And I had two options: try to climb out, which would require getting past the Black Pullet's maw.

Or descend into the tunnels behind me.

The decision was easy, for at that moment the Pullet was rapidly gaining purchase and digging itself out from under the broken roof, and though my sword had been slammed even farther into its neck, the monster was no worse off than before. Its claws knocked away bricks bit by bit, and its breath heaved hotter than the wind and reeked of carrion.

So, in a burst of speed, I threw myself into the lightless depths of a catacomb unknown.

CHAPTER NINETEEN

Moonlight from the caved-in roof did not extend into the catacombs. I instantly cast an awareness spell, silent words trilling over my tongue and the net flying out, out—

It hit the Pullet.

And the spell exploded. Magical threads shriveled up and tangled through my muscles.

I stumbled, choking. I couldn't cast that spell—I didn't think I could use *any* magic on the creature. It would simply backfire again.

I lurched to the left wall and, using my one hand to guide me, I scurried farther into the tunnel. If this was like the bull temple, I would hit queens' guards soon—and maybe I could hide behind one. If this was like the *dogs'* catacombs . . .

I prayed it was not.

A shrill scream pierced the darkness behind me. It bounced off the limestone walls.

Ice rolled down my spine. The Pullet was still coming after me.

I hurried my steps. Soon I could see absolutely nothing, and the heavy air clogged my lungs. But I jogged on—I had no other choice. If I could just reach *something*, I might have a chance. . . .

Yet nothing came. For all I knew I was walking right by potential hiding spots, but my feet and my one hand touched nothing except chalky stone.

And behind me, talons tapped, golden feathers shook, and breath huffed. The creature was close, but *how* close was impossible to gauge.

Faster, I ordered myself. *Faster.*

My toes suddenly bumped something. My hand lurched out—and connected with stone. Fear shot up my throat, and I had to bite back a scream. Was this a *wall*?

I sidled right, dragging my hand . . . dragging . . .

Until I tumbled forward. It was not a wall—thank God—and when I crept forward, I found something even better than a queens' guard: an *alcove.*

It was narrow, barely enough space for me to squeeze into, but it was there nonetheless.

Just as I wrestled my body into the tiny space, my back knocking against something strangely soft and familiar, a yellow light filtered into the tunnel.

I clamped my hand over my mouth, trying to stifle my breaths. To contain my pounding heart.

The glow brightened, sweeping side to side, and I realized with twisting horror that the Black Pullet could see in the dark. Like Oliver, it had yellow, *glowing* eyes.

Its scuttling claws slowed as it neared me.

Then it was in front of me, talons clacking and head swinging from side to side. It paused, black scales quivering and so close I could pluck a golden feather from its wing.

For several endless moments the tunnel was sprayed in pale light, and I stared with trembling eyeballs at the wall opposite me. Vivid murals spanned from the floor to the ceiling: paintings of a farmland crowded with the usual, rigid Egyptian people. Yet between each person there was a black-and-white ibis, its beak curved and majestic.

My breath hitched in, my eyes widening. Oliver had mentioned a god with an ibis head: *Thoth.* This was Thoth's temple . . . and this had to be the bird catacomb that Oliver could not find.

Then another thought hit, and my eyes bulged even wider— for what had Oliver told me about the ibis? *They once protected Egypt from a great winged serpent.* A great winged serpent like the Black Pullet.

And at that moment the winged serpent was resuming its stalking steps and carrying its yellow light away. But not before I glimpsed a shadowy alcove across from me . . . and a small, canvas-wrapped mound inside.

A mummy, and if I was right, there was one directly behind me too. And more throughout, if this catacomb was anything like the others.

The Pullet's scaly tail flicked past, and I squeezed my eyes shut.

Awake, awake, awake, I thought. *Return to your bodies. Wake up and fight—awake!*

A pulsing light appeared behind my eyelids, and my soul slid through my veins—climbing, reaching for my heart.

Wake up! Awake!

The light shone brighter, and my magic continued to trickle inward. I had never felt power like this, so warm and . . . yet almost dampened.

And still the light burned brighter until it scorched red behind my lids.

Then a soft huff sounded, and my heart turned to stone.

This light wasn't magic.

I snapped my eyes wide—just in time to see the Pullet's fangs lurch at me. A scream cycloned over me, raising my hair and coating me in static and moisture.

I fell back, stumbling over the ibis mummy . . . and hitting a wall. Another scream and another snap of teeth. It filled every space of my sight, of my hearing, of my heart.

But the Pullet's head didn't *quite* fit into the alcove.

I ducked down, my hand landing right on the bound mummy's chest . . . and then my fingers poked through the canvas wrappings.

The ibis moved. It wriggled—it *was* awake—but it was bound too tightly to break free. These wrappings had not decomposed like the dogs'. My fingers curled into claws, and I shredded the fabric. . . .

The Pullet reared back for another attack, and my sword gleamed in its throat.

I dived forward, and in a single move I grasped the hilt and kicked off the monster's chest. I tumbled back into the alcove, and hot blood sprayed over me. Then, with a slash, I cut the ibis free.

It burst from the bindings, bone wings and desiccated flesh spreading wide.

"Attack," I roared, but I didn't need to. The mummy knew what to do. Its long beak snapped right for the hole left by my sword, and *stabbed*.

The Pullet screamed, staggering backward.

I lurched across the tunnel, swinging beneath golden wings before I ducked into the other alcove. This bird wrestled its bindings too; I arced my sword out . . . and sliced away more cloth.

And just like the other ibis, it careened straight for the Black Pullet. Light swept every which way, blinking and swinging as the Pullet struggled to fight the birds. But they swooped and stabbed, effective and vicious.

As I gaped, trying to find the perfect moment to *run*, more ibises wriggled from their alcoves. They wrestled free from their bindings, and in moments there were ten ibis. Then fifty. Then *hundreds*.

So I moved. Raising my sword high, I bolted into the tunnel and aimed back toward the entrance. The darkness crowded in, shaking with the Pullet's keening wails, but I didn't slow. I trusted my feet to get me back to the broken temple.

And soon moonlight shimmered over bricks and fallen stone. The Pullet's cries were far behind, almost drowned out by the flapping of bone wings.

I reached the rubble, shoved my sword behind my belt, and climbed. Using broken stones and crumbled roof, I leaped and grabbed and hauled myself ever higher. The moon was so bright and so brilliant.

Then I was back to what remained of the temple's roof and jumping into the dunes. A distant *Pop! Pop! Pop!* hit my ears as I launched into a run.

The copper lines around the obelisk must still be working . . . but where was the thunder from Joseph's electricity? Why was no blue light blazing in the distance?

Terror welled in my throat, and I hurtled over the sand. The shattered skeletons of my army crunched beneath me, and as I sprinted, I severed all my necromantic leashes to these dogs.

Sleep. Sleep. Sleep.

The magic kept me going. A leash cut for each footfall and a burst of strength through my body.

The noises of battle grew louder. Clashing weapons and indistinguishable shouts.

I reached the pyramid and slowed to a gasping stop. Rounding the stones would bring me to the imperial guards, but going up would at least let me *see* the battle before I entered.

So I dug my heels into the first step and tucked in my head, and I charged up the pyramid. Each step brought more sounds into focus.

Boom! A pulse bomb detonated.

Which meant the mummies were to the final line.

I moved even faster. I pushed *everything* I had into my legs. My strength, my magic, my life—I had to get to the Spirit-Hunters. To my friends—my family.

I crested the pyramid. The battle crashed over me.

And the truth did too.

We were losing. Three of the copper lines had been dug up and smashed apart. The mummies scurried over . . . and toward the final line.

Beside the obelisk, Joseph was doubled over. The crystal clamp shone in his hand, but he wasn't able to squeeze. Daniel and Jie flanked him, pistols and fists at the ready. . . .

And beneath his balloon, waiting like a cat beside a mouse hole, was Marcus.

I jumped. In a leap that carried me two levels down, I rocketed through the air and drew the world's magic to me. My feet slammed down; my knees crunched. Onward I moved, gathering in the magic of the stones, of the night, of the sand. I called it to me just as I had two days ago, and I damned the consequences. I just inhaled . . . and *ran*.

But then light exploded, sand flew, and thunder crashed over me. Mummies flew back—only to be instantly replaced.

The final copper line was finished.

And a single mummy darted through, spear out and aiming for Joseph's back.

"No!" The scream ripped up my throat. *"No!"* I lashed out with my magic, aiming for the mummy, trying to sway its spear. . . .

But I was too far. Too slow.

The spear cut through the air.

And Daniel stepped into its path.

CHAPTER TWENTY

With a single twist of his body, Daniel blocked Joseph from the spear.

And the spear impaled him.

Right through his heart, until it thrust out the other side.

Screams blistered inside me and tore out, rattling and unearthly. I ran and dived as fast as I could. I threw my magic at the mummy—at the spear. *At any goddamned thing that would stop this moment.*

But nothing stopped it.

The guard wrenched back his spear, and it yanked free from Daniel's chest. Daniel spun around, limp but reaching.

His eyes locked on to mine. His lips parted.

He hit the obelisk.

His body slid down.

And he stopped moving.

Jie reached him, tumbling to her knees. Her screams melted with mine as Joseph's electricity exploded into the lines of mummies.

I hit the sand and hurled myself forward. All I saw was Daniel. All I thought and felt and *shrieked* was Daniel. My Daniel.

I dived at him, Jie's sobs meaningless to my brain. My hand grabbed his face. Blood was everywhere. I tried to gather it up, as if I could push it back into his chest.

But he wasn't breathing. His eyes were still. His lips frozen.

He wasn't dead, though. He *couldn't* be dead. I shook him. I screamed at him.

And all the while, electricity sizzled and held the mummies away.

"Daniel, Daniel, Daniel." Jie's cries sounded over and over. She rocked back and forth, and I wanted to screech at her to *stop!*

Because he wasn't dead. I wouldn't *let* him be dead. There had to be some way to change this. Some way to go back. Some way to bring his soul here, where it belonged.

I clutched the side of my face. It was warm with his blood; the sharp stench seeped into my skull.

And my eyes landed on the obelisk. Like me, it was streaked with Daniel's blood . . . and as I stared at it, it shifted and swayed.

It shimmered golden. Like a sunray trapped in moonlight and covered in blood.

By blood and moonlit sun.

Suddenly the phrase made absolute sense. I could cross the curtain. These obelisks—which had reminded me of sunbeams each time I looked upon them—were gateways to the spirit dock. But they had needed blood and moonlight to open. . . .

Now this obelisk had both. Sprayed with Daniel's blood, I could cross into that realm.

I shoved to my feet, roaring at Jie to hold Daniel. Keep him safe. Then I staggered to the obelisk and *slammed* my bloodied palm against it.

I fell through the curtain.

Instantly, Joseph's electricity and Jie's sobs vanished. Everything was silent. Too silent after all the violence bursting in my chest.

The dock spanned ahead of me, empty.

Where was Daniel? He should be here. He had just died, and he should be *here*.

"Daniel," I screamed into the stillness. *"Daniel!"*

Nothing.

So I kicked into a run. The wood thumped beneath my boots, and the slats smeared beneath me. I swung my arms and drove my knees high. I ran and I ran and I ran.

Until a silhouette appeared before me. An ambling stride. A lanky build.

He paused, his head cocking as if he heard me. . . . His lips twitched up.

But then he blinked and resumed his unhurried stride.

351

"Daniel!" I shoved my body harder, but for every slam of my heels, he stayed the same distance ahead.

But I didn't stop.

Not until my body betrayed me. My legs tangled together. I plummeted forward, my single hand lurching out to catch me.

My face hit the dock. Wood stabbed my cheek. My teeth chomped through my tongue, and blood splattered onto the deck.

I dragged my head up.

Daniel walked on, his pace constant, his silhouette never vanishing.

His name shredded over my vocal cords. "Daniel, Daniel, Daniel." I screamed it, and my tongue gushed blood.

But still he walked on.

Then came the sound I knew would arrive eventually. A muffled baying, far out over the black waters.

Gritting my teeth, I staggered upright. The Hell Hounds could not have my soul, and they could *not* have his.

Daniel was mine. He was *my* Daniel, and I would not let this death claim him.

I shambled back into a run, shouting for him. Begging him to wait.

Even when ice gusted into me, I stumbled onward.

Even when howls splintered my skull, my course stayed true.

But the Hounds would reach me at any moment. Their frozen storm kicked at me from behind. Harder, colder, and louder with each second. They would claim my soul and blast it into a million pieces.

But they couldn't shatter an already-broken soul.

And then I saw the opening—the jagged hole that cut into the dock. I could keep going. I could escape the Hounds. . . .

I lunged low, hitting my knees and *sliding* over the wood. My pants shredded, my legs sliced open, and I choked on the blood that surged from my tongue.

I reached the hole; I toppled through.

The Hell Hounds' fury screeched overhead, exploding through my eardrums. Ice clawed into my hair and yanked chunks from my scalp.

But my eyes were blanketed in darkness. My hearing cloaked in thunder.

I hit the boat.

You found the way.

I snapped my head up, and in the gloom a figure formed.

It was the jackal—yet he had the body of a man. He sat on a bench at the opposite end of the boat. In his hand was a pole that sank down into the gentle waves. His tanned chest was exposed, and he wore nothing but a small flap of fabric around his legs.

"You," I snarled, pushing to my knees and gulping for air. "Take me to him."

He is gone.

"I saw him!" Blood hit the boat's floor. "Take me to him."

You cannot reclaim his soul.

"Of course I can." I scrubbed my left hand on my pants, ripping flesh off my palm with each vicious wipe. "I know what you are, *Annunaki*, and I know that you hold the power of life and death." I thrust my face at him. "I want life."

The jackal cannot do this for you.

"Yes you can!" I screamed. "Why would you show me this boat if not for this moment? You knew it would come to this."

The jackal did not know. He only showed you the boat so you could bring him the Pharaoh's clappers.

A harsh laugh broke through my lips. The boat shook. "I don't have the clappers, and even if I did, why the hell would I bring them to you?"

They are not meant to be in mortal hands.

"Then," I growled, "you shouldn't have given them to us. Was it you? Were *you* the one who fell in love with a human?"

The jackal would never do this. Mortal souls are weak, and that is why the balance has been disrupted.

"Balance?" I repeated. "I don't give a damn about balance or clappers or you. If you will not take me to Daniel, then I will find him myself."

No.

A new voice flamed through my mind, and the boat tilted back. I lurched around—and froze. A second Annunaki had joined us. It was the god Oliver had mentioned. The god with the head of an ibis but the body of a man.

"Thoth," I whispered, shock briefly overcoming my fury.

Yes. The ibis head bobbed.

And rage instantly curled back through me. "You are the god of balance, no? So *you* take care of this."

Only the jackal may enter the earthly realm. His eyes rolled, just like a bird's but with fire flickering inside. *And even the jackal may not interact directly. He is nothing more than a messenger.*

I shook my head. I didn't care, and I was wasting time. But when I tried to rise, both Anubis and Thoth blasted their thoughts at me—so bright and loud, my body locked into place.

The jackal and the ibis do not care about you, yet Hathor's clappers were never meant to be in the earthly realm—

"So punish Hathor. Not me."

Hathor has been punished. Two layers of Annunaki thoughts, like fire searing through my brain. *She was punished more harshly than you can even fathom, mortal. Yet now the imperial clappers have* chosen *you, and the queen's clappers have* chosen *your demon. The magic within them has spent millennia drifting and seeking the ones who could bring them home.*

"Ridiculous," I gritted out. My arms would not move. My legs were trapped in time.

It is fact. The clappers made their choice, and now you will do as required. You will return the clappers here. Then you will restore balance. The one called Marcus has broken it. You will fix it. And your demon will fix it too.

"No. *No.* You took the purest of all souls—the only person in this world who truly wanted to be *good.* You think that is balanced? If so, I do not want your balanced world. You may bind my body in place, but you will have to hold me for an eternity before I will *ever* be your pawn or do your bidding. I do not care how much you punished Hathor. It can never be enough. The clappers and the Black Pullet should never have existed—and Hathor should never have fallen for a mortal she could not have."

My eyes bored into Thoth. I fought against the power that trapped me.

"I came here to find the man I love, and that is *all* I will do. I have made my choice, and it is for *me*. The balance of the world may crumble for all I care. I will have my Daniel back, and you. Cannot. Stop me."

With those final words, I *pushed* against Thoth with my mind. Against Anubis. Against anything that was not my choice.

I was not a pawn.

I was a queen. I was an empress.

My hand shot up. Movement rippled through me, through the boat. My eyelids lowered, and when they popped back up, the ibis was gone.

So was the jackal.

On wobbly legs, I jumped up and grabbed the dock. But I was so weak. I had to swing my legs—back, forward, back—but even that did not give me the momentum I needed.

A hand appeared before me.

My gaze leaped up . . . and met sea-blue eyes. Elijah. It was my brother, and though his body looked like Marcus, his soul did not. Nothing about my brother's spirit felt like the monster outside.

Elijah gripped my wrists and hauled me out. My belly scraped over the dry wood, but soon I was upright.

And my arms flew around his neck. My brother.

"I've been waiting for you, El."

"Help me," I mumbled into his chest. But then I trembled

back a step, trying to see beyond him.

Daniel's silhouette was gone.

I clutched at my heart. No matter how many breaths I gulped in, my lungs would not stop shaking. "W-where did he go? *Where did he go?*"

"He left the dock." Elijah stroked my hair. "He passed into the spirit realm."

"No." I shook my head, a desperate swinging that made the dock spin. Made tears scorch down my cheeks. "He was right there." I pointed ahead.

"I'm sorry, El." Elijah's eyebrows lifted, a pitying look that I wanted to scratch away. It was not *time* for pity. Not yet.

"He has passed on," Elijah added. "Daniel crossed from the no-man's-land, and now he's out there." He gestured to the black waters around us.

My breath hiccuped. Left, right—I searched every wave and ripple for some sign of him. . . .

"So I must use the boat then." I pivoted back to the hole.

But I instantly stopped. My nose hit an evening suit, and I rolled back my head to stare into Clarence Wilcox's face.

"You," I breathed. He looked so much like Allison.

I grabbed his jacket. "Why didn't you tell me about her?" I screamed. "You should have warned me!"

"You do not understand," he shouted back.

"I *do*! She made this happen. I wouldn't be here if not for her. *Why didn't you tell me?*"

"Enough." Elijah yanked me back. "Clarence has been so

357

focused on protecting *you*, so intent on helping me keep watch of this spirit dock, that he lost sight of his sister." He wrenched me around, and his fingers dug into my elbow. "I promise you he feels enough agony."

"He may feel shame," I snarled, "but that does not mean I forgive him. Or forgive Allison. Let *go*." I snapped my arm free. "I will take the boat, and I will find Daniel."

I kicked into a stalk, shoving past Clarence.

But the boat was gone. The *hole* was gone.

I rounded back on Clarence, whose brows were drawn tight with sympathy.

"Where is the boat?" I demanded.

He lifted one shoulder. "That is the way of the no-man's-land. You may find it again. Or you may not."

"And even if you *could* find the boat," Elijah said, moving to Clarence's side, "and even if you *could* find Daniel's body, it would do you no good. Daniel's body and his spirit are cleaved. You cannot hew them back together."

"Don't lie to me." I stared into his blue eyes—so familiar, so foreign. "You tried it. With a spell from *Le Dragon Noir*, you tried to return Father's soul to his body—to his *skeleton*. I will do the same. At least Daniel's body is still fresh and whole." Spinning on my heel, I resumed my stride.

"It will not matter," Elijah called after me.

I ignored him and pushed my legs into a march. The golden curtain was as absent as the boat, so I could only guess I had come very far into this no-man's-land.

But not *too* far. There was never too far for Daniel.

I moved faster. And faster. Soon I was sprinting, and each step thwacked hollowly on the wood.

"Miss Fitt." Clarence's voice whispered behind me. "I implore you: stop walking."

I twisted my head slightly. Somehow he was keeping pace with me. Silent. Ghostly.

I only ran faster, until each breath was agony and each step thunder.

"You do not want this." Elijah's voice snaked into my ears, but when I glanced back, neither he nor Clarence was there.

I returned my gaze forward.

And I slammed into a body. Clarence's face leaned into mine. I bolted back around—but Elijah blocked me.

"Let me go!" I shrieked, lurching back at Clarence. "Let me go—"

"NO." Elijah's voice boomed out, shaking through the stillness of the air and scratching over my skin. "Look at what became of me!" He slammed his palm against his chest. "Look at what I have done." He flung his arm at Clarence. "You will become this if you do not *stop*."

"And," I growled, "I do not care. I have come for Daniel's soul, and I will *take* it."

"But he will not be the same," Clarence murmured. "Your Daniel is no more."

"What do you mean? Your soul is here, and it is the same—"

"And our souls have not passed judgment," Elijah

interrupted. "We are still on the dock, but Daniel is out there now." He jabbed a finger at the endless water. "When Clarence and I are eventually judged, our souls will be stripped bare. Soon . . ." He glanced at Clarence and swallowed.

"Soon," Clarence agreed. "Soon *we* will have to face the scales ourselves. We have clung to this dock to keep you safe. We have used our resolve and our desire to stay here, where we could protect you from the Hell Hounds and guide you on the dock . . . but once we enter the spirit realm, our souls will be ripped apart and judged piece by piece."

I stared at Clarence, not understanding. "But how could Daniel already be judged? Yet you are not?"

"We were not ready to die," Elijah whispered. "Daniel was."

"He died willingly," Clarence said. "When a person enters death by their own choice, they cross the dock in moments. Fragments of a moment."

"His . . . own choice." My breaths came in, faster and faster. Daniel had jumped in front of a spear meant for Joseph.

Just as he had jumped from the airship.

My life's nothin' compared to yours. That was what he'd said a few days ago.

But he was wrong. His life was worth everything—how could he not have known that?

"Eleanor." Elijah spoke my name with an inescapable heaviness. "What you will find will only be fragments of Daniel—good, bad, ugly, or clean. . . ." He lifted one shoulder. "There is no way to know what parts of his soul now drift toward the final afterlife, and if you try to fuse those remnants back into his body, you won't have a complete human. You will have *something* back . . . but it will not be your Daniel."

"I do not *care*," I croaked, but my knees were beginning to shake. "I would rather have a piece of him than none." I gasped . . . and gasped again. The air felt too cold. My lungs too small.

"But would Mr. Sheridan want to be summoned back?" Clarence pressed. "Would *he* wish to return to a shattered life?"

"No." Elijah's head shook, but the movement seemed hazy and slow. "Daniel gave his life willingly. If you bring him back, you will be dishonoring that choice."

My legs stopped working. It was as if they'd forgotten how to exist. How to *be*.

Elijah's and Clarence's faces disappeared, and the dock drew close.

I hit the wooden slats—my knees, my hand, my chest . . . my face. Each piece of me was broken.

I had no reason to keep going. None.

I could not even utter the words, for speaking them—even forming a coherent thought in my brain—would give it power. Would make it *real*.

And this could not be real.

Not my Daniel.

Not *him*.

I would not get to say good-bye. I would never touch his face or hold his calloused hands. I would never look into his grassy-green eyes or hear him say "Empress." I would never howl at him in rage or kiss his lips with need.

Because he is gone, and I cannot bring him back.

The words flickered through my brain, and with them came the truth. It engulfed me. Submerged me. I had no idea which way was up or how to draw in my next breath—not without Daniel to dive in and show me.

Back and forth, we had saved each other. He had rescued me, and I had rescued him . . . but not this time. I could not save him this time.

And he could not save me.

Because he was gone.

It confounded me. How could someone be alive one moment and then simply *dead* the next? When I had left, he'd been beautiful and vibrant. When I had returned . . . lifeless and cold.

And I knew with sick, disgusting certainty that this was my line. My limit: I could not take away what Daniel had chosen— not when I loved him. Not when his choice had been an honest, pure one.

"You have to go back now," Clarence said, his voice a gentle whisper.

I stared at the wood. "No."

"You have to," Elijah agreed. "It's time to say good-bye to us . . . and it is time to end this."

"*No.*" My head shot up. "Not yet."

Clarence smiled sadly. "There are people waiting for you, Miss Fitt."

"Jie," Elijah reminded. "Joseph, Oliver——"

"Oliver is gone," I snapped. "I broke our bond, and he *left* me."

"Oh, El." Elijah knelt beside me, his hand cupping my elbow. "Oliver came back."

I blinked—and then blinked again. But Elijah's face held no deception, and when I glanced at Clarence, he was motioning behind me.

"Look," Clarence said. "Your demon has returned, and he has brought you an army."

I whirled around.

And a cry writhed in my throat. The curtain was only twenty paces away, and though a battle raged beyond the golden glow, Oliver stood at the forefront.

He punched against the curtain, a noiseless scream erupting from his mouth. Again and again he tried to heave his way through the obelisk.

And tucked into his belt was a set of ivory clappers—they were smaller and less ornate than the ones I had carried. But they were clappers all the same, and the army that raged behind him was one of lithe mummies with swords.

Oliver had summoned the queens' guards.

"Go to him," Elijah whispered. "Go back and save those who remain."

I nodded, and with the power of my own arms and my own legs, I rose. I tipped my chin high and drew my shoulders back, and I inhaled.

But when I turned to say good-bye to Elijah and Clarence, they were gone.

And in their places were a jackal.

And an ibis.

I started. Then panic set in. "No. *No*. If you have lied about Daniel's soul—if this was all a trick to—"

The jackal and ibis have not lied, they said together.

"But . . ." A sob shivered over my lips. "My brother? Clarence? Were they ever really here?"

No response came, and behind me, the sounds of battle raged.

Retrieve the clappers, the Annunaki said. *Return them here.*

Teeth clenching back tears, I glanced into the earthly realm. To Oliver's bloodless face—to his palms beating against the obelisk. Then I flung my eyes back to the gods. "I will do this, but not for you or your goddamned balance. What I do is for *me*. And what I do is for *Daniel*—the one you took away from me. The one I can never have back."

Then I twisted toward the curtain.

And I marched ahead.

CHAPTER TWENTY-ONE

The battle thundered over me. In the space of a gasp-
ing breath, my eyes took in everything: clashing swords,
hammering feet, and Jie's wailing sobs. The queens' guards
swirled their swords faster than my eyes could follow.

But they were severely outnumbered.

I stumbled into Oliver. His face was flushed with relief, but
I spared him no words, only a nod of soul-deep thanks before I
staggered the two steps to Daniel.

His body was already stiffening. His lips blue. The blood on
his chest was brown and congealed. And his head stayed on Jie's
lap as she continued to rock back and forth, screaming for him
to wake up.

I couldn't watch. Instead, I honed in on Jie's face. On her
weeping eyes.

"Where's Joseph?" I shouted.

No response—I wasn't even sure she heard.

But Oliver did. "Marcus has him." He motioned into the fighting guards. "He collapsed right before I arrived, and Marcus reached him before I could."

"I have to get him." I swooped down and hefted my sword off the blood-covered sand. Daniel had died to protect Joseph; I would *not* let that sacrifice be for nothing. "You stay here and keep Jie safe."

"No." Oliver yanked the clappers from his belt. "I will get us through." He thrust the ivory toward the attacking queens' guards. Then he snagged my sleeve and yanked me onward.

The queens' guards opened a path.

And we stepped into the battle.

Imperial spears stabbed at us; queens' swords arced up. Tattered arms and shriveled skin blurred. It was an endless roar of slamming bodies and clanking weapons. Each step brought bronze armor and spear tips into my face, but always, swords would streak up and sling away the attacks.

On and on we moved, until I finally caught sight of Marcus. Just as he had done in Philadelphia all those months ago, he had Joseph by the collar, and he *dragged*. Joseph's feet left two long trails in the sand. His eyes were closed.

I couldn't tell if he was still alive. It didn't matter; I was coming for him.

But the queens' guards weren't fast enough for me.

I shoved into the fray alone. I thrust and parried and

screamed at the mummies to sleep. My magic blazed over my sword, blue and brilliant, and Oliver's power scorched around me. Each mummy I met blasted back, briefly frozen. Each spear I hit snapped beneath the fury of my blade and my magic.

Until we finally reached the edge of the battlefield. Mummies gave chase, but Oliver's magic and the queens' guards kept them at bay.

I lurched into a run. Marcus was almost to his balloon two hundred paces away. He was almost to the boulder on which it was fastened.

And Joseph's eyes stayed closed.

I screamed Marcus's name. My heels kicked up sand. Moonlit dunes and crumbling ruins melted within my vision. But I wasn't fast enough. Never as fast as I needed.

Marcus reached the boulder and slung Joseph across it. Then he knelt to his boot.

Silver flashed in his hand. A knife. Which meant Joseph wasn't dead yet—and Marcus was finally doing what he'd planned all along.

But just as light glimmered on the blade, a second shimmer caught my eye. A movement in Joseph's hand.

A crystal clamp.

Marcus stood, his back to us.

"Stop!" I shrieked.

"Attack!" Oliver bellowed beside me.

But slow. We were *so* slow.

Marcus reared back with the knife.

Not again, I thought. I would *not* let this happen. So with all the strength and soul I could summon, I threw my sword.

Tarnished and ancient, the sword was carried in a perfect line through the air by my magic. . . .

It sliced into Marcus's back. All the way to the hilt.

His knife fell. He staggered into the stone . . . but immediately shoved himself back up. When he twisted around, blood bubbled from between his teeth.

For the tiniest space of a breath, I saw him as Elijah. My brother impaled.

But then he smiled, and his hands rose. This was *not* Elijah.

Magic rammed into me. Cloying and putrid, it charged over me—over Oliver and the queens' guards.

I swayed back . . . and then clutched my throat.

I couldn't breathe. Magic coated my throat, choked off my airway. My lungs heaved and fought, but there was nothing coming in. Nothing going out.

Shadows crossed my vision. *Just a little air,* I pleaded with my body, thrusting magic against him. I fought the oil sliding through me. I *pushed* it back out. . . .

But it didn't work. Marcus continued to chant . . . and smile . . . and *dig* his fingers toward us. And the sword in his back began to push out of his body. The flesh mended with each passing second.

My legs buckled, and panic seared through my brain. Was *this* the end? A single spell to suffocate us?

Just as I tumbled toward the sand, I had enough time to

see a dark figure rise up from behind the stone. Behind Joseph.
Behind Marcus.

She lifted her arm, and a distant *crack!* pierced the fog
inside me.

Blood exploded from Marcus's forehead.

His spell lifted.

And I thrust back to my feet as Oliver staggered up beside me.

Crack!

Blood burst from Marcus's chest, and Allison's pistol
smoked. She fired again. And again. Yet somehow, even as each
bullet broke through him, Marcus stayed upright.

He was *so* strong.

But so was I.

My hand shot up. Power lanced out. Straight at Marcus's
heart, I poured every ounce of my soul into the assault. And I
stumbled closer and closer.

Then from the boulder, lightning exploded. In agonizing
slowness, Joseph gathered himself upright. Yet, though his body
listed, his hand stayed steady. His electricity stayed true.

Like a thousand spiderwebs, my magic and Joseph's sizzled
over Marcus's body. Then Oliver's power unleashed, and Marcus
was nothing more than a beacon of blinding light.

Yet no matter how much energy I shoved into my attack, it
wasn't enough. I could feel Marcus pushing back. Even as our
souls wrapped around his, he wriggled and writhed free.

My feet carried me, shambling through the sand, toward
Joseph. I was draining too fast, and even though I sucked at the

world around me, the world had nothing left to give.

Marcus was taking *his* power from the sand, the wind, the stones.

I needed the power of the crystal clamp. I needed electricity.

I reached the stone, my left hand slung clumsily out toward the lines blazing from Joseph's fingertips. I laced my fingers through his. . . .

Electricity tore from me. Blistering and trembling, it sliced through my veins and gathered in my heart—then surged from my right wrist. Smoke filled the air. Flames licked up my sleeve. I could barely see, and I certainly couldn't hear.

But I could feel. Somehow, with the power of electricity, Joseph and I had stabbed into Marcus's soul. I felt each of his heartbeats. I understood the scale of his power. And even his thoughts trickled around inside me.

And that, more than anything else, *terrified* me.

For Marcus was amused. Eventually our power would run out, and he simply had to wait until that moment. Then he would crush us. He had two souls to lean on. He had the Black Pullet's soul too. And he had the very soul of the earth.

We could not stop him, and he found it funny that we even tried.

Horror choked through me, spiraling around the electricity. I looked at Joseph. His eyes shone blue, but there was fear within. We *weren't* strong enough.

Crack! More pistol shots, almost lost in the eternal thunder of our electricity.

My eyes crept right. The world swam, and each fragment of

a breath was torture. I met Oliver's gaze, glowing with the pure magic of who he was.

As I watched, the light in his eyes dimmed and dimmed. He was stopping—and I couldn't blame him. He had already given more than he needed to. He had come back, and my soul would never forget.

Save yourself, I thought, though he could not hear me with our bond broken. I hoped he might see the want in my eyes. *Save yourself, Ollie. Please go while you still can.*

The slightest tug wound through my gut. Then the flicker of a thought nestled inside my brain. Somehow, despite our broken bond, he still managed to meet my mind with his.

And what he thought was simple: *No.*

At that moment the sword popped from Marcus's chest and hit the sand. Then the bullet in his forehead spat out. The bullet from his heart.

And again, the hint of Oliver's thought flamed inside me.

No.

Oliver's magic cut off. In two impossibly long strides, he came to me.

He grabbed my wrist.

And his vast demon soul hurtled through me. Instantly, the electricity doubled. Tripled. It grew so hot, I lost all sense of where I was or who I was. My body became a distant, fleeting thing. A vessel much too small for all this raw power gathering inside.

Three spirits laced together as one. Joseph. Oliver. And I. Power boiled in my brain, beneath my ribs, behind my eyes. My clothes burned—my eyelashes, my hair. Everything *ignited*.

And our power hit Marcus's attack. For an endless fragment of a second, it was a balanced collision of souls.

But then the scales tipped too far. In a heavy, clicking *twist*, all the electricity shifted.

And Marcus could not stop it. His eyes widened. His mouth fell open with silent screams. His skin caught fire, melting over sinew and bones.

Elijah's skin. My brother's body was crumbling before my eyes.

Oliver felt that loss too—it sang through our shared electricity. A high-pitched shriek of grief for someone whose soul we had already lost . . . and whose body we now lost too.

But we did not stop pushing against Marcus. Skin flayed off his skull. His yellow eyes spun and rolled . . . and then burst. They exploded outward. Blood sprayed.

Then, bit by bit, his lungs and guts scorched and popped. The red muscle ignited . . . and then shaved away.

Until there was nothing left but a skeleton and a pulsing, festered heart.

Joseph's fingers all furled in, save one, and then he *thrust* a final whip of electricity at Marcus.

And his heart exploded. Black, oily blood spewed on the sand, on the bones, over us.

And the necromancer Marcus Duval collapsed in a pile of charred bones.

Chapter Twenty-Two

There was a long silence that seemed to fill the earth after that.

No one moved. No one spoke.

But then screams slithered into my ears. Into my consciousness.

Allison. She sobbed for mercy at our feet, begging us to help her.

"He took my life," she screamed. "You must get it back! You must get it back!"

I ignored her. I could not even look upon her. She turned to Joseph. To Oliver.

But none of us had any mercy to give. She had dug her own grave, and now she could lie in it.

I stumbled to Marcus's blackened, ashy bones. Elijah's bones. I brushed them gingerly aside. I would save them; bury them somewhere here in this ancient, timeless necropolis.

But first . . .

I found the ivory clappers. Clean and white, both hands were now open. No souls left inside.

I swooped them up and turned to the frozen battle behind us. "Go home," I whispered.

It was the only phrase I could rasp out, and in a great lurch of movement, the imperial guards left. They radiated in all directions, bounding for their tombs all across Egypt.

The queens' guards followed.

"Here." Oliver's voice was a broken, rattling thing. "Take these too." He offered me the queens' clappers . . . and my gaze slid up his dusty, ripped sleeve to settle on his face.

To stare into his hazel eyes. *Hazel*. Not gold.

"Oh no," I breathed, gripping for his arm. Then his chin. "Oh my demon, what did you do?"

"I did what needed doing." He tried to look away—but my left hand cupped his jaw. Tears pooled in his gold-flecked eyes.

"Oliver, Oliver." I pulled him to me. My arms clutched his shoulders, and I held him as tightly as I could. "Oh my demon."

"I am your demon no longer, El. I am just . . ." His voice broke. He sank his face into my neck. "I am just a man now. A man with no magic. A man with a . . . a *man's* soul."

And as he began to weep, I wept too.

He had given up his demon soul to save us all. The electricity from the crystal clamp had blasted it away, just as it had in Paris—but a thousandfold worse. Oliver's immortality was gone, his soul shrunk and shredded to a human size. My demon would never, *ever* go home. He would never touch magic again or cross the curtain or be anything but Oliver.

No matter how many times I uttered the words—*Thank you, thank you, thank you*—it wasn't enough. It would never be enough.

"Eleanor." Joseph's croaking voice cut into my brain. His hand lay weakly on my shoulder. His second hand moved to Oliver's. "The Black Pullet . . . returns." His head swiveled toward the pyramid.

I had forgotten the creature entirely. Again.

Eyes swollen, I strained to see. . . . Black scales—as thick as velvet in the graying dawn light—slunk over the sand. Several bone ibises continued to peck at it, but it barely seemed to notice. It simply moved toward us.

Toward me—for with the clappers, I was its master now.

"Stop," I whispered.

It froze, yellow eyes shuttering. Then its breath huffed out. It spiraled in on itself and laid down.

The ibises continued their meek attacks.

"Sleep," I ordered them. Then I turned my eyes to Joseph. Tears streaked through dirt and blood, and there was a hollowness in his gaze.

The pain of the living. The guilt of the survivors.

We would carry it with us forever.

"Come," he murmured, shuffling toward the pyramid. Toward Jie. Toward Daniel.

Oliver and I followed, Allison's cries for mercy howling after us. As we trekked on unsteady feet over the dunes, I paused only once. Beside the Black Pullet.

Its head was as long as I was tall. Yet it did not seem dangerous now. Its eyes brimmed with a sadness I understood.

I rested my left hand on its serpentine snout. "You were just a pawn," I whispered, my words carried off with the wind. "I am sorry you were never given a choice."

Then I resumed my stumbling journey to Daniel's side. His head was still in Jie's lap, and she still hunched beneath the obelisk.

But she was silent now. Stiff as stone. Empty as the rest of us.

Joseph fell to the earth beside her. I fell beside him . . . and Oliver beside me.

And together we wept on. For all we had fought.

For all we had given up.

And for all we were never meant to lose.

At the first rosy light of the wicked dawn, we burned my inventor's body.

I looked into his face for the last time as he lay atop pine crates—a makeshift funeral pyre. The wind dusted sand over him, and as I brushed a final kiss over his waxy lips, flies buzzed on his chest.

Death was so coarse. So unforgiving.

I wanted to brand his face in my memory. I wanted to remember the shape of his hands, the lines of his jaw, and the sunny color of his hair.

But there was nothing left of Daniel in this corpse.

After Jie doused the crates in alcohol and Oliver found an ancient urn among the dunes, Joseph spoke.

He spoke of how he had met Daniel—in New Orleans. How he'd never seen a mind so sharp or a moral compass so true.

"All he ever wanted was a second chance," Joseph whispered over the wind. "A chance at redemption. I *pray* he knows he had it. He redeemed himself a thousand times over." Joseph scratched at his bandages, inhaling before he went on . . . but then his brow furrowed; his hand dropped; and he stared into Daniel's face. "You gave too much in the end, Daniel. Too much."

"Too much," Jie repeated. Then she set fire to the wood and moved to Joseph's side. As the flames licked up, they held each other. Just seeing the two of them without Daniel at their side was almost too much. . . .

I looked at Oliver. He stared at Daniel's body with a horrified interest. It was as if he was seeing the future ahead of him—the future of all mortal souls. And he did not like what he saw of death.

I turned away.

I could not watch Daniel's face eaten up by flames. I could not smell his flesh turn to ash. I could not look upon him as just another corpse.

I had seen too much death; I wanted to remember him *alive*.
So I left my friends to bear witness.

Yet as I summoned the Black Pullet to me and the poor serpent slithered my way, I saw Oliver turn his gaze east, to the rising sun. His brow wrinkled, his lips parted . . .

And a hint of wonderment gleamed in his hazel eyes. As if he *did* like what he saw of life.

"Come," I mumbled to the Black Pullet, and we shambled to the obelisk.

A slash in my hand. *By blood.*

A bright granite sunbeam. *By moonlit sun.*

Though it was moonlit no longer, I dragged my palm down the obelisk . . . and crossed the spirit curtain.

I stepped wearily onto the dock. It looked as it always did. Truly timeless, truly disinterested in the world of mortals.

And before me, a long-legged ibis and a scruffy jackal awaited.

I took two steps toward them and flung all four clappers at their feet. Then I turned to go—ready to leave this world behind forever.

But as I twirled around, my gaze caught on the Black Pullet. Its golden eyes pulsed with fear. Its feathers shook. I ran a soothing hand over its wings.

And without thinking, I plucked a single golden feather.

Then I twisted back to the gods. "When the Hell Hounds come, do not give them the Pullet. It did only as it was commanded, and you have taken enough innocent souls today."

Its heart must be judged like all creatures, the jackal said as the Pullet, still trembling, walked slowly down the dock and out of sight. *If the heart is pure, the soul will live on for a time.*

I licked my raw lips. Daniel's heart was pure. I hoped his soul would live on.

"What of my brother?" I asked. "Or Clarence? Do their souls live on? Were they ever really *here?*"

As before, I received no response. But both gods blinked. It was as if they were leaving that truth up to me.

So I chose to believe it *had* been Elijah and Clarence. I chose to believe they had helped me on my path. And I chose to believe they could hear my final whisper of good-bye.

Then I locked eyes with Anubis. With Thoth. And I drew back my shoulders. "You think your bright souls and endless lives make you better than we are. Wiser. And perhaps you are right. Perhaps your cold detachment from our mortal world makes you stronger. But you make mistakes just as mortals do. Hathor made one—for love.

"So I will tell you something, *Annunaki.*" I spat the word. "Mistakes make you strong. Love does too, and that is why I am stronger than any of you. Never forget it. I am *not* your pawn, and I never will be.

"I will see the world alone. I will start Daniel's school alone. And I will make a home without him. But I will never, ever stop loving him."

I curled my left fingers inward. "I can still make a fist, and breath still burns in my chest. So look at my face. Look at my mortal soul, and *remember* it. You did not crush me, and you will have the rest of eternity to think on it."

I did not wait for an acknowledgment—I did not need one.

I pivoted around and stepped back to the spirit curtain.

My life. My choice.

CHAPTER TWENTY-THREE

The easy chatter of happy families bubbled around me as I wandered past a statue with its nose eroded off. Almost three months since leaving Paris, and I was already back again. But this time I was simply a tourist seeing all the places Daniel had wanted to see.

I had saved the Louvre for last—and the Egyptian wing of the Louvre for the *very* last. After spending almost eight hours in this old palace, I had seen every item there was to see, and my brain was a jumble of brushstrokes and weathered statues. Yet now that the Parisian sun was slinking down, I had reached my final destination.

As I strode into the tiny room, there was only one other person there: a girl with unruly brown hair and a furrowed brow.

She did not pause her careful inspection of a weathered statue, and I bustled right past before stopping at a chest-high glass case.

Inside was a small, black statuette of a jackal. He was surrounded by shards of pottery and bits of broken jewelry.

I arched an eyebrow. "They did not even give you your own case. How that must annoy your inflated sense of self-worth."

The girl nearby turned wide eyes on me. Clearly she was curious as to why a sunburned young woman felt the need to speak to display cases.

Or perhaps she was merely fascinated by my mechanical prosthesis. I did not blame her—it *was* impressive.

I tapped the glass with a wooden finger so she could get the full effect of Daniel's genius. Gears whirred within the mechanical palm—almost silent, yet not quite. And as the grease spot shimmered in the sunset's glow, a fond smile tugged at my lips. It was, I thought, the best part of my new hand.

I cleared my throat, my eyes returning to Anubis. "Do not think that because I am speaking to you that I have forgiven you. I have not, and I never will. Yet I once saw my father at the spirit curtain—and I feel quite certain he was able to hear and feel what I said. As such, I would like to think pieces of Daniel may still exist and that he too can hear me."

Reaching into my dress pocket, I withdrew Daniel's tarnished spyglass. *Clack-clack-clack.* It opened and I began to speak.

We miss you, Daniel. Obviously, we do. The flight from Saqqara was . . . brutal. Grief filled every space of your airship. It sat where you sat. It lay in your bed. It held my hand . . . and it would not let us forget what we had lost.

Not that we want to forget. You are . . . no, were. No—are. You are the only one for me.

Joseph and Jie took a steamer back to America. In their last letter, they told me they had found the perfect location for a school. It is an old estate in North Carolina, and they have already begun calling it 'The Institute.'

Now, before you demand to know where we acquired enough funding so quickly, I shall tell you: it was provided by a Mr. and Mrs. Lang. They say they knew you, and they are quite eager to see the Sheridan Institute come to life. Mrs. Lang, in particular, has been immensely helpful. She has aided Jie in filing three of your patents already! One for the pulse pistol, one for the goggles, and one for the crystal clamp. Jie says they have to wait to submit paperwork on my mechanical hand, as they must sketch it and I am not there.

But I will go there as soon as I finish touring Paris. And then London—and Vienna and Rome, of course. It is a good thing I pulled that feather off the Pullet. I daresay, I would have run out of money long before I ever reached Munich.

Speaking of Munich, I am very displeased with you for never mentioning how much it would hurt *when Herr Doctor Quitterer sewed on the mechanical hand.*

Blazes, Daniel. It was worth it in the end, but really. Blazes.

While we are on the subject of suffering—and in case you are curious—I do not know what became of Allison. Last I saw her, she was old and wrinkled. She begged for our help at Saqqara; we ignored her, and we left her.

The Wilcox family has suffered so much, and yet there can never be too much suffering for Allison. Not to satisfy me, at least. If it hadn't been for her betrayal, I would not be standing here speaking to a statue.

Yet I have learned something, Daniel. From you.

Vengeance solves nothing. None *of us was a winner in the end. Not Marcus, not me, not Joseph. And of course, it was you who paid the price for our sins. You—the only one who never sought revenge against his wrongdoers.*

We will never forgive ourselves, you know. Joseph, Jie, and me. We miss you so much.

I miss you so much. And I love you.

I always will.

Tears ran down my cheeks, but I didn't mind. They were as common as spring rain these days—and I hoped just as cleansing.

Thwump! I smacked the spyglass shut, and ever so gently I laid it atop the glass. Then I withdrew my humming mechanical hand and scowled at the Anubis statue.

"You are all he has now. All that Mama, Elijah, Father, and Clarence have, so please, look after them. It is, I daresay, the least you can do after all you have taken from me."

The statue's eyes flashed gold. My scowl only deepened. . . .

But then my eyes settled back on the spyglass. My face relaxed with a sad, broken smile.

I would never forget my Daniel Sheridan. My inventor. My

scalawag. I would always remember the freedom in his smile and the power in his touch.

"I love you, Daniel," I whispered. "Too."

"Jennifer!" A woman's voice cried behind me. "Hurry up!"

I blinked, realizing the girl with unruly curls still stood beside me, gaping.

"Must you always be so strange," the voice went on, shouting from the next room over. "You are holding up your classmates, and no one else wants to see the Egyptian exhibits."

I shot a glower at the fussy-looking teacher. Then I shifted my gaze to the girl's blue eyes.

"Jennifer," I said softly. "Since you have listened to my monologue with such rapt attention, I will give you a piece of unsolicited advice."

A blush rose on the girl's cheeks, but she did not stop me as I powered on.

"Contrary to what your teacher might suggest," I declared, "it is perfectly all right to be strange. For ever after, you will be glad you did what *you* wanted instead of what everyone else expected. No doubt you wonder how someone as young as I can possibly know this, but trust me: I have seen more deadly, dark, and . . . *lovely* things than you can possibly imagine."

The girl narrowed her eyes skeptically.

I shrugged one shoulder. "You may listen to me or not. It is your choice. But"—I raised one mechanical finger at her—"should you ever decide you want a more interesting curriculum than what you're currently receiving, you might consider the

Sheridan Institute in North Carolina. I've heard they have the best teachers in the world. Certainly they are the strangest."

I flashed her my most rakish grin (of which I was certain Daniel would approve), and in a flurry of skirts, I strode from the exhibit and left the Louvre behind.

When I stepped into the orange glow and bustling insanity of a snowy Rue de Rivoli, there was a lightness in my step that I had not felt in months. Years, even.

People in winter clothes swarmed among carriages and horses dusted with snow, and as I pushed into the evening traffic, I couldn't help but murmur an old favorite quote. "The web of our life is of a mingled yarn, good and ill together."

"El!" The tenor voice trickled into my ear. I scanned winter-flushed faces and carriages. . . .

"Over here, silly girl."

I spun around and found Oliver sauntering toward me. He wore a lazy smile and his top hat askew. "Finished?" He twirled a hand toward the Louvre. "Because I know of a lovely place on Montmartre, if a Bohemian meal would interest your palate."

"I *am* finished here, and I *am* famished." My lips lifted, a sad but freeing smile. "Has Laure arrived yet?"

He shook his head no and slipped a hand into his coat pocket—a *new* coat that was part of a *new* suit in a handsome, chalk-gray color. He withdrew a silver flask. "Care for a drink?"

"Yes, please." I smiled wider. There was only water inside. No more alcohol for my former demon.

Oliver wasn't happy or settled or certain of himself, but he was working toward it. Each day, he struggled to understand mortality a bit more—to sort out what *he* wanted from this new life of his.

And so was I. So were most of us, I supposed. We waddled through life blindly, hoping to find something—and some-one—worth fighting for. I had found it; I had lost it; I would find it again.

I took a gulp of icy water from the flask (to a few horrified stares of passersby—I winked at them), when Laure's voice trilled out, "Miss Fitt! *Je suis ici!*"

I twisted back toward the busy street, and my eyes landed on Laure's face. She waved excitedly from the window of a hired cab.

And I grinned at her. A wide, absolutely genuine grin.

Miss Fitt. It was who I was, and it was who I would always be.

Miss Fitt. Misfit. Forever.

ACKNOWLEDGMENTS

This entire series has been a labor of love, and it only exists because so many people worked *so hard*. To start, I am forever grateful to Maria Gomez and Barbara Lalicki for first acquiring the Spirit-Hunters and bringing them into the HarperCollins family. Of course, it was Karen Chaplin and Alyssa Miele (who is not related to the vacuum company) who kept my prose from getting too boring and my plot from getting too twisty as the series progressed—while Rosemary Brosnan made sure those ladies didn't get too twisty either. I am forever grateful to Cara Petrus, who designed the most *stunning* covers for my series—under the watchful eye of Barbara Fitzsimmons. Olivia deLeon and Sandee Roston were my publicists-in-shining-armor, while Kim VandeWater, Lindsay Blechman, and

Diane Naughton handled all the marketing voodoo (it's magic and I'm sticking with that). A thousand more thanks must also go to all the amazing copy editors who slaved over my misuse of ellipses, to Jon Howard, Josh Weiss, Andrea Pappenheimer, and—of *course*—Susan Katz and Kate Jackson. HarperCollins transformed my heaps of boring words into an entire trilogy of beautifully gleaming books.

The truth is, though, that Eleanor and the Spirit-Hunters would never have found HarperCollins if not for Sara Kendall, Joanna Volpe, and Danielle Barthel. Thank you for all your patience, your constant dedication, and your awesome *you-ness*. I'm so grateful I get to be a part of New Leaf, and I feel so blessed to have you in my court.

For my *anam cara*, Sarah J. Maas: Death is only the beginning. And I mean that in the least creepy, most Mummy-reference-way possible. You taught me to tap into my deepest, darkest feelings and pour them onto the page—and my writing has been more powerful and more fulfilling ever since. You're amazing; this book exists only because of your endless cheer-leading through every single daunting chapter; and I love you forever and ever and ever. And then some more.

I have to extend a *gigantic* thank-you to Erin Bowman, for always having an ear ready when I need to vent, a shoulder ready when I need to sob (So. Much. Sobbing. During this book), and a hand ready when I needed to get off the floor and keep writing. You're a neighborhood watch of one.

For Meredith McCardle: we've come a long way in a few

years, and I'm so glad we're on the road together. I'll have to write another series in Paris so we can tour it again. Or, how do you feel about Venice next time?

Thank you *again* to Biljana Likic (and also to Mufei Jiang) for help with the Latin. Who knew an ancient language could be *so hard*? I'd have been lost without you.

For Maddie Meylor: You and your family are the coolest bunch of readers a gal could ever meet. I'm so glad we're friends and that you love the Spirit-Hunters as much as I do. I hereby declare Daniel as your official fictional boyfriend.

To Kat Zhang, Dan Krokos, Amie Kaufman, Erica O'Rourke, Amity Thompson, Katherine Brauer, Julie Eshbaugh, Leigh Bardugo, Marie Lu, Alex Bracken, and Jodi Meadows— you guys have been the best friends a gal could ever ask for, and I honestly can't imagine writing a book without you to cheer me on. Thank you for always being there.

Many thanks to my husband, Sébastien, for his tireless support and hundreds upon hundreds of delicious meals (though if I ever see another zucchini casserole, I might strangle you). This is only the first series, baby, so get ready for an entire future of dinner-based slavery. Oh yeah, and *je t'aime*.

For my parents, my brother and sister, and aaaaall of my huge extended family: thank you for always believing in me, always backing me up, and always thinking I'm the best writer in the entire universe (I'm looking at you, Mom and Dad). I'm so lucky to have such a warm, loving family.

For every librarian, every teacher, and every bookseller who has ever crossed my path (and the ones who have yet to cross it too): you're the number one reason my books reach young readers. Thank you, *thank you* for doing what you do and sharing the stories that you love.

Finally, I want to thank my readers—old and new. Since the first book released two years ago, I have been *constantly* humbled by all that you do. Your emails, your tweets, your letters, your fan art, your presence at events—everything is downright awe-inspiring. Each time I hear from you, I remember why I write. These books are for you, and I can never thank you enough for your love and support.